Ray Furness

ON HELIGOLAND

A PITCHFORK PUBLICATION

Order this book by email from pitchforkproduct@aol.com

Note for Librarians: A Cataloguing record for this book is available from Library and Archives Canada at www.collectionscanada.ca/amicus/index-e.html

Printed in Victoria, BC, Canada.

ISBN: 978-1-4251-4528-6

www.pitchforkproduction.com

Pitchfork Production is a small independent and non-vanity publishing company which aims to provide a discerning section of the public with works of quality which may otherwise be ignored in the highly commercialised "blockbuster" climate of much current production. We commission and pay advances to our authors in the usual way and they are in no way involved with the organisation or publishing decisions of the company.

Pitchfork Publication
5 Orchard Court
Rose Hill
Oxford
OX4 4HJ

The publication of On Heligoland is the final responsibility of Pitchfork Production who benefited in the case of the present work from the services of Trafford

www.trafford.com

10 9 8 7 6 5

"Sir Edward was very popular with all who visited Heligoland, and was fond of relieving the boredom of his honourable exile on the rock at the mouth of the Elbe by amateur dramatic entertainments."

(The Times)

"Sir Edward was very popular with [illegible] visited the island, and was fond of [illegible] his [illegible] of his honourable exile on the [illegible] the mouth of the [illegible] circumstances."

—*The Times*

☙ *PRELUDE: ONE* ❧

New Year's Eve – Heligoland, 1889

The four sat upon the chesterfield, the women distraught and ill at ease, William simpering.

'I faithfully promise,' said Teddy, 'that if we do look awful I'll get Harry to smash the plates. I would not wish to bestow a photograph of ravaged debauchees to posterity!'

Mr Taylor looked under his black cape, took a slide from his box and inserted it. Frances saw his hand move towards the rubber ball and waited for the familiar exhortation to watch the birdie and then the flash – but it was not the explosion of magnesium which transfigured the room.

There was a sudden uproar at the door, commotion, disturbance, shouting.

She saw with great clarity a man in a heavy coat run across the floor, his face covered by a black wide-awake.

He drew two pistols from his pockets, and the flat detonations cracked and reverberated around her as Florike's head burst into blood, Charlotte jerked back screaming and Teddy, the blood pumping from his neck, fell across her with a ghastly smile.

PRELUDE: TWO

London, before Christmas

Tetchy and irritable, George waited until the last bell had been rung and the foyer emptied.

He had sought an usher: had he not seen a tall, attractive young woman with dark hair about to enter a box? Had any message been left?

The usher was sorry: there had been no message and the box in question was empty. He also begged the gentleman's pardon as the music was about to begin and he must close the doors. That gentleman in the corner had also been making enquiries.

George looked and saw a pale, round-shouldered man frowning and obviously uncomfortable.

'Reverend Heywood?' asked George, moving rapidly towards him, 'have you seen my cousin?'

The Reverend Heywood introduced himself in great agitation: no, he had not seen her and had been waiting over half an hour.

The muffled strains of the Pilgrims' Chorus reached them. George impetuously thrust his card into the clergyman's hand.

' There may have been an accident. You wait here a bit longer, and let me know if she turns up.' He hurriedly took his top hat and cloak from the cloakroom and hailed a cab for Eaton Square.

The night was restless, he was tormented by irrational fears. Had she been robbed? abducted? murdered? He had visions of his cousin gagged and bound in an opium den in Limehouse whilst furtive Chinese coolies sought her extradition hellwards to Shanghai.

The following morning, Sunday, he informed the police that

his cousin had not appeared the previous evening and that he was concerned. The rest of the day was spent wandering under a slate-grey sky, kicking the dead leaves that remained in Regent's Park and drinking porter as he listened to the chimes of the Swiss clock in his Eaton Square drawing room. In the evening he played patience and retired early.

Frances, where are you? His affection for her had deepened into something which, he felt, must be love. Her dark hair, winning smile and generous figure hovered before him.

' I love you, Fan,' he said out loud. 'Don't talk guano, George,' he replied.

On the following morning he decided to absent himself from his office and take an extended Christmas and New Year holiday. The police reported nothing. He caught a train to Salisbury and, at Codbury St Mary, made enquiries.

The clerk in the ticket office haughtily explained that he could not be expected to remember every young woman who had bought a ticket to London, but suggested that a recent photo be displayed which might jog the memory of passengers. The police had also suggested a similar ruse, that a photograph be hung in Her Majesty's Theatre.

He arrived at Capewell House in the middle of the afternoon and informed an alarmed Mrs Lovell what had happened. Perhaps Frances had been knocked down and was lying in hospital?

The police had no information, he explained, and walked with his dog Mops in the gathering dusk. That evening Mrs Lovell suggested that Dympna might know of a possible friend with whom Frances was inexplicably staying.

Dympna the cripple? It was a long shot, Mrs Lovell agreed, but worth trying. They also looked at photographs to select the best to display at the station and the theatre.

There was Frances in a group of young maidens in diaphanous draperies, looking amorous; Frances looking stern as the Valkyrie Sieba; Frances wearing a mantilla and looking seductively over a fan: this intrigued him. She looks too Spanish, said Mrs Lovell sagaciously.

He finally chose one of her in profile, her hair twisted on top of her head, with one curl curved above her right cheek. She was wearing a choker or scarf tied high across her throat, decorated with arabesques twining on a light material. Her dark blouse had high puffed sleeves. She looks very lovely, he thought, but reprimanded himself for talking guano.

This photograph was to be displayed at the station and a similar one, with shoulders bare, would adorn the foyer of Her Majesty's Theatre.

☙ *PRELUDE: THREE* ❧

Winter. On the water

It was a woman's voice, a voice that was mellifluous, yet fractured, melodic, yet strained, a mezzo soprano with a low tessitura.

Frances sat bolt upright and listened intently. It was a song that she knew, a song by Schubert and entitled 'Auf dem Wasser zu singen', 'To be sung on the water'.

A figure was standing in the blue grotto, and it was Millicent Freshet.

'Quiet!' Frances cried, 'Quiet! Listen!'

The voice floated through the night air, a nocturnal cantabile:

'Now through the gleam – of watery mirrors -
Glides, like a swan, the rocking boat.
Ah, on the waves of soft shimmering gladness -
Glides now my soul, a swaying boat.
For from the heavens - now on to the waters,
Dances the glow of the dusk on the boat.
Ah- time now vanishes - dewy its pinion -
Vanishes now, on rocking waves.
Tomorrow – tomorrow – let time disappear –
Vanish on shimmering wings from me now –
As I – did then – and shall do ever –
Till on a high – and gleaming wing – I too shall vanish – from change and from time…'

'No!' screamed Frances. A dreadful premonition had seized her.

'Millicent, no!' But the figure, dressed in what looked like flowing draperies, had walked into the bluish water, fallen face down into it, and disappeared…

CHAPTER ONE

They walked arm in arm from the Hotel Belvedere whose pleasant pavilion had faced the beach and afforded splendid views of sunsets, of ragged bands of orange in the west, and made their way towards the quay; a calm grey sea lay beneath a low, cloudy sky, a reassuring neutrality moistened by a gentle drizzle.

The first whistle had already sounded and they hastened towards the Prinz Eitel-Friedrich.

'It'll be a very smooth crossing, Fan,' said her father, gazing down at her and smiling. Her cheek brushed across his damp tweed ulster; she did not open her elegant swan-necked umbrella, studded with small jet beads, but sought with difficulty the line of demarcation between sea and sky.

'I shouldn't by rights be sending you to Heligoland unchaperoned,' he joked, 'but I can't imagine you'll end up in any fleshpots over there, and Teddy and his wife will keep an eye on you. I can't see what else he's got to do on that god-forsaken Rock of his. Mind you, he used to be quite a masher – very charming, so be careful! Bracing walks for you, my girl, and sea bathing on the Düne. Keep on the south side where the ladies dip in the briny and no straying across to the gentlemen's section now!'

She smiled wanly.

'I've had your luggage sent on board and here's the ticket for your private cabin. You'll be there in under three hours but I thought you'd like the chance of stretching out in comfort. Should be a decently clean bunk, we're in Prussia now after all. And Heligoland's ours, don't forget, so you'll feel quite at home over there.'

The second whistle blew, making her jump; she put her free hand to her bonnet and the umbrella slipped into the crook of her elbow. Her father laughed when he saw it.

'Fat lot of good that'll be, Fan, with a gale eight blowing! But I'm sure Teddy's wife will have all sorts of sensible togs for you to wear.'

He suddenly looked serious.

'Have a good rest above all. Put all that Bayreuth business out of your head. Why you wrote that wretched letter I'll never know. You can sing to the seagulls out there – much healthier, if you ask me.'

He bent to kiss her and she felt his wet moustache on her lips.

'There's a telegraph cable to the mainland now, thanks to Teddy, so we can keep in touch that way. Or write to the British consul in Hamburg, The Honourable C.S. Dundas, Hohe Bleichen 50: Teddy knows him. I'll be travelling through Prussia for the next few weeks, in mufti of course, but I'll be here to meet you at Cuxhaven on your return. Then it's back to England for both of us. Don't hang about the deck, Fan, I hate these protracted leave-takings.'

They reached the steep gangplank as the bell clanged, the final whistle shrilled. She kissed him again, and embraced him, then walked swiftly up on to the deck. The waters churned below and seaweed and refuse slapped against the quay wall; gangplank and anchor were raised, the engine throbbed and a black flag streamed from the smokestack.

Her father waved and blew her a kiss, then turned on his heel and walked along the jetty, disappearing behind the harbour master's office. She stood holding the clammy brass railing in her gloved hands and a freshing wind tugged at her skirts; they passed the lighthouse at Neuwerk, the three lightships, the pilot ship. She felt the swell of the open sea at the river's mouth and, stepping over the high brass step, she walked along the rubber mat and went below to find her cabin.

A purser in a dark blue uniform and cap gravely took her ticket and escorted her down a dark, confined corridor then, saluting, handed her the key to number seven. She entered the poky room and was reassured by its cleanliness; she locked the door and dashed water onto her face from a small washbasin. She took off her skirt and her elastic-sided boots and lay down on the crackling sheets of the narrow bunk.

'Öd und leer das Meer…' She felt the waters of the German Bight surge against the starboard side of the Prinz Eitel-Friedrich; the crossing would not be quite as smooth as her father had kindly suggested. She closed her eyes.

To Heligoland.

And to its governor, Sir Edward Hennicker-Heaton…

The engines throbbed beneath her; salt spray spattered the round porthole; spindrift, she mused, spindrift…

She heard muffled voices in the corridor outside, voices speaking in German, in English, in Frisian, voices that blurred and receded. She lay as if in a grey cocoon, moving across the grey swell of the North Sea, conveyed to the Rock, banished almost. She had deferred to her father's wishes. Fire-girt it was not, but laved by water, sprayed by storm, scoured by flailing winds in winter, salved by summer suns, its red sandstone pitted and hollowed in a bristling air.

She unbuttoned her blouse and loosed her corset a little, breathing more deeply. I am carried in a coffin of mahogany and brass across the salt slap of the sea, a black scarf tugging in the wind above, a stricken princess…

Nonsense! Far too much imagination, as Papa would say.

Simply a failed singer going for an autumn holiday to a British crown colony in the North Sea some fifty miles from Cuxhaven. Or so her Baedeker told her, her handbook for travellers, a dark red volume now in one of her boxes stowed safely in the luggage compartment, 'Northern Germany as far as the Bavarian and Austrian Frontiers, with excursions to Copenhagen and the Danish Isles'.

Holy-land, was it? Hertha and her rites, or was that Rügen?

The sacrifices, the sacred cows, the veiled goddess?

No, Sir Edward and Lady Hennicker-Heaton: oilskins,

waterproofs and sou'westers, the wind buffeting them as they strode to the lighthouse, a surging grey sea beneath, her hair stiff with salt or blown back like a dark halo around her face.

(He had commented on her hair, had he not? Her lustrous eyes also, and had pinned to her breast that huge silver star that the Bey of Tunis had given him, and I wore it all the evening, much to the discomfiture of his wife and his reproachful father-in-law.)

Forget it, father says, put it behind you. But it is not so easy, remembering, and wondering...

(The Master plucked us in springtime, did he not?)

She turned on her left side and closed her eyes, listening to the throb of the engine below, the dash of the spray, the creaking woodwork and sought in vain for heaviness of limb, the melting of mind into mother-of-pearl, into mental vacuity.

I am held in dead air, moving through bands of grey watered silk towards an unknown place where he is not, cannot be.

(Yet did he not die beside water? Brackish, though, southern and slack, mirroring and exuding decay. And I? I?)

She moaned softly and turned to face the grey eye of the porthole, an eye of water and grey rheum. She reached out and pulled a small curtain across: the cabin darkened.

Forget, forget...She turned back onto her left side; the tiny tick of her gold watch, close to her ear, brought a strange comfort, a listless acceptance which dispelled reminiscences, recriminations.

The afternoon shaded into numb oblivion, a lassitude rather, a mental suspension, and she dozed, her lips parted, her hair loose upon the pillow as her island appeared on the horizon and drew closer to her....

* * *

'Is Tied uptustaun, jung Wicht! Wi bünt ankomen.'

She woke with a start as the purser knocked on the cabin door; she drew back the curtain and saw the massive red sandstone cliffs through the spume-streaked glass.

The ship had stopped and she heard movement outside, voices, footsteps, shouting. She hastily dressed, combed her hair and checked her reticule for the coins her father had placed there to pay for the ticket to board a small boat that would take her from the ship to the landing stage on the island. She had enough money in her purse, for her father had explained that Teddy would take care of all her expenses whilst she was his guest, and 'there'll be precious little else to squander your money on!' She could run up a bill with Teddy if there were any items that she might need, toiletries and so on.

They use German money there although it is a British possession – Teddy would explain. She left her cabin and went on deck: the red cliffs rose perpendicularly out of the sea to a height of some two hundred feet and hundreds of seabirds wheeled about them in a clamorous cackle of noise, straining against the wind, tirelessly buoyant and gliding in circles.

A crowd of people was standing on the beach from which long duckboards ran into the sea to meet the small boats from which the passengers disembarked. Her luggage, she noticed, had been shouldered by two burly sailors who carried it into one of the waiting boats, bobbing on the tide.

She gathered her skirts and was helped down the steep metal ladder into a boat with ten other passengers. They were rowed to where the duckboards stood above the slapping water; she was again helped out of the boat clutching her reticule, bonnet and umbrella and nimbly walked through the rising wind across to the beach which was lined, she noticed, by several hotels. Her cases and boxes had been stowed upon a handcart, and a sailor was touching his cap and bowing before a tall, fair-haired man dressed in a tweed suit and light summer overcoat.

He turned and saw her, smiled, and moved to greet her, holding out his hand.

'Miss Frances Prince? Welkoam iip Lun! I'm sorry I don't have a plumed governor's hat but it's a very modest posting.

'I'm Edward Hennicker-Heaton. How was the crossing?

'"Come unto these yellow sands," well, grey at least! I really must sort out the beach here.'

He put his hand under her arm and helped her onto the stones; a rough causeway led onto a narrow esplanade where a Strandbazar advertised its wares.

'Sir Edward, it is most kind of you to go to this trouble.'

'Teddy, please. I've known your father for years, we were at the Crimea together. I was so sorry to hear of your dear mother's death, Jack told me all about it - he was heartbroken, poor chap. You've got her eyes, I'm told, but I can see his features in you, also his colouring. He's so proud of you and your singing.'

She gazed at the sea which was chattering among the rocks and running along a low ledge, curling and translucent. 'I don't sing any more.'

'I don't believe that. We'll get you to join in our amateur theatricals, they're great fun. Now, there's something I have to confess. I've booked you into the Conversationshaus, see it? That long red-brick hotel with the huge windows looking out to the sea? It's only for a few nights. My wife and children are away in Berlin, and I've used the opportunity to have reparations done in Government House and I didn't want you to be subjected to all the inconvenience of workmen hammering and plastering all day. The island is certainly full of noises at the moment, and of a very disagreeable kind! I've also given the staff time off and it would certainly set tongues wagging here if the governor had a charming young lady under his roof without a female companion. I hope you don't mind awfully.

'I'll take my evening meals down here with you so we can enjoy our lobster and Chablis together. The work should be over by Monday and Augusta and the tribe will be back in the evening. I'm sure Jack won't mind. It's an excellent hotel – I put guests up there if Government House is full. It's not pretentious, like the Stadt London, and the food is excellent. Agreed?

'Of course.' She felt that she was blushing for some reason, and she felt the salt tang on her lips when she ran her tongue along them. She gazed across at the bath-house and a pool where a few hardy children were still bathing; their screams, like rags of sound, drifted across to her.

'Excellent. Now I'll introduce you to the manager and tomorrow we'll do a bit of mountaineering up the one hundred and ninety wooden steps leading up to the Oberland and my palatial residence. I've got the morning free and I'll show you my domain. I'll come round tonight, say seven thirty.

'I'm trying to inculcate good British habits here, otherwise they'd be eating at four o'clock in the afternoon. Hello, I think the wind's getting up. Hope you don't mind a visit from the gentle zephyrs!'

She held on to her bonnet as a strong gust blew from the sea. Sir Edward called for the lad wheeling the handcart to stop at the Conversationshaus and carry her luggage up the steps and through the glass doors into the foyer.

'Must dash. Herr Jensen speaks good English, but Jack tells me that your German is excellent, although they speak an impenetrable dialect here. Sort yourself out and I'll be round later. I've booked you a room at the front, hope the sea doesn't keep you awake. You'll certainly hear it in Government House, I assure you!'

He bowed, smiling, and hurried along the esplanade, his coat blowing in the wind.

* * *

Herr Jensen was most solicitous.

He was a stocky man in a tight frock coat; his face was ruddy and a golden pince-nez cut deeply into a somewhat fleshy nose. He greeted her effusively as an honoured guest of Sir Edward and he insisted that she inform him immediately of anything she required.

The heavy trunks were already stowed in the best bedroom at the front, he explained and, pointing to a slim pale girl who bobbed a curtsey and then stood with her hands clasped before her, Stine would carry up the small valise and act as lady's maid if Fräulein Prince so desired. Fräulein Prince must feel completely at home in the hotel. He had nothing but respect for Sir Edward who had done so much for the island and he was flattered to think that he and Sir Edward were on such friendly terms. But she must be tired after the journey?

No, she demurred, I am well rested.

Sir Edward would come that evening for dinner, he explained, and the best table had been reserved for them.

He turned to Stine and, in the local dialect, gave a peremptory order. The girl, angular and awkward in what seemed to Frances to be national costume and a starched apron, her hair in plaits coiled about her ears, picked up the small valise and led the way up a handsome staircase of light polished wood which smelt pleasantly of beeswax. They walked along a long, light corridor and arrived at a large door on the left which Stine unlocked, standing demurely to one side. She stood impassively until Frances smiled.

The girl curtseyed and silently withdrew.

The room was commodious and, she noticed, heated by a heavy green-tiled stove in the corner; the carpet was also dark green and woven into an intricate pattern.

She moved automatically to the large windows which gave out onto the narrow esplanade beyond which the Prinz Eitel-Friedrich rode at anchor, the beach, the landing stage and an uninterrupted expanse of grey, choppy sea extending to a darkening horizon. She heard the wind moaning gently and noticed that the windows were double ones with wooden shutters outside. She turned to look at her room.

A large portrait of Queen Victoria, she noticed, hung upon the wall opposite the bed, a four-poster surmounted by an ornate and heavy tester. There were neither blankets nor sheets but an eiderdown quilt and a wedge-shaped pillow. There was a dressing table, a large wardrobe, and a solid writing desk with elaborate dolphin-shaped legs in dark wood, also a sofa and several chairs.

She looked at the washbasin and washstand in the corner; a commode was discreetly hidden behind a screen. An ornate oil lamp stood on the writing desk and candles in heavy brass candlesticks stood on the dressing table and a small occasional table next to the bed.

My realm, she thought, my domain and, searching in her valise, she extracted a small box of Neptun Cigaretten and a box of lucifers. These were not easy of ignition but she succeeded in lighting one and gratefully inhaled the fragrant tobacco.

What would Papa say? That it would ruin her voice?

That's gone, anyway. No more flower-maidens for me, well, one was enough...

She pulled up a chair and sat with her back to the stove, gazing out at the darkening sea, the German Ocean, heaving and sighing in the dusk.

I am on this thin sliver of rock surrounded by vast waters, she mused, the land of Hertha and her rites, the holy-land. The wind had grown appreciably stronger and she rose to close the heavy velvet curtains, but then caught sight of her reflection in a long cheval glass. A glass coffin, she thought, seeing her form contained within the narrow oblong mirror: the stricken princess is – but then she stopped.

* * *

At seven o'clock she rang for Stine and requested hot water which came ten minutes later in two large Delft jugs. She dismissed the girl and washed herself perfunctorily at the washstand, wondering of what the facilities for intimate ablutions would comprise in Government House. She changed into a lace blouse and a dark grey skirt and dressed her hair in a French pleat.

She stopped once more before the cheval glass: a tall, dark, shapely English woman stared earnestly back at her.

Rain pattered against the windows and the wind boomed in the stove.

She threw a shawl around her shoulders, stepped out onto the landing, locked the door and, after placing the key in her reticule, descended the stairs. It was just after seven thirty.

Sir Edward was waiting at the bottom of the stairs, talking and laughing with Herr Jensen.

He was taller than her father, also slimmer; she noticed his fair mutton-chop whiskers, his rather girlish lips and lively grey eyes. He had changed into a light grey suit, not evening wear, and wore an elaborate watch chain on his waistcoat. He smiled when he saw her, and took her arm.

'How's the room? We could have put you into the Stadt London up on the Oberland, but I prefer it here.'

'It's a very handsome room,' she replied, smiling at Herr Jensen who summoned the maître d' hotel to take them to their table in the dining room. There were few guests at dinner; Sir Edward acknowledged their bows and gestured to them to remain sitting.

'The Germans are so deferential and insist on standing on ceremony,' he joked, 'I keep telling them to regard me as a kind of head boy but they are in awe of authority and see our dear Queen hovering above me. Right, let's sit by the window. Shall we close the curtains? Not much of a view now.'

'No,' said Frances, 'I rather like to see the rain on the glass and hear the wind outside. It's cosy here. What was that flash out there?'

'It's the lighthouse. You can't see it from here as it's behind us, as it were, on the Oberland, but you can see the light it gives out, it's very powerful.'

They sat at the table and an impeccably dressed waiter approached.

'I was serious about lobster and Chablis,' he said, 'but obviously the choice is yours. The seafood is excellent here, however, and I love the lobsters. The wine cellar's good, too. If they do remember me for anything in particular I hope it will be for getting some good wine across from Hamburg. Charlie Dundas sends it across for me and I make sure he gets his crustaceans in return. But before the Chablis let's have a bottle of champagne to celebrate your arrival.'

He spoke to the waiter who returned with a bottle of Veuve Cliquot in an ice bucket; Sir Edward insisted on opening it himself. He carefully removed the foil, untwisted the wire and held his napkin over the neck of the bottle while extracting the cork. He poured a glass for each of them; the pale liquid frothed and sparkled in the tall glasses. He looked her in the eyes and smiled.

'Welkoam iip Lun!'

The wine pearled and pricked her palate, and she drank gratefully. 'I am very glad to be here, Sir Edward.'

'Teddy, please! Or Edward if you think Teddy is too familiar. Augusta doesn't like our English frivolity and can't stand Teddy, but William and the two girls - they're twins, don't you know – don't seem to mind. Or, rather, Beatrice doesn't, but Charlotte's rather more fastidious. Augusta doesn't really like it here and wants to get off the Rock. There's a posting coming up in Newfoundland and she wants me to go for it, but I'm not keen on rotting away in St. John's. I like it here very much and I've made some very good friends. The duties aren't onerous and I have time for my translating and my acting.

'If you want something to send you off to sleep I'll lend you my *Prince Bismarck's Letters to his Wife and Sisters*. Now, you must join our little theatrical group. We did *The Tempest* last summer. I think I was a creditable Prospero, but the Miranda was awful, poor girl. You would have been marvellous, I'm sure!'

She looked at the silverpoint on the black windows, the light stabbing the rain-soaked darkness. 'I'm not much of an actress,' she murmured.

'Or you can give us a recital some time. Jack says you've been to Beirut and sung there.'

'No, Bayreuth.'

'Fine. We have a good Erard here, frightfully out of tune, but I'll get somebody across to fix it. Can't rise to a proper orchestra, I'm afraid, but we can do the Palm Court sort of thing. My son scratches on the fiddle reasonably well, Bea plays the piano and Charlie the flute.'

He refilled her glass, also his own. 'An die Musik!' he said. 'I've got quite a bit of sheet music up in the house, quite interesting stuff. We can all sing "Das Lied der Deutschen" which a chap called Hoffmann von Fallersleben wrote when he was over here on the Rock; he actually stayed in this hotel, and there was a bit of rantipoling, I gather! It's arranged for solo voice with piano or guitar accompaniment. The Conservatives don't like it, but I think it'll catch on. Heine was on the Rock too, but couldn't stand the English Sunday and read the Bible out of sheer despair.'

She frowned. 'I don't sing any more.'

'What a pity. No acting, no singing. So it will have to be tableaux vivants. I can see you in white draperies gazing across the waters like Iphigenia in that painting by Anselm Feuerbach. Or we can do Odysseus and Calypso by Böcklin. I saw it a couple of years ago in Switzerland. I could stand on a rock, a dark figure swathed in sombre black and you can be the nymph Calypso and her lyre, sitting on the shore. Somewhat cold for you, however, if you wear her diaphanous wisps! I'd love to do 'The Island of the Dead', marvellous painting – do you know it? – but cypress trees are in short supply here!'

Had the champagne loosened his tongue or was he always so loquacious, so carefree, careless with the proprieties?

She placed her hand over her glass to prevent his filling it again, but he removed it gently and insisted that she drink at least one other. He drank quickly, almost greedily.

'Does your wife also enjoy acting?' she asked.

'Augusta? Lord, no. She thinks it's rather infra dig. She helps me in the translations, though. She did most of the Bismarck book, met the old boy at Varzin. I wonder how long he'll stay in office with the new Emperor. People wonder, too, about this place. Apparently the Germans have started to build a canal from the North Sea to Kiel on the Baltic and when it's finished little old Heligoland will be of great strategic importance to the Germans. But I mustn't bore you with politics. Tell me about Jack –

‘Ah, the lobster’s here! Marvellous! Look at the lovely silver hammer to break the claws and the elegant fork to extract the succulent flesh!’

A silver dish arrived at the table. Six lobsters, nestling on fragments of ice and dark strands of seaweed, garnished with lemon, were presented, and Sir Edward rubbed his hands with relish. Fresh glasses were brought and the Chablis placed in the cooler from which the empty bottle of champagne had been removed. The waiter sought to open the bottle but Sir Edward, as before, insisted on doing it himself. He raised his glass and smiled.

‘To Merrie olde England! Long may the Union Jack fly over this island!’

The wine was excellent, and both of them set to in crunching, extracting and eating. Sir Edward waxed lyrical.

‘I designed a pretty little postage stamp using their national colours, red, green and white. It has the Queen’s head on it and the currency in farthings and pfennigs. You’ll see these colours everywhere: I’m quite happy for them to fly their flags if they wish. But not on Government House!’

‘My maid here wears these colours,’ she remarked, ‘a pink blouse, green skirt and white apron.’

‘Stine? Yes, a strange child. There was some nasty business a couple of years ago and I had to pass a very heavy sentence on one of the German sailors who tried to molest her. The poor thing escaped and fell down the cliff near the North Horn. She was badly injured and hasn’t spoken since.

‘How I adore lobster! I could eat it until the proverbial cows come home. Bismarck adored it too. He enjoyed the good things of life, as I do, and people used to send him pâté de foie, and caviar and so on, but he liked my lobsters best of all. I’ve got a letter in the house where he waxes eloquent about the marvellous moment when he first broke open the fine claw of this excellent shellfish!’

He was sampling a fragment of white flesh which he had balanced on the end of his silver fork. The wind outside reached gale force; the panes rattled and the windows were awash with water.

'How many – how many people live on Heligoland?' Her question was trite, she knew, but she sought the neutrality of statistics.

'Two thousand, and I pride myself on knowing nearly all of them. In the summer, of course, we get the visitors here, but it should settle down now that the autumn's upon us.' He spoke at length, and she dutifully listened, of his island, his Rock, of its progress under his governorship. He spoke without arrogance, but with pride; he spoke of his many German friends, his warm relationship with Bismarck, his conviction that he had helped in no small manner to cement Anglo-German friendship.

A great tiredness overwhelmed her and she refused more wine.

Cultural links were just as important, even more important, than merely political ones, Sir Edward continued, flushed and animated. He was making a collection of all the references to Heligoland in English and German literature. One curiosity was an essay which his wife had come across written by the philosopher-poet Friedrich Nietzsche when he was a fifteen year-old schoolboy.

'Have you heard of him? He's not a very exemplary individual, I believe, and a bit extravagant in his thinking. A Danish chap, Georg Brandes, was telling me about him. Apparently he's had some kind of breakdown. I haven't read his stuff, I'm told it's a bit rum, but my son was reading *Thus Spake Zarathustra*. Well, Augusta met this elderly gentleman who had taught Nietzsche in a very good school and had kept the draft of the essay the young lad had written. It's called *Capri und Helgoland* – quite a juxtaposition, eh? The red cliffs, it's all there! Probably got it from Heine, though.'

Frances nodded and suddenly jerked her head upwards: she was dozing.

'I'm awfully sorry, I do feel rather tired.'

He looked at her attentively.

'Good lord, don't apologise. I'm being most insensitive. I'd completely forgotten you'd come from Cuxhaven this afternoon.'

He finished off the bottle of Chablis, draining his glass rapidly. The waiter stepped forward with a glass of cognac on a silver tray. Sir Edward downed it in one gulp, then stood up.

'Must get back to Oberland, up those hundred and ninety steps. Jensen always keeps me a room here in case the weather turns atrocious, but I can make it.'

She rose, unable to suppress a sense of relief that he would not be spending a night in the Conversationshaus and also a feeling of bewilderment that she should feel this.

'I'll call for you tomorrow at ten and we'll explore my fairy realm – not quite a Domdaniel but very beholden to the elements!'

He stooped to kiss her hand.

'Sleep well, through wind and storm.'

She blushed and watched him walk to where the coats and hats were hanging. She saw Herr Jensen help him into a yellow oilskin and south-wester, fetch a lantern and escort him to the front door, carefully opening it against a ferocious wind and then shutting it rapidly, bolting it top and bottom.

* * *

She was not of a nervous disposition, but slept badly.

The wind wailed and shrieked past the hotel, booming in the stove, and torrents of rain hurled themselves against the double windows and the shutters.

She had undressed by candlelight and slipped into bed beneath the plump eiderdown quilt which she had pulled up to her ears. The impressions of the day reasserted themselves in an intrusive pattern: the Hotel Belvedere at Cuxhaven, her father's leave-taking, the cabin on board Prinz Eitel-Friedrich, the arrival on the Rock, the meeting with Sir Edward, the meal, his animated conversation and that intertwining of the erudite with the louche which intrigued and disturbed her.

Her heart was pounding in her breast and she felt dehydrated, although she had drunk moderately. The stove still gave out heat and she lay with her right arm outside the quilt, but the sound of the wind and the grinding of the sea kept her awake for a long time. Sleep came shortly after midnight, but strange dreams tormented her.

She was approaching the island, the Island of the Dead as portrayed by Böcklin, a painting that she had indeed seen with her parents when they had visited Basel shortly after she had taken up her professional singing career. It was she who was now that figure in white standing in the boat which was approaching the gloomy shore, but then she was naked and it was Sir Edward who was rowing the boat, laughing and shouting 'Domdaniel!'

She knew that the island was a place of punishment, of retribution; they were approaching the beach where she saw a temple and a tall woman in black who would, she knew, plunge a knife into her heart.

Then she was fully dressed and drinking tea with her father in Cuxhaven, and a figure she knew to be Charlie Dundas was laying various postage stamps upon a table, stamps which bore an image of the tall woman on the island who was, she knew, the Guardian of the Temple.

'You must lick them first,' her father had said, 'and then you will be saved.'

A vast torrent of water had entered the room and she was gasping for air – here she woke with a start.

The gale had not abated and she heard the moaning wind, the driving rain. She lit a candle from her box of lucifers: it was half past three.

She covered herself up and held her little gold watch in her fist, once more feeling reassurance from the tiny ticking. She drifted into an uneasy sleep; the candle guttered and she woke at dawn to find a sorry mass of grease upon the bedside table. She rose and pulled back the curtains to find a grey world of water and tumultuous sea before her.

She shivered, put on her negligé and sat gazing out; the beach before the hotel was deserted and the smaller island, the Düne, she glimpsed to her right, a mere blur in the rain, scarcely able to assert itself against the waters, a grey smattering of sand.

At seven Stine entered with coffee, rolls, slices of cheese and sausage; she averted her gaze and removed the contents of the close-stool, replacing the used chamber pot with a clean one. The tepid stove became warmer, and Frances sat close to it, refreshed by the steaming infusion of coffee.

What would the day bring? There would hardly be a chance for a long walk. She would write to Papa using one of Sir Edward's pretty Heligoland stamps in red, green and white with Victoria surmounting both farthing and pfennig. She hoped that she would find books to read in the hotel for she had brought none apart from her Baedeker.

She rose and stood again before the cheval glass. She tilted back her head and placed her hands behind her neck, moving back the heavy weight of her hair. 'Well, Mariana,' she murmured, 'I should be kneeling before this liquid mirror, seeing the clear perfection of my face, but this is no moated grange and I'm a long way from the south. But there are Northern heroines too.' She frowned, turned away from the mirror, completed her toilet, brushed and coiled her hair and, after dressing, stepped out onto the landing.

Boots and shoes stood neatly polished outside certain rooms; on the wall at the end of the corridor she noticed a framed piece of tapestry with the following embroidered inscription: 'Grön is dat Land/ Rood is de Kant/ Witt is de Sand/ Dat is de Flag vun't hillige Land'. She smiled ruefully and gazed through the window at the flying rain and the wild waste of waters outside.

She descended the staircase and was greeted by Herr Jensen who bowed and, speaking in German, expressed his commiseration at the inclement weather. She replied in that language that she was glad to have reached the island before the gales had arrived. It will blow itself out before evening, he answered.

The lounge was sparsely occupied. She noticed two large ladies dressed in black bombazine, a gentleman in naval uniform, a slim young woman dressed in a blue and white striped dress who was reading a newspaper through her lorgnette and another man who was staring into space; his hair had been carefully combed over his skull to conceal a thinning scalp. She wished them good morning and crossed to a smaller, darker room which smelled strongly of cigar smoke and was dominated by a gloomy painting entitled 'Die Wacht am Rhein' which portrayed the sombre figure of Germania leaning on a sword and looking down at that river whilst an eagle hovered above.

This was obviously the library. A handsome ormolu clock stood on an occasional table, and next to the clock she found Sir Edward's *Prince Bismarck's Letters*; she opened it and saw on the fly-leaf a dedication, in purple ink, to 'My dearest Augusta, from her loving Teddy'.

Was his wife not Augusta? She turned a few pages: his English was fluent and although she did not know the German original she imagined that the lucid and easy style combined accuracy with elegance. A scholar, then, as well as an actor, a civil servant, a soldier? A lover of lobster, of Chablis too, she thought to herself, smiling. And she suddenly looked forward to seeing him.

The library was well stocked with books in English, German, Dutch, Danish and Frisian: Sir Walter Scott stood beside Goethe, Dickens beside Bosboom-Toussaint, Theodor Storm beside Tennyson. She looked at Spielhagen's *Stormtide* and Wilhelm Jensen's *Ebb and Flow* and a selection of Theodor Storm; she took down Fritz Reuter's *From My Early Years* but soon laid it aside.

There were many heavy volumes commemorating the Prussian victories over the French in 1870. She settled down by the window with a volume of Tennyson; the wind had dropped somewhat but the rain still fell steadily and she saw a boy in oilskins run to the hotel entrance.

She tried to find 'Mariana in the South' but was interrupted by a waiter bringing her a letter in purple ink. She opened it.

'Dear Miss Frances, would you mind awfully if we postpone our tour of all I survey? The weather's beastly and I don't want you to catch your death of cold too early. I'll see you later, however, for dinner at seven thirty. Affectionately yours, Teddy.'

She gazed out at the agitated waters, at the black groynes running down to the sea, and heard the chinking of flag ropes slapping against the poles. 'Break, break break,/ On thy cold grey stones, o Sea!' Let it be so.

She read for the best part of an hour when suddenly she saw a young woman sit down on the sofa opposite, her brown silk dress billowing around her.

'Miss Prince?'

'Yes?' She put down her Tennyson and gazed at her interlocutor who was nervously tugging at her gloves; her boots were wet and raindrops glistened in the heavy, fair bun at the nape of her neck. Frances noticed hazel eyes and a pale, sensuous mouth.

'My name is Millicent Freshet – Teddy said you were coming across.' She was about Frances's age; she was ill at ease and, after having removed her gloves she nervously tugged at her collar, first the right side, then the left.

'Are you a relative?' Frances asked, noticing the informal appellation.

'No, nothing like that.' A strange smile twisted her lips; she gazed at the dripping windows.

'I think the rain's easing,' she said, 'it can be awful here. I was in Bergen once, but it's worse here. Miss Prince, may I ask you a favour?'

'Of course, what is it?'

'I know I shouldn't talk to a complete stranger like this but I would appreciate your help if it's not too much of an imposition.'

'Please continue.'

Miss Freshet looked down at her boots, then looked straight at Frances.

'I live up at the telegraph station with my father. My mother died some years ago. I've spent most of my life here, but also used to visit relations in England, in London and Gravesend. They discovered I had musical talent and I took piano lessons, but there's little chance over here to play, although I sang a lot.

'An American lady, a Miss Landauer, came here on holiday,

heard me singing and said that I should have my voice trained: she offered to help financially and I did have some lessons in Germany. My father wasn't too keen, though, and insisted that I give up the idea and stay here to look after him.

'Then William – Teddy's son – heard me at one of our glee-clubs and said that I was wasted here and must go back to Germany for proper training.

'I'd kept in touch with Miss Landauer who would certainly take me back. Father isn't at all happy. Teddy says I should do it, that art comes before everything, but I really feel there's too great a risk. I enjoy singing, but know full well that I'd never make the grade. I've sung a bit with Beatrice – she's the musical one, Charlotte less so – and Teddy gets wildly enthusiastic, but I know deep down that I'm not good enough.'

She paused. Frances stared at the ormolu clock and said nothing; the rain had stopped and muffled figures hurried along the narrow esplanade.

'Now comes my request. Teddy said you'd been singing in a German opera house and that your father is very fond of you and that you have a wonderful future stretching before you.

'Please, Miss Prince, please give me your honest opinion of what my voice sounds like. Teddy's got a lot of sheet music in the House – there's Spohr, I know, and Mendelssohn galore – and if you could give me an honest opinion I'd be eternally grateful. If there's a fee involved I could certainly – '

'Nonsense,' Frances snapped. Then she stood up and, in a more emollient tone, she took her leave of Millicent Freshet and hurried from the room.

* * *

Luncheon was a miserable meal spent in bitter self-laceration. Miss Freshet's face, its startled wild-eyed hurt and surprise at her rudeness hovered before her, delicate in its blushing, as delicate as the rosy lining of that great sea-shell which had adorned her parents' mantelpiece.

She scarcely tasted the pickled herring and rye bread, the glass of pale beer that she toyed with, and went to her room to sleep. But recriminations, memories, guilt and distress prevented sleep; she rose, wrapped a warm cloak around her and gathered her hair into a large Tam o' Shanter which her father had brought her from the Isle of Lewis. A brisk walk was in order. She left the Conversationshaus and turned to the right along the esplanade.

The air was cold and wet, and a choppy sea sucked back across the grey sand. She had a clearer view of Düne, three quarters of a mile to the south where a ferry was now plying, low in the water with passengers and merchandise.

She crossed the Marcusplatz with its cluster of deserted hotels, their dripping tables and chairs empty before them, and noticed the hundred and ninety wooden steps leading up to the Oberland, the towering cliff behind her, sodden after rain and criss-crossed by countless gulls, fissured and streaked by droppings.

We'll wait till tomorrow, she thought, I shall climb you tomorrow. She stopped at the Strandbazar and gazed at rudimentary maps displayed on the counter: was she now on the 'Lung Wai', the Long Road or Way? There was also a 'Gesundheits-Allee', a 'Bindfaden-Allee'; she wondered whether Edward – Teddy – had tried to impose English names. She wished to buy a map and some postcards but then realised that the very little money she had was in her reticule in the hotel.

She explained in German to the assistant, a stout flaxen-haired young woman with a cast in her left eye, that she was a guest in Government House and that all bills should be sent there. In censorious silence the assistant noted down the exiguous amount.

Sepia portraits of August Heinrich Hoffmann von Fallersleben lined the walls, together with those of Heinrich von Aschen and Jacob Andresen Siemens, names that were unfamiliar to her.

'Wer sind - ?' she began, turning to the silent assistant, when a gentleman in German naval uniform suddenly stepped before her and saluted.

'Siemens is the man we must thank for saving our island – I

mean your island – from poverty. May I introduce myself? Captain Herbert von Kroseck at your service.'

He was a broad-shouldered man in his late forties; his weather-beaten face was framed by a greyish Newgate frill and his eyes were blue and piercing.

'I think I saw you in our hotel this morning. You are obviously taking the air after such bad weather.'

His English was faultless, tinged with the slightest German accent.

'Siemens,' he continued, 'had the good idea, some sixty years ago, of promoting Helgoland – or Heligoland – as a maritime spa. The local people thought he was mad – who would come here and pay to throw themselves into the cold water? And who would risk the crossing? But it paid off.'

'And the other gentleman?'

'Dr von Aschen? He became our spa doctor and soon Heligoland was on the fashionable map. And now Sir Edward continues to look after us well. May I escort you up the steps?' They had both left the Strandbazar and von Kroseck offered her his arm.

'No, thank you. Sir Edward will show me the Oberland tomorrow.'

'You will be walking one mile by a third of one mile! But English ladies are great explorers and you will walk from the Nathuurn to the Sathuurn very quickly. I mean, from the Horn of the North to the Horn of the South. And the Kartoffel-Allee is not as busy as Piccadilly, I can ensure you!'

'You speak excellent English, Captain von Kroseck.'

'But yes, I am on a British Crown Colony, am I not? I also studied in England and went to a Naval College at Greenwich.'

They were walking along the 'Lung Wai' and gazed at the deserted bathing place. 'This is called the "Rothes Meer", the Red Sea,' Kroseck explained, 'because the red clay makes the water look red. Do you like bathing, gnädiges Fräulein? But of course you do. The English are sea creatures, amphibians I think.'

'No. I don't particularly enjoy inundation.'

She stared at the grey, uninviting inlet; primitive steps had been hewn into the rock and a rope balustrade hung sodden on rusty supports. The air grew chill.

'I think I shall return to the hotel,' she murmured.

'Of course. I shall be dining at the Princess Alexandra this evening and am at your disposal if you seek company.'

'Thank you, but I am dining with Sir Edward.'

'Of course.' They retraced their steps and Captain von Kroseck accompanied her to the Conversationshaus.

'I wish you a pleasant Sunday with our Governor. Lambrecht's Wettertelegraph is usually reliable and this excellent barometer promises better weather tomorrow. There will also be a new moon tonight but do not look at it through glass if you want good luck. Auf Wiedersehen, Miss Prince.'

He saluted and walked briskly into the late afternoon.

* * *

She dozed until six and then, gazing from the window, she noticed the new moon in the west, a sharp line of silver, high and slender above the sea.

'Well, Captain von Kroseck,' she mused, 'what tribulations await me now? And how did you know my name?'

Pictures of Millicent Freshet returned, a nacreous fish caught in the swaying nets of memory, and other, darker, destinies. She frowned, rose, and rang for Stine for her water.

She stripped and washed herself thoroughly; the cheval glass showed her again a dark, tall young woman, now divested of outer garments, of bodice, corset, petticoats and under-hose, her pale flesh mellowed by the light of the oil lamp and candles.

My silver dagger shall hold the coil of my hair tonight; she fetched her hairpin and adjusted her hair, noticing as she did two faint smudges of dark hair in her armpits.

A vivid memory suddenly asserted itself, visual and olfactory, of Fräulein Lorenz, another of the solo Flower Maidens, raising her arms to sing and tempt, and displaying an abundant tangle of twisted, sweat-caked hair…She turned away from the mirror in disgust and washed herself yet again with the now tepid water that remained.

(But it was on *my* breast that he placed the silver star…)

She chose her burgundy silk dress and also her creamy lace stole that hung across her bent elbows as she stood before the mirror, her hands clasped before her waist.

Muffled voices sounded from below, also laughter; she descended the now familiar staircase and saw Edward exchange pleasantries with a young woman, the one, she felt sure, she had seen reading the papers in the lounge that morning.

Edward came towards her, smiling.

'Miss Frances! Delighted to see you! May I introduce Miss Ingeborg Frostrup, a Danish guest. My island used to be Danish but the Danes backed the wrong horse when we were fighting Boney so we seized it. But Miss Frostrup has forgiven me long ago!'

Frances smiled yet barely concealed a pang of displeasure at the thought of spending an evening with Miss Frostrup, but the young Dane explained that she was dining elsewhere tonight, at the Princess Alexandra. She shook hands and smiled; she was ash-blonde and her eyes were the colour of smalt.

'You can't eat better than here,' said Edward, leading Frances to their table. Champagne, she noticed, was already standing in the ice bucket.

'Just to celebrate day number two for us!' he laughed, uncorking it. 'Real Veuve Cliquot! I admire the Germans but I can't stand their Sekt. So, Prost!'

They clinked glasses and she rejoiced in the sparkling freshness, the piquant needles of effervescent wine, the departure of Miss Frostrup and the reassuring awareness of how her dress and stole suited her.

Edward rubbed his hands in delight.

'Well, tell me about your day. Not so bad here, is it? I even organised a new moon for you.'

'I did very little. I sat in the library and received your letter. You were quite right to postpone our expedition.'

'And then Miss Milly arrived and you had an earnest tête-à-tête.'

She stared. 'How do you know that?'

'I know everything,' he laughed, 'my spies are everywhere. No, Jensen mentioned that she had come to the hotel, so I assumed it was to see you. About her singing, I expect.'

'I was most rude to her. I must see her again to apologise.'

'You will. I'm going to throw a big party after Government House is open for business again. Do try to hear her sing. She's a strange girl. It will mean a great deal to her to have a professional listening.'

She frowned and looked down at her napkin. 'I'm not a professional.'

'But you sang in all sorts of opera houses, didn't you?'

'I only sang in one, which wasn't really an opera house, more of a, well, temple. I had previously met a conductor called Hermann Levi when I was in Munich with my parents and he heard me and invited me to sing in a work called *Parsifal*, in Bayreuth. I only appeared there for one summer. I was a so-called Flower Maiden, and had to dance as well as sing. That was all.'

'You're too modest, Frances. You brought great pleasure to many. Keep the singing going. I'm only a silly amateur, but you have a real gift, real power.'

'Power? What sort of power?'

'You can bring joy, alter people's lives.' He refilled their glasses. 'My, we are getting serious, and so early in the evening! What else did you do?'

'I had a brief lunch, then went for a walk round the Unterland. I met a very courteous German naval officer.'

'Did you indeed! Von Kroseck, I expect. I'd heard he was here. There's something going on: the new German Emperor likes to play with toy boats in the bath and they're thinking of boosting their navy. He was here, by the way, as a child, and loved it. I'd heard too that the Brandenburg is steaming round the island. Von Kroseck's a clever man.'

'He knew a great deal about the island. He was most solicitous and offered to give me a guided tour. A handsome man, too.'

'Ah! Now I'm jealous! But, Miss Prince, don't forget that your Governor has the droit de seigneur on this island! Oh lord, that sounds a bit off! I mean, I have the privilege of escorting you around the Oberland and nobody else!'

He drained his champagne glass and refilled it, hers also.

'I've ordered some fresh oysters from Cuxhaven – they came across with you yesterday. We can have lobster again, or try some excellent fish, halibut say, or turbot, Steinbutt. But the choice is entirely yours, of course.'

Her gorge rose at the thought of swallowing oysters, those briny twists of slime, and she declined; the fish, however, was tempting and she ordered turbot.

The moon had set and the lighthouse pulsed behind them in the darkness. She refused another glass of champagne and Edward finished the bottle quickly.

'Frances,' he said, 'may I call you Frances?'

'Of course.'

'I can't say how splendid it is to have you here. Jack has so often sung your praises and, well, I thought, yes, a proud father and so on. But I agree wholeheartedly with his encomium!'

'You've only known me for about five hours,' she said dryly.

'Is that all? A vision of delight steps on to my barren Rock and transfigures it! I would prefer Aphrodite on her shell, but would not inflict the grey North Sea on anyone in such dishabille!' His eyes glittered in mischievous delight.

Very well, she thought, I shall spar with you, sir.

'I'm sure Miss Frostrup and Miss Freshet enhance the beauty of your realm.'

He laughed vociferously. 'My blest pair of sirens! My sphere-born harmonious sisters! Fröken Frostrup writes poetry in Danish and in Heligoland dialect – or Halunder spreek - quite impenetrably! My son is smitten by her, I believe.'

'I look forward to meeting your children and your wife.'

Yes, it'll be jolly when they're back. Augusta will have bought up half of Wertheimer's I expect. I'd better requisition the British Navy to carry all the stuff across.

'Beatrice will have half a dozen new bonnets and all of them will end up blowing across to Schleswig-Holstein. Charlotte will have at least twenty boxes of books for my library.

'Augusta will cast a reproachful eye on the new wallpaper in Government House and demand that we start afresh. William will seek out Fröken Frostrup and they will sit and read the poetry of Emil Aarestrup. William tells me that he's a highly sophisticated love poet, a daring immoralist, in fact, and an aesthete whose worship of the beauty of the female body is expressed in his mastery of poetic technique. A good excuse, it seems to me, to dally all day with Inge.'

' "We read no more that day",' she murmured. He caught the allusion. 'Well, Francesca!' he laughed, 'this isn't exactly Rimini but there'll be plenty of dark winds to blow you about here! Ah, would I were your partner in crime!'

He had ordered a dozen oysters which arrived on a bed of ice and dulse with red, deeply divided fronds. He swallowed them with relish.

'Ah, bliss! Oh edible bivalve mollusc!'

She shuddered.

'I've never been able to eat them.'

'You don't know what you're missing,' he rejoindered, 'who knows, we may find a pearl for you!'

'I have pearls enough,' she replied.

'My tutor at Oxford once told me,' he continued, wiping his mouth with his napkin, 'that he couldn't stand anything to do with the Baroque. Apparently the word "baroque" comes from the word "barroco", a rough pearl, you know, with excrescences. And it's the same word as "verruca", or wart. But I'm sure your pearls are round and smooth, liquid and lustrous!'

She felt uncomfortable and was glad when the fish course arrived.

'I think Pouilly-Fuissé tonight,' Edward suggested.

'Did you meet my father at Oxford?' she asked.

'No, Jack and I met later, he was at Oxford before me. We met in the army. I was a captain in the Coldstream Guards and was ordered to the Crimea in eighteen fifty-four. Jack and I got together when we were on the staff of the Earl of Cardigan.

'We were at Alma, at Balaclava and then Sebastopol. I was slightly wounded there, nothing to speak of though. We both won the Crimea medal and clasps and I got some Turkish medals and, believe it or not, the decoration of the fifth class of the Medjidie.

'When we do our amateur theatricals up here I sometimes bring them out for effect. Augusta doesn't like it if I pin them on to people for fun. I pinned one onto Tasso, once, our Newfoundland, for a joke, but she was very disapproving. I say, are you all right?'

A wave of nausea swept through her, suffused her, a greenish churning; she felt her palms grow clammy, her brow bead in perspiration.

(The huge, silver star of the Bey of Tunis on her breast, the undisguised hatred of the haughty woman at his side and then, later, his comments on the dreadful portrait which Renoir had done for him and which she later saw – a feverish head, obsessive, expiring, a face decomposing, drained of colour, the eyes rheumy, the lips pursed in a sickly awareness…It makes me look like a foetus, he had murmured, an embryo of an angel, perhaps. Or am I not like an oyster, an oyster swallowed by a gluttonous sybarite, an Epicure? What do you think, Miss Prince? And he had touched her hair and run his fingers over her cheek on the Rialto Bridge at dusk. A decomposing face, a feverish head, an embryo-oyster curdled in coagulating slime…)

'I'm sorry, Edward. It was just, well, something upset me. The thought of the oysters, perhaps.'

He put down his napkin and looked at her in contrition.

'Fanny, I've been insensitive and ungallant. Do please forgive me.'

He ordered the waiter to remove the oyster shells.

'If you prefer to be alone I'll quite understand.'

'No, please, it'll pass.'

She smiled weakly.

'Do try to eat a little of the fish,' he urged her, 'it's very light and the flakes are very digestible.'

But she could only toy with it.

The rest of the meal passed in desultory conversation about trivial matters; she sipped a little of the wine. At ten o' clock she pleaded a headache and he escorted her to the foot of the stairs.

'If you can face it I'll come round at ten for our walk. But if you feel indisposed I shall quite understand.'

'I'm sure I'll be fit enough then,' she reassured him, and gave him her hand, which he kissed.

As she went up the stairs she saw him light a cigar, take his half-Hunter from his waistcoat and look at it. He then ran down the steps on to the esplanade and she saw the red tip of his cigar disappear into the darkness.

* * *

Again, the night was miserable. The bedroom seemed to be overheated and she lay perspiring beneath the heavy eiderdown.

She dreamt that she was being engulfed by a vast oyster shell which sucked her into a gelatinous mass within; she was drowning in 'The Red Sea', a pool of blood from which Captain von Kroseck was trying to fish her; she was in Venice with Miss Frostrup who unbuttoned her blouse and bodice and took out a pearly breast whose nipple was an emerald. 'This is for Edward!' she said, laughing.

Frances got up, grateful for the proximity of the commode. She returned to bed and, as on the previous day, she fell into a deep sleep from which Stine, bringing her breakfast, woke her.

She drew back the curtains; the sky was clear and an orange ball hung over a placid sea. After a leisurely breakfast and her morning ablutions she dressed, putting on her worsted skirt, stout boots, thick blouse and woollen jacket; she arranged her Tam o' Shanter before the mirror and smiled as she glimpsed her elegant umbrella standing in the corner.

She left it and went downstairs at ten; Edward was smoking a cigar in the lounge. He extinguished it and came towards her with a smile, his arms outstretched.

'The gods smile upon us!' he said, 'Perfect weather to blow away the cobwebs. I stayed up rather late last night over grog with Herbert von Kroseck in the Princess Alexandra.

'And Miss Frostrup?' she asked, archly.

He laughed.

'No such luck! She retired early and left me and Herbert to it.'

He offered her his arm, which she accepted, and they stepped forth into the bright Sunday morning.

'I am wearing my "Patrick" coat in your honour,' he smiled, 'it's a new one, good English stuff, none of your loden here. It's also waterproof they tell me. And my glengarry matches your Scottish bonnet!'

He cut a dashing figure and was obviously in high spirits; they walked up the shallow wooden steps and stopped half way to catch their breath, gazing down at the Unterland below, the landing stage, the Düne.

'We used to be one island,' he said, 'we were originally joined by a neck of land but a violent storm in seventeen twenty severed the link and the Düne's been sailing along independently ever since.'

The sea glittered under the sun and the perpendicular red cliffs up which they were climbing, fissured and scoured, seemed more welcoming beneath the screaming gulls.

He pointed down to the harbour below, the Marcusplatz and Strandbazar.

'Do you see that small tower down on the right? That's what they call the Rathaus, it's just a small administrative office manned by a couple of my chaps. It would make more sense to have Freshet down there, but he likes it up on the Oberland and so that's where the telegraph office is. Vorwärts!'

She smiled and they continued up the steps; the gulls cackled and soared, and the wind tore at her tammy. They reached the top and the Oberland stretched before her.

Her first impression was that she was standing on a vast ship, a ship a mile long which stretched to a tapering prow in the distance. The sea sparkled below and the surf creamed amongst the rocks; she stood on a green deck of grass held by the reddish sandstone which rose steeply from the waters below.

To the right she saw the settlement, a cluster of small houses, some of brick, others of wood, and above them, standing proud, she saw a large house above which the Union Jack fluttered in the wind. Behind the house, on a small rise, stood the church, stern and isolated. To the left, in front of her, she saw the lighthouse; a rough track led from there to the island's tip, the Nathuurn, where stood an isolated reddish stack, streaked with gull droppings.

'They call that the North Horn!' he said, pointing. 'There are all sorts of grottos here, and rocks and caves. They all have odd names, the Nun, the Monk, the Pastor and so on. If the weather holds we can have some Illuminations with Bengal lights, we can hire boats and visit the grottos. It can be jolly spooky though!

'Now, Miss, pay attention. I have a plan. We'll take the Falm – the main path to you! – to the lighthouse and you can meet McBride who'll bore you to death with high-powered, gas-filled electric filament lights, feux éclairs, flint glass and mercury floats, of which he's inordinately proud, and then we'll move on to the church for eleven o' clock service and you can meet the Reverend Timothy Heywood who'll give a sermon on fortitude and Christian charity.

'You'll meet most of the English there, and after that we'll move on to the telegraph station for a glass of grog and a bite to eat with Freshet. And yes, you can talk to Millicent and beat your breast in contrite debasement. I'm sure your apologies will be quite redundant anyway.

'Then we'll walk back along the cliffs to Government House which you can visit in all its primitive glory; you can also salute the flag and think of England. Then I'll escort you back to the Unterland, leave you to rest, then come round to your hotel at the usual time for our evening repast. Is this in order, gnädiges Fräulein?'

'Agreed, mein Gouverneur!'

Why was she in such a good mood despite having slept so badly? She strode along the springy turf of the Falm at Edward's side, her arm in his, feeling the tweed of his "Patrick" overcoat, amused by his voluminous glengarry, his golden side-whiskers, his girlish mouth, his lively, animated way of speaking. Rabbits fled as they approached; she saw the white bobbing scuts, the pellets on the grass.

The Rock had done well, she learned, during the Napoleonic wars but experienced bitter poverty when the English business-houses closed and the inhabitants lost their monopoly over piloting. Without pilotage there was little source of income until Siemens had his bright idea of establishing a Seebad.

He, Edward, had been appointed Governor some twenty years ago; he had reformed the constitution, modernised the bathing arrangements and encouraged farming. 'They've got about three hundred sheep here now and goats as well – you can hear them coughing over there!'

They approached the lighthouse, a squat, red brick building surmounted by a large white dome and thick glass windows; a small garden towards the cliff edge showed the remains of a vegetable garden and much tussocky grass, rippling in the wind. Edward went to the solid wooden door and hammered on it.

'Hullo, Hamish, it's me and a fair maid from England!'

McBride opened, a stocky bald man with a weather-beaten face and sparse ginger beard and dressed in his best Sunday uniform, immaculately ironed. He invited them in and he and Edward discussed shipping, the Brandenburg, the weather.

'I'm sure Miss Prince would love a tour of inspection, Hamish, but we're off to the kirk. We now have electricity here, don't we, Hamish? No coal-cresset beacons like in Cornwall. No more acetylene mantle-burners or whatever they were, and the clock-machinery revolving the lens is run by electricity too. We've got the strongest light in the North Sea.'

'Thanks to you, Teddy,' grunted Hamish.

'Well, perhaps. Anyway, we're off. Street lighting on the Falm next, Hamish! Better than the Potzdamer Platz by a mile!'

They stepped out into the sun, and the wind blew her skirts before her; she held Edward's arm and they walked swiftly to the Episcopal Church of St. Michael and All Angels.

Edward led her to the front pew which was reserved for him, his family and the local dignitaries.

The church was full and, to the right of the altar, Fanny saw Millicent Freshet playing the harmonium. She wore a dark blue moiré silk blouse and dark skirt and her hair was drawn into a bun in the nape of her neck as it had been the day before. She looked at Frances and started, then smiled wanly.

She stopped playing as the Reverend Timothy Heywood entered from the left, a tall, bespectacled young man with round shoulders and a slight limp, his hair lank and untidy.

The service was much as she remembered the Anglican service to be, and she felt a stab of guilt at not having worshipped for many years.

The hymns were familiar; 'O God our help in ages past' was a favourite, and it was delightful to hear Edward sing loudly in a high tenor voice. And she sang with him in her high mezzo-soprano; she felt her breasts rise and a column of air and praise pass through her throat and open mouth. Edward turned and smiled at her as he sang. She smiled too, but also knew that her voice had been sadly neglected.

The sermon was uninspiring and her thoughts wandered; she held her tammy in her lap and gazed at Millicent Freshet who was looking at the preacher.

You wish to devote your life to art? Beware, foolish girl, of the dangers awaiting you. Live for happiness, not art. One longed for me once as I sang and danced for him. He placed a silver star upon my bosom; he told me I should come to him. But then he died...

She suddenly felt Edward's thigh pressing, it seemed, against her skirt. The pew was not full as Augusta and the children were not there, but it seemed that this pressure was deliberate. She was sitting on the edge of the pew, constrained by its hard wooden handrail and could not move to the side. And the warmth of his leg was not entirely displeasing to her.

After the service Edward stood by the door of the church next to the vicar, whose cassock flapped in the wind, and greeted the celebrants effusively: Mrs Ohlson, Mr and Mrs Morris, Commodore Phelson, Miss Lavender, Mrs Wilson, Mr Robertson, the Misses Payne…He knew them all and exchanged pleasantries, introducing them all to Frances who felt acute embarrassment at his fulsome praise of her putative accomplishments.

The sun beat down but the wind was strong and it was only with difficulty that the Reverend Heywood managed to close the door after the last of the worshippers had left. Frances suddenly caught a glimpse of Millicent Freshet who sought to hurry away. Edward paused, smiled awkwardly, then called after her.

'Now, Milly, no French leave, we're coming to see your father, the old reprobate, for a grog and a bite to eat.'

Frances felt the sun and wind in her face; the sea beat beneath, surging and soughing in the rocky cavities. The three walked towards a lonely house on the edge of a cliff, the women's skirts blowing wildly, their hands holding bonnet and Tam o' Shanter. Edward ran ahead of them and reached the telegraph station first, hammering on the door for Bill to open.

* * *

The two women sat in the small drawing room and gazed out at the sea which had grown steely grey since clouds had covered the sun.

The meal had been frugal and uncomfortable, for Millicent's father was taciturn and, it seemed to Frances, censorious. Edward had talked enthusiastically about gutta percha wire and the success of the new telegraph cable which now linked them to the mainland, seeking obviously to dispel Bill Freshet's morose reticence; when Millicent rose to remove the remnants of the meal he winked at Frances and insisted that Bill show him the new double-lever sending key which had been supplied from London.

‘We’ll leave the ladies to it, Bill, and you can tell me all about your double-current duplex arrangement. We’re in the vanguard of progress here, Fanny! What Heligoland does today the world does tomorrow!’

The two men left the room, Millicent returned and the two sat in silence. A large vessel appeared like a smudge far out on the horizon; a brass ship’s clock ticked on the mantelpiece above the empty grate. Then Frances spoke.

‘I wanted to apologise, Millicent, for being somewhat abrupt with you when we met before. The fault was entirely mine, and I do hope you’ll forgive me.

‘It’s just that, well, you touched quite inadvertently on certain memories, certain experiences, that were painful. It was all tied up with singing, with devoting oneself, or exposing oneself, or being vulnerable somehow, and also guilty.’

Millicent fingered the buttons on her blouse and stared out at the sea.

‘No, I was to blame. I shouldn’t have intruded. I just felt, I just – I’m sorry.’

Her voice died away and Frances saw tears welling in her eyes. She held out her hands to the girl, but Millicent ignored them; the wind rattled the shutters which were hooked to the wall outside.

There is desolation of spirit here, Frances thought, and she rose and knelt before her partner, seizing her hands and holding them in hers.

‘I shall listen to you, Millicent, and we shall sing duets together, if you wish. Edward would love to encourage you, I know.’

Again that twisted, almost ugly smile moved across the girl’s lips.

‘Did he say so? Well…’

They heard voices outside the door and both stood together, moving towards the window which was now speckled with raindrops.

The two men entered; Edward was in good spirits.

‘I’ll get you a new Morse machine, never fear,’ he said to Bill, ‘Frischen’s been doing some interesting things in Germany. Ah!

Observe! The fair and the dark!' he chortled, moving across to the two women and placing his hands on their shoulders.

'A charming picture. Right, Mendelssohn duets it shall be. "I would that my love could express itself just in a single word". I told you Heine was here, didn't I, Fanny? He felt a cloud of leaden boredom weighing down on him and crushing his skull. More fool him!'

It seemed to Frances that Millicent had winced under Edward's touch.

'Yes,' she said, 'you did.'

'We'd better move. Thank you, Bill, for feeding us and showing us the instruments. We won't stay for tea as the rain's started to fall and I want to show Fanny my refurbished residence.'

Bill Freshet fetched their coats and Edward helped Frances into hers; he showed Millicent the "Patrick" label on his, but there was no smile on that pale, large mouth.

They hurried through the squally shower across to Government House; he offered his arm but she chose instead to hold her tammy with one hand and her skirts with the other.

The house, an imposing brick building, stood four-square on a slight rise and was surrounded by a low wall; a shingle path led through stunted shrubbery past an ancient piece of ordnance upon wooden blocks and the flag pole to the portico surmounting a heavy door. Edward withdrew the key from his pocket and opened the house. She entered and stood in the large hall which smelt of fresh paint and varnish.

Two portraits caught her eye, one of Queen Victoria as a young girl, the other a large and stirring canvas of a hussar in full charge. The floor was tessellated with black and white tiles, and an elegant staircase led off from the left.

He led her to the reception room, the drawing room, the dining room and a room which he called the ballroom; the wallpapers, stained glass and heavy furniture pointed to the influence of William Morris.

'We're up to date here!' he smiled when she drew his attention to the Gothic influence.

'I went to Red House once, my brother was quite friendly with Madox Brown and when they set up their decorator's studio he put some money into it. Now in the ballroom here I've fixed up a stage, do you see?'

She noticed a raised dais and various silk screens at the back of the room.

'It was a bit cramped before and I had the devil of a job persuading Her Majesty's Government to provide the funds, but I explained that it was very important to impress the Germans with Shakespeare and so on. We'll put on the German classics too, which I've been translating. I tend to leave the day-to-day running of the place to the chaps in the office. Let's see if the Erard's been tuned.'

The grand piano stood in the corner; he opened the lid and ran his fingers along the keys. The tone was pleasing, and he extemporised skilfully. The room was cool and she shivered as the autumn rain fell more steadily against the large uncurtained windows. He stopped.

'Right, no more tickling the ivories, that's enough for one day!'

He led her upstairs to a long gallery with several bedrooms leading off.

'Now, you can take your pick. And the marvellous thing is, we have piped running water here and splendid water-closets. And take a look at this!'

He opened one of the bathrooms and pointed with a flourish to a magnificent cast-iron bath surmounted by an enormous geyser. 'It's a Shanks Independent Spray Bath,' he explained, 'made in Glasgow in eighteen seventy-five. It's almost as big as a ship's boiler! And we've also got somewhere something called a "Wellgunde", a kind of rocking-bath you can put inside the bigger one.'

He laughed in obvious delight.

'You can pretend you're a Rhinemaiden, how about that? I also saw a marvellous thing in Hamburg called an "Undosa", a kind of motorised bath for rocking up and down. Just think, you could lie here in beautiful hot water and splash about, luring us poor men to our doom with the stormiest, bleakest weather outside! Ah, civilisation!'

She felt strangely discomposed, standing close to him in the empty bathroom and stared at the bottles of 'Divinia' perfume, the bars of 'Lilienmilch' and tins of Sarg's tooth powder. And suddenly he put his arm around her waist.

'Edward, Teddy, please…' she stammered, blushing. She turned away from him.

'I just wanted to say,' he said, 'how marvellous it is to have you here. We'll have some splendid times this winter, I feel sure. Don't worry if your Uncle Teddy gets a bit carried away. It's my nature. I expect Jack told you.'

'No,' she said dryly.

'Right, let's go down and look at my study.'

They went downstairs and he led her along a dark corridor to a room at the side of the house. The first impression was of a room choked with heavy furniture, pride of place being a massive writing desk on which stood a bronze figure of Siegfried, naked and standing at full length with his sword raised. On the base was inscribed 'Enemies surround us'. Edward fingered it irreverently.

'Augusta bought it for me as a present. But I prefer those,' he added, pointing to the wall.

In a fine gilt composition frame there hung a picture of sea nymphs disporting with a dolphin.

'I wouldn't mind a frolic with those in the "Wellgunde" tub!' he joked. 'I think it's an Adolphe la Lyre, I picked it up in Paris.'

His library was extensive, with equal numbers of books in English and German; she also saw literature in Frisian, Danish and Dutch as well as the classics in Greek and Latin.

'I'm translating Schiller at the moment,' he explained, 'fancy being the Maid of Orleans?'

'No,' she answered.

Her mood had darkened and he sensed this. The visit to the other rooms, the servants' quarters, the kitchen, the utility rooms, was perfunctory; they left the house and walked past the straining flag along the steps down to the Unterland.

'Seven thirty, I hope,' he said quietly. 'It'll be the last time at our table as the tribe comes back tomorrow and I'll obviously have a lot to do. But on Tuesday I'll get the men to carry all your stuff up to the house. You can have the best guest room and your own water closet and bath. If Jensen can spare Stine she can live in as your own personal maid.'

'Yes,' she said, 'seven thirty.'

* * *

She sat before the dressing table mirror, brushing her hair vigorously.

She felt annoyed at Edward for his suggestive improprieties and also at herself for admitting such prudish disapprobation; a feeling of swollen listlessness also reminded her that the menses were imminent.

She would wear her hair loose, she decided, and changed into a lace leg-of-mutton sleeve blouse (which, she knew, showed off her figure to advantage) and a dark blue velvet skirt; at her throat she wore an onyx cameo brooch which her mother had given her.

She descended at a quarter to eight, wishing not to appear too eager, too punctual. Edward was sitting in the lounge reading The Times and smoking a Manoli cigar; he jumped to his feet and smiled as she approached.

'Charming as ever! Heligoland obviously suits you! Now, Uncle Teddy has an admission to make.

'I've been naughty, hogging you all to myself and not sharing you with more people. So I thought I'd invite some worthies to join us, Tim Heywood our Reverend, Miss Lavender who's been on the Rock since time immemorial, and Herr Garer. Tim teaches the English contingent as well as looking after our souls and Herr Garer teaches the Germans. I'm quite happy for him to do this and he doesn't make any trouble. He's a bit of a pedant but knows an enormous amount about my domain.'

'As much as Captain von Kroseck?' she interrupted.

'Much, much more. They're sitting at the table – mustn't keep them waiting!'

Was this barb directed at her? Was she relieved that she would not be alone with Edward this evening? Was she disappointed at not having the Governor to herself? They entered the dining room and she saw the three of them sitting at a table by the window; the two men rose as they approached.

The Reverend Heywood she had already met; he had changed into a dark suit and a white choker and stood in the stooping posture which she had noticed in church.

Why, she asked herself, do Anglican clergymen have such a bad posture, standing like submissive question marks? She turned to Herr Garer, a stocky, middle-aged man dressed in a brown tweed suit; he had broad cheekbones and small bloodshot eyes, and his hair was cut en brosse. Miss Lavender smiled up at her through faded, light blue eyes. She was a frail old woman dressed in black, resting one gnarled hand in her lap and the other on the head of a silver-topped cane. Frances sat between the Reverend and Herr Garer; there was, she noticed, no champagne.

'I recommend the lamb if you want a change from sea food,' Edward said, 'then we can try some of the capital claret I got over from Hamburg.'

'They live well in Hamburg,' announced Herr Garer, 'it is a fine city.'

'Are you from Hamburg, Herr Garer?' Frances asked.

'No, I am from Mecklenburg-Strelitz,' he explained, speaking in a rather halting English, 'and therefore a subject of the Grand Duke Friedrich Wilhelm.'

'But he doesn't mind living under the benign stewardship of our dear Queen,' smiled Miss Lavender.

'He's got a new boss now,' laughed Edward, 'a new Emperor!'

'My allegiance will always be to the Grand Duke,' insisted Herr Garer. 'I am a Mecklenburger, not Schwerin, but Strelitz.'

'I am a philatelist,' said the Reverend Heywood unexpectedly, 'and Herr Garer kindly provides me with postage stamps from that Grand Duchy when it issues them. I still lack the eighteen sixty-four one-third silbergroschen dark green unused.'

'Tim likes the Heligoland stamps,' commented Edward, enjoying the soup that they were all now drinking. 'Did you know that Queen Victoria's bun has a tiny lock of hair depending from it in some issues, and that makes a huge difference, apparently. "The farmer's daughter hath soft brown hair – Butter and eggs and a pound of cheese!"

' Now,' he continued after having scrutinised the three bottles of claret that had been brought to the table, 'do you know that our Euphemia had beautiful brown hair in her early years: her sister showed me her portrait once.'

Miss Lavender blushed in a winsome manner and looked down at her lap.

'How long have you been in Heligoland, Miss Lavender?' asked Frances, intrigued and strangely envious.

'My father was a naval officer and we settled here shortly after the island was officially ceded to Great Britain. I stayed here after his death and never returned to England. So I have been here over seventy years. I was here long before Teddy.'

'She told me once she had tea with Foseti,' joked Edward.

Frances looked puzzled. Herr Garer laughed out loud and tucked his napkin behind his starched turned-up collar.

'Heligoland was originally called Fositesland,' he explained enthusiastically, 'after the god of that name. He, Fosite, often called Foseti, was a son of Baldur and Nana. He was a god of justice. In the mythology of Iceland he is called "Forseti", that is, the one who sits before an assembly, and hence a god who passes judgement. He was a wise ruler, but his temple was destroyed by St. Ludger in the eighth century. My friend Timothy will not agree, but I say that Christianity did much harm in Frisia.'

The Reverend Heywood smirked and smoothed the crumpled tablecloth.

'My friend Otto delights in goading me,' he said. 'He knows that one of Ludger's attributes is the swan and, like Lohengrin, he appears over dark waters to bring light into heathen darkness.'

'"Mein lieber Schwan!"' Edward carolled, much to the astonishment of the waiter who brought the lamb.

'Have you seen *Lohengrin*?' Frances asked the curate, who looked away.

'No, I have not, alas.'

'But I have!' announced Miss Lavender, 'and I saw Wagner too.

'It must have been about fifteen years ago when I was visiting my sister and her husband in Hannover. They managed to get tickets for the opera and it was a marvellous occasion. I remember a beautifully sung Elsa, I think her name was Fräulein Weckerlin. We caught a glimpse of Wagner who seemed enraptured by the production. I'm told that he later invited Fräulein Weckerlin to sing Gutrune in the *Ring*.'

'What did the old boy look like?' asked Edward, eating greedily.

'He was a shortish man but his head was very impressive, especially the chin.'

'I do not like his music,' said Herr Garer, his mouth full of potato, 'his operas are far too long and far too noisy.'

'Very German, then,' quipped the Reverend, sipping his claret. 'I, too, saw him once when he came to the Albert Hall in London. I was not impressed by the man, who looked ill at ease and had the manner of a charlatan. The Albert Hall was about half empty. It was a dispiriting occasion, with excerpts from the *Ring*. They had to play the Ride of the Valkyries twice because one of the tenors was hoarse and couldn't sing. I would not care to see the *Ring*, a farrago of bombastic vulgarity. *Parsifal* I reject utterly. It is an affront to Christianity, a disgusting work.'

'A work you know intimately?' asked Frances, turning deathly pale, her heart pounding violently.

'No, I have never been to Bayreuth, nor would I wish to. My friend the Suffragan Bishop has been, however, and has written a pamphlet condemning the work. The celebration of the Holy Eucharist on the stage is utterly offensive and the endless meditations on blood are tasteless. There is also much vulgarity in it.'

Frances rose to her feet, trembling.

'Forgive me, I must just retire for a moment,' she stammered, laying down knife and fork.

The three men got to their feet, and Miss Lavender attempted to rise, but Frances restrained her.

'Can I help you, dear?' the old woman asked solicitously.

'No, I'll only be a moment, do please sit down.' She walked unsteadily to the retiring room set aside for the use of ladies, and burst into tears.

The blood, ah, the blood, a gaping wound…Her blood too, she could feel it on her thighs, flowed in sympathy, in strange concinnity.

(Blood spurted too, in *Tristan and Isolde*, he told her, as Tristan tears off the bandages, the blood spurting to greet the woman in whose arms he would die. But the polluted blood of Amfortas is deranged, shrieking in hideous torment when the chalice is uncovered. And Amfortas too tears open his bandages! Here flows the blood that poisons me, unsheathe your swords and thrust them in, deep, deep, up to the hilt! Prattle, you inane fools, the Master told me of these things, his flower-maiden. He told me of blood and redemption, he spoke of my loveliness, he pinned the star to my breast, here, here…Ah, the wound, the blood…)

She buried her face in her hands, sobbing, and then made her way upstairs to her bedroom.

Here she placed the strips of absorbent cloth close to her bleeding body and sought her phial of tincture of opium which she always took at these times of the month, and lay down. After fifteen minutes she rose, washed her hands and face in cold water, dabbed eau de cologne on her skin and descended.

Edward, she noticed, was waiting at the foot of the stairs.

'Touch of the vapours, was it? Come and finish your meal, Fanny. I hope Tim didn't say anything that upset you, he's a pompous ass, I know.'

She rejoined the group and apologised for her indisposition; Herr Garer recommended the local schnapps, which she declined.

She ate little, almost nothing. The Reverend Heywood was silent and avoided her gaze; Miss Lavender looked at her in sympathy.

Edward was holding forth on the impending reopening of Government House and was planning a grand reception, a firework display and a nocturnal illumination of the grottos. 'I'll try to get Queen Victoria across and Vicky, poor thing,' he cried, his manner expansive after an excellent dinner and the claret. 'Then, if our Queen wants to see her favourite grandson your new Kaiser will get an invitation too, but he must be civil to his mother.'

Herr Garer was not very enthusiastic.

'Kaiser Wilhelm the Second has not forgiven the Grand Duke of Mecklenburg-Strelitz for his dilatory support of Prussia in eighteen sixty-six and his disapproval of Prussia's annexation of Hannover.'

He became agitated and lit up a large cigar. Edward looked at him.

'Better not light up, old boy, Miss Prince still looks a bit green about the gills.'

'Not at all, please continue,' she said, 'and would you mind if this modern woman smokes too?'

She reached in her reticule for the box of Neptun Cigaretten.

'Marvellous,' cried Edward, 'and I'll have a Manoli if Miss Lavender doesn't object.'

'Not in the least,' came the frail reply.

'Have a Manoli, Tim,' urged Edward, pulling out his cigar case and holding a candle in order that Frances might light her cigarette.

'No, thank you, I do not smoke,' he replied. The curate looked reproachfully at Frances and turned to Edward.

'How are Augusta and the children?' he asked, 'and when do they return?'

'Tiptop, thank you, and they're coming home tomorrow on the Eitel-Friedrich if the old tub doesn't sink to the bottom of the North Sea with all the goodies they'll be bringing. I'm going to need a team of strapping young men to heave it all up the steps to the Oberland. Then Fanny – I mean Frances – joins us on Tuesday. If we've broken all the backs on the island then Herr Garer can dragoon the schoolchildren to help.

'You look a bit peely-wally, Tim, you could do with some exercise. How about carrying Frances's trunks for her?'

'It would be a privilege,' came the muted reply, 'but Dr Graevenitz fears I may suffer from phthisis and recommends that I spare myself.'

'Where is Graevenitz?' cried Edward, 'I haven't seen him in months. What good's a sawbones if he's not here to tend to our ailments?'

'I am told,' said Miss Lavender, 'that Dr Graevenitz is in Berlin for a holiday, but that Dr Saphir will be his locum.'

'Right,' said Edward, 'so no falling over cliffs, please, till Graevenitz gets back, no swimming across to the Düne in case the Kraken gets you. We'll all keep fit – Garer, you look as though you could lose a bit of weight. Physical jerks every morning at six outside Government House for all islanders.'

'Does that include me?' asked Miss Lavender mischievously.

'Of course, Euphemia, you'll lead the ladies in graceful and delicate exercises. Frances is an accomplished dancer, don't you know? But be careful in case Fröken Frostrup insists on Scandinavian exercises with hoops and rings and so on.'

Herr Garer laughed vociferously and choked on his drink, a glass of Jägermeister; the Reverend Heywood sat impassively.

At ten o' clock Miss Lavender rose to her feet and Edward summoned Herr Jensen to provide a boy with a lantern to escort her up the steps to the Oberland. The Reverend Heywood would have none of it and insisted he would take Miss Lavender home. Edward kissed the old woman graciously on the cheek and shook the clergyman's hand.

He returned to his cognac, to an inebriate Herr Garer who was now speaking in German to Frances, mopping his perspiring brow with a red handkerchief.

Bismarck, he was arguing, had made life impossible for Vicky, the Princess Royal, after her husband's tragic death last year. He, Garer, would not forgive the Hohenzollern for what they had done to Germany.

He rose unsteadily to seek the jordan in the gentlemen's room; after his return Edward took him by the arm and intimated that it was getting late and that Miss Prince was exhausted. He helped the German into his lodencoat and Jensen stepped forward to organise assistance for the nocturnal ascent.

Frances sat and finished her Neptun cigarette; through the large window she saw the moon, fuller now, low over the sea.

Edward ordered another cognac and was glad when she asked for a small one. She sat bent forward, her arms folded across her stomach to relieve the griping spasms that had gripped her.

'Hope the evening wasn't too bad,' he smiled. 'Miss Lavender's a dear and Garer's all right, got his heart in the right place. Tim's a bit of a prig, we all know that, but he's very lonely. I don't think he'll stay with us much longer, keeps on about moving back to England. You do want to stay, don't you, Fanny? We can easily get hold of Jack if you can't bear the sight of another lobster. But I do hope you'll stay.'

She had crossed her legs in an unladylike manner and was gazing at her black patent leather shoes. Her feet were small, and she was proud of them.

Would it not seem churlish to leave just as Edward's wife and family were coming? Did she wish to go back just yet? What would her father say if she turned up in Cuxhaven? Thoughts, like moths, fluttered through her mind. Should she stay here in the hotel? But Edward would not hear of it.

He was an engaging man, delightful in many ways, but he touched her too frequently, and took liberties. Perhaps she was becoming as priggish as Heywood. She shuddered.

Had he seen her dance, had he heard her sing, he would

not, perhaps, have been as peremptory in his rejection of that miraculous work.

‘Feeling all right, Fanny?’

She smiled at him and finished her cognac.

‘I’m feeling tired. Thank you, Edward, I look forward very much to Tuesday. I hope Augusta is prepared.’

‘Of course she is. The house will be full of servants tomorrow. I’ll send Jörg round Tuesday midday to bring up your possessions. There won’t be any other guests in the house for a while, and we’ll treat you like royalty. You’re a very precious young woman.’

He looked quickly round the dining room, which was now empty, and kissed her freely and fully on the mouth.

* * *

☙ CHAPTER TWO ❧

The infusion tasted brackish, and Frances frowned as she tasted it.

'Swallow,' ordered Lady Augusta Hennicker-Heaton. 'I insist that my daughters drink it every month as I did when I was a young woman.

'I make it myself from arnica, Iceland moss, yarrow, valerian and sage, also balm-mint. They do not grow here, of course, nothing does, but my herbalist in Berlin sends me herbs, roots and bark.

'God is an apothecary who provides us with all we need. I take a heaped teaspoon of the prepared herbs and steep them in a quarter of a litre of water, boil it, and let it draw for three minutes. It should be taken half an hour before breakfast.'

'Thank you,' said Frances, 'but I'm sure that everything will be fine in a couple of days.' She smiled at the Governor's wife who sat opposite her and was looking at her intently.

Frances was resting on a dark green chaise longue in the bedroom at Government House (the best guest room, Edward had claimed).

The flux of blood had been severe as she had climbed the one hundred and ninety steps that Tuesday morning, and she had held the railing tightly as Jörg, an enormous man in homespun trousers, boots and a blue nautical jersey had carried her possessions from the Unterland to the Oberland, from 'bedeeln' to 'boppen' he had called it, as though they weighed nothing; he had overtaken her as she walked carefully upwards, disappeared at the top of the steps with her boxes and cases, returned, come back up, gone back down, returned…

A stern woman had opened the door to her and had escorted her up to her room; there were still workmen in the house and the servants scuttled to and fro.

There had been no sign of Edward, unless he were ensconced in his study, but she knew he would have come to greet her had he been in the house. Or had the memory of that Sunday kiss inflicted him, as it had her, with acute embarrassment? It had been a kiss compounded of cigar smoke and cognac, yet his lips had been yielding and moist. And hers? And hers? Her heart had beaten wildly, she had sensed this, as she stood watching him leave, and she had then mounted the stairs. The cheval glass had shown her a flushed countenance and eyes preternaturally bright.

The night's sleep had been interrupted by blood and *Parsifal*. Forget, forget, put it behind you. But how could she? Do flowers bleed? What had he inhaled from the breath of her lips? The smell of blood? 'Let me blossom for thee, stroke thy cheeks, let me kiss thy mouth…I am fairest! Nay, I! I smell sweeter! Nay, I! Yes, I!…' She had tossed and turned, vividly remembering how guiltily she used to read her grandfather's bible at the onset of puberty and how puzzled, baffled, intrigued she had been by the description of the uncleanness of women in Leviticus. Shall I, she had wondered, be put apart for seven days when I have my issue of blood? What man should sit upon my bed and be unclean? My father? If any man lie with me and my flowers be on him, shall he be unclean? But what flowers are these? She had been haunted, she remembered, by the image of a black bloom of blood growing from her vulva and had turned to her friend Sophie for enlightenment, but Sophie had known no more than she; guiltily they had both read Leviticus, the Song of Solomon. Then, she thought, I became a flower, but a flower of death, for he died…

Towards dawn a gentle breeze had risen from the sea, wrinkling the grey waters and stirring the flags on the island; at seven the smell of strong black coffee had wakened her from a shallow sleep.

She had later sat, that Monday morning, in the library, resting, dozing, embowered in the fragrance of Neptun cigarettes, her feet on a large, soft pouffe, immersed in Tennyson, in "Maud".

The day was windy but bright; figures passed by on the esplanade outside and a few small boats bobbed on the waters near the landing stage. Her mind was not on the poem and she had constantly thought of Edward's mouth on hers, her agitation, her bleeding. She had gazed out of the window and had suddenly caught sight of Miss Frostrup standing by the Strandbazar in a dark, tight-fitting coat with matching bonnet, a knot of golden hair gleaming at the nape of her neck. She had been laughing in an animated manner and talking to somebody whom Frances had been unable to see, hidden as he was by a projecting corner of the building. She had been leaning on an elegant umbrella, but it was not, thought Frances, as stylish as mine. She had been talking to a man, Frances had been sure of this.

Was it Edward? Her heart had beaten violently, and she had put down her book; she had stood and walked to a corner of the window to get a better view. It had indeed been a man but not Edward, for he had been wearing a German naval uniform. It was Herbert von Kroseck, and the two had been sharing a joke, Miss Frostrup had thrown back her head in amazement, and Frances had seen the flash of her teeth as she laughed. The naval officer had offered her his arm and the two of them had disappeared from view behind the Strandbazar.

Moody and discomposed, Frances had paced the library and had found herself reading The Times, particularly the discussion of The Lord Playfair's Amendment Bill to the Merchant Shipping (Fishing Boats) Act and The Lord Thring's Infectious Hospitals Bill. But this would never do. She walked upstairs, stanched her blood, seized her cloak, her beret and her dainty opera glasses (she had put them on her chain around her neck in case she wished to study the cliffs, the birds, the caves) and stepped outside.

The sun sparkled on the sea in the fresh October light; she had walked to the landing stage where the ferry boat was about to leave for the Düne, also known as the Hallem. She had fished the required sixty pfennigs from her reticule and had slipped her gloved hand into the colossal grip of the ferryman who had helped her into his boat; there would be no other passengers.

The ferryman had spoken to her with a very pronounced accent which she had not understood; she had averted her gaze and looked at the sand-island which they were rapidly approaching and which grew closer with every stroke of his oars. On arrival he stepped from the boat and pulled it up the wet sand; he had then pulled out a large turnip-watch from his inside pocket, held it close to her and pointed to four o' clock; this was the time when he would meet her and row her back.

She pulled up her skirt and stepped on to the beach; fish nets were drying in the wind and she inhaled the smell of fish and tar. She had walked along the shore past a few fishermen's cottages, seeing no one, apart from a silent child who had stared at her. A boat lay upturned on the sand, and the wind whispered in the tousled marram grass. Then, suddenly, she came upon it: a carved figurehead of a woman which had been fixed to the low wall of the lifeboat shed.

The figure, of painted wood, represented a woman whose head was thrown back so that her turquoise eyes stared upwards in a transfigured gaze; her fair hair hung down and partly concealed her thrusting breasts. The nipples, Frances had noticed, were green, and the paintwork was fresh, with no sign of sand or lichen. A mermaid, Frances had murmured, and well looked after. And she had felt a curious reluctance to think of the figure staring at night, in alternate light and darkness as the lighthouse illuminated it. The gleam of the gold hair which half encircled the neck had made her think of Ingeborg Frostrup, as did the tilt of the head upwards; she was glad that the smile of the mermaid did not disclose her pearly teeth.

She had struck inland along the sandy path through the restless grass; a track led to a small Russian Orthodox chapel surrounded by rusty iron railings.

She had opened with difficulty a creaking iron gate and entered a small cemetery commemorating the loss of all hands when the Russalka sank in eighteen eighty. The ship was Russian and a single headstone, surmounted by a St. Andrew's cross with slanting bar, listed the names of officers and men. The chapel had been locked, and she had turned to leave, but suddenly started.

A figure in black sat on a rudimentary bench, staring at her: it was the Reverend Heywood. He had risen to his feet when he saw her looking towards him, he had blushed, and doffed his clerical hat.

'I am sorry to have startled you,' he had murmured.

'I am sorry to have disturbed your meditations,' she had replied. She had gazed down the track to the beach, the cottages, the figurehead, the slate-grey sea, the Rock beyond. They had both stood in silence, then he had been the first to speak.

'I hope, Miss Prince, that you will forgive my uncharitable remarks yesterday, my somewhat churlish behaviour. I feel strongly about certain matters and occasionally give the impression of unfriendliness. I should, as a Christian clergyman, show more humility.'

Frances felt that her aversion to him was not assuaged, yet she had sought to reassure him that she had not been offended by his rejection of *Parsifal*.

'I know that it is a difficult work for some,' she had murmured (and how trite it had sounded), 'but there are some who find it – miraculous.'

He had gazed down at his shoes, still holding his hat in his hands.

'Perhaps I shall see it,' he had said, 'and you might, Miss Prince, give me some advice on how I might prepare for it. I am sure that much study is needed. You could, perhaps, sing some of it for me, although Terpsichorean gyrations would, I feel sure, be lost on a man like me. And I am no King Herod demanding distraction.'

She had shuddered, feeling her flesh creep.

'I think I have already explained that I have given up music and drama, Mr Heywood.' She had felt weak, remembering that she had eaten nothing at midday, but she had refused to sit lest he should take his place next to her.

'Do you read Russian, Mr Heywood?'

'Alas no,' he had replied, 'again I fear I must disappoint you. All I know is that the ship was called the Russalka and that she was lost in a violent storm. All were drowned. They lie buried here. I have taken it upon myself to look after the chapel and to see that it is whitewashed and kept in good repair.'

'Russalka is a water nymph,' Frances had explained, talking more to herself than to him, 'like Undine.'

She had rounded on him.

'Have you read Fouqué's charming story, Mr Heywood?'

He was looking at the sea.

'I have no time for secular reading. Elementary water spirits fall outwith my purview.'

'And the figurehead?' she probed, 'is she Russalka do you think? Or do you avert your gaze when you approach her? I feel that I can see a passing resemblance to Miss Frostrup.'

A strange, sly smile had played about his lips. 'Again, this is outside my purview,' he had murmured.

'The affinity felt by the female sex for water has always baffled me,' he continued, 'it is water and the spirit that I preach, not water and the female form, the female soul.'

'But is not Mary herself associated with the water, the sea? Is Mary not the stella maris?'

'No,' he smirked, 'this is false etymology, a false gloss of a Hebrew name. But we know that artists and dreamers prefer the beauty of metaphors to the rigours of scholarship. Mary and the sea, the tides, the moon – very well. This is Papist self-indulgence. True knowledge comes from prayer and devotion, not excrescences.'

'Does art, does music, mean so little to you?'

'The highest music, yes, for it shows us realms that approach the divine. But modern music – Wagner above all – I find contaminated. We have already spoken about this, Miss Prince, I know, and I have apologised for my rudeness yesterday. But Wagner is a man without love, one bent only on his own self-aggrandisement. I know you esteem him highly, but I cannot share this enthusiasm. I am not interested in coups de théâtre, Miss Prince, but in truth and its incarnation in Our Lord.'

She had turned away from him and had sought in vain to hold back the tears that were bursting from her eyes, tears of anger, of frustration, bitterness, embarrassment, annoyance. She had wept uncontrollably, her shoulders shuddering.

He made a move to comfort her; she had sensed this and had thrust him away with her free hand, the other clutching a sodden lawn handkerchief. He mumbled apologies, solicitude, but she had refrained from turning to him. She rested her forehead against the whitewashed wall of the chapel and her sobs subsided.

'Miss Prince, let me take you to Rasmussen. He will row us across immediately, we need not wait for the ferry.'

'I wish to wait,' she had told him, blowing her nose, 'and I want you to go.'

From the corner of her eye she had seen him bow stiffly, then make his way across the grass to the beach.

The October sun still sent her its warmth and she stood for five minutes leaning against the wall. She had seen the Reverend Heywood call at a small cottage from which a fisherman had appeared, and the two men get into a boat and row across to the Rock. She was weak from lack of food, tired, and all too aware of the discomfort of menstruation, but the thought of sitting in a boat with her adversary had been intolerable.

She had sat and dozed on the bench for a quarter of an hour and then noticed the ferryman rowing between the two islands. She walked down to meet him, passing close by the figurehead, Russalka, and her mood improved. She had suddenly had a naughty vision of the Reverend Heywood touching the wooden breasts, and she also recalled her dream of Miss Frostrup scooping out a pearly breast tipped with an emerald eye.

She looked across at the ferryman and suddenly saw the Prinz Eitel-Friedrich rounding the tip of the Düne and making its way towards the Rock; smoke streamed from its stack and she heard the jangling of the ship's bell, and, unexpectedly, the boom of a cannon up on the Oberland, fired in salute.

The ship had arrived early and she saw the small boats row out to where she lay at anchor, saw passengers descend into the bobbing dinghies, then stepping out on to the duckboards. She had put the opera glasses to her eyes; their powers of magnification were not great, but she saw a tall woman in black being greeted on the duckboards by a dignitary whilst a young man and two girls stood behind her. The group had walked along the landing stage; there had been much activity, many boxes and trunks were being lifted, carried and deposited on the shore.

Her heart had pounded as she looked for Edward, but he was nowhere to be seen; she imagined him in scarlet uniform with gold frogging, wearing a pillbox hat, and applying a taper to the ceremonial cannon which had boomed out over the bay. She had looked for some five minutes, seeing the crowd disperse and the boxes stowed on several handcarts. The ferryman landed and she stepped into the boat; he had rowed vigorously and she sat gazing down into the dark green water, at fronds of twisting bladderwrack.

'Goodness and truth dwell but in the waters: false and base are those who dwell above,' she murmured as the landing stage approached. She slipped her remaining coins into the ferryman's calloused hand as he helped her on to the duckboards; then, hurrying, she strode past the nets, ropes and lobster pots towards the lights which were now burning in the Conversationshaus.

At seven thirty she had decided not to eat alone in her room (for she had always felt an aversion to eating whilst looking at a bed) but dressed casually and descended the staircase.

The smell of beeswax was wholesome, as always, but raucous laughter from the dining room had made her frown. Herr Jensen had hurried towards her, perspiring and exuding a strong smell of pomatum.

He was, he explained, in a distressed and embarrassed predicament. A group of Hamburg merchants, men of business, had requested that the dining room be set aside for a private function that evening: they had come across on the Prinz Eitel-Friedrich that afternoon and had neglected to inform him in advance. He had not wished to offend them as they were influential people who might invest considerable sums of money on the island.

He knew that Miss Prince would not be dining with the Governor this evening and wondered if she would mind dining in her room. Another solution would be for her to eat in the library which he would put entirely at her disposal. It could be her own chambre separée. There was a gentleman in there studying old maps but as he was not a guest of the hotel he, Herr Jensen, would ask him to leave. Did she perhaps know him? It was Kapitän von Kroseck.

She felt a pleasant sensation at the news, and had told Herr Jensen not to incommode the gentleman, she would not mind a bit if he stayed. Herr Jensen had thanked her profusely and ushered her in to the familiar room.

Herbert von Kroseck was standing at a desk where maps of Heligoland were displayed; he recognised her immediately and smiled, holding out his hand.

What a pleasant surprise it had been to see her again! Had the citizens of Hamburg driven her from the dining room? They were indeed a resourceful and energetic people, representatives of a new Germany. She had described Herr Jensen's embarrassment and the reasons why the staff were carrying in table linen and cutlery. He declared that he would depart that instant in order that she should enjoy her meal in peace. She had insisted that he should stay and that she did not wish to interrupt his studies.

He had looked at her. It is true, he said, that he ate in the Princess Alexandra, but he would gladly join her for a meal if she would permit.

It would be a pleasure, she said, blushing. Captain von Kroseck had ordered a bottle of dry white wine, and they had stood and drunk a toast.

'The Queen!' he cried, his eyes twinkling, 'the Queen!'

But how had her day been? She had explained that she had had a quiet morning and had also caught a glimpse of him and Miss Frostrup from the hotel window.

Yes, Ingeborg was an old friend of his. They had walked along the cliffs and she had made preliminary sketches of that famous stack, the Nathuurnstak. She was an accomplished painter in watercolours.

A very talented young woman, Frances had commented.

Yes, she had had exhibitions in Copenhagen. Sir Edward had encouraged her and he had bought some of her work. What would the island do without him! His family had returned, did she know? Had she heard the cannon? It was a little piece of fun, but Sir Edward personally fired the salute when Lady Augusta returned. (Here she had smiled to herself.)

He asked if she been at the landing stage when they had arrived. No, she had been on the Düne. Ah yes, the Hallem, our little sister island. But there was very little to see there. She had seen the figurehead, the Russian graves and the Reverend Heywood.

Herbert von Kroseck had laughed at this. Yes, he is often there. Mischievous people say he goes across to check that Russalka is in a good state of repair and that he gives her a new coat of paint every month or so. This is why her bosom is so white.

Now she had laughed too. He had claimed that it was the chapel he was in charge of! Ask Sir Edward, Herbert von Kroseck replied, it was he who told me about the Reverend Heywood's little hobbies! He and Miss Frostrup should get on well together, she had quipped, with their interest in painting. She had noticed a similarity between Russalka and Miss Frostrup – had this been the Reverend's doing? He had smiled at this and winked at her: Now, Miss Prince, let us not be too over-imaginative!

They had both eaten plaice caught, the waiter insisted, that afternoon. She had asked the Captain if she might ask a question. Of course, he replied. What sort of woman was Sir Edward's wife? Frances was in awe of her before she had even met her.

She comes from a very good family, he explained, von Strachwitz, Baltic aristocracy from the Courland. Her father, General Waldemar von Strachwitz, had fought with great distinction in the Wars of the Liberation. She was a highly intelligent woman, much more intelligent, he suspected, than her husband. He, Herbert, esteemed her highly, but did not think that there would be too much – what was the word? – rantipoling when she was back in Government House.

Frances had burst out laughing at this. His English was amazing! How on earth did he come across such a word?

It was one of Sir Edward's, Herbert von Kroseck explained. The Governor was full of such outlandish expressions in both English and German. The children are sometimes embarrassed by him, although he tends to spoil them. William is, well, you will meet him. Beatrice seems flighty but is talented; Charlotte is deep and studious, but, I think, unhappy. He then suggested they should drop formalities, telling her his Christian name. She in turn told him she was called Frances. A charming name. His sister was called Franziska.

Frances had then asked him about his family. Small landed gentry from Oldenburg. Lady Augusta Mechthild von Strachwitz-Hennicker-Heaton looked down her aristocratic nose at him. The von Krosecks had farming friends in England and he, Herbert, had been to school and college there.

He had always loved the sea and had made the navy his life. He was wedded, so to speak, to the Imperial Fleet and did not have a wife.

He had then asked her about her family. Oh, military, she explained, related some way back with the Orange-Bromeheads. Her father had been in the Coldstream Guards and had met Teddy – Sir Edward – on the Crimea. They'd been friends ever since.

Her mother had died some three years ago and she was an only child. Her father, she said, blushing, doted on her.

He had every reason to, Herbert had said, and had asked her where her father was now. He was somewhere in Germany. He was a military attaché of some kind, and she thought he was in Berlin.

And why had she come to Helgoland? Herbert asked. She, well, had had a difficult time, one way and another, and her father had thought she needed a holiday. So here she was, she had laughed, dining with an unmarried man in a chambre separée!

He had laughed at her frankness, and her feeling of guilt at such flirtatiousness had been transient. She enjoyed his company and the evening had passed agreeably. Gales of laughter had floated across from the dining room.

They are obviously having a very convivial evening, Herbert commented, raising his glass. When Hoffmann von Fallersleben was here they all sat at a long table in there and drank many toasts. His, von Fallersleben's, had been to German women. Now, Herbert continued, in my view English ones are equally adorable and so I drink to you, Frances.

This he had done, and she had smiled across at him. After the meal they drank cognac, and he had left after kissing her hand. He had wished her all the best for the following day's move and assured her that Lady Augusta had a heart of gold, despite her austere manner.

She had gone to bed happy and did not feel the normal agitation that precedes the prospect of change, however slight. There were no dreams of blood, and she had drifted into sleep, hearing from a long way off bibulous laughter and footsteps on the corridor. She had thought of Edward and their imminent meeting but only with the faintest feeling of embarrassment. With Lady Augusta back in Government House dignity and decorum would surely prevail.

Yet there had also been the slightest feeling of regret at the impending intrusion of this tall woman in black, this high priestess of the Rock, into Edward's realm. Domdaniel, she had murmured, before turning onto her left side to sleep.

* * *

'Miss Prince?'

Frances jerked herself out of her reverie.

'I am sorry, Lady Augusta, I was daydreaming. I'm sure, as I said, that I will be perfectly all right by tomorrow, but I appreciate your concern.'

Lady Augusta was a handsome woman with iron-grey hair scraped back into a bun; her features were dignified, her skin pale and unwrinkled, her eyes piercing. She wore a severe gown of dark-grey silk and her waist, still slim, was encinctured by a dark belt. An eyeglass hung on a long gold chain about her neck.

A priestess indeed, Frances mused, a chatelaine, a guardian. She reminds me of…No, she reminds me of no one. She visits me. She thinks I look anaemic and is kind enough to seek to relieve my natural pains.

The room faced west and was suffused by a strange orange light from a sun low over the waters. Lady Augusta stood; Frances tried to rise but the older woman forced her to sit. 'There is still a great deal of disorder in this house. Sir Edward will take no notice, but I shall. I am punctilious, he is not. If you require anything please let Frau Stoeven know, our housekeeper. If you require the services of a lady's maid this can be arranged.

'We dine punctually at six thirty with drinks beforehand in the drawing room. I like to eat at midday but my family prefers the English custom. You will meet my children then. If you are still indisposed I can order a servant to bring you a meal here.

'Do not neglect to take my infusion. Thyme is also a good antidote to abdominal cramps: it may be taken internally or externally. Dinner is informal, we do not dress. Auf Wiedersehen.'

Frances rested for a while, then rose and sat on a window seat, gazing at the sea which moved restlessly beneath the late afternoon light.

What was it, she wondered, that had brought Sir Edward and Augusta von Strachwitz together? Where had they met? She idly speculated on their courtship, then reprimanded herself for such indelicate conjectures.

She looked back into the room. It was smaller than the one in the hotel but more elegantly appointed, with rosewood furniture, a Turkish carpet and pink satin wallpapers. The bed was less pompous and had a graceful tester. The greatest delight, however, was the adjoining bathroom with piped water, a water closet and the enormous bath.

She blushed when she remembered standing there with Sir Edward last Sunday afternoon, and how he had embraced her.

It had meant nothing, she convinced herself, and neither had the kiss.

She pulled herself together and decided to write to her father before dinner, and sat at a dainty escritoire. The house was supplied with electricity from its own generator, but it was light enough in the room with its tall windows.

She described her stay in the hotel, the meeting with Sir Edward and others, her first impressions of the island, the return of Lady Augusta and the impending dinner with the family.

'Do not worry about me at all, Papa. I am feasting on lobster practically every evening and Sir Edward is most solicitous. I have also met a delightful German naval officer who is most attentive. There is much rantipoling here so I shall have no time (or inclination) to think about the past. Your affectionate daughter, Fanny.'

She sat for a while, then put on the overhead light which flickered alarmingly but then suffused the room with a mellow glow. She dressed in a mutton-sleeved blouse and skirt, and coiled her hair into a chignon. There was no cheval glass but a pier glass had been fixed between two of the windows.

She looked at herself: a tall, attractive woman stared back at her. Would he greet her with a kiss if his wife were there? 'Auf in den Kampf, Torero!' she laughed, and went downstairs punctually at six o' clock.

* * *

She entered the drawing room which she had briefly visited on Sunday, a room spacious and handsome and now cheered by a flickering log fire in the hearth. Her eye was immediately drawn to a large painting which had not been there before and which hung over the fireplace, a painting of Bismarck leading Napoleon the Third towards King William of Prussia at Sedan. Lady Augusta had seen her enter the room and came up to her.

'You are admiring the painting? It is by Wilhelm Campenhausen. I purchased it in Berlin. Although we are on British territory, Miss

Prince, I like to remind my husband of German victories. Queen Victoria would most certainly approve.

'My husband, by the way, is not here and sends his apologies. He is away on business and does not know exactly when he will return. Did you see him leave?'

She had not, and felt in equal measure both relief and disappointment. A butler brought drinks on a silver salver.

'Sherry? I do not drink it but Sir Edward insists that we pour it.'

She took a glass of amontillado and was aware that three young people were looking at her.

'May I introduce my children? William, Beatrice and Charlotte, come forward.'

They moved towards her and she shook hands with them, the young man first, and then the two girls. William was tall and willowy with his father's looks, she thought, but attenuated, and the handshake was limp and condescending. He was dressed in a light-grey suit with a rich mauve cravat, and an elaborate watch-chain hung across a sunken abdomen.

The girls were both in green silk dresses; Beatrice was fair, was the shorter of the two and had her mother's eyes which sparkled, however, with irreverence; Charlotte was darker, her features were pleasing but disfigured by a mulberry birthmark beneath her chin and on the left side of her throat.

An awkward silence prevailed; the fire crackled in the grate and the wind moaned outside, catching the flag in the dusk and twisting it to and fro.

It was William who spoke first, summoning the butler to bring another glass of sherry.

'Well, what do you think of our exile, Miss Prince? I wouldn't arrogate to myself the status of Napoleon but can guess what he felt on St. Helena.'

He spoke with an affected drawl which she found unpleasant.

'I like it here,' she replied, 'I used to spend school holidays on various Scottish islands and have always loved the sea.'

'The sea's fine, but I wish that Pa would get a posting in the Caribbean or somewhere like that.'

He wandered to a window and stared out into the gathering darkness, lighting a small cigar.

'I believe you are a singer, Miss Prince,' said Beatrice, 'Papa has told us about you.'

How many more times, Frances thought, do I have to disabuse my listeners of this expectation?

'Your father is too kind. I sang for one season, but then gave it up.'

'Pa won't have you slacking, Miss Prince,' drawled William, flicking a speck of tobacco from his lapels, 'he'll have us all doing *H.M.S. Pinafore* when he gets back.'

'Papa doesn't like Gilbert and Sullivan,' said Charlotte, blushing, 'he thinks it's too trivial.'

'He enjoyed *The Mikado*,' said Beatrice, 'he wanted to put it on over here once, don't you remember?'

'He's not fussy, he likes quite a few things,' quipped her brother, 'he took me to a play once in London where there was this talk about a woman having a thermometer in her corsets to measure how hot her passion was. Wow!'

'Have you been to the theatre in Berlin, Miss Prince?' asked Lady Augusta, looking coldly at her son.

'I'm afraid not,' she replied, 'but I saw some plays in the Hoftheater in Munich, Paul Heyse, I think.'

'Ah yes, I forgot you were in Bavaria. Bayreuth, was it not?'

'Yes, it was.'

'Prince Bismarck told me once that Wagner had written to him demanding that he, Bismarck, should burn Paris to the ground. I am no friend of the French, but am not sorry that Prince Bismarck did not heed this request.'

'Papa said he would take me to Paris,' said Beatrice, taking a small sip from a glass of lemonade.

'French culture is alien to me,' continued Lady Augusta.

'At least there's something happening in Paris,' commented William, taking another glass of sherry.

'You should experience what is happening in Meiningen first,' insisted his mother. 'The Duke of Sachsen-Meiningen has an excellent troupe and high standards of acting and production.'

'There is to be a new play put on in Berlin called *Before Sunrise,*' explained Charlotte, awkwardly, 'it's by a young writer called Gerhart Hauptmann.'

'Not another Ibsen, I hope,' muttered Lady Augusta, 'I'm told that *Ghosts* is disgusting. I cannot tolerate this kind of thing. What life must be like in these Norwegian coastal towns I shudder to think.'

'What happens in it?' asked Beatrice.

'I would not care to say,' came the reply.

'Sounds like Heligoland to me,' smirked William, 'I'll ask Pa to write a play about us. Miss Prince would love to be in it, I'm sure.'

'Don't be preposterous!' snapped his mother, 'Please forgive him, Miss Prince, my son has a somewhat undisciplined imagination.'

'When Pa gets back we must decide what play to do,' said Beatrice, 'I don't really care for Schiller and we've done Shakespeare.'

'Here comes the rain again,' said William gloomily.

The butler drew the curtains and Lady Augusta left to check the dinner arrangements; they sat on sofas and gazed into the flames.

'I really can't stand the idea of another winter here,' said William, flicking ash into the grate.

'It won't be too bad,' said Charlotte, quietly, 'I've brought lots of new books to read.'

'Don't let Ma see them if they're racy,' giggled Beatrice.

'I've been reading Baudelaire,' commented William, 'really hot stuff. "Je suis comme le roi d'un pays pluvieux" – you can say that again, but there are no lubricious ladies contorting themselves before me. I say, Miss Prince, I am sorry.'

'Please don't apologise,' she murmured.

The caked coal collapsed and a tongue of fire spurted up the back of the grate.

'Dinner is served,' announced the butler. Lady Augusta entered and led Miss Prince into the dining room; the three children followed.

Grace was peremptory and Frances looked around the room; it was darker than the drawing room and a large crystal chandelier hung over the massive oak table.

The centrepiece was a silver epergne modelled on the quadriga above the Brandenburg Gate, an ornament of which Lady Augusta was inordinately proud.

'I picked this up in an auction in Berlin,' she explained.

'I'm sure Sir Edward will like it,' said Frances, unfolding a stiff damask napkin.

The tablecloth was faultlessly ironed and the meal, when it came, was excellent: bouillon and beef marrow, sole au vin blanc, pheasant and pineapple. The wine, Rhenish, prickled on the tongue. The conversation veered this way and that and was finally dominated by Lady Augusta and her views on Bismarck and the Kulturkampf. William frequently yawned behind his napkin, and the girls' attention was manifestly elsewhere.

'We retire early here,' Lady Augusta explained at the end of the meal, 'I do hope you will sleep well. You will find a well-stocked library which you are free to use. Do you require anything? An infusion, perhaps?'

Here the girls giggled, much to their mother's annoyance.

'No thank you, Lady Augusta, I have sufficed.'

'Breakfast is an informal meal,' Lady Augusta explained, 'Sir Edward likes the English habit of leaving chafing dishes with hot food on the sideboard. I do not, but I submit to his wishes. Sleep well.'

And, unexpectedly, she came across to her English guest and kissed her on the forehead.

* * *

The night was overcast but the lighthouse, stabbing the darkness, covered the sea intermittently with a scaly silver, a finger of wrinkled argentine.

Frances sat in her room on the chaise longue next to a small tiled stove which, as in the Conversationshaus, was heated; she had drawn back the curtains and was staring into the darkness.

A disturbing thought presented itself to her, an image, rather, of Russalka leaping forth in the light, and jumping back in the darkness. She thought of Edward and found his absence puzzling. Surely he would have told her that he would not be there when she arrived? But why should he? Had he fled, she wondered, because of her? But she reprimanded herself promptly for this arrogance – what right had she to presume anything of the sort?

His kiss had meant nothing, it was a spontaneous token of affection, nothing more; he would kiss Miss Frostrup, Miss Freshet and countless others in a similar way. Miss Lavender too.

She smiled wryly and turned to the pile of books that Lady Augusta had carried to her room: the homilies and patriotic verse of Pastor Gerok, Spielhagen's *Hammer and Anvil*, various writings by Clausewitz and the poetry of the Heligoland writer Hans Frank Heikens. She opened the poet and attempted to read, but gave up almost immediately.

A grey blast of boredom seemed to strike her from the Gothic print and she put the books aside. She reached for her reticule to extract the Neptun cigarettes but then realised that she had no lucifers, and the thought of seeking a fidibus and going down to the drawing room to gain a light from what might remain of the fire was distasteful to her.

Should she ring for a servant? The thought of Frau Stoeven's bleak disapprobation dissuaded her, however, and she returned to the window and the pulsing silver thrusts; the wind had grown stronger and she could hear the flag thudding and straining at its pole; the sea groaning beyond.

She thought of the telegraph station and of Millicent Freshet, standing too, she felt, by the window and gazing into the darkness. Perhaps she would move, with heavy golden hair blowing in the wind, in streaming draperies, towards the edge of the cliff and hurl herself downwards into the inky waters…

Frances shivered at these strange fantasies and closed the

curtains; a clock, the handsome one on the landing, standing beneath a print of Alfred Kandler's 'Allegorie der Elektrizität', struck nine.

Oh well, she thought, bed it is – but suddenly she heard movement outside the door and noticed that a small lilac-coloured envelope had been pushed underneath it. She bent down, picked it up and opened it.

'Dear Miss Prince, Willy and I are off to the Stadt London hotel for what Willy calls a nightcap. We'd be delighted if you came too, if you haven't turned in, that is. It's up here on the Bopperlun so we won't have to struggle down those awful steps and back. We'll be waiting for you outside the front wall by the cannon. We'll give you until nine fifteen, then go. Charlotte doesn't come so it will be just the three of us. Ma doesn't approve, but she'll be in bed with Pastor Gerok. Affectionately yours, Bea.'

Frances paced the room in indecision.

Should she leave the house with these young people? What did she have in common with them? How old were they? William was in his mid-twenties, the girls some four years younger. Did she wish to spend an hour or two in a hotel with them? She felt an undeniable antipathy towards William, but it was kind of them, was it not, to have invited her. She looked at the improving literature on the table and hesitated no longer.

She seized her cloak and velour beret and stepped from her room. The house was quiet as she descended the stairs, crossed the hall and went out into the night. The wind had dropped somewhat, but rain hung in the air; it was very dark and a few scattered lights marked the settlement where the hotel must be.

She made her way towards the gate and noticed the light of a dark-lantern, also the glowing light of a cigar where she surmised the cannon might be. She heard voices talking quietly, then a giggle.

'Jolly good, Miss Prince, here we are!' she heard Beatrice say.

The glowing cigar point described a figure of eight in the darkness.

'This way, Miss Prince, but be careful, we can't have you falling arsy-versy in the Stygian gloom.'

Beatrice took her arm and the two women followed William along a narrow track, then along the Falm towards the settlement. The hotel loomed before them, its globular lamps muted but welcoming in the wet air. William went up to the brass-handled front door and opened it for his companions.

It seemed to Frances that she was indeed in London. There was electric light and the walls of the foyer were covered with prints of Balmoral and various gloomy Scottish scenes; Queen Victoria and Prince Albert looked down on all those who entered.

The manager, somewhat casually dressed, Frances thought, came to greet them.

'Evening sir, evening Miss!' he said when he saw the siblings; he turned to Frances and gave a slight bow. 'Welcome to the Stadt London, little bit of England!' he said.

'This is Miss Frances Prince, a friend of my father's,' drawled William, divesting himself of coat, gloves and hat, 'she's a famous singer, don't you know?'

'I am honoured,' smiled the manager; Frances detected a faint smell of whisky.

'Please come through into the lounge, there's room by the fire.'

The lounge was sparsely filled with people Frances did not know, sitting in deep leather chairs.

'Ah, bliss!' groaned William, sitting down and stretching out his long legs towards the fire. He drew out his cigar case, also cigarettes, which he offered to Beatrice.

'They're Jasmatzki Elmas,' the girl explained, taking one, 'I like ones with the gold tip. Please don't tell Ma, she'll have a fit.'

'I certainly shall not,' said Frances, 'may I have one?'

Beatrice smiled conspiratorially and handed them to her; William had ordered drinks, whisky for himself, cognac for Frances and a glass of Hollands gin for his sister.

'I feel,' he drawled, 'as though I were in civilisation again. There's a splendid billiard table round the back, but I'll never forgive Pa for shutting down the gaming tables. Unlike him to suffer from an attack of bleak probity, I must say. Moral rectitude is all very well in its place, I suppose, but there are limits. When I was in London I played Railroad Euchre with some American chaps and lost a lot of money.'

'Silly boy!' commented Beatrice.

'Do you play cards, Miss Prince?' he asked, yawning.

'I'm afraid not.'

'A pity. We could have a jolly evening playing faro or bezique.'

'Pa taught me how to play beggar-my-neighbour,' said Beatrice, 'we played for buttons, I remember. I didn't have any buttons left and wanted to take the cotton one off the waistband of my petticoat, but Pa said he preferred the pretty glass ones I had on my blouse.'

'He would,' said William, taking a sip of his whisky. 'I think he's got a collection of buttons and ribbons and things in a secret drawer. He loves dressing up and he probably gets pleasure from appearing as a woman, wearing silk and things like that. He's got Paul de Kock's *The Lady with the Three Pairs of Stays* in his library, I've seen it. Do you remember the French maid we had briefly before Ma got rid of her? I recall Pa joking about what kind of corsets she was wearing and saying how the German girls now wore Thalysia undergarments because they were healthier and didn't endanger the prospects of the Germans of the future. He said he preferred the Parisian ones, though, and could tell from her figure that she was wearing French.'

'Stop it!' cried Beatrice, her eyes sparkling mischievously, 'what will Miss Prince think?'

Frances, however, did not heed her. I know another, she thought, who, malicious tongues insisted, longed for pink silk underwear trimmed with lace. Did he really write those letters to her as his detractors claimed? Was her name Bertha? How we delight in smearing the great with our own sordid dirtiness. He loved perfumed loveliness, attar of roses, but not as a voluptuary, not as a Sybarite. For there was ravishing beauty, was there not?

'Ah, I smell sweeter! No, I! I blossom lovelier! No, I...Canst thou not love and cherish? Then I must fade, must perish...'

She gazed for a long time at the red blooms of fire, and light gleaming in the highly polished andirons, hearing the two chatter and laugh as from a great distance. I was young then, she thought, so young, not much older than Beatrice here. She looked across at her companions: should she suggest that they drink less rashly? But who was she to interfere? The waiter replenished their glasses with generous measures; she, Frances, took no more. There was much that was maundering in their conversation, so much so that she picked up a dog-eared copy of Punch and left them to their ramblings. She read in a desultory fashion and was suddenly aware that William's now incoherent soliloquy was interrupted by a squeal of delight from his sister as someone sat down on the couch next to Frances. She put Punch down, turned, and saw a tall, slim young woman at her side. It was Ingeborg Frostrup.

* * *

'Well, what a surprise!' drawled the young man. Miss Frostrup smiled at him knowingly and took one of Beatrice's cigarettes.

'Is it? I often see you here, do I not?'

'Do you know Miss Prince?' Beatrice asked. The two women shook hands.

'We have met, I think,' said Frances.

The young Danish woman was striking, there could be no doubt. Her hair was silver-blonde, gathered and tied in a black bow at the back; her features were fine and delicate and her complexion was flawless. Her eyes were of an almost cobalt blue and she wore a dark blue dress which drew attention to her slim figure and remarkably long legs which she crossed and stretched before her, as did William. She inhaled the fragrant tobacco gratefully and turned to Frances.

'They are leading you astray, I see.' She spoke English well but with a marked Danish accent.

'I hope,' she continued, speaking to William, 'that your mother does not know you are here.'

'Lord,' he groaned, 'I am of age.'

'Is Sir Edward not with you?'

'Pa's away somewhere. Anyway, he prefers the Conversationshaus. I can't face staggering down those steps, and the Con. house is too German for me.'

'I like the Princess Alexandra,' said Beatrice, 'but the season's dead now. No more balls with summer visitors, just the same old crowd. Remember dancing the cotillion with the American sailors, Willy?'

'Can't say that I do,' came the reply.

'I believe you paint?' asked Frances, irritated by the trivial conversation of brother and sister and turning to Miss Frostrup.

'Who told you this?'

'Captain von Kroseck.'

'Ah, of course, our observant German! Yes, I do.'

'And you exhibit, I believe?'

'Yes, I have. Have you heard of Thorvald Bindesböll?'

Frances shook her head.

'The Skorgaard brothers?'

'I'm afraid not.'

'We are thinking of founding a group called "Frie Udstilling", free exhibition. We wish to break away from academic painting and introduce a new, fresh element. My friend Jens Ferdinand Williamsen has met Gauguin, so we are not as provincial as you may think. I believe you are a musician?'

'No. I sang once, very briefly.'

'Pa says you have a brilliant voice,' said Beatrice, finishing her glass of Hollands.

'Sir Edward is a connoisseur,' remarked Miss Frostrup, drinking whisky. 'He is an artist manqué. He has given the island so much. I once lived in the Danish West Indies. Very well, the climate was beautiful but culturally there was nothing.'

'"Give me the sun, mother, the sun,"' groaned William. He

had been drinking more whisky, his eyes were bloodshot and his features puffy.

'You like Ibsen, I see,' commented Miss Frostrup, tapping her right foot against the fender. 'I hope you are not implying that Sir Edward did some terrific damage to your health?' She laughed, a strange, shrill laugh and blew smoke through her mouth.

'Smoke, boy! Smoke away, boy! Poor William! Now, we shall get Sir Edward to put on *Ghosts* and poor William will be Osvald Alving. Yes! The Reverend Heywood can be the pastor! And who can play Regina?' Here she stopped. 'But I am talking nonsense. I am sure that Lady Augusta does not approve of modern theatre.'

'My mother,' murmured William, his speech badly slurred, 'my mother - '

Frances rose to her feet.

'I think it is time we went home. I am glad we met, Miss Frostrup.'

'Please call me Ingeborg. I shall lend you some Amalie Skram. You must read *Constance Ring*. I shall show you my paintings. But you are right - the boy here has drunk too much, and his sister too.

'I am sorry Sir Edward is not here, he thinks highly of my work. He is a delightful man in so many ways.' She was standing, now, and kicked William smartly on the ankle.

'Cigar out, boy! Stand, boy! Walk, boy!' He rose unsteadily, as did Beatrice who looked pale and was perspiring profusely.

'Take them both, Miss Prince, and tuck them in. Then sing them a lullaby!' She laughed her shrill laugh and left the room.

Frances led the two away and retrieved hats, coats and lantern.

She guided them through the Falm and then supported Beatrice who was violently sick after gagging and retching. She extracted the key from William's pocket, opened the door and led them quietly upstairs to their rooms.

Pastor Gerok, she reflected ruefully, would have provided a far more wholesome experience that evening, and she went to bed reprimanding herself for accepting the invitation to accompany the two and for not displaying a keener disapproval of their behaviour.

The meeting with Ingeborg Frostrup had unsettled her. Edward – where was he?

* * *

She went down to breakfast shortly after eight o' clock; the dining room was empty except for Charlotte who was sitting alone. The chafing dishes, as promised, stood on the sideboard. Frances lifted the lids but was not tempted by congealed bacon and rubbery fried eggs; she helped herself, however, to some kedgeree.

'Are the others not down yet?' she asked disingenuously, taking her place opposite the silent girl.

'No,' came the reply.

'Lady Augusta?'

'She's been and gone. She says you must ask Frau Stoeven if you need anything, or ring the bell and a servant will come from the kitchen.'

Frances ate in silence and Charlotte averted her gaze. The room faced north and was chill; Frances drank some tea, and then had to speak. 'I am thinking of going for a walk, the day is fine. Would you like to come with me?'

'Yes, if you wish.'

'Then I'll wait for you at the front door, say in an hour?'

'Very well.'

The wind was brisk and from the south-east, but the sky was cloudless. The two women walked out of the gates past the cannon, then struck off to the left, towards the lighthouse, leaving the settlement to their right and the steps down to the Deelerlun, the Unterland, behind them.

Frances looked back at the landing stage below, the fishing boats, the Düne, and thought briefly of Russalka, then put all this behind her and strode along at Charlotte's side. The girl walked quickly, and in silence. After five minutes Frances had to speak.

'I believe you read a lot, Charlotte.'

'Yes, I do.'

'What do you enjoy reading?'

'Everything.'

'Do you prefer German, or English? Your mother doubtless advises you what to read.'

'My mother lets me read what I like. I prefer German. It probes more deeply.'

Is the child really only an adolescent? thought Frances, is she really related to Beatrice and William? Yes, the physical resemblance is there, but strangely transfigured.

The wind tugged at their cloaks; Frances was wearing her tammy and Charlotte a small, tightly-fitting black bonnet with blue ribbons. The sea boomed in the caves below them and sucked back rattling over the shingly beach; they approached the cliff edge but kept a safe distance from it. The sea ran smooth, glaucous and swelling far out, flecked with spume as it dashed and spattered amongst the boulders at the island's edge.

'Have you tried to write anything yourself, Charlotte?'

'Yes, I write poetry, but it is not good. My father likes it, though.'

'He is a good judge, you should let him encourage you.'

'He says you are a good singer, Miss Prince.'

Frances gazed at the shrieking gulls, wheeling and swooping above them.

'He is kind to say so, and perhaps I was once, but not now.'

They walked in wind and sunlight towards the lighthouse where two bent figures were tending the sparse vegetable patch. This is a domain suitable for her, thought Frances, a figure in a tower gazing out at the wild emptiness. Or a Miranda, staring with wild blowing hair at shipwreck.

'Have you ever acted in your father's productions, Charlotte?'

'No, I cannot act. I help him sometimes. He reads things to me and we talk about them.'

'Your father is a very remarkable man.'

'Yes. It is said that he is.'

She lapsed into silence and Frances was pleased to see Hamish McBride coming towards them.

He greeted them gruffly.

'Ye're gettin' quite weatherbeaten, Miss Prince, we'll make a Haluner of you yet, but Miss Charlotte never gets colour in her cheeks, always peely-wally with all that book readin'. It's a braw day for a walk, though.'

'I've always wanted a proper look at the Nathuurnstak,' said Frances, 'I saw the Old Man of Hoy when we were in Caithness, once, the top of it at least.'

'It's a stack all right,' said McBride, 'but don't go too near the edge of the cliff to look at it, it's crumbling away and we don't want another bad accident like that poor lass last year.'

'Who was it?' asked Frances.

'It was Stine,' said Charlotte abruptly.

Frances remembered, yes, the silent girl in the hotel.

'Did she fall down the cliff, Mr McBride?'

'Aye, maybe she did. I keep telling your father, Miss Charlotte, that he must fence around the whole island, but he's got other things on his mind. He's away, I hear?'

'Yes,' said Charlotte.

'In Germany, I expect? There's something going on, the Germans are taking quite an interest in the Rock. That naval captain of theirs isn't here for his health.

'Don't forget now, keep well away from the edge or you'll be down below with the selkies.'

He doffed his cap and strode back to the lighthouse; the sea sparkled below.

'Let's link arms,' said Frances. She felt the need to be physically close to the strange girl, and the lighthouse keeper's warning about the friable state of the cliff had unsettled her.

The girl said nothing; they linked arms and strode through the gusting wind across the short cropped grass. Goats scattered as they approached, bucking and bleating, and the cackling gulls strained and soared above. It seemed to Frances that the wind was forcing them to the edge, whipping their cloaks about them and bent on whirling them into the thundering foam below. And then they stopped. They gazed at a spike of rock, contiguous with the cliff which rose from the churning surf, red sandstone which was streaked with the droppings of a million gulls; beyond it, serrating the sea like an enormous blade, rose the Horn.

A monstrous block, rusted and ribbed with white striations, reared from the booming sea – this is what Frances saw, a fang of fire transfixed and held in the roaring light. What Charlotte experienced she could not tell, she, however, gasped at the colossal pillar of stone, of marl, towering before her.

A blade, or an arm, she felt, thrust from the depths, rusty with blood, cicatriced and streaked. But what fearful form had driven it upwards? And to what sea creature did it belong? To what body in the depths was this a limb? Or a stabbing horn? The surf churned and spume flew in the wind, the sun beat the sea to hammered gold, and a wild exuberance seized her.

She suddenly felt Charlotte withdraw her arm; the girl slipped down upon the tussocky grass and sat with her hands clasping her knees, her cloak like a cloud around her. She stared fixedly ahead.

'I would love to see the full moon shining on the sea here!' cried Frances, 'think of it, the moon lying like thick silver upon the water! And this pillar, this tower, this figure, this – tusk rearing upwards!'

She was abnormally exultant, but Charlotte shivered and sought to gather her booming cloak about her, and Frances heard a moan, a sobbing ululation. She stared at the girl.

'Are you all right, Charlotte?'

'No – I am – unwell – I wish to go home. Please help me.'

Frances pulled her to her feet; the girl shuddered, her teeth were chattering. They stumbled over the grass and reached the Falm; it was then that Frances noticed a bent figure, rooting in a potato field. It was Miss Lavender who, arthritic, nevertheless straightened herself as she saw the two approach.

'Do you have sal volatile, Miss Lavender?' asked Frances, 'I think Charlotte is unwell.'

'Come inside,' said the old woman, opening the door to her cottage, 'let her rest here.'

They entered the low room, the fire flickering in the grate almost invisible in the slanting rays of the October sun which flooded in through the small window.

Frances helped the girl across the room and onto a couch; the old woman fetched salt of hartshorn.

'Inhale this,' she commanded; Charlotte breathed in the pungent ammonia and threw her head from side to side.

'It is green sickness, nothing more,' said Miss Lavender, 'Charlotte always was prone to anaemia.'

Frances looked around the room, a room filled with somewhat shabby furniture, bookshelves, faded prints; a mirror whose silver was badly stained partially reflected the small, windy garden. To have lived here, she mused, on this sliver of rock, for a lifetime, surrounded by a groaning sea, a sea darting into caves and grottos, a sea of steel beneath the moon…

She pulled herself together.

'I can easily walk back with Charlotte, it is not far.'

The old woman offered broth, also a nip of whisky.

'Sir Edward keeps me well supplied,' she joked, 'and I thank the good Lord every day that your father is Governor of this island, Charlotte.

'There is a rumour going round here that Germany has an eye on it. I shall soon lie buried behind the church, and I hope to lie in British soil, not under the Prussian eagle.'

Her faded blue eyes, dusted with horn, gazed at the girl on the couch.

'Your fire is comforting, Miss Lavender,' said Frances as the old woman bent to heap some driftwood on it. Crackling, spitting, the salty wood spat out spurts of flame, ghostly in the amber midday light.

'It is life,' she replied, holding the projecting mantelpiece with gnarled hands for support. The half blind mirror threw back a faded countenance, a sunken visage framed with a halo of silvery hair.

'I must get back,' said Charlotte quietly, rising to her feet.

Frances felt loath to leave, preferring to talk to the old woman and help her prepare her meal. She fetched Miss Lavender's silver-headed cane which stood against the wall.

'Is there anything I can do? Charlotte can easily walk back to Government House on her own.'

'It is kind of you,' said Miss Lavender, 'but I see that you feel uneasy about leaving her.'

'I can easily walk back on my own,' said Charlotte, moving towards the door.

'I shall ask my neighbour Mrs Wilson to walk with you,' Miss Lavender murmured, 'I have an old ship's bell hanging by the door, and when I ring it she comes across. I feel happy to know that I can call on her.'

She looked at Frances. 'Would you mind ringing it, dear?'

Frances stepped out into the wind; clouds had gathered and their shadows flew over the island. She beat the bell with a small brass hammer that hung at its side.

* * *

The broth was warmed on a blackened trivet fixed over the fire; Frances fetched a home-made loaf from a dingy kitchen and leaves of rock-samphire which made an acceptable salad.

'Not as good as Government House fare,' smiled Miss Lavender. 'Do call me Euphemia, and I shall call you Frances if I may.'

'Of course. I have always loved the name Euphemia.'

'It's become very popular,' said the old woman, 'but I predate all the Effies that you hear of now. I think Miss Euphemia Gray was very surprised when I told her my name.'

'Miss Gray?'

'Yes, before she married John Ruskin. My father was friendly with the Gray family.'

'Did you ever meet Ruskin, Euphemia?'

'Yes, once, but that was much later, after he gave a lecture in

London. My sister was keen to meet him, she was quite shameless and introduced herself to him.'

'A pity you did not speak to Wagner!' cried Frances, her eyes sparkling, 'then that would have been a very special bond between us!'

'My sister met him when he was in London in 1855, I think it was. I was already established here on the Rock but Selena and our mother were living in Portland Terrace, near Regent's Park. They used to walk in the park quite a lot and Selena told me that she became intrigued by a man she used to see taking a large dog for an occasional run. He would call out "Gipsy, here!" in a strong German accent. She saw him feeding the ducks and when she and mother visited the Zoological Gardens they saw him there, and he recognised her and smiled at her.'

She paused.

'Forgive an old woman's meanderings. This cannot be of any interest to you.'

'Please, please go on!' cried Frances.

'Now you must not think that my sister was importunate or impudent, but she smiled back and felt it would be nice to see him again, and she started to look forward to her visits to the park. One day Gipsy bounded into them, and the stranger excused himself for not keeping the dog under stricter control. His English was halting, Selena said, but he was courteous and gave them his card, on which was written "Herr Richard Wagner". He was not very well known in England then, but Selena was keen on music and had heard of him, and was intrigued.

He told her and my mother that he had seen them in the Zoological Gardens which he visited every afternoon, raised his hat and wished them good day. Selena was determined to meet him again and, when mother was resting the following afternoon, she slipped out and did, in fact, meet Richard Wagner in the Gardens. They met frequently after that, using some subterfuge or other. They went to Westminster Abbey, to St. Paul's and also to the Guildhall. Apparently he was fascinated by the figures of Gog and Magog, saying that they reminded him of Fafner and Fasolt!

'He only stayed till June. It was an unhappy time for him, he said, brightened only by Selena's beauty. I think he was quite fond of her from what she told me.'

Fond of her…Frances felt herself blush and pressed her hand to her breast, trying to assuage the pounding of her heart. Fond of her…But me he loved, he loved!

What foolishness to be jealous of something that happened some thirty-five years before! And strange, strange it was that she had come to the Rock to escape, and yet to find him everywhere…

Euphemia rose to make coffee and Frances did not restrain her. She gazed into the fire and scarcely noticed that Euphemia had returned with two fragrant cups.

'Sir Edward gets me coffee beans too,' she smiled.

The two women sat in the gathering gloom; Euphemia dozed fitfully and Frances tended the fire. How strange that Charlotte's indisposition had led her into this house, with its ghosts and echoes, the man and the dog, the Zoological Gardens, and Gog and Magog, survivors of a monstrous brood, the offspring of demons and infamous daughters.

This gentle soul opposite, she thought, tells me of strange things. For there were giants on the earth in those days…But to me he spoke not of giants but of one who mutilated himself in madness and who now looks in an azure mirror for the advent of the lovely boy whom I and others must tempt with love, with our loveliness, our fragrance, our tender breasts…

Euphemia stirred and moaned gently, and Frances kissed her on the forehead, wrapping a rug around her withered legs. She picked up her cloak and hat from the wooden chest on which they lay and stepped out into the wintry dusk.

* * *

Drinks were served punctually at six o' clock in the dining room; Lady Augusta looked most regal in a dark green silk, a small golden aigrette in her hair.

'Thank you, Miss Prince, for looking after Charlotte. I believe Miss Lavender gave her a febrifuge?'

'She felt that Charlotte suffered from anaemia,' replied Frances, taking a glass of sherry from the silver tray.

Lady Augusta led her across the room to where a tall gentleman was standing; he bowed and she noticed thinning hair scraped back to conceal a balding head. She remembered having seen him somewhere and smiled as he kissed her hand: he was sun-tanned and clean-shaven. Lady Augusta introduced a Dr Reershemius from Bremen, an African explorer.

'I salute you as a subject of your Queen,' he said in excellent English, 'and a subject of the greatest Empire the world has ever seen.'

'Dr Reershemius has just returned from Angra Pequena,' explained Lady Augusta. 'Is there no hope of finding Lüderitz now?'

'No, alas,' replied Dr Reershemius, 'I fear he drowned at the mouth of the Orange River. The prospect of finding diamonds was too much for him. He sought wealth and power, but the waves rose and claimed him.

'How I envy you your Cecil Rhodes, Miss Prince! He effortlessly claims whole areas for the British Crown, and has a vision of Africa as a British colony, from Capetown to Cairo! But we are beginning to colonise it too, from East to West.'

A trite tune came into Frances's mind: 'To Africa, to Cameroon, to Angra Pequena!'

'Have you travelled widely, Dr Reershemius?' she asked politely.

'I was with Dr Carl Peters in Zanzibar. We live in interesting times, Miss Prince.'

From the corner of her eye Frances saw Beatrice and William enter the room. The young man looked unwell, with bloodshot eyes and puffy skin; he went to the window and lit a cigar.

Beatrice came across to where they were standing, looking fresh and charming in a pale pink dress with a white bow at the back. She began talking in an animated and precocious manner to Dr Reershemius; Frances excused herself and went across to where William was standing.

'Spare me Pequena and piccaninnies,' he groaned, drinking whisky.

'Or the Danish West Indies?' she joked, mischievously.

'Well, all right. I'll get Ingeborg to introduce me to some people, then I'll start a business in Christiansted or Fridriksted or some such place, and I'll get very rich. Then I'll sit on a balcony watching the coons slaving away and drink aquavit.'

'I hope you'll invite me,' she quipped, but he did not respond and gazed at his cigar.

'Pa's having a great time, I expect. I wish he'd take me with him, I can't stand much more of this.'

'Surely you can get a position in England, can't you? Or in Germany?'

'Oh God, not there. Ma's relations hate me and I can't stand Berlin, all that marching about. Pa wants me to try for the Foreign Office, but I'm not keen. I went to his old college in Oxford but, well, things didn't work out.'

He lapsed into silence. The sun was setting; an orange eye flamed beneath brows of grey on the sea's rim.

They sat at the small, round dining table, Dr Reershemius at Lady Augusta's right, William on her left, and Frances and Beatrice completed the circle.

They dined off langoustines and steamed fillet of turbot in white wine, followed by a light syllabub. Dr Reershemius was moved to praise the Rock and its Governor.

'The lobster trade flourishes, the tourists arrive and culture prevails. Sir Edward has created a paradise here, a light shining in the darkness.'

'My husband is a man of vision,' explained Lady Augusta, 'generous with his time to a fault.'

'He helps and encourages,' added Frances. 'I met a young girl, a Miss Freshet, whom Sir Edward wants to have trained as a singer. I was reluctant at first to listen to her, but Sir Edward persuaded me that I should.'

Why had she said this? It seemed as though a film of ice were forming in Lady Augusta's eyes.

'Miss Freshet has no voice to speak of. Sir Edward was only wishing to be kind. The truth would have been kinder. Beatrice sings far better.'

'No, Mama,' said Beatrice eagerly, 'Millicent has a much more beautiful voice.'

'There is no style, no Kultur,' continued her mother, 'it sounds like a milkmaid's to me.'

'It sounded pleasant enough when I heard it,' said William, 'but, there again, I can't judge these things. Cabaret is all I can stand. A charming diseuse, a chanson or two.'

He stared morosely at his glass.

'My son elects to prefer French culture,' said Lady Augusta disdainfully. 'We give him the best of German and English, but he prefers the products of Latin degeneration.'

'Sir Edward told me you used to play the violin,' said Frances, seeking to come to the young man's aid.

'I'll spare you that dubious pleasure,' he muttered.

'Willy used to play jolly well,' chimed in his sister, 'Bach partitas and things like that.'

'The children put on a small concert for the new Kaiser some years ago when he visited us as Crown Prince,' explained Lady Augusta. 'We call it Hausmusik. He was delighted. It was a trio for flute, violin and piano by Spohr. Charlotte played the flute very well. There were also recitations from Shakespeare, Schiller and Körner.'

'How charming, very charming!' Dr Reershemius smiled benignly across the table. 'A perfect example of Anglo-German rapprochement! What a remarkable island this is! A veritable jewel hanging on the bosom of Ran, the sea goddess!'

Beatrice giggled, but a severe look from her mother restrained her; William ordered more wine. The moon, now fuller, had risen.

'Der Mond ist aufgegangen,' hummed Beatrice, 'Papa liked that song. If he's back and there's a full moon we'll hire boats and go around the grottos. We'll have Bengal illuminations too.'

'I heard from a friend in Bavaria,' announced Dr Reershemius, 'that their poor king built a Venusberg grotto on an artificial lake.'

'I wouldn't think he would be interested in the mound of Venus,' said William with a sickly smile.

'We shall take coffee in the drawing room,' snapped Lady Augusta, 'Beatrice, see if Charlotte needs an infusion. William, you are unwell. Please take your leave and retire.'

Brother and sister rose to leave, and the three adults retired to the comfortable fire of the larger room.

* * *

Dr Reershemius spoke of Livingston and Cecil Rhodes, his particular hero, of Dr Carl Peters, of Lüderitz, Vogelsang and Nachtigal; Frances strove to appear attentive, but her thoughts were elsewhere.

She stared into the fire and thought of Euphemia Lavender in her lowly cottage, of Charlotte and also of William, whose faux pas had shocked and unsettled her. She thought above all about Edward.

Was it prurient to speculate on the marital relationships between him and his wife, on their love-making? How did he behave with his children? What would happen to William? And suddenly Millicent Freshet came vividly to mind, sitting in silence in the telegraph station on the edge of the cliff whilst below, in the darkness, the sea heaved and swelled.

She was glad when the clock struck nine and Dr Reershemius rose to take his leave.

'We shall meet in Ovambo-Land!' he cried, taking her hand and kissing it.

'I think not,' she muttered under her breath as she went upstairs after Lady Augusta had kissed her goodnight.

On the mat in her room there was another letter. 'Wasn't it awful? Willy and I will wait for you by the cannon until nine fifteen, then we'll go to the Stadt London. Willy's in a bad way and needs to be cheered up. Do come. Affectionately, Bea.'

Frances put down the note. She had hoped, had she not, to relax in the tub (Frau Stoeven had the geyser working if ever she needed it) but she also felt concern for William and an obscure need to keep an eye on him. The thought of meeting Miss Frostrup was, however, disagreeable.

Did the age gap between her and William (five years, was it?) and between her and Beatrice (eight?) necessarily mean that she could be neither confidante nor friend? The thought, however, of acting in loco parentis was manifestly absurd.

It was nearly nine fifteen. She threw herself onto the chaise longue and picked up Pastor Gerok, but then, immediately, she jumped up, seized her hat, coat and reticule and slipped from her room. The clock chimed the quarter as she hurried down the stairs; she did not wish to miss brother and sister as she was not sure that she could find her way to the hotel in the darkness on her own.

She jumped the last steps, but her ankle twisted beneath her. She stumbled, put out her arms, and fell headlong. She lay on the carpet, flushed with pain but more with embarrassment, and struggled to stand upright. But she was intently aware of a stabbing spasm in her right foot and hobbled to a large chair which stood by the ornate free-standing clock.

Footsteps approached, and Frau Stoeven appeared, alerted by the noise and expressing signs of disapprobation.

'I had a stupid fall,' groaned Frances, 'I – I wanted to look at the night sky and tripped over myself.' She tried to stand but the pain was excruciating.

Frau Stoeven came to her aid. She supported the young woman under her right arm and led her slowly, awkwardly, up to her room.

The night was torture, red with pain and disturbing memories. Frau Stoeven had helped her to undress, and washed her ankle, which was badly sprained. With unconcealed disapproval she had fetched the tincture of opium at Frances's request, but the laudanum brought little relief. The weight of the quilt pressed down on the swollen flesh, and every movement exacerbated the painful torment.

Yet memory also prevented sleep, the memory of that open trapdoor on the stage, her stumbling, sprawling. Had it been an accident? She had racked her brains constantly, trying to make sense of what had happened. The rehearsals had gone well, but even better were the performances, yes, so lovely. And he told me that the Flower scenes were the only ones he sat through completely because the perfection of the performances refreshed him every time he saw them. Did he not shout Bravo! from his box, and was hissed for it!

But the evening came when I was dancing and, during the transformation scene in Klingsor's garden I suddenly stumbled and fell into the trapdoor that opened before me. The other maidens masked me, seeing what had happened, and the audience did not know.

Then the cab took me, with my foot badly sprained, to the house on the corner of Wahnfriedstrasse where my parents were staying. Thank God that there were three rest days, so I rested and made a full recovery. But I danced carefully, afterwards.

He came to me, his flower-maiden, and was tenderness itself, giving me flowers which I kept until they were stalks, husks, dust. Why was the trapdoor open? Was it she? Was she jealous? But no, this is madness...

Towards dawn she slept and was wakened by the girl bringing coffee and rolls, also by Lady Augusta herself.

'I hear you fell on the stairs? Your ankle is sprained? Let me see.'

The puffy, inflamed joint was examined carefully; shooting pains splintered and tore.

'Comfrey is an excellent vulnerary,' explained the Governess. 'I have a tincture in my garden house. I shall also make a warm poultice. If you wish I can have it put in the bath. This must be tomorrow. I have to let five hundred grams of dried leaves stand in five litres of water overnight. I shall then have them boiled.'

Frances smiled and winced.

'Thank you, Lady Augusta, I am sure that my ankle will get much better if I rest it for a couple of days.'

'Let the girl help you into the bathroom and fetch your clothes. I shall return with the tincture of comfrey.'

Frances finished her breakfast and the girl supported her to the wash basin, averting her gaze as Frances removed her nightdress and started to wash. There was something familiar about her pale features, her plaited hair and somewhat angular movements, and Frances suddenly thought of Stine.

She washed herself thoroughly, enjoying the Lilienmilch soap and Divinia perfume; the geyser had heated the water to an acceptable temperature. How pleasant it would have been to lie full length in the Shanks tub! She promised herself a luxurious bath when her ankle permitted it and hobbled with the girl's help back into the bedroom.

'What is your name?' she asked her.

'Elke,' came the quiet, almost whispered reply. Clothes, stays and hairpins were fetched and Frances dressed, foregoing silken hose and her patent-leather shoes. She hobbled back to the chaise longue, her right hand on Elke's shoulder, and sat with her leg on a small footstool. Elke applied powdered French chalk to the puffy ankle and stood silently, waiting for further instructions. The silence became oppressive.

'Do you know Stine, the girl who works in the Conversationshaus?' Frances asked.

'Yes.'

'Are you friendly with her?'

'Yes.'

Elke's pale features assumed, Frances thought, an expression of discomfort; she gazed at the pier glass, then at the floor.

'She was a good girl,' continued Frances, desperate to communicate with the wan creature who stood opposite her, 'but I believe she has been unwell. Has she met with an accident?'

'No,' said Elke, urgently now, as she heard footsteps approaching outside, 'there was – nothing.'

Lady Augusta knocked and entered; Elke bobbed and withdrew at a gesture from her mistress.

'I have the tincture,' the latter announced, 'and shall bring the compress tomorrow.'

* * *

The morning passed pleasantly with the reading of The Times which Frau Stoeven had brought up at Lady Augusta's request from her husband's study, together with novels by Dickens, Mrs Gaskell, Anne and Charlotte Bronte and Hall Caine. The latter novelist she did not know, and started *The Deemster*, but a knock at the door interrupted her.

It was Charlotte, wearing a plain dress and cloak, who brought a small posy of fuchsias, borage, pale asters and feverfew.

'I do hope I am not interrupting you, Miss Prince, but we were told at breakfast that you had had an accident.'

'Come in, Charlotte, what a pleasant surprise! I foolishly ran downstairs last night to go out and look at the stars but missed my footing and sprained my ankle.'

'The stars are lovely here,' said Charlotte, 'but I think it was overcast last night.'

She smiled weakly.

'You looked after me once, Miss Prince, and now it's my turn. You have enough to read, I see? My father has a good library and books regularly come from Hamburg and London.'

She noticed *The Deemster* in Frances's lap. 'You are reading Hall Caine? An interesting young writer from the Isle of Man. Reassuring that an island like that can produce a promising young writer, is it not?'

'It is,' replied Frances, 'and perhaps Heligoland will be proud of Charlotte Hennicker-Heaton one day.'

Charlotte blushed, and looked down.

'My father says such things, but it will never be.'

'Nonsense!' laughed Frances, 'Millicent Freshet must sing, you must write. There is much talent here and your father is right to recognise it.'

'My sister plays the piano,' Charlotte spoke quietly, 'and my brother used to play the violin.' A strange expression flitted across her face. ' There is also unhappiness here.'

Frances sought to change the topic of conversation.

'A quiet girl, Elke, looked after me this morning. We started to speak of Stine, but your mother interrupted us.'

'Stine?' asked Charlotte, sharply. 'You spoke of her?'

'Your father mentioned to me an incident with a German sailor,' Frances continued, 'and Elke said she knew her.'

'Elke is her half-sister,' announced Charlotte, severely.

'I shouldn't have told you. Please keep it secret. I don't want my parents to know. She will soon give in her notice and find work elsewhere, but it would be better if nothing is said. Did you speak of Stine?'

'I simply mentioned her name. I thought I saw some similarity. But of course I shall say nothing to your mother. Does your mother disapprove of Stine?'

Charlotte had turned pale and was gnawing her bottom lip.

'Stine was involved in an unfortunate incident and tried to kill herself. My mother does not want to think about these things.'

'But your father punished the man responsible most severely, did he not?'

'My father punished a German sailor, yes. He was sent to prison on the mainland. I visited Stine when she was ill and tried to help her. She does not speak. My visits were acts of Christian charity, nothing more. Let me order you some luncheon, Miss Prince. Or would you like to try and walk downstairs?'

'A light luncheon would be very pleasant,' said Frances.

Charlotte left the room, and Frances stared out of the window; a dove-grey bell of cloud hung over the island. She had embarrassed Charlotte by her reference to Stine and sensed that something was being concealed. But she must not meddle.

She returned to *The Deemster* and read for five minutes until a tall, bony woman entered, carrying a large tray of cold meats, fish, bread, beer and a large glass of port wine. She also noticed, shuddering, that Lady Augusta had sent up another phial of tincture of comfrey.

After luncheon she dozed, but strange dreams afflicted her. She saw Stine standing on the Nathuurnstak, the North Stack, stretching out her arms towards her, arms that writhed like snakes; she, Frances, knew that she had to prevent a shadowy figure from reaching the girl, a figure in a dark cloak, and the sea was rising to drown them all, the sea which could only be repulsed by her dangling her pink bonnet by its ribbons over the side of the cliff.

She was wearing a veil against which insects were battering; the dark figure, whom she knew to be William, had reached Stine and was setting her on fire.

Frances cried out and woke with a start, her heart pounding. Her ankle was also throbbing: had she rested her other foot over it? She turned to the window; a face of cotton wool was pressing against the glass, a dumb countenance of vapour, of fog, dissolving and reforming, a moving silent mouth. She struggled to get to her feet, using the sturdy ashplant which Lady Augusta had thoughtfully provided. She hobbled to the window; banks of fog were enveloping the island, a soaking, clammy deadness in which she heard the doleful booming of the foghorn. Her father had warned her about this.

'If it's not blowing a gale it'll be shrouded in mist. Remember the holiday we had on Unst, Fan? Good practice for a stay on Heligoland!'

She smiled ruefully and stood for a long time gazing on the strange dead world outside the streaming panes.

Unst, yes, the isolated house near the Horns of Hagmark, the intrepid journey (so it seemed to her, being ten years old) to Muckle Flugga. Her father had wrapped her in his ulster and held her tight. Had her mother been there? No, she had stayed in the hotel at Baltasound.

'To the Faroes, Fan!' he had cried, 'then to Iceland! Come, my Nordic princess, to the land of ice and fire!' But it was not to be.

She turned away from the window; the fog had thickened to a dense, sodden opacity which unsettled her. She decided to take a bath, her ankle now no longer throbbing, and rang for Elke; it was, however, the bony woman who appeared, ignited the geyser and ran the bath when the water was sufficiently hot. She added bath salts and essences.

Would gnädige Frau require help getting in and out? No, Frances explained, she could manage by herself. The woman brought red Turkish slippers for her to wear, should she need them: Lady Augusta had thoughtfully found slippers that would fit comfortably. Or should she order supper to be brought up that evening?

No, she would make an effort to appear in the drawing room at six o' clock.

The woman left, and Frances entered the steaming bathroom, gingerly lowering herself into the welcoming water. She luxuriated in its warm embrace and remembered Edward's arm about her waist, his kiss upon her lips. She feared his return, yet also longed for it in equal measure. Firmness on her part would avoid embarrassment and obviate compromising, equivocal situations.

She sat and soaped her breasts with fragrant Lilienmilch and thought of her father. What had he called Edward? A masher, was it? She imagined the two of them as young lieutenants, dashing and gallant, and reprimanded herself for feeling attracted to a man of her father's age. And yet...She pulled herself upwards and, sitting on the side of the bath, swung her legs over and placed her feet on the mat. Her ankle was still swollen but she could touch it without undue discomfort. She dried herself, stood up and used the ashplant to walk into the bedroom. She dressed herself in her burgundy gown and slipped a white silk stocking over her right foot, then stepped into the Turkish slipper. She pinned her hair into a coil and gazed at herself admiringly in the pier glass.

Would she not have felt neglected if Edward had not flirted with her? Was she averse to coquetry? She wondered when she would see Herbert von Kroseck again; he would, she knew, be most solicitous. Perhaps he would be standing in the drawing room?

She dabbed her finest perfume (French, not German) behind her ears and on her wrists, then made her way awkwardly towards the door.

* * *

Her heart sank as she saw Herr Garer talking volubly to Beatrice, but she advanced slowly towards him, holding out her hand.

'I heard of your fall, Miss Prince. I hope that your foot is not too painful.'

'Not at all, Herr Garer.'

Lady Augusta advanced and bade her sit.

'William is indisposed and will not be joining us. Charlotte, however, will soon be here. I shall give you a poultice for your ankle later.'

Beatrice came up to her and kissed her on the cheek. She was wearing a light green gown which suited her; her eyes sparkled mischievously.

'Herr Garer is a dreadful flatterer, Miss Prince, he says I am an excellent linguist.'

'But you are, Miss Hennicker-Heaton!' he cried, 'you have mastered "de Halunder Spreek" as though you had been born on "deät Lun"! And your Hochdeutsch, like that of your father and Miss Prince, is excellent!'

He was in high spirits and had availed himself freely of the glasses of sherry being offered to him.

Frances sat and gazed at the window against which the fog was pressing.

'My knowledge of Plattdeutsch is very limited, Herr Garer,' she murmured.

'No, Miss Prince, they speak a Frisian dialect here, not Platt! I shall write down for you all the similarities between the way they speak here and what you will hear on the islands of Amrun and Föhr. Have you visited them?'

She groaned inwardly. No, she had not. She was relieved when Charlotte entered, and she smiled at her; Charlotte smiled quietly in return and came across towards her.

'The posy was pretty,' said Frances, 'thank you.'

Lady Augusta, dressed in black, stood close to the Erard.

'The fog is getting thicker,' she announced, 'the island will be cut off until it lifts.'

'We are in Niflheim,' cried Herr Garer, 'and you can hear the monster moaning!'

The foghorn boomed, and Beatrice burst out laughing.

'You can summon creatures from the deep, Herr Garer! Just think of all the drowned sailors coming up from the sea and gibbering outside our windows! How spooky!'

'The thought is inappropriate and disrespectful,' snapped her mother.

'Not far from here, off the island of Borkum, the dreadful tragedy occurred. I refer to the loss of the Cimbria with four hundred and thirty-seven lives. You have not forgotten this, Beatrice, I hope. There was a thick fog, just like this. Sir Edward was deeply affected by it. The pride of the German passenger fleet – he knew many of the people who lost their lives. It is some six years ago now. Do you remember, Miss Prince?'

'Of course she does,' cried Herr Garer, 'it was a shocking thing. The British freighter Sultan rammed the Cimbria in thick fog on January the nineteenth. It sank within fifteen minutes. The British skipper failed to stop and sailed to Hamburg. It was indeed dreadful. There were many Mecklenburgers on board, also Jews. There was much porcelain, beautiful porcelain by Meissen, Schwalb, Schlackenwerth. And Moritz Strauss went to his death with his gold coins. The gold now lies in the mud.'

He fell silent.

'Let us move to the dining room,' ordered Lady Augusta. 'Miss Prince?'

Frances sat sunk in reverie. Yes, she had heard of the disaster, for he had spoken of it, in Venice, as they walked across St. Mark's Square to stare at the wintry lagoon. He had been deeply shocked by the loss of life, the loss of Imperial Germany's largest passenger liner. The liquid realm of lustral radiance, he claimed, would be invaded by weapons of war, by ironclad engines of extermination – there is now no fructifying seed in the water, but hot missiles of annihilation. The Cimbria's loss was a tragic accident, certainly, but it was hubris to build so vast a ship and regard it as unsinkable. A thin rain had fallen and they had sat beneath dripping arcades, staring at the grey afternoon. He had held her left hand. And then he had kissed her.

She pulled herself together and, taking the arm that Herr Garer had offered, she walked with the two girls and the dignified older woman into the dining room.

* * *

Fog shrouded the Rock in sodden grey cerecloths for the next four days, when a brisk north-easterly wind swept it away in rags, in strands of thinning vapour, and a world returned, damp, yet viridescent and orange as the sun shone on land and water.

Frances, her ankle now fully restored, longed to escape from Government House and to walk to the Nathuurnstak by way of the telegraph station. She wished to avail herself of this new means of communication to contact her father, and sought Bill Freshet's expertise; a deeper motive, however, was her desire to see Millicent.

She had found the Mendelssohn duet 'I would I could utter my love for you' in a music cabinet next to the Erard in the drawing room and wished Millicent to look at it with the aim of singing together with her. In private, of course, not in a concert. She felt guilty about not having been more supportive of the girl before, she also felt curious to learn more about her; there was also, deep down, a suspicion, ill-defined, faint, scarcely articulated yet somehow prurient that the girl's condition was one of a discomposure caused somehow by an illicit relationship, an enthralment which caused profound distress. She would use the excuse of sending a telegraphic message as a means of entering the house and seeking a conversation with Millicent.

After breakfast she dressed in cloak, tammy and stout shoes and left the house, avoiding both Charlotte and Beatrice who were arguing in the drawing room; William was nowhere to be seen.

The air was cold, and a bright October sun bathed the cliffs in hues of madder and magenta; the gulls screamed in whirling acclaim as she struck out along the familiar path between the potato fields. Down below, or 'bedeeln' (she used the local term now, smiling to herself) she saw the usual activity at the landing stage, the boats bobbing on the water, the figures walking along the esplanade, and heard the shouts and hammering carried by the wind; on the Düne (or 'Hallem') she saw fishermen repairing boats and nets; Russalka, however, was hidden from her.

Up here, 'boppen', the settlement was busy, and gusts of laughter drifted from one of the hotels. She left the Falm and walked along the cliff towards the telegraph station, her face cold yet glowing in the wind-washed light, her cloak billowing about her.

The sea boomed in the caves below and threw fangs of emerald water into their recesses; a restless turmoil prevailed, welcome after the damp death that had drenched them; clouds sailed high in the air above.

She remembered the Sunday walk with Edward, the pleasure of his presence and the unsettling sensation of his thigh against hers as they sat in church. Where was he? Lady Augusta had kept silent, and the children were not forthcoming; they were probably ignorant of, even indifferent to, his whereabouts.

She scanned the horizon as if she expected a yacht to appear, flying the British flag, but the horizon was empty. Borkum lay, where? To the south-west? She shivered and thought of the watery grave, the dense compacted mass of sand and shells holding the crumbling Cimbria. 'Those were pearls that were his eyes…' What had Teddy, had Edward, quoted to her on her arrival? Edward and Millicent, they spun and danced through her mind in esoteric pattern, framed by silver sea and throbbing sun, a medallion of agate and nacreous glimmer, a locket holding in strange symbiosis the English Governor and his subject.

Her thoughts, she knew, were whirling and wild as she walked briskly along the cliff, feeling now the sun on her back, her legs walking with ease, her arms swinging at her sides. She was very close now to the telegraph station, and suddenly a sensation of unease, like fronds of vapour, enveloped her. She went to the door and knocked; she stood and waited, gazing at the glinting sea, and knocked again.

The sounds from within were unmistakable: voices raised in anger, in anguish, in vituperation and pain. She could hear the man's voice raised in fury and the woman's in supplication.

It was the father and his daughter, she knew this, but was unable to distinguish the words clearly. She listened, appalled yet fascinated by the violent emotions within. Did she, could she, hear the words 'whore', 'eat his bread', 'nothing', 'station', 'innocent'? And, horribly, 'trull'?

There was the sound of a blow being struck, of a wail of grief, of sobbing pain. And then the man's voice was raised to such a volume of intensity that she heard, unmistakably, the sentence: 'You're all butterflies one day, slatterns the next…' The woman's wailing became a moan, then died away.

Frances fled, holding her skirts as she ran. She rested, breathless, by a large boulder at the very edge of the cliff, her heart beating furiously.

What could have caused such anger? She recalled Bill Freshet's surly, taciturn nature, but what had caused such a furious altercation between him and his daughter? The sea swelled below her, its surface marbled by shifting patterns, traceries caused by eddies and currents beneath. She stood for a long time, narrowing her eyes against the sun; her eyelashes caught the rainbow iridescence of its light. Millicent, Millicent…

She was reluctant to return to Government House and walked towards the steps, then down, down to the Unterland, the 'Deelerlun'; on an impulse she walked up the steps to the Conversationshaus, was greeted by a surprised Herr Jensen and ordered a light collation in the dining room.

She enjoyed a small carafe of red wine and settled herself in the library with a Neptun cigarette, resting in a large armchair. She took stock of all that had happened to her on Heligoland: a delightful Governor who took liberties and ignored the conventional proprieties; his dignified, austere wife; their children, one showing undeniable signs of degeneration, the others twins unusual in the degree of their differences.

She had met poor Millicent and her violent, abusive father; a supercilious English clergyman who rejected a work of sublime beauty as blasphemous; a handsome, charming German naval officer; a garrulous pedantic school-master; a Danish woman artist; a lighthouse keeper; a frail, old lady who had spoken of him, the one she had come here to forget. She had met a girl struck dumb and rendered mute by some deep trauma – and, again, the nagging suspicion asserted itself that the young degenerate was, in some way, involved.

And a more unsettling thought took hold of her – that his father had been implicated in Millicent Freshet's predicament. Had Edward not simply encouraged her but made advances to her? Was it this that had incurred the wrath of her father? 'You're all butterflies one day, slatterns the next…' But no, she must rein in her imagination, it was inappropriate, inadmissible, unbecoming to speculate thus.

She left the hotel and walked in the brown and silver October light, along the Lung Wai to the Strandbazar where she saw again the morose assistant, the cast in her eye even more noticeable, and browsed amongst the maps and books, dipping into Hans Frank Heiken's *The Severe Winter of 1840-1841 on Heligoland* and reading descriptions of storm, ice and deprivation. What would the coming winter bring? she wondered. She, surely, would be home long before then, back in Wiltshire with the dogs.

She wandered down to the landing stage and saw the duckboards standing in the water in readiness, the boats neatly arranged on the sand. The Prinz Eitel-Friedrich was on time, she learned, and she sat on a bench, watching the crowd gather, the hotel porters with their handcarts.

The smell of fish, of weed and of coal, the sound of voices clear in the cooling air, the sight of the tangle of ropes and nets seemed preternaturally vivid to her, as though there were an aura of finality about it.

And there, rounding the headland it came, the vessel that had brought her to this island so recently, yet so long ago. She stood up and walked with the crowd for the air was indeed cool and the sun cast long shadows. The boat sounded its horn, the bells clanged and she saw the passengers waiting to disembark.

Would Edward be among them? She could not see him but watched the figures climb down the ladder into the waiting boats, being rowed across, then helped onto the duckboards. There were very few visitors, it seemed, and the Governor of the Crown Colony was not among them.

If he does not come back in the next three days I shall leave, she said to herself as she walked back up the steps. I shall telegraph the Honourable Charles Dundas and tell him that I shall be arriving in Hamburg. He can book me a room in the Hamburger Hof and I shall wait for Papa there. She gazed down at the sea below, at the Hallem.

'Farewell, Russalka,' she murmured, and turned her steps to Government House.

At the doorway Frau Stoeven met her with the news that there would be no formal dinner that evening as the family were otherwise engaged; a meal would be brought up to her room. She bathed, rested, read; the bony maid brought lobster bisque, a rack of lamb, vegetables, fruit and a bottle of claret, also cognac.

She ate the meal and sat by the window, staring at an almost perfect half-moon, golden, low above the sea. A hunter's moon, she murmured, and there, there were the fingers of light laid on the sea by the lighthouse. And she suddenly felt a great longing for Edward, an illicit longing, she knew, but irresistible. There was nothing for it, however, but to go to bed with *The Deemster*. A judge on the Isle of Man if not a Governor here.

She stood before the pier glass and looked at her pretty silk nightdress with its lace collar and cuffs, her dark, well-brushed hair, her regular features, her full mouth, and she traced the outline of her lips with the little finger of her left hand. 'To bed, sleepy-head,' she whispered, knowing full well that it was not sleep that she sought. But Hall Caine would make her eyes tired, and oblivion would enfold her.

She turned and pulled back the quilt. There, on the sheet, was a folded piece of paper. She picked it up and unfolded it. There was something written in purple ink and, astonished, she read the following:

"Goodnight, sweet Prince,
And flights of angels sing thee to thy rest!"

CHAPTER THREE

She entered the dining room punctually at eight o'clock for breakfast and there he was, tucking into a pork chop. He jumped to his feet and held out his hands towards her.

'Fanny! How lovely to see you!'

He kissed her on the cheek, brimming over with good spirits.

'Hope you didn't mind my little joke, couldn't resist! I hope the rest won't be silence! Sit and eat something, breakfast is a very important meal. Did you know that George the Fourth had on his deathbed two pigeons, three beefsteaks, three quarters of a bottle of Moselle wine, a glass of champagne, two glasses of port and one of brandy? Ah, there were giants on the earth in those days! I keep telling Willy to have a good breakfast, but he never listens. I don't know what the girls eat. You've met the tribe? I heard you had a fall – is it better now?'

'Yes,' she answered, blushing furiously, her heart pounding in her breast; she took some devilled kidneys and sat opposite him.

'Well, Fanny?'

'Yes?'

'Would you like another joke?'

'Not just now, Edward.'

'Teddy, please!' he urged her, standing up from his place.

'Now,' he continued, 'lift up your napkin. You might find something there, a message perhaps.'

'Edward, please.'

'Your Governor commands you, lift your napkin.'

She did as he commanded and found a letter which, to her delight, was from her father.

'Two men dance attendance on you,' he cried, his eyes shining.

'Edward, where did you get this?'

'Ah, that would be telling! I saw Jack a couple of days ago and he asked me to bring it to you. I obeyed.'

He threw down his napkin and lit a small cigar.

'I'll leave you in peace and shut myself away in the penetralium. Can't wait till six this evening. You must help me plan a big reception to launch the winter season. Don't let those lovely kidneys get cold'. He strode from the room.

Frances eagerly slit the envelope with a clean butter knife and read the following (there was neither date nor place):

'My dearest Fanny, thank you so much for your letter which I received this morning. It was splendid seeing the head of Queen Victoria on the stamp, and the Reichspost did the rest most efficiently.

So, Teddy is treating you well? I never doubted it! I loved the word "rantipole"! You got it from him, doubtless! He's a charming man, but be careful – even your mother fell under his spell for a while. Augusta is the salt of the earth; I don't know the children but have heard that his son is a bit listless. Take him for a bracing walk or two! There are also the two girls to keep you company. The lobsters are famous and I'm told that Prince Bismarck used to send for them. Things don't look too good for him at the moment and I'm told that he'll soon be out. Caprivi will probably succeed him. I won't bore you with all this, however.

I'm well, and doing a useful job (I think!), but don't know how long I'll be here. The Hamburg address will always find me. I do hope you're having a good rest there and can forget RW. What happened had nothing to do with you, the man was overworked and was also prone to seizures. Anything might have caused it – he'd probably just received a bill from his gondolier. Don't mention RW to Teddy for Heaven's sake, he'll probably hit upon the idea of putting on *The Flying Dutchman* and have you throwing yourself off a cliff into the sea after him!

Seriously, Fan, you are very precious to me and I long to see the colour in your cheeks again and a spring in your step. How's your "Halunder spreek"? I can see you wearing the red-white-green national costume – it would become you! Don't turn too many heads, my darling daughter, I'm sure there's a swain in Wiltshire pining for you! We'll do the London season when I'm back.

LATER. Well, I can save myself the cost of postage! Teddy is here, unexpectedly, on some dark gubernative business and he's offered to take the letter with him. He reassures me that you look well and have the German fleet scuttling themselves for you! I should have had you chaperoned, Frances my girl!

Bless you, darling, and take care of yourself. Your ever loving Papa.'

Frances finished her breakfast, then went into the deserted drawing room. She felt strangely agitated: delighted, and yet disturbed, at seeing Edward again, amused and yet annoyed at his little joke of the previous evening (had he entered her bedroom? felt amongst her nightclothes?), happy to hear from her father yet also intrigued, and somewhat upset at the news that her mother 'had fallen under Edward's spell for a while'. She gazed into the mirror, frowning.

Did Papa mean that Edward and Dulcie had been close before her parents' wedding, or after it? Had there been a tendresse before her birth, or after? A flirtation merely, or something more? When had this happened? Where? She had never felt close to her mother whose cool, almost chilling elegance had discouraged extravagant displays of affection. Had Dulcie and Edward – no, this was impossible. Had she, as a young child, been unknowingly present at a clandestine meeting? No, no, it was tasteless, it was improper to speculate thus. Father had simply meant that Edward was a lady-killer, no more. And this she knew already, did she not?

She heard footsteps outside and turned from the mirror; Beatrice entered the room.

'Hello, Miss Prince, how are you? Isn't it splendid having Pa back again! Sorry we didn't see you last night but Mr Russell, you know, the gentleman who owns the Stadt London, invited us over for dinner, the family that is.'

Frances suppressed a pang of resentment, of disappointment at not having been invited also, but smiled at the young girl.

'Pa asked me to slip that note into your bed last night before we left, hope you didn't mind!'

'Not at all, it was an amusing thing to do.'

'He asked me once to put a toy spider into Mademoiselle Couturier's bed, all black and hairy, she nearly had a fit!'

'Mademoiselle Couturier?'

'Yes, that was her name, a French governess whom we had briefly, but Ma didn't like her and she left.'

'Your father has a droll sense of humour,' murmured Frances.

'Yes, Willy calls him a wag.'

'Where is your brother?'

'Pa and he are shut up in the study. I expect that Pa's trying to persuade him to take up a position somewhere. Charlotte's reading in her room as usual. I say, Miss Prince, would you like to accompany me to the office down below? Pa's secretary, Herr Stahl, is off at the moment and I said I'd take these letters down for him. It's a nice morning, but the wind's getting up. I'll wait for you by the front door at nine o' clock if you'd like a walk.'

Frances remembered the Rathaus, an unassuming building almost on the shore.

'Yes, thank you, I'll see you then.'

The two walked through the wind and streaming light down the steps; the sea was choppy and spurted across the sand and the shingle almost on to the Esplanade, and the boats had been dragged well back on to the dry land.

The Rathaus was a gloomy office where the two assistants, Mr Strang and Mr Osborne, sorted out the mail and dealt with the expedition of dispatches to and from London, also to the British consul in Hamburg; Queen Victoria's portrait hung on the wall, as did a discoloured painting of the Crystal Palace in all its glory.

Beatrice immediately attached herself to Mr Osborne, the

younger of the two officials, and Frances introduced herself to Mr Strang, but he had known about her arrival already, telling her the exact time of her arrival on the Rock.

'We have little else to do here,' he explained, 'except keep a look out for new faces. Mr McBride and Mr Freshet rule above, and Mr Osborne and I guard Her Britannic Majesty's territory down below from our cubbyhole here.'

'I expect the arrival of the Prinz Eitel-Friedrich is the climax of your day,' joked Frances, noticing the schedule of the ship's arrivals and departures, summer and winter, pinned to the wall, together with a railway timetable of trains for the Venlo station, Hamburg, via Harburg, Buxtehude and Stade.

'It's obviously a busy time when the steamer calls,' continued Mr Strang, 'but private boats also call in here. When Sir Edward has official business on the mainland he usually goes by yacht. We know that Sir Edward's been writing a lot to the consul, also the ambassador, but that's official business and I'll say no more.'

'We know how often the Reverend Heywood goes across to the Düne,' chimed in Mr Osborne, 'with his paintbrush at the ready.'

'Isn't he restoring the Russian chapel?' asked Frances.

Beatrice and the young man laughed.

'Well,' said Mr Osborne, his eyes sparkling, 'a certain figurehead's more appealing, I would say. More of a bosom friend for our Minister.'

Beatrice giggled, but Mr Strang looked censorious.

'That's enough of that, in front of Miss Prince and Miss Hennicker-Heaton. There's no respect amongst the young these days.'

A bell shrilled in the adjoining room.

'Excuse me, Miss.'

He went next door; Mr Osborne expressed contrition, but, Frances noticed, also winked at Beatrice. The two women said good day and he opened the door for them against a rising wind.

They clutched their bonnets and hurried past the Strandbazar whose awning was flapping wildly; a light metal chair which had been standing outside one of the deserted guesthouses skidded across the Marcusplatz; papers flew in the wind.

'Here we go!' cried Beatrice, unable to conceal her exhilaration, 'we'll be blown out over to the Düne next! Mother started to keep chickens a couple of years ago but the whole henhouse full of Buff Orpingtons was blown over the cliff into the sea!'

The wild wind had excited her and she laughed and chattered as they struggled against a ferocious south-wester that swept the high clouds across the sky. They forced their way up the one hundred and ninety-four familiar steps, pausing for breath twice and gazing at the wild ferment of water crashing over the landing stage and drenching the steps of the Conversationshaus.

'Good thing we're up here!' yelled Frances, 'I wouldn't like to be out there in this!'

She suddenly saw in her imagination a figurehead ripped from its mooring and, breasting the tumultuous waves, coming finally to rest in a place of placid repose, a moon of milk dripping into a silent sea.

'Don't let's go home yet,' shouted Beatrice, 'let's go to the Princess Alexandra for something to eat – I expect Willy's in there after a wigging from Pa.'

Frances agreed, albeit reluctantly, for she did not want a repeat of what had happened after the night in the Stadt London, but she was determined to exert a restraining influence; they lifted their petticoats and ran up the steps as dark, boiling clouds overwhelmed the island.

* * *

The Princess Alexandra was a light, commodious building, one solid enough, however, to withstand the ferocious buffeting that was now visited upon it. William was sitting in the lounge reading Punch and smoking a cigar; a stout young woman who had been sitting next to him rose and left the room as Frances and Beatrice approached.

'How was it, Willy? Did Pa give you a bad time? Was that Florike just leaving?'

'Answer to question one: it went reasonably well; answer to question two: he didn't; answer to question three: yes, it was.'

Beatrice kissed him on the cheek, he winced and shrugged her away.

'Do sit down, Miss Prince,' he drawled, 'and don't take it amiss if Florike left without greeting you, she's very shy, there's nothing personal in it.'

'She mothers him,' laughed Beatrice, 'and her parents are fabulously rich from coffee in the Dutch East Indies. How about it, brother mine? A lovely town house on the Keizergracht, a summer residence in Scheveningen? But I fear the Zuiderzee can't compare with Jolly Jutland as far as looks are concerned!'

William ignored her and ordered a large pot of coffee and a bottle of cognac.

'Ignore her, Miss Prince. Miss van Egmond is a friend who keeps me in touch with the poetry on the continent, this time it's Dutch.'

He held up a copy of Albert Verwey's *Persephone*.

'I told Pa I wouldn't mind being a writer, but he wasn't too happy. He said he understood my feelings about the arts, and he sympathised with them, but it was far too precarious a life. He suggested I could be a journalist, possibly for The Times or the Vossische Zeitung in Berlin. But that's not for me. I could I suppose be an arts correspondent, or music critic, that might be fun. Charlotte showed me something from the English Illustrated Magazine by George Bernard Shaw, something about that place you went to, Miss Prince. What do you think?'

Frances looked at him. He had dressed neatly for his interview with his father in an elegant suit and stiff white collar, and his cravat was fixed with a sparkling pin, yet she could not ignore the unmistakable signs of dissipation in the unsteady, flickering eyes, the tobacco-stained fingers, the general nervous debility.

Outside, she thought, the elemental world batters us and the fishermen pull in their boats and nets to protect them from the storm, yet here I talk to a young neurasthenic who wishes to write of beauty, of loveliness, to stand where I once stood, but to stand also by that grave which I have never seen, shall never see…No, he must not do this.

'I think your father is quite right to warn you about the arts,' she said, 'and art criticism must be just as bad. You'd have to survive on a pittance.'

'Ma's got lots of money,' said Beatrice, taking a sip of brandy, 'they've got huge estates up in Livonia or wherever it is. How about it, Willy? You can be a landowner near the Prussian border, galloping in furs over the frozen wastes. Miss Prince and I will visit you and listen to the wolves howling at night!'

'I give up,' he groaned, helping himself to the cognac. The rain streamed horizontally past the rattling windows; a girl heaped logs into the large fireplace and started a blaze; sparks flew upwards.

'Sir Edward must have all sorts of contacts,' Frances continued, 'surely he could find something?'

'The thought of being our man liaising with the Akhund of Swat doesn't appeal to me,' he replied. 'Perhaps I'll just ask Pa for my inheritance and live as a dandy. I shall appear in apparel of exquisite cut and in the palest shades, cerulean blue, lilac, or shell-pink, and wear a curly-brimmed bowler, high stiff collar and jewelled tie pin.'

Frances burst out laughing.

'What a bird of paradise! I wonder what the locals would think!'

'Good God, I wouldn't stay here! I've never met such a bunch of peasants. Result of centuries of inbreeding. I don't know how Pa stands it here. If you want a piquant flirtation with the girls here they'll either start knitting you jerseys or chucking themselves off the cliffs in terror. Absolutely no finesse, no savoir-faire.'

'I think we should go back,' said Beatrice suddenly, 'they might be expecting us for lunch.'

'How can we go back through this awful weather?' he moaned.

'The hotel has a sulky,' said his sister, 'we can take it in turns to ride through the rain.'

Frances got to her feet, glad of Beatrice's suggestion and keen at all costs to avoid a dissipated luncheon with a morose young man; the girl, she knew, was anxious to deflect attention from what her brother had, and also might, inadvertently let slip. Or had the expression 'throwing themselves off cliffs' simply been a turn of phrase?

'You can stay here if you like, Willy, I'll say that you were otherwise occupied.'

'Occupied, well, yes…Pa's alright, isn't he? Always occupied, always doing things.'

He poured another cognac.

'Lording it over us, our benign Governor. Takes his pick. Probably has a harem in Hamburg or a bordello in Berlin.'

'You're very disrespectful,' said Frances sharply.

'Ingeborg told me he'd importuned her, but she slapped his wrists for him. Now, Pa, I thought, what will Ma say, bad boy. But Ma knew all about silly Milly, didn't she, Bea?'

His speech was badly slurred, and the cigar slipped from his fingers; he sat slumped in the corner of the leather armchair.

'Leave him,' said Beatrice urgently, picking up the cigar and throwing it into the fire, 'he can make his own way back later.'

The two women waited by the door for the sulky, a light two-wheeled carriage drawn by one of the few horses on the island. Beatrice insisted, in the rain-lashed doorway, that Frances go first and then, as the older woman stepped into the carriage and seized the reins, she cried that it would be better if she remained with her brother. She gave the mare a smart slap on its sodden rump and the carriage disappeared through the rain.

* * *

Frances requested that her luncheon, a collation of cold meats, dried fish and potato salad, be brought to her room.

She ate without tasting the meal, then pulled the chaise longue across to the tiled stove which radiated a comforting warmth. She sat and thought of the morning just passed, her father's letter with the unsettling statement concerning her mother and Sir Edward,

William's obscure references to cliffs and suicide attempts, his account of what Ingeborg Frostrup had putatively claimed, and then the mention of Millicent and something that Lady Augusta knew. How was Sir Edward involved in this? Had there been a flirtation as there had been, ostensibly, with her mother? Had there been more than this?

She stared out at the driving rain and the sombre afternoon, the sea mountainous and booming. Was a febrile, perfervid, prurient imagination at work here, fuelled by inebriation? But why had his sister reacted as she had? And why had she returned? To chastise? To warn? William may have been guilty of some impropriety with Stine, but Teddy, Edward, was, in her father's own words, a 'masher'. He enjoyed flirting. What harm was there in this? Was she becoming priggish? Suspicious? Vindictive, even?

She shuddered as she thought of herself growing old, petty, reproachful...Her twenties were drawing to a close and she was rapidly approaching the age when – what? She pulled a rug over her legs and lay on her back to doze.

But the wind prevented her. It had increased in intensity and was now shrieking past the house, tearing at shutters and roof-tiles; shrubbery flew past and the windows creaked and throbbed.

How often did they have such gales at this time of year? She wondered what the Rock and the Düne looked like under a fresh powdering of snow – or would rain and sleet assert a sodden grey? She thought of the Nathuurnstak, a froth of white waves at its base, the screaming wind ripping at its flanks. A savage sea, a shattering wind...Her thoughts turned to the Cimbria, to the wrecks lying broken and shattered. Those rocks off the Scillies – were they called the Manacles? She suddenly remembered a photographic plate that her cousin George had shown her, the wreck of the Minnehaha in January 1874, a vessel that had taken fourteen months to bring guano from South America to Falmouth.

'This is a good photographic plate,' he had said, 'Alexander Gibson took it, but you can also see it's been extensively retouched, I think the sails have been added.'

She had not known what guano was.

'It's bird shit, Fanny, in enormous quantities, excrement of sea fowl if you prefer, a kind of manure. And Minnehaha, laughing water, brought it half way across the world to lose it in the sea off St. Mary's! Nine of the crew were drowned, also the pilot and the captain whose headless body was washed up weeks later.'

She had hated the word 'guano' after this, the senseless scraping and gathering of excrement to be taken across the world and then lost at sea. She remembered hearing when she was young of the loss of the Schiller, too, lost one dreadful night in dense fog like the Cimbria, and of the wreck of the Deutschland with its nuns…Layers upon layers of wrecks.

We stand and gaze, in our frocks, our smocks, our bonnets, from the safety of the shore at stricken vessels, at brigantines with splintered masts, tangled rigging, shredded sails…

The warmth of the stove made her drowsy; the wind threw rain against the glass, and she drifted into a half-sleep: she seemed to be on a vast, luxurious ocean-going liner, descending a handsome staircase. And he had been with her, but said that he was her father. He had led her across a garden into a conservatory, into sultry, steaming air, and had placed his hand upon her left breast.

'This is where the orchid will grow,' he said.

'A garden?' she replied, 'on a ship? Upon the sea?'

And she knew without doubt that there would be dreadful wreckage as they struck the Retarrier reef. Or was she seeing this on one of George's photographic plates? A lazy slap of water over an exposed fang…

She stirred and woke in darkness. After rising and closing the curtains she put on the light which flickered, was extinguished, then returned. She pulled the bell-rope and, to her surprise, it was Frau Stoeven herself who brought the tea. She wished to inform the English guest that the dinner that evening would be more formal and that she should dress accordingly; the dinner would be in the ballroom at the long table as Sir Edward wished to make an important announcement. There would be many guests.

Would the bad weather not deter them? Frances asked, pouring herself some Mazzawattee tea. Frau Stoeven shrugged her shoulders, went to light the geyser, and departed.

Frances laid out her cream silk dress upon the bed, her matching gloves, shawl and shoes, and decided to wear her pearls and pearl earrings. She stepped into the bathroom and saw the 'Wellgunde' rocking-bath standing in the corner.

She smiled to herself.

'Well, Rhinemaiden, let's try this for a change!'

It was heavy, but she lifted it into the Shank's tub and pulled it under the brass taps; 'Wellgunde' soon filled with hot water to which she added her favourite bath essences. She undressed and stood in the smaller bath, then lay backwards in it. The pressure from her feet and shoulders caused the bath to rock gently back and forth; waves of soft, warm soapy water caressed her.

She held both sides and closed her eyes. Had not Edward described a motorised rocking-bath? 'Undosa', was it? Strange, strange the strands of associations. 'Wellgunde', 'Ondosa', Russalka, Melusine...How men associate us with water, with drowning, with oceanic feeling, the water womb, the sucking vagina...

She no longer rocked the bath but lay supine, her body almost covered by fragrant water, the fingers of her right hand gently feeling her softly moistening cleft. She lay and succumbed to waves of sensuous pleasure, and thought of Edward: had he fondled Millicent? Ingeborg? Had he thrust his manhood into them, Neptune with his trident?

She lay there, gently caressing herself till the water grew tepid; she stepped from the rocking bath and dried herself. A flushed and striking countenance appeared as she wiped the steam from the bathroom mirror.

* * *

Many voices echoed from the drawing room as she approached, laughter, animation. She knew that she looked her best in her cream, low-cut gown, her hair swept up and held by a golden comb, and she entered the room with confidence.

She immediately saw Edward, wearing full dress regimentals, medals and spurs; he smiled at her across the room. Lady Augusta was at his side in severe black; a brilliant diamond flashed from her choker. She spotted Beatrice and Charlotte, but William was nowhere to be seen.

The room was full of people, some of whom she half remembered; Edward came across and introduced her to Mrs Wilson, Mrs Ohlson, Commodore Phelton, the Morrises, Mr Robertson, the Misses Payne…Hamish McBride she knew already, did she not? Also Bill Freshet? Frances gazed closely at the latter.

'Is Millicent not here?' she asked.

'No,' her father responded curtly, 'she is indisposed.'

'Such a shame!' laughed Edward, 'I was looking forward to seeing Millicent again.'

Bill Freshet said nothing, but moved across to where the butler was standing with a tray of drinks.

'Miss Lavender also sends her apologies,' Edward explained, 'she was not up to coming out on a night like this. Can't say I blame her! The hall is full of dripping umbrellas, waterproofs and galoshes!'

The Reverend Heywood was standing in a corner and greeted her discreetly; Frances nodded briefly and turned to talk to the Commodore. She accepted a glass of sherry and smiled as Commodore Phelton held forth about the Kiel Canal. Frances looked over his shoulder and noticed that Mr Osborne was flirting with the younger Miss Payne, a gaunt middle-aged spinster who was blushing and simpering; her sister stood in silence. Mr Strang was also present and was deep in conversation with Mrs Wilson. Commodore Phelton was a bulky man with halitosis who feared the imminent build-up of the German fleet. The Germans were not a sea-faring nation, they should stick to the Baltic and leave the British the sea which was their birthright.

A dark young man joined them whom Frances did not know; he introduced himself as Dr Jonathan Saphir, locum on the island until the return of Dr Graevenitz. Commodore Phelton moved away, and Dr Saphir complimented Frances on her appearance, saying that she was a credit to the island and an advertisement for its health-giving properties.

Frances thanked him, glad to be relieved of the company of the Commodore whom, to her delight, Edward had led away to his daughters.

'Haven't you noticed,' said Dr Saphir, 'that there aren't any Germans here apart from Lady Augusta?'

'And the children,' said Frances, 'who are half German, are they not?'

'All the children have British nationality,' explained Dr Saphir, 'as do I.' He was sorry that William was not present, he was concerned about that young man, as was Dr Graevenitz. The symptoms were obvious – neurasthenia. But he must not give away medical confidences and much preferred to enjoy the company of the healthy, beautiful young woman at his side.

The gong sounded.

'May I escort the jewel in the expatriate crown to dinner?'

She graciously offered him her arm and they moved into the ballroom, where the long dining table had been laid. Several candles burned in the candelabra which were reflected in the polished wood; there was much silver and crystal.

Edward stood at the head, with Lady Augusta on his right; Frances found herself between Dr Saphir and the Reverend Heywood who said grace, after which they sat.

The Rhenish wines were excellent and the glasses were refilled with remarkable frequency; Frances enjoyed the shellfish and bacon chowder, the smoked trout pâté with dill, the slices of grilled halibut. Dr Saphir flirted outrageously, ignoring Mrs Wilson who sat on his right and devoting himself entirely to the young, attractive woman on his left. Frances was relaxed, enjoying the attention being lavished on her by Dr Saphir who spoke volubly, his lustrous eyes with their dark lashes constantly straying towards her décolletage.

'Your pearls are very pretty, Miss Prince, are they an heirloom?'

'My mother gave them to me when I was twenty-one.'

'But, Miss Prince, you are not yet that advanced age! I am

a doctor, an expert, and believe me, your epidermis is that of a seventeen year-old!'

'Thank you, Dr Saphir, but you are some ten years out.'

'Never! I am never wrong! Skin, eyes, hair, all speak of the first flush of youth! Now, medical men are often painters, they know how to represent flesh on canvas. I dabble myself a little.'

Frances felt that the conversation needed to be regulated.

'Miss Frostrup paints, does she not? Now, there is a beauty!'

'No!' he cried, 'there is something of the albino about her!'

'But her eyes are not pink, are they, Dr Saphir? They are the colour of your name, surely!'

'Naughty, Miss Prince, naughty!'

He had been drinking heavily and accidentally knocked a glass of wine over Mrs Wilson's lap, who screamed and burst out laughing.

'Dr Saphir, really! You gave me quite a turn!'

'Let me help you undo your bodice to let you get some air!'

Mrs Wilson screamed again.

'Excuse me,' said Frances, and turned to the Reverend Heywood who had been sitting silently throughout the meal.

He seemed preoccupied and had eaten very little and drunk even less. He suddenly spoke.

'You look very beautiful, Miss Prince, I agree with your neighbour. But I have not his easy flow, his silver tongue, his – Levantine loquacity.'

'I am relieved.'

'I must again beg forgiveness for my churlish behaviour on the Hallem. All I ever seem to do is annoy you. Please forgive me.'

He looked down at his plate, and Frances felt a pang of pity for him, his awkwardness, his priggishness, his obvious unhappiness.

'There is nothing to apologise for, Reverend Heywood,' she said, looking him straight in the eyes.

'My name is Timothy,' he murmured.

'And mine is Frances.'

He smiled at her, and his expression suddenly acquired an appealing vivacity.

'We clergymen are such wet rags,' he continued, 'particularly Anglican clergymen. I wish I could be more, well, more life enhancing. All I want is to bring joy, to praise all things, but it is not easy.'

'You bring us the Good News, Timothy,' she said, feeling strangely drawn to him, 'that brings great comfort to many.'

'I long for beauty,' he cried, 'but the Pale Galilean casts a chill shadow over me.'

She frowned, perplexed.

'Don't you see,' he continued, 'the Greeks knew that the worship of physical beauty brings us closer to God. Beauty is part of the divine trinity. But the Christian must be suspicious of physical beauty, for it is corruptible, it perishes, prey to the worm. The loving countenance of a mother, a sister or – dare I say it? – a dear wife is but transient, and the skull is already grinning beneath the flesh.'

'No, Timothy,' cried Frances, strangely upset, 'there is love – you will love, and forget death. Love art! Love music! When I sang I knew that my song would end, but there was such intense loveliness that I seemed to be above time. I'm sorry, I'm not putting this very well.'

'Man is in love, and loves what vanishes,' he murmured, 'what is there more to say?'

A delicious pudding wine, served with a syllabub, terminated the meal, and a decanter of port began to circulate. Dr Saphir, much to Frances's relief, was deep in conversation with the woman sitting opposite him, Mrs Ohlson, an attractive widow in her late forties. Frances smiled at Timothy and raised her glass.

'To beauty!'

He clinked his glass with hers, and also smiled:

'To beauty!'

The conversation buzzed and flowed around them until Edward stood up and struck the table with a small gavel. He smiled and looked around the room, then, with a clear voice, proposed the loyal toast. There was a scraping of chairs and a shuffling of feet.

'The Queen!'

They then sat down, and Edward started to speak.

He greeted them as his friends, his Halunders, and thanked them for coming through such wild and windy weather to Government House. He regretted the fact that he had not been able to collect them all individually, possessing neither horse nor carriage of his own, but also suggesting perhaps that it was no bad thing as they might all have been blown over the edge of the cliff into the North Sea and even the estuary of the Elbe had he tried.

He read out apologies for absence from Miss Lavender, also from Albert Russell, manager of the Stadt London who could not get away; other names were mentioned whose absence he regretted. (He did not mention Millicent Freshet, Frances thought, sipping crème de menthe.)

But it was splendid seeing so many of his friends, his countrymen, and, as well as entertaining them, which was always a pleasure, he wished to mention a couple of items. Firstly, he wished to put their minds at rest about the rumours that were circulating concerning the sovereignty of their island. It was not in the interest of Her Britannic Majesty to cede Heligoland to Germany. Heligoland would remain British as long as he was Governor and he intended staying on the Rock for the foreseeable future (this statement was greeted by a burst of applause).

We are Halunders, he declared, and we are British, as much a part of the Empire as Tristan da Cunha, Pitcairn Island or the Falklands – and much, much closer to London than these! Here he raised his glass and drank to 'The Empire!', a toast that was enthusiastically celebrated.

He came to his second point. It was always a delight to welcome new visitors to the Rock, and he wished to drink to the health of Miss Frances Prince. Many of them had already made her acquaintance, he added, but it was now his great pleasure to welcome her formally, the daughter of an old friend and a young woman of talent, refinement and beauty. There were cries of 'Hear hear!', the scraping of chairs and the toast 'Miss Prince!'

Frances remained seated at her table, blushing a deep crimson.

The guests sat down and Dr Saphir winked at her salaciously; she felt acute embarrassment.

Thirdly, Edward continued, he wanted to warn the assembled company that he wished to organise, weather permitting, a nocturnal boat trip around the island, with illuminations and fireworks. A clear sky, quiet sea and a full moon would be ideal, and he would sort this out with the Clerk of the Weather. He would also need help with boats and torches. The severe gale nine which was battering them at the moment would blow itself out in a couple of days, and he would order Hamish to force the mercury upwards in his barometer and keep the horizon clear.

His last request was for all the colleagues to think about the next theatrical performance and to consult with the German Halunders. He had certain ideas which he was keeping to himself for the moment. We are a florilegium of talent, he concluded, and a group of dear friends who extend the hand of friendship to all those who seek that which is noble and true. His last toast, he cried, was to Anglo-German friendship, the blending of two cultures in a harmonious vision of peace.

They rose to drink, and Frances saw him gallantly kiss his wife on the hand.

'Long live Lady Augusta!' cried Mr Strang to enthusiastic applause; Lady Augusta bowed her head regally, and the dinner came to an end.

The foyer was full of servants helping the guests into oilskins, galoshes and sou-westers, and fetching umbrellas and lanterns. The rain had eased, but the wind was still very strong and it was with difficulty that the butler pushed open the door and held it against the buffeting from without.

Edward shook hands and kissed cheeks; Timothy Heywood came forward to Frances and shook her hand warmly before leaving, and she took pains to avoid Dr Saphir, who clumsily sought to embrace her.

She walked into the drawing room where a fire was still burning in the grate. She felt light-headed and flooded with happiness, joyful in the knowledge of her beauty, at the memory of Edward's compliments, and proud that he should single her out for praise, he, the Governor.

She heard Lady Augusta go up to bed, the last stragglers say their farewells and the butler bolting the heavy door. She sat in the leather armchair next to the fire, crossing her legs and pulling her shawl more tightly about her. Had the dress been too revealing? She recalled the lustrous eyes of Dr Saphir purposefully examining her pearls, and she smiled as she remembered Timothy Heywood's unexpected compliment. 'You look very beautiful, Miss Prince.'

For Edward, yes, I adorn myself. I did it for another, once, who brought me his star. But then…

She stared into the embers, knowing that Edward would come and find her. She heard footsteps, and he entered the room.

'Well, Fanny, how was it? I thought it went well, didn't you?'

He sat down in the chair opposite and lit a Manoli cigar with a fidibus.

'It was a lovely evening,' she said, 'and thank you for your words of welcome. They were quite unnecessary, though.'

'Nonsense, Fan! If I see a lovely woman on my island I welcome her to public acclaim. You've certainly conquered our one and only Israelite and even Tim Heywood seemed to respond to your charms, I could see it from where I was sitting! Still, with the Old Testament on one side of you and the New Testament on the other you should be in good hands.'

He stood up to unlock the tantalus that was standing on the sideboard, pouring himself a generous glass of whisky.

'Will you join me?'

'A very small one, Teddy, you've been so generous already with excellent wines and liqueurs.'

'My hospitality allowance is rather meagre,' he laughed, 'so I supplement it from my own pocket. But don't tell my wife that!'

'I'm sorry William wasn't present,' she said suddenly, taking the glass from his hand, and aware of the tips of his fingers.

'Will's had to go away for a day or so.'

'And Millicent?' (Why had she asked this?)

'Bill said she was unwell. She doesn't enjoy good health, poor thing. But let's think of you!'

He smiled and his laughing eyes betrayed nothing.

'Are you getting bored here, Fan? It was with you in mind that I hit on the idea of the trip around the rocks and the illuminations. We've done it before, but I think you'll enjoy it.'

'Yes, Beatrice mentioned it, she liked the Bengal lights, and they sound fun.'

'If there's no wind,' he explained, 'they give a steady and blue coloured light. We use phosphorous and flares and things for the other colours.'

He threw more wood onto the fire, which crackled and flickered; a pink glow suffused the room. With what light, she wondered, did the King illuminate his Venusberg? The blushing, rosy lining of that great seashell, darkening to carmine, to almandine. "Turkis and agate and almandine" was it?

'Penny – or pfennig! – for them!'

'Sorry, Teddy, I was dreaming – a line by Tennyson passed through my mind.'

'How agreeable! I see you very much as the Lady of Shallot gazing into her mirror and waiting for me to pass! Or Mariana in her moated grange!'

'Yes, you are right, I love that poem.'

'Well,' he smiled, yawning, 'you've no need to pine and feel a-weary, wishing that you were dead, for he certainly cometh!'

He held out his hands to pull her to her feet.

'Time for bed, my Princess…'

She felt unsteady and leaned against him; he gently laid his arm around her waist and moved with her to the door. It seemed as if she were hovering over the ground, so gently did they glide out across the tessellated floor and up the stairs.

She was aware of the ticking of the grandfather clock in the hall, that her heart was beating. Had Edward, on her right side, cupped her left breast with his left hand? Had she, sighing, buried her face in the side of his neck? Had he opened the door of her bedroom and carried her across to the bed, laying her gently on it?

Had she felt his lips upon hers, and heard quiet words whispered in her ear?

Or was it imagination only, the vapour of a dream?

* * *

She woke at dawn with pounding heart and throbbing head; the wind was moaning past the windows and she rose to relieve herself and also to drink water. She returned to bed, confused and contrite, embarrassed and distraught.

She had had tangled dreams of Dr Saphir and Timothy, both of whom were making her give a speech that was greeted by jeers and derision, and Edward had appeared in drawers of yellow nankeen, carrying "Wellgunde" in which was lying a doll named, she knew, Millicent.

Tossing and turning she felt ashamed of her frivolous behaviour, her overindulgence in wines and ardent spirits, her impropriety, and vowed to spend the coming day reading in silence. Or should she not flee? It would be a simple matter to board the Prinz Eitel-Friedrich, sail to Cuxhaven, catch the train for Hamburg and wait for her father.

She took breakfast in her room and gazed out at flailing shrubbery; trees, she realised, would have little chance of survival here. The Union Jack twisted and writhed, the weather vane spun on its pivot and the sea ground and crashed below. She hung up her cream silk dress which, to her chagrin, had stains of wine on the bodice. Serves you right, my girl, she muttered, flaunting yourself and drinking immoderately. Pastor Gerok it is for you today! Or what other works of supererogation would atone?

The bony woman tidied both bedroom and bathroom whilst Frances gazed at the agitation outside.

She should never have come to this island. It was too concentrated, too inbred, inward-looking. She should have sought distraction in a big city, London say. Yet was she not supposed to escape the blandishments of the metropolis for fear that there would, even in London, be too many echoes, too many reminders?

Her father had been most distressed at her illness and felt that Heligoland was the ideal place for recuperation where the Governor, his friend, could keep an eye on her. An eye on her, yes, and his hands…

She flushed at the memory of her weakness and vowed never to let Edward take advantage of her again. But what had he actually done? Had he carried her to bed? Had he done more?

Her ill humour was compounded by the realisation that she had lost one of her pearl earrings, a gift from her father. The maid had not been able to find it, and she would have to ask Frau Stoeven if it had been found elsewhere.

She felt a great need to flee the house, to avoid meeting Edward at all costs and, although the wind was still as strong, and the sea was frosted with surf, she seized her cloak, beret and gloves and hurried outside into a shouting, buffeting world.

She struck off towards the Sathuurn or South Horn, a part of the island that she had not yet visited; the cliffs were lower than in the north, but she chose not to look at the Nathuurnstak on that day.

The wind tore at her with great scooping movements, but the cold, clear air blew away the fumes of wine, the self-laceration, self-exculpation. The sea was indeed awesome to behold; great rollers roared in against the island's flanks and collapsed in a cauldron of churning spume. Rags of cloud blew across the sun; razorbills and cormorants wheeled and screamed above. The Deelerlun lay to her left, but nobody was attempting to battle up and down the steps in such a wind; the Hallem seemed deserted but she suddenly caught sight of Russalka, serene above the wild tumult of fish nets which the wind had caught.

You stand there serene, she thought, in rain and storm whereas I…She suddenly thought of Timothy, and Herbert von Kroseck's amusing description of the clergyman's devotion to Russalka's bosom. Herbert. It would be pleasant to see Herbert again; he was delightful company. But Edward, Edward – had he really fondled her?

She strode against the wind across ground that was still wet after the rain, across moss, through low blueberry bushes. To the Sathuurn and then back. She approached the promontory but then she noticed a figure standing there, gazing at something. It was Ingeborg Frostrup. Frances turned abruptly to retrace her steps. But Ingeborg had seen her.

'Løb ikke vaeg, Fröken Prince, jeg spiser dig ikke!' cried the young Danish woman, 'Don't run away, I won't eat you!'

Frances joined her, holding out her hand.

'I don't want to disturb you,' she said weakly, 'you looked preoccupied.'

Ingeborg was holding in her hand a small, dark, convex glass.

'It's my Claude-glass,' she explained, 'Teddy gave it to me on my birthday. He said it once belonged to Corot.

'I'm trying to reduce the proportions of the landscape, to abstract the subject from its surroundings, subduing the colours, reducing the intervals between the lights and the darks. I had planned to come out here and sketch later, but I think the canvas would be blown to Copenhagen with the easel and brushes!'

She wore a dark coat and beret, her blonde hair blew across her smiling teeth, and she brushed it back out of her eyes with an abrupt gesture.

'I like this part of Teddy's realm,' she said, laughing, 'it does not have the drama of the Nathuurnstak, naturally, but the blending of rock, fissure, bracken and sea is pleasing.'

She put her glass into a satchel which lay on the grass and slipped her arm through Frances's.

'Let us walk as sisters, or we might get blown off the cliff! Now, we shall drink coffee in my house and I shall show you my paintings. Or do you have other commitments?'

No, Frances had none and would like to see Ingeborg's work. They struggled against the wind to a small wooden house standing apart from the others, and went inside.

Why do I not like her? thought Frances as she stepped through a low door into a room full of nautical artefacts: sea chests, green glass balls, a ship's wheel, pieces of flotsam, and a fishing net strung across the wall; an iron stove spread an agreeable warmth and Ingeborg, tearing off her coat, threw more logs onto it.

'My studio is next door,' she explained, grinding coffee beans and placing a jug on the stove. An oak table had many books scattered across it, also sketches; one, a greenish dawn light on the sea, with rust-coloured clouds, impressed Frances, who picked it up.

'I tried to get the effect of staining,' explained Ingeborg, 'the sun as a wound upon the vernal sea.'

She stood on tiptoe to reach two large cups on a high shelf, and Frances admired her svelte figure, her long legs; her hair, now loose, was silver-blonde. She poured them both a glass of brandy and offered Frances a small, slim cigar. Frances accepted, and Ingeborg removed a book from the chair next to the stove.

'Please sit here,' she smiled, 'I shall remove Wilhelm von Gloeden's young ephebes for you. Have a look at them while I leave you for a moment.'

She left the room and Frances opened the book, an album of photographs. She was startled to see that these were of young men, taken, she read, in a Sicilian landscape, near the village of Giardini Naxos. The young men posed in unselfconscious innocence; one was standing leaning against a spear which pointed upwards, complementing his pendulous penis which hung from a luxuriant tangle of dark hair; another young man, his flaccid member hanging between his thighs, mended a fishing net; other photographs showed naked youths from behind, their buttocks tight and perfectly rounded; another showed a young man in profile, holding a large ball. A clothed figure was von Gloeden himself, standing leaning against a wall, dressed as a Sicilian pirate, his hair in a bandana.

Frances felt herself blushing; the photographs had unsettled her. Ingeborg entered, having brushed her hair and coiled it round her head.

'Do you like the photographs? I bought them for Herbert who met von Gloeden once in Sicily and wanted the pictures. Isn't it a shame!' she laughed, her eyes glittering like icy sapphires, 'we all pine for our handsome German captain but his interests, well, lie elsewhere. Er ist ein Urning, unser braver Kapitän.'

Frances put down the album and stared into the fire. Ingeborg handed her the coffee, which she drank automatically. Urning, yes, from Venus Urania, but the love of Urning is the love of man for man, or woman for woman, physical in some way.

'I am wedded, so to speak, to the Imperial Fleet, and do not have a wife.'

But this was merely a turn of phrase, surely? How could such a man remain indifferent to a woman's charms? Did Herbert prefer the slim-hipped young boys of Giardini Naxos to a woman's loveliness? She had been fooled into thinking – but she stopped.

Ingeborg had sensed her unease.

'He is a handsome man. We poor maidens can still enjoy his company. He will flirt with us, with you, with me, with Beatrice. We are women of the world, I think, but Beatrice must be careful not to fall in love, at her age.'

Frances sat up with a slight jolt.

'Beatrice? Is there a liaison between the two? Surely not!'

Ingeborg smiled slyly.

'They have been seen together – nothing can be concealed on this island!'

'Does Sir Edward know?'

'Oh, Teddy is rather casual in these matters, is he not? But let me take you into the studio.'

Frances let herself be ushered into an adjoining room; this, Ingeborg explained, had originally been an outhouse but she had had it extended. The walls were covered in her work; the ceiling was high and admitted a pale northern light. Canvasses were strewn over the floor and leant against the walls, brushes and paints covered the tables. But Frances was distracted by the thought, the news of a relationship between Herbert and Beatrice, and scarcely did justice to the work displayed.

The colours were predominantly rust-red and green; a bold hand, Frances saw, had captured the island in all its moods, and the sea had been portrayed with great skill, its metallic brilliance, its wrinkles, its skin, its placidity and turmoil; one small canvas struck Frances particularly forcibly: it was of a cave with icy, dark green fronds depending from its roof, half concealing a gelatinous pink mass. Ingeborg smiled.

'This is not successful. William likes it though. He says it is an embryo in a womb of ice. He has an unhealthy imagination. I simply wanted to juxtapose the almost invisible foetus of an octopus with an alien, Arctic setting. They are sometimes washed ashore here. A foetus, a throbbing ball of invisible slime. But it is a pretentious piece of work. I thought of giving it to William if he wants it, but you may have it, Frances.'

A feverish head, obsessive, expiring, a face decomposing, drained of colour, the eyes rheumy…A foetus, an embryo of an oyster, an oyster swallowed…

She turned away, pale, her stomach knotted.

'Thank you, no, William will appreciate it more. I must go now. Thank you for showing me your work.'

She took her leave from a coolly smiling Ingeborg and walked back through the wind which, although strong, had abated.

* * *

Edward was expansive that evening, drinking Hock and Seltzer in the drawing room; it was to be a small family gathering without guests.

Frances had deliberately dressed demurely in a severe grey skirt and a deep pink crêpe de chine blouse buttoned to the throat. She wore no jewellery, but had blushed when Edward presented her with the missing pearl earring.

'One of the maids found it on the stairs,' he smiled.

'My father gave them to me,' she murmured awkwardly.

'Good old Jack. Don't tell the girls or they'll be clamouring for the Crown Jewels.'

'I don't think Charlotte is interested in baubles,' had been her reply.

'Thank God for that!'

Lady Augusta entered wearing pale green; the three children, unusually, entered behind her.

'Now listen, chaps,' said Edward, standing before the fire, 'how's this for a plan? Full moon and quiet sea – perfect. No moon but quiet sea – fine. We still go. Full moon and choppy sea – hmm. Possibly, possibly not. No moon and rough sea – no. Hamish tells me that the prospects look good and Herr Jensen, having consulted Lambrecht's Wettertelegraph confirms this, as do the old crones who prophesy with seaweed and starfish and such like. Don't you just love the local word for starfish: "Füffut" or five feet! Anyway, those who divine such things by haruspication and copromancy predict good weather. So we shall visit the Monk and the Nun and all the other petrified worthies.

'Cheer up, Fanny!' (She had been looking down at her shoes.) 'I suggest October the twenty-fifth. If the sibyls get it wrong and it's a wretched night I'll have them summarily executed, shot at dawn behind Government House. Tim can perform the last rites, administer extreme unction and we'll bury them at sea.'

'Tim's not a Papist, Pa,' chortled William.

'But he's hardly a Pastor Manders,' replied Charlotte.

'Tim's liturgy is spot-on,' continued their father, 'bells and smells but no kow-towing to Rome.'

'I have never understood the Anglican church,' said Lady Augusta, 'it is so diffuse, embracing everything. There are far too many compromises, it lacks Lutheran sternness.'

'There lies its strength,' continued Edward, 'it's comprised of chaps who've tacitly agreed not to ask certain questions. Things like the existence of God and so on. Ah, the dinner's ready!'

They walked though into the dining room where mulligatawny soup was served, followed by lamb en croûte, with ices as dessert.. Beatrice looked very pretty, Frances thought, her hair shone with youthful health and her complexion was radiant.

'Herbert can come in our boat,' she cried, 'then he can tell us all about the sea and things.'

'I'm sure Captain von Kroseck has other things to think about,' said her mother, pointedly.

'I'll get Rasmussen to sort out all the boats,' said Edward, 'we'll get a jolly crowd together. I'll get Hartmann across from Hamburg to do the illuminations.'

'The lights can be very spooky,' said Beatrice, excitedly, 'and Charlotte was very scared once, weren't you, Charlie?'

Charlotte looked down at her plate.

'I thought a drowned thing was coming out of the sea, but it was only the light shining on a great mass of weed. It was a bluish light.'

She fell silent. Frances wondered whether or not she should mention Ingeborg Frostrup's painting, but felt that she should not, and gazed at Edward. He had ordered more claret, which he drank with relish, as did his son.

'I've seen some odd-looking people on the Düne,' said William flippantly, 'they've got receding foreheads and chins, watery blue bulging eyes and odd, deep creases at the sides of their necks. They've got greyish skin, covered with what look like scales. Be careful, Charlie, that they don't swim over here and claim you as a bride.'

'Is there not a new play by Ibsen about a woman who is betrothed to the sea?' asked Frances, 'I thought I'd heard of it in Germany.'

'Yes,' murmured Charlotte, 'she remembers a man wearing a pearl as a tie-pin, a large bluish white pearl that looks like the eye of a dead fish.'

'Very droll,' said William, 'how about it, Pa? That could be the next pantomime here.'

'I forbid Ibsen,' said his mother firmly. 'I have heard that *Nora* is a most scandalous play. The emancipation of women is a nonsense.'

'You're right, Ma,' drawled her son, 'I've just read a book about this. It's by an American, Dr George Beard, and he reckons that we're getting so nervous now because of modern civilisation. We're all neurasthenic now because of steam power, the telegraph, the sciences and the mental activity of women. I'm his man.'

'What do you mean?' cried Charlotte angrily, 'do you want us to sit around sewing antimacassars all day? Are we not supposed to think, to write, to work?'

'Of course we can think and write and so on,' retorted her sister, 'but for Heaven's sake, who wants to be a blue-stocking? I'd much rather play the piano than work as a female stenographer or whatever they're called, or study.'

'I wish to study,' cried Charlotte, her cheeks flushed, 'I shall go to Zurich and study jurisprudence.'

'Jurisprudence? Law?' exclaimed her mother, 'what is the purpose of that?'

'To help those who are unable to help themselves and to bring justice into the world,' came the reply.

Silence fell over the table; Edward lit a Manoli.

'Let's go back to the drawing room. I'll think about the next play after the illuminations.'

William rose unsteadily, and Charlotte excused herself; the five of them went to the other room and sat around a cheerful fire.

'Please forgive my daughter,' said Lady Augusta, 'she is a rather modern young woman.'

'I'm a modern man,' said William, reaching for the tantalus and pouring a generous glass of whisky, 'neurasthenic. It's the age.'

'Nonsense,' snapped Lady Augusta, 'you read too many of those odious French novels in those yellow covers.'

Beatrice giggled.

'I'm modern too, ain't I, Miss Prince?'

'I'm not quite sure what the word means any more,' said Frances, gazing into the flames. Edward reached across to his daughter and twisted her ringlets between his fingers.

'You're a poppet,' he said, 'you're charming, witty, intelligent, graceful and musically gifted. A perfect daughter.'

Frances heard Lady Augusta draw in her breath, sharply.

'Now Fanny,' he continued, 'whom would you like to invite to the royal barge? Herbert von Kroseck, doubtless, as he turns all the ladies' heads.'

'He'll sit next to me,' said Beatrice, her eyes shining, 'I have first choice.'

'Miss Prince may sit next to Edward,' announced Lady Augusta, 'I shall not be with you. I do not like nocturnal boat trips in the autumnal air.'

'I thought,' said Frances quietly, 'that the Reverend Heywood might like to join us.'

'Capital idea,' said Edward, 'then we can invite Ingeborg.'

'Or Millicent?' said Frances suddenly.

'If you wish,' said Edward, drawing on his Manoli. Lady Augusta rose; a gibbous moon hung orange over the sea.

'Do not be late, Beatrice.'

She kissed Frances on the forehead and swept from the room.

* * *

The calendar confirmed that there would be a full moon on October the twenty-fifth, and Edward decided the following: that, were the weather good, and the sea calm, the assembled company would gather at the landing stage at nine o' clock. Rasmussen had ten boats at the ready, and Ralph Hartmann had placed the Bengal lights and the other illuminations around the island in the various caves and grottos. A hunting horn had been procured and he, Edward, would blow it at eight forty-five to confirm that the expedition would take place. If the weather were unpropitious, then Rasmussen would not gather the boats; if it were uncertain, then a blast on the horn would confirm that they would set forth; silence meant that they would not.

Charlotte, if she came, would be accompanied by Mr Osborne (to Frances's great relief Dr Saphir was not invited to sit in their boat); Ingeborg had gladly accepted, as had Timothy. William asked to sit next to Millicent, to whom an invitation had been sent. But Frances was ill at ease, and felt that she had to see Millicent before the twenty-fifth; she reprimanded herself for having badly neglected the young woman who was, she knew, profoundly unhappy and was certain not to accept the invitation. Or would her father prevent her? But why should he? Frances was restless and waited for Millicent to reply, but there was silence.

On the morning of the twenty-fourth William told her that Edward held his 'hebdomadal' meeting with those in positions of responsibility on the island and that Bill Freshet would be there. It would be held in the Rathaus and Millicent would be alone in the telegraph station. This was the chance for Frances to see her, and she watched to see Hamish McBride and Millicent's father walk towards the steps and go down to the Deelerlun.

She seized her cloak and beret and went forth. There was a light breeze which rippled the short grass; a mellow sun burnished a coppery sea. Frances approached the telegraph station with a sense of trepidation, and knocked. There was no reply. She walked round the building and, standing on tiptoe and holding on to the sill, she peered in through the narrow window.

It was the room where they had sat that first Sunday, and what she saw shocked her deeply.

Millicent was lying motionless on a threadbare couch, her dishevelled, matted hair in strands across her pale features, features, however, which were discoloured by what looked like bruises. She wore a dirty, ripped grey dress and was barefoot; one arm lay limply over the edge of the couch, the other was bent across her body, and her clenched fingers were clutching her throat. Her eyes were open, staring fixedly at the ceiling.

A dreadful thought flashed through Frances's mind: is she dead? But no, her breast was moving, almost imperceptibly. A great fear overcame her, she slipped from the window and, picking up a small stone, she stood on tiptoe once more to rap upon the glass. Millicent started up with a look of terror.

'Millicent, please, let me in!' Frances cried.

The girl inside shook violently, then swung herself off the couch. It was then that Frances noticed, as the tangled hair had slipped across her face, that Millicent had a deep gash across the forehead.

Frances ran to the front of the house and waited for the door to open; a grey ghost stood before her in a dark, cold corridor.

'Millicent! What has happened? You look – most unwell.'

The girl stood in silence, motionless; Frances took her by a thin arm and led her back into the drab sitting room. Here, she thought, I knelt before her and held her hands in supplication. If only I had been more helpful then…

Millicent moved as though she were an automaton, she was very cold, and shivered. Frances sat her down upon the couch.

'Let me bathe your wound. What happened? Was it a fall?'

But she knew immediately that it was not a fall. She noticed the bruises on the cheek and neck; the hazel eyes were dull and unseeing, the pale mouth (sensuous, once, it seemed) was drawn back, the lips revealing brittle teeth. The top of the dress was badly ripped, revealing white flesh, and the girl clutched the rent fabric, her fingers twitching spasmodically.

'Please, please, go,' she whispered, scarcely audibly. Frances bent towards her.

'No, I must help you.'

'He will be back soon. You must go.'

'But I can't leave you here like this! Come with me, back to Government House,' Frances cried, wildly, 'there you can rest.'

A dreadful smile twisted that strange mouth into a fearful rictus.

'I would not be welcome there. Not after - '

A great sob burst from her; Frances threw her arms around her and held her close.

'Surely Edward - ,' she began, but then fell silent. It was Edward, she felt sure, who had caused this grief.

'Go, go, please,' implored the afflicted girl sitting beside her; she had forced herself from Frances's embrace and was wiping her eyes with her sleeve.

'Please, please come to me if you are in distress. I can take you from the island, as far as you want, to Hamburg or to London.'

Her voice trailed away, her attempts at encouragement were desultory and trite, and fell as dead leaves. Millicent sat in waxen immobility; Frances rose and kissed her tangled, matted hair and hurried from the house.

* * *

After a solitary lunch she felt a great need for a walk, to feel the air, to put her thoughts in order. She felt sure that Edward was in some way responsible for what had happened, that he had had an affaire with Millicent of which her father had violently disapproved. Had not William hinted obliquely (albeit drunkenly) at something of which Lady Augusta had knowledge? 'Silly Milly…'

Lady Augusta had disapproved of Millicent, had she not? What had her father shouted? And there had been the sound of a blow, and a fearful cry. 'You're all butterflies one day, slatterns the next…' Had she misheard? Had her prurient imagination not fabricated a sordid liaison?

She found that she was climbing down the familiar one hundred and ninety-four steps, and walking along the esplanade to the landing stage. Water slapped lazily against the wooden posts, and fronds of seaweed rocked and coiled. The ferryman was sitting in the boat and shouted something about the Hallem. She nodded, reached out her hand for him to take, and stepped into the swaying craft. She gazed at the ferryman's back, the glaucous water, the approaching island. And Herbert von Kroseck? Was Ingeborg correct, or merely malicious? Was he, a homosexual, playing with the girl's feelings? And if so, why?

The ferryman jumped into the shallow water and pulled the boat crunching on to the sand; she lifted her petticoats and followed him. He pulled out his turnip-watch as before and pointed to the time. Four o' clock, she remembered. He grunted and rowed away.

She set off to walk the Düne, to dispel these dark suspicions that assailed her. She crossed the sands where jellyfish were dissolving in pools of purple-ganglioned slime, and bladderwrack crackled in the sun; an old woman was sitting knitting outside her cottage; the fishing nets billowed gently in the mild air. A small boy was playing with a starfish, Edward's 'Füffut', she recalled.

How could she believe that he was involved in dishonourable behaviour towards Millicent? Was she not enmeshed in a net of misunderstandings? And there she was, Russalka. The figurehead gazed into the quiet afternoon, spick and span, immobile and yet suffused, it seemed, with an indwelling life in the whispering silence. The wood was polished and smooth, and the eyes were clear and bright.

Your sailors loved you, tended you, washed you, she murmured, and yet you took them down, all of them, to a watery grave. Do their ghosts now visit you, in the moonlight after storms, brushing the seaweed from your hair, the sand from your eyes? No, you are not Ingeborg, despite your golden tresses, she is too bright and brittle.

Then, looking round in embarrassment, she stood on tiptoe and kissed the cold, damp, wooden lips; then, blushing, she stepped backwards and wiped her mouth.

Well, she thought, I hope nobody saw that! What would Papa think of a daughter who's kissing wooden statues! Perhaps her lips will be warm one day and mine will be cold, as cold as Millicent's. Pull yourself together, Frances.

She suddenly thought of the scurrilous rumours concerning Timothy Heywood's devotion to Russalka, the louche suggestion that he contemplated the whiteness of her bosom after seeing to the upkeep of the chapel; she frowned and turned away.

She walked inland, slashing at the longer grass with an arm of seaweed that she had picked up from the beach. I shall seek those strange sea creatures of whom William spoke, with watery bulging eyes and wasted gills, they will take me from here.

Ah, Millicent, you and I, like silver swans, will fly away. Your loveliness will be restored, and we shall sing together. Yet swans sing, she remembered, when they die…We shall dip our heads into the crystal water, and float to paradise. But there was also a handsome swan killed by a headstrong boy in a forest…

She walked on and reached the sea; turning left she gazed into the sun which hung over the Rock. The Nathuurnstak stood immediately beneath it, an orange disk contiguous, it seemed, with the thrusting blade. She could make out the silver pin-points of gulls soaring serenely; to the left, along the cliffs, stood the telegraph station, and to its left, on a slight rise, was Government House, and then the settlement. The sun was dipping behind the stack now, and she shivered. Should she leave them all? Had these people not distressed her, intrigued her, annoyed her? But she was now entangled by them, and flight, she knew, was impossible.

She must, above all, seek ways of helping Millicent, to satisfy herself that Edward was innocent of any misdemeanour. It would not be easy to leave him, there was much that was admirable about him, much that was loveable.

But if he were a reprobate, a seducer? But was he not her father's oldest friend? Yet had her father not suggested that there had been a tendresse between Edward and Dulcie? No, stop, stop. To tear out these thoughts, to lie in saurian repose on the rocks, or float with jellyfish, brainless, drifting, remote from ratiocination, amoeba-like…

She walked back past the chapel and sat for a while on the low wall. Or join the dead beneath the whispering grass. To walk into the sea, to watch the sea creep over her shoe, her petticoats, her bodice, a pearly, swirling embrace. Into her mouth, her eyes...

She watched the ferryman cross; he had come early, and she was glad of this. She walked to the shore to meet him. As they crossed between the two islands she gazed down into the water, but no mermaids beckoned to her. Only a mad English woman, she thought. At the landing stage she explained that she had come without any money, but that Edward would pay. Please send the bill (sixty pfennigs) to him. The ferryman grunted, doffed his cap, and hurried towards the orange ball that was sinking into the sea.

* * *

The morning of the twenty-fifth was cloudy and still, but by midday the clouds had dispersed and the sun gleamed from a sapphire sky.

The previous evening had seen only a very small gathering at dinner; Edward had not been present, neither had William nor Beatrice, but Charlotte had attended and spoken most courteously to Mr Strang, who had been invited. Lady Augusta had encouraged Mr Strang to talk of the Crimea, and he had been delighted to learn that Frances's father was, during that campaign, Captain Prince of the Coldstream Guards, in which regiment Mr Strang had served.

'He was a very popular officer, Miss Prince, and the men respected him greatly. I was at Balaclava and often saw your father. A very gallant gentleman.'

Frances had glowed at this praise for her father, and the evening had passed delightfully. The memory of Millicent's plight, if not forgotten, had been relegated, eclipsed, by the feeling of pride at her father's achievements, and she had felt grateful to Mr Strang for his kindness.

'I remember him on horseback charging ahead of us. Even the French cavalry couldn't compete with him!'

Lady Augusta had spoken disparagingly of the French cavalry, a mere flash in the pan, no more. Her father had fought in the Wars of the Liberation: the French were despicable. They had been defeated in Leipzig, at Waterloo, and, finally, at Sedan. The horrors of the Commune had demonstrated to the incredulous world the depths of barbarism to which they had sunk. Charlotte had attempted to salvage some remnants of French culture from her mother's castigation, but Lady Augusta would have none of it. Her offspring may be Francophiles but she, their mother, rejected the race out of hand as being irredeemably degenerate.

Mr Strang had listened dutifully, not wishing to contradict, stirring his coffee with a silver spoon. He had remembered, he said, a German summer visitor, a Saxon, describing how his mother had fled from Leipzig with him when he was a babe in arms. She had later described the bombardment, the incendiaries, the plunging, whinnying horses, the marauding soldiery; she and her son had barely escaped with their lives.

How fortunate, Frances had thought, that she had been spared these things. Mr Strang had spoken of the Crimea again, of the stagnant Putrid Sea, a name which Frances had found amusing. Slack, brackish waters, Frances had thought, reeds stinking and whispering in the dead air.

Mr Strang had kissed her hand most respectfully as he left.

'You should have told me,' he said, smiling, 'that you are Captain Prince's daughter. I even think I see a likeness! I do hope that your father will visit us soon. Then we can grokka, drink grog together.'

Frances had slept well, but had woken early and lain in bed, thinking of the day to come. No putrid sea, no foetid waters beneath a baking sun, but a sea from whose waters oars rose sparkling in the moonlight: this is what she would seek. And Millicent at her side, two sisters. Had Papa not told her that she had had a little sister who had died when she was three days old?

The morning had passed in reading, the afternoon in walking. There had been no formal dinner because of the sundry preparations; she had dressed warmly in her thick coat, velour beret, boots and muff, and had met William and Beatrice at the front door punctually at eight thirty.

At the top of the steps they could see lights below, lanterns and torches, and heard excited laughter, shouting and singing. A glorious full moon hung over the sea, the moonlight trembling on the water like shoals of silver fish.

William led them down the steps; they were joined by others. A blast from a hunting horn echoed from the landing stage, followed by a burst of applause.

'Pa's in his element,' laughed Beatrice, 'he ought to be running a circus.'

'I think he is,' replied William morosely. The horn then played ten jaunty notes, heroic, joyful. Frances laughed out loud.

'It's Siegfried's motif!' she cried, 'your father is a genius!'

'He's been practising it for long enough,' muttered William, pulling up his fur collar, 'driving Ma to distraction.' A rocket burst like a golden chrysanthemum over the sea and collapsed in a rain of sparks; a crackle of shots reverberated along the bottom of the cliffs. The air was keen but Frances felt a delicious thrill of child-like excitement. A cannon boomed from Government House behind them.

'Who fired it?' she cried.

'Ma got Hamish McBride to do it,' said Beatrice, giggling.

They went down onto the Lung Wai; dark figures were gathering at the edge of the sea. Frances saw Edward and ran to greet him. He was surrounded by revellers and grog was much in evidence.

'Now,' he commanded, 'obey your Governor! We have ten boats. In the Royal Barge, a vessel of burnished gold, will be seated your Pontifex Maximus, Edwardus Porphyrogenitus with his Queen, Francesca. Also Beatrice, his daughter, symbol of pulchritude itself, and Herbert of the High Seas. Herbert?'

'Here!' a voice cried from the darkness, and Frances saw him slip his arm around Beatrice's waist.

'Then the son of his loins, William the Conqueror, and – who is it to be?'

'I think it's Millicent,' said Frances, suddenly concerned. 'Millicent?'

There was no response.

'Very well, William is free to grokka on his own. Now, Timotheus? Our spiritual guide, shepherd and psychopomp?'

'Present!' called a voice, and Timothy Heywood approached with Ingeborg.

'You have a charming partner1' cried Edward, 'the Queen of Denmark, Tove herself. Oh, that I were King Waldemar!'

He kissed Ingeborg lightly on the lips.

'Now,' he cried, 'is Charlotte here, daughter of gravitas? With Mr Osborne, our trusty vassal?'

Mr Osborne stepped up to the little group.

'No Miss Charlotte, I'm afraid,' the young man lamented, sobbing theatrically.

'Join my son and heir,' commanded the Governor. 'Two stalwart Vikings, Jörg and Martin, to row us?'

The two approached and saluted; Frances recognised the giant who had carried her boxes up the steps.

'So, that means two, four, six and eight, plus two Herculean oarsmen. Please give your names to Rasmussen!' he called to the waiting crowd, who were jostling and laughing behind him, 'we don't want anyone to go astray. And no hanky-panky! Keep your Hüllihait in moderation!'

A roar of laughter followed this mock admonition. Frances noticed that the Royal Barge had Chinese lanterns on prow and stern and that rugs and furs had been spread across the wooden seats; a chest of bottles showed that grog would not be lacking, and there was also a tin box full of Plumtoort and Sockerstruuwen.

'Some confectionery for the ladies!' laughed Edward, helping Frances down the ladder and settling her into the stern of the boat; the dark water slapped and the reflections of the Chinese lanterns snaked and trembled.

'How about a painting, Inge?' he cried, 'to remind us of our mystery tour? "Nocturnal expedition", perhaps?'

'Why not?' she replied, archly, sitting close to Timothy, 'but I cannot paint these Romantic mystery pictures. You need Caspar David Friedrich, or, better, Carus.'

'A ghostly bier,' said Timothy dreamily, 'night journey to Avalon.'

He smiled at Frances who suddenly remembered – what? – a dream? 'The Island of the Dead', was it?

Another rocket burst over the sea, scattering crimson sequins of light.

'A bombardment!' cried Herbert, 'volle Kraft voraus!'

Mr Osborne suddenly pulled a pistol from his overcoat pocket and fired a shot into the air: this was the prearranged signal.

'Away!' shouted Edward through cupped hands; Jörg thrust his oar against the landing stage and pushed the boat out into the night.

* * *

Into the night? Or into an inky darkness transfigured by moonlight which shimmered like silver mercury on the water, and towards caves illuminated by vivid green and vermilion light where figures loomed in fearful clarity, petrified figures in hortative, beguiling or minatory attitudes.

Looking back, after the numbness of that horror had given way to shock, to grief, to self-recrimination, it seemed to Frances that there was an inexorability about it all which held, as in a frame of iron, that garish picture that would return to haunt her and which would, ultimately, never be expunged.

She remembered Edward's warmth against her, how he offered her a drink of whisky from his hip-flask, how she had removed her black fur muff and laid it on her lap, how he had playfully thrust his hand into it.

She saw Timothy looking at her with enormous eyes, she saw Ingeborg and Mr Osborne laughing and joking, she saw Herbert and Beatrice whispering, sitting very close, she saw William slumped in the stern, drinking grog.

They rounded the Sathuurn and met the swell from the west, but Jörg and Martin rowed vigorously towards a mysterious green glow – the first of the caves, where a Bengal light flickered in luminous viridity. The sea washed into the cave, and the two oarsmen skilfully brought the boat in as close as they could to where a gnarled excrescence of sandstone stood at the entrance, gaunt in a grey-green posture. This was "The School Master": the figure seemed hunched and, from a rudimentary hand, a finger of rock was raised in bleak admonition before a group of stones representing his pupils.

'Herr Garer!' called somebody from a boat behind them; this was greeted with raucous acclaim and applause.

'Don't worry, Tim,' shouted Edward, 'your turn's next!'

Timothy smiled wanly, his face strangely patterned by the light from the Chinese lanterns which swung and flickered. The boat moved on through the darkness, through a black sea mottled with liquid silver towards a garish phosphorescent light; in this cave stood "The Pastor", a rock whose sides seemed to hang in folds suggestive of clerical garb; an arm was hinted at, raised in blessing.

'Pax vobiscum,' Timothy murmured, then fell silent.

Ingeborg had now moved across to sit next to Herbert and, to distribute the weight more evenly, Beatrice had been asked to join the clergyman. The young girl was manifestly vexed by Ingeborg's boldness and drank the grog that her brother handed her. Mr Osborne saw his chance to offer to put his arms around her for warmth; she readily agreed.

'Now comes the fisherman and his wife,' called Edward, ' "De Fesker en siin Wüf".'

A reddish glow illuminated a deep cave or grotto where two figures seemed to stand, one gaunt which could be seen to have a pipe in its mouth, the other a dumpy, rounded mass of rock. Martin explained in halting Hochdeutsch that it would be possible to land and enter this cave, the floor being shingle and not soft sand; it was decided that they would not, and they rowed onwards, towards the Nathuurnstak.

Edward had finished his whisky and was drinking grog with William, Herbert and Ingeborg who were passing the bottles around with much merriment; singing could be heard close by from one of the other boats.

The moon hung high above and the sea was beaten silver. Frances remembered how she had felt strangely exhilarated, light-headed; it seemed that she were rowing across not water but glass, a silver mirror through which the boat cut silently; the revelry of the others receded and she – and Edward – were alone in a world of crystal light.

She sat close by him and rested her head on his shoulder; Beatrice would not see. And if she did? And Herbert? Ingeborg Frostrup had beguiled him, the Urning. And Timothy? He sat alone, dreaming of – whom? Russalka? Were Russalka's breasts bleached now by moonlight? Let him visit her and love her – the man I love is now beside me.

She dreamily lifted her head from Edward's shoulder and pulled off her velour beret to let her hair flow free; she laid her head back and closed her eyes. Would Timothy dare to stroke it, to press it against his lips? He, even he, had surrendered to my beauty…

The oars creaked and the water swelled silvery in the moonlight. Then, as from a great distance, she heard Ingeborg's tinkling laugh, a laugh of glass. 'Yes, there it is, the grotto of love! We shall have some sport here, I think!' Frances opened her eyes.

The grotto of love, Edward had explained to her earlier, was a grotto which could be reached also from the cliff above by a narrow fissure into which rudimentary steps had been cut, and could therefore be reached by land as well as by water.

'It sounds romantic!' he had laughed, 'but gets its name from certain, well, suggestive shapes and also because the young adolescents of the island frequently visit it to escape from their parents and indulge in clandestine embraces. We can certainly go ashore there and you can make out the two lovers, the one obviously a woman and the other, equally obviously a man. We'll see what Hartmann has managed to rig up by way of lighting. Who knows, Fanny, what adventures may befall us in the bower of bliss!'

Now she saw it, a bluish light which radiated from the grotto. She lifted her head from Edward's shoulder and stared at it; she saw the blue light running into the cave and receding; she made out the two sandstone figures, one of which could be construed as a reclining woman and the other, a rock which displayed a rigid protuberance, was her lover. But she saw something else. And she heard music, the sound of singing, in German.

It was a woman's voice, a voice that was mellifluous, yet fractured, melodic, yet strained, a mezzo soprano with a low tessitura.

Frances sat bolt upright and listened intently. It was a song that she knew, a song by Schubert, and called "Auf dem Wasser zu singen", "To be sung on the water".

A figure was standing in the blue grotto, and it was Millicent Freshet.

'Quiet!' Frances cried, 'Quiet! Listen!'

The voice floated through the night air, a nocturnal cantabile:

'Now through the gleam of watery mirrors
Glides, like a swan, the rocking boat.
Ah, on the waves of soft shimmering gladness

Glides now my soul, a swaying boat.
For from the Heavens now on to the waters,
Dances the glow of the dusk on the boat.
Ah time now vanishes , dewy its pinion ,
Vanishes now, on rocking waves.
Tomorrow – tomorrow – let time disappear ,
Vanish on shimmering wings from me now,
As I did then and shall do ever
Till on a high and gleaming wing
I too shall vanish from change and from time...'

'No!' screamed Frances, for a dreadful premonition had seized her, 'Millicent, no!'

But the figure, dressed in what looked like flowing draperies, had walked into the bluish water, fallen face down into it, and disappeared.

In uncontrollable agitation Frances stood upright in the wildly swaying boat; Edward seized her arm.

'Sit down, Fanny, for God's sake!'

Herbert too sought to restrain her. Beatrice screamed and Timothy sat, staring with a ghastly expression at what had happened.

'Quick!' yelled Edward to the oarsmen, 'get to her and pull her out of the water!'

Shouts were heard from other boats and rowers spurted forwards. But Frances was horrified to see William tear off his coat and dive into the sea.

'Come back!' his father screamed, his face a mask of frozen terror. They were close to the beach and the shadow of the cliff fell over them; all Frances could see from the light emanating from the grotto and the pale Chinese lanterns was William's head in the water and his arms bent in swimming.

'Fire rockets!' shouted Edward, 'get the lifeboat from the landing stage!'

But rockets had been bursting into the sky in abundance, and what good could the lifeboat do? Frances could just make out how William was diving, re-emerging, diving, re-emerging, then lifted his hand.

'She's here!'

Martin yelled for a boat hook which one of the other boats provided; rowing furiously they reached the spot and Frances saw Jörg thrust the boat hook into the sea and pull.

A sodden figure emerged, but lifeless, this Frances knew; Millicent Freshet's body was dragged and pushed into the boat. Herbert laid her on the floor, pumping her meagre, bony chest with his hands, then pulling her arms this way and that.

Was there a death rattle? A shuddering spasm as life fled?

'No, no!' cried Frances, rubbing the heart, the limbs, the lips with grog, with ardent spirits.

She seized the furs and sought to rub the body with them as though a touch of animal warmth still resided within them, a trace of life with which she could revivify the dead woman. But she knew that it was hopeless.

'Get help!' yelled Edward, seizing the pistol from Mr Osborne and firing it recklessly into the air. But Millicent Freshet was beyond help.

* * *

A silent flotilla accompanied the dead woman around the island and back to the landing stage. William had been hauled up into another boat; Beatrice sat shuddering and weeping in the arms of Herbert von Kroseck; Ingeborg sat close to Edward and Mr Osborne, staring fixedly in front of her; Timothy sat with his head buried in his hands.

Frances cradled the dead woman, wiping her tangled salty hair from her face, kissing the pale, cold lips. Pale they had always been those lips, but now they were completely drained of colour, drained of life. She wrapped her in furs and held her tight.

I heard you singing, did I not? Why? Why? Why? What drove you to this? Did your father – but no, no. The moon hung silently over them, the breeze became stronger. She dared not look at Edward lest she saw – what? One who was in some way responsible? One who had kissed those pale lips, touched these limp dead breasts when once they were warm?

She shuddered as she thought of those dead hazel eyes beneath the lids, eyes that would soon melt into milky liquescence. She kissed the gash on the dead forehead; no blood would ooze from it. Freshet – a small stream of fresh water…A rush of fresh water flowing into the sea. She wept, bitterly.

Look, Millicent, my tears flow for you, my dead sister.

At the landing stage Martin ran to fetch a stretcher on to which the body was gently lowered. Edward demanded that torches be lit, that he should carry one and lead the procession; William, now in a shapeless overcoat, seized the other. The bier was carried to the steps, and Jörg and Martin gently bore it upwards; many people followed in silence.

Frances walked with Edward and they made their way to the telegraph station. But it was deserted, in darkness; the door stood open, and the only sound was the tapping of the telegraph key. The cortège halted and waited in the rising wind.

'We shall take her to Government House. She shall lie there.'

The ghostly procession moved towards the house; Frances held Edward's free arm. They reached the door where a terrified Frau Stoeven met them.

'Summon my wife,' the governor commanded. The body was taken into the ballroom and reverently placed upon the large table. Edward lit candles and placed them at her head and feet. He dismissed them all, even William, even Frances, and stood in silent devotion.

* * *

CHAPTER FOUR

She walked through the silent woods on a mild, still December day, breathing the cool scent of slow, leafy decay; Mops ran ahead, scenting furtive sylvan life and tunnelling deep into the black leaf-mould. She had a hazel switch in her hand and slapped it against her thigh as she walked; the cawing of crows above was the only sound she heard in the dull afternoon. She wore a grey cloak over her dress, fastened at the throat with a silver chain; her loose, dark brown hair flowed from beneath her velour beret.

Many trees, dying, were choked with rampant ivy, she noticed, and there was also much fungus in evidence, bracket fungus and livid orange-spot and, beneath the trees, fly-agaric. She kicked them with her boot and strode on, throwing the stick for Mops to fetch.

They reached the edge of the wood; Tilshead lay beneath them and her home, Capewell House, standing by the small stream which glinted in the light of a low sun. Smoke drifted comfortably from the chimney of the house; the afternoon was turning to evening dusk.

She walked down to the small wicket gate and entered the garden where Mops, barking furiously, scattered the wood pigeons which fluttered up to the roof; she walked over the crunching gravel past the fish ponds and the sundial and reached the back of the house where she scraped her boots and opened the door, restraining Mops and calling him back for her to wipe the mud from his paws.

She hung up her cloak and hat and sat on a large ottoman, removing her boots and slipping into a pair of dainty slippers. She walked along the passage into the kitchen where Mrs Lovell was preparing the afternoon tea. She was a stout woman in her late fifties, a woman who lived in the house with Frances and cousin George who was in London for most of the week; she had lit a fire in the drawing room and would bring in the tea when it was ready.

Two letters had come, she explained, fetching the cake and warming the pot, both from foreign parts. They were lying on the table in the hall. Frances walked across the cool tiles to the loo-table standing beneath an ornate boule mirror; the letters were lying on a silver tray. She picked them up and took them into the drawing room, settling down by the fire in her favourite chair. Mrs Lovell had lit the gaslight and the mantel glowed in a cheerful incandescence.

The letters both bore foreign stamps, one, she noticed with a start, bore the head of Victoria in a red, white and green pattern, the colours of Heligoland; the second bore the stamp of Imperial Germany and was in her father's hand.

Her heart began pounding in her breast; she gazed into the fire and did not look up as Mrs Lovell brought in a tray of tea, scones and slab cake. Mops sat before her, his head in her lap, and gazed at her soulfully; she absent-mindedly patted his head and noticed that the garden was now in darkness, the shrubbery bunched in silent masses against the French windows. She scarcely touched the tea and was chided good-humouredly by Mrs Lovell who came in after half an hour to remove the tray.

Frances crossed to the bureau and fetched the elegant silver paperknife which her father had given her as a present. She slit open his letter first and read the following:

'My dearest girl,

I have reprimanded myself more than a dozen times for not having written more frequently, but things are moving on the diplomatic front and I am in daily conversations with the ambassador here, also with Prince Bismarck. It all sounds very pompous, doesn't it, if I say that your Papa is a very important man, even indispensable at the moment! But that's what I seem to be.

But how are you, dearest Fan? I'm so glad that Charlie Dundas was able to help and that you got back from Hamburg safely. You young women are quite intrepid, there's nothing stopping you! But what a beastly business it was.

Teddy was obviously very upset, and hates anything like that. Who doesn't? But he always wants life to be fun, one huge carnival, and that poor girl's suicide must have destroyed his faith in the human capacity for mirth and merry-making. But he's resilient and probably planning the next round of junketing. I'm just sorry that you saw it all.

I want to shield you, darling, from the jagged edges of the world, for you are very precious to me. But I'm sure that George's company and Mrs Lovell's excellent cooking will put you back on an even keel.

Now, there is another rather tiresome matter. I was longing to get away from this great ponderous city and come to Tilshead for Christmas to walk with my lovely daughter over Salisbury Plain and to see the roses in her cheeks again. But, but, but... The ambassador, Sir Edward Malet, wants to wrap up some very important business by the end of the year, and nobody knows how long Bismarck has to go. Things are rather delicate and I am required to stay out here until the end of December. This grieves me very much, as you may realise. I shall make every effort to escape by the first week in January. It might be tied up by Christmas, but I doubt it.

One way out might be for you to spend Christmas with George in his London house, do a few shows and have a jolly time. Or you could invite some friends to Capewell House and have Christmas there, playing charades and things. The Scottish tribe would also love to have you.

Oh dear, this sounds as if I'm trying to parcel you off somewhere, but I feel quite inadequate as a father. Dearest, dearest Fan, we'll jaunt off together in the New Year, I promise. How about the Riviera? There you'll turn all heads, marry a rich American and sail away in his yacht.

Bless you, my darling, and take care,
Your ever loving Papa.'

She put the letter down and, in great agitation, opened the second, turning immediately to the end to see who had written it. It was from Beatrice. Frances threw a large log onto the fire and settled down to read.

'Dear Miss Prince,

I didn't know your address but found it in Pa's special book on his desk. He's been in a very bad mood, mooching about, no rantipoling, so I thought I'd give you our news, such as there is.

It's been awful since you left. We had that terrible inquest on poor Millicent, the coroner came across from the mainland and it was held in the Rathaus. Suicide whilst the balance of the mind was disturbed. But all sorts of malicious rumours flew about involving poor Willy.

Do you remember that strange girl Stine? Well, she had a sort of fit and started to talk all sorts of nonsense about Willy, how bad he was, we couldn't make head nor tail of it. We had a girl working here called Elke who was related to Stine and Ma threw her out thinking she was a spy.

Then people started to say that Willy had had an affaire afterwards with Millicent! Can you believe it! He went through a very bad time, poor brother, but he's now working with the English consul in Copenhagen, a Mr A.P. Ingliss, just a clerical job. Pa found it for him.

Pa said that poor Millicent was driven to do what she did because her father was abusing her, and nobody knows where he is. Bill Freshet was known as a brute and a bully and some said that he was jealous of any man she wanted to marry.

It's scandalous, saying Willy drove her to it. Do you remember how brave he was, trying to save her? Ma kept well out of it, but Pa really suffered. She tried to take his mind off things by reminding him of his plans to get a lift installed between Bopperlun and Bedeeln, but his heart isn't in it at the moment.

Millicent is buried in the churchyard next to that actress, you know, the one who was struck by lightning on the Düne after escaping the outbreak of cholera in St Petersburg. The Reverend Heywood was not keen to give her Christian burial, but Pa insisted.

It's very irksome, all this. And it's very boring here now, for Charlotte is away too, travelling with one of Ma's relations, a Gräfin von Strachwitz. They wanted to know if I wished to go away too, but Charlotte only wants to study and I'm not keen on that. They've been to Zurich where Charlotte made a good impression but the professors said she was not yet ready for study, and one of the Gräfin's friends said they should go to Berlin to meet a lady, a Frau Salome, lovely name isn't it, who had studied in Zurich and she could perhaps advise Charlotte.

If they'd gone to Paris I might have gone too, or perhaps not. For, I can now tell you, I'm very much in love with Herbert who comes to see me when he can. Don't tell Ma for Heaven's sake! Let this be a secret between us!

One more sad piece of news is the death of Miss Lavender. She had a bad fall when it was icy here and never really recovered. So she's buried outside the church too. The Reverend Heywood started to do the service but was taken ill. He's not a well man and people wonder about his mental state. He sits all the time by the Russian chapel on the Hallem, but Mr Osborne says he stares at that figurehead all the time. Aren't men strange creatures!

Dear, dear Miss Prince, it would be so lovely to see you again, and I'm sure that Pa would welcome you with open arms. Now, I'm going to be very naughty and let you into a secret. Charlie and I, well, we're going to be twenty-one on Christmas Day, believe it or not, and it would be absolutely wunderbar if you could come across and celebrate it with us. Willy's come across from Copenhagen so it should be fun. But I expect you'll be in great demand at home.

I'm playing the piano quite a bit, nothing much else to do, and helping Pa with things. Mr Osborne gets quite impertinent and I think he's keen on me, but Herbert is the one I truly love. Oh Miss

Prince, I can't tell you how happy I am when I see him, and he's such a gentleman. He's interested in everything and asks me all sorts of things. Ma came across us once unchaperoned and got a bit annoyed, but Herbert made it up to her by having beautiful lilies sent across from the florist in Cuxhaven. Ingeborg Frostrup fancies him too, I'll bet, as she gives me some funny looks when she sees us together. She said to me once that she hoped I wouldn't be disappointed. I expect she means Herbert has a girl in every port, you know what sailors are.

I really mustn't ramble on. I'm sure Pa would send his fondest love if he knew I was writing this.

Do come at Christmas if you can. I know you can't invite yourself but if you could come I'll suggest to Pa that he might invite you. I'm sure he'd jump at it. By the way, Miss Lavender left you a few bits and pieces in a sealed box, so it would be a good opportunity to collect it. You also left your lovely umbrella with the black beading behind. It's very pretty, where did you get it?

Yours affectionately,

Beatrice Hennicker-Heaton.

PS. There's a new man in the Telegraph Station called Mr Brass. He's so thin that Pa says we should stick him in the lighthouse and use him as a telescope.

PPS. I'm playing some very nice Haydn canzonets and Pa sings them with me, or bellows them, more like. "High on the giddy bending mast, The seaman furls the rending sail" and so on. "Tis Britain's glory we maintain!" We overdo that bit and Ma gets quite annoyed. "Hurly burly Hurly burly!" Come and keep the peace, Miss Prince.'

* * *

She scarcely tasted the delicious meal that Mrs Lovell had prepared, and forgoing the pudding she carried a glass of claret across into the drawing room and sat gazing into the fire. Mrs Lovell ate in the kitchen and lived in a small room upstairs; George, who worked in marine insurance, usually lived in his London house during the week and came across to Capewell House at weekends. The only sound was the ticking of the clock, the crackling of the fire and the dull sussuration of the gas.

Capewell was her father's house but George had lived with them after the death of his parents. His earlier interest in shipwreck and nautical disaster had been channelled into insurance of vessels and their cargoes; he specialised in particular average. He was two years older than Frances, nearing thirty and still a bachelor; he was thick-set, dark, and inclined to portliness.

Frances sat alone; Mrs Lovell brought in coffee and wished her goodnight. There was no wind, and the silence of the night was oppressive. No grinding sea, but the plain stretching for miles where she had walked as a girl with the two dogs Hector and Lucy. Why had both letters referred to Christmas? She sighed deeply, and her left hand played with the pendant that hung from her neck.

Beatrice, Beatrice, why did you write me that letter? The night of October the twenty-fifth arose before her in angular horror, etching its acid into her brain. The moon of mercury draining into the black sea, the caves, the phosphorescent lights and flaming barrels of tar casting a flickering glare onto the twisted, irregular shapes, the lapping waters, the lanterns, the gloomy sapphire of that last grotto, the grotto of love – and then the woman, singing. 'Now through the gleam of watery mirrors – Glides like a swan the rocking boat…And I too shall vanish – from change and from time…' Selber entschwinde der wechselnden Zeit…

The rest had the quality of a nightmare: the sodden corpse, the ghostly procession up the steps, the body of Millicent Freshet laid to rest in Government House, the candles at her head and feet. And then the following days, days of turmoil, wretchedness, grief.

Edward had, bewilderingly, unaccountably, insisted that she leave the island as soon as possible for he did not wish to afflict her with the inevitably distressing investigations that would ensue.

But would she not be required as a witness at the inquest? There were so many witnesses, he had continued, his face strained and pale; all had seen what had happened. The flight of Bill Freshet surely pointed to his guilt. Frances had meekly acquiesced with Edward's wishes, loving him and yet not understanding him, wishing to be near him yet not wising to importune him with her presence.

Her departure was precipitous, her belongings were packed and carried down the steps to the Rathaus, and a telegraphic communication with Hamburg alerted the consul to her intended arrival on October the twenty-ninth. There were no more family dinners and the children she scarcely saw; on the morning of her departure she bade farewell to the weeping girls, but William did not appear. Frau Stoeven regretted that Lady Augusta was indisposed and unable to see her.

Frances had walked down the steps and gazed down at the Prinz Eitel-Friedrich waiting below. A mass of seaweed had been washed up on the beach and stank in the late autumnal sun, a mass of glittering flies. She sought Edward in the Rathaus but Mr Strang took her aside and explained that the Governor bitterly regretted not being able to see her; he would be writing very shortly. This, then was the end.

She sat upon a crude wooden bench and stared at the sea; snatches of conversation drifted over towards her. 'Vaar… Doghter…Jongwüf…verdrink…boös, sloh…' - 'Father… daughter…virgin…drunkard…bad…wicked.' Yet there was also 'Söön…ünredelk…Barbaar…'- 'Son…depraved…barbarian'. Ignore it, she murmured, it is ignorant gossip.

She had suddenly noticed a tall, dignified figure standing before her, a figure in black and in a cloak, a large hat and veil. It was Lady Augusta.

Frances jumped to her feet and the Governor's wife lightly placed a gloved hand on her shoulder.

'Forget this unfortunate incident. The young woman led a tragic, empty life. She had no talent, and sought solace in fantasies. Her father was brutal and possessive. The relationship was abnormal. I have grown fond of you, Miss Prince, and do not wish your memories of our island to be stained by waste, baseness, senselessness.'

She had kissed Frances on both cheeks.

'Live as a proud daughter of a proud nation. Think of us and return in happier times.'

She had turned and walked back through the piles of weed, the ropes, nets and lobster pots. She did not look behind, she did not wave.

* * *

Frances slept badly in the silent house; the shutters rattled as a rising wind moaned in the chimneys and at the windows. She dreamt of grotesque rocks and twisted shapes, of fissures and collapsing cliffs; she was the actress Malwine Erk and was fleeing the cholera in St Petersburg, knowing that she would be incinerated in lightning on the Düne; snow was piled high against the lighthouse which became a monstrous phallus.

She woke with a pounding heart and lay on her back, staring into the darkness. What state of decomposition had Millicent's body now reached? Had her eyes turned to slime, her mouth to mildew? She groaned and turned on to her left side.

Rain fell before dawn and pattered on the laurel bushes below. Frances dozed and heard Mrs Lovell rise at seven o' clock to clean out the fireplace and lay the breakfast. She heard Mops bark as the postman delivered his letters; she dressed and went downstairs.

There were no letters for her, and she frowned over her toast. What had she expected? A letter from Edward inviting her to his realm? What word did he use? Domdaniel? She walked into the study, a room lined with George's pictures of shipwrecks, and read again yesterday's letters from Germany, but Mops followed her expectantly and sat at her feet, his tail thump-thumping the floor.

'It's too wet,' she explained. But the rain had stopped.

She walked with him through the grey damp air, through the

wicket gate into the wood, then out on to the road that looked down upon the plain, a featureless expanse that stretched to the horizon, interrupted by sparsely populated hamlets. Almost the sea, she thought, the grey autumnal sea, a grey mirror.

She thought of Miss Frostrup's glass, its muted tints, the reduced intervals between light and dark, and felt a pang of resentment at the Danish woman's beauty, her talent, above all her proximity to Edward.

But I, too, have beauty, do I not? And talent I had once, well, yes, once. And suddenly she stopped, opened her mouth, her throat, and to Mops' amazement, sang.

It was a creamy, liquid sound, a liquescence of pearl and amber that trembled in the dead air.

'She never told her love – She never told her love – But let concealment like a worm in the bud – Feed on her damask cheek...' It was one of the Haydn canzonets Beatrice had mentioned and, subconsciously, Frances had recalled them, for she had sung them with Herr Winter at the piano.

'She sat – like Patience on a monument – smiling, smiling at grief – Smiling, smiling at grief...'

How poignant it was, how passionate! How radiantly expressive the second 'never'! How plangent the note, the tone of the first 'grief'! And yet how untrained was her voice, her breathing, her control. Once she had sung it beautifully.

She remembered Herr Winter looking up from the pianoforte with a dark, intense look, a look of unconcealed longing, also her mother's stern disapprobation. For Dulcie had sat listening, intent on protecting her attractive daughter from lascivious advances. He had loved her, she knew, and she had been drawn to his sensitivity and his devotion to the art of music. He had left a bunch of violets in her coat pocket, she remembered. When was it? Eight, nine years ago? There had been love letters, too, long since destroyed. There had been one kiss, in the dim practice room in the Conservatoire, a gentle and fluttering presence on the lips. That was all.

David Winter, accompanist and repetiteur. Was he not writing an opera, *Cupid and Psyche?* Was it not dedicated to her? She smiled ruefully. He is now happily married, I expect, and teaching music in Leipzig or Berlin, whereas I tramp through grey, damp Wiltshire and, like a mad woman, sing in a badly neglected voice to no one but a dog on a deserted road.

Dulcie had disliked Herr Winter intensely.

'I do not wish my daughter to consort with impoverished Jewish musicians.'

With whom, then, should I consort? Your art must come first. Art, well…

But was it not my art, my singing that drew him to me, the supreme one, the one who, whom I - ?

Did my beauty do this? Is beauty lethal, then? Or was it, as father said, a heart attack brought on by those immense achievements? But she, his wife, the High Priestess ran, I know now, with such violence into the door that it split, because she knew, she knew that it was her fury that had killed him. No, no, think of something else…

She strode on; Mops was far ahead, chasing rabbits. A fine drizzle fell and she tucked as much hair as she could beneath her beret.

Another priestess called me a proud daughter of a proud nation. Yes, high on the giddy bending mast, that's where I should be.

She suddenly thought of Edward and Beatrice at the Erard, and a pang of intense longing overcame her, for the island, for its Governor. She would stand with him on the top of the lighthouse and gaze with him through the telescope at Wangerooge and the tower there.

Had he melted my mother's icy reserve? Had he kissed those lips that father had kissed? Or was it simply a tendresse, a bunch of violets in a coat pocket, a chaste touching of lips?

The rain fell more heavily and she called Mops, who had disappeared. I shall need my umbrella, the black pretty one with the jet beads which I bought with him in Venice; he had stood in the haberdasher's shop and the owner had knelt before him:

'Maestro, che honore!'

And I felt proud, yes, to know that I walked with him, sang for him, danced for him.

The plain had disappeared under a blanket of rain; Mops reappeared and she hastily retraced her steps after the bounding dog.

* * *

The early afternoon was gloomy; Frances had changed her wet clothes and was wearing her leg-of-mutton blouse and a grey skirt. She had dried her hair and wore it in a chignon, held by a silver comb. She lit the gas and sat by the fire. The room was warm and still, and she fetched one of her cousin's pictures of shipwrecks.

The Aquatic, yes, she knew, had sunk in bad weather off Heligoland, losing its cargo of grain. It had been bound for Hull from Hamburg but now, in the photograph, lay wrecked on its side, the sails ripped, the masts splintered, the rigging torn and tangled.

Suddenly she heard a knock at the door, which Mrs Lovell answered. She heard voices, then Mrs Lovell entered the drawing room.

'There is a gentleman to see you, Miss Frances. A clergyman.'

She showed Frances the card: it was, as she knew it would be, from the Reverend Timothy Heywood. She jumped to her feet and looked at herself in the mirror.

'Please show him in.'

He had left his coat and hat in the hall, and entered the room; his face seemed paler and drawn, but a smile of great loveliness spread over it when he saw her. He shook hands warmly, then they both sat on opposite sides of the fire. He sat with his legs pressed together, and nervously played with a twisted handkerchief in his fingers.

He had been, he explained, visiting friends in Winchester, where he had been to school, and then he had come to Salisbury to look again at that cathedral which he loved above all others.

Then, on an impulse, he had taken the branch line to Codford St. Mary, and from there a conveyance had brought him to Capewell House. Beatrice Hennicker-Heaton had previously given him her address. (Surely not really a sudden impulse, Frances thought.) He sincerely hoped that he was not intruding? Not at all. She led a very quiet life, and it was good to see old friends. Yes, he said, we are friends.

Frances rang for Mrs Lovell to bring tea, and the two sat in silence. Then he spoke.

He spoke of the horror of October the twenty-fifth, his shock, his grief, his sadness and his anger at Millicent's act of self-destruction. He spoke of his reluctance to allow Christian burial to one who had wilfully thrown away God's most precious gift, but also of Sir Edward's plea for clemency and firm insistence that Millicent lie in the churchyard.

He spoke of days of numb depression, his inability to perform satisfactorily his clerical duties, then of the death of dear Miss Lavender and his collapse and the assistance given to him at the graveside by the Lutheran Pastor Niep.

He had passed through a dark night of the soul, he murmured, gazing not at Frances but into the fire, and had longed to speak to a dear friend, but there was no one. He had asked the Governor for an extended leave of absence and Sir Edward had graciously concurred, bringing a young curate, a Mr Eliot, from the mainland as his locum.

He had visited his elderly mother in London and his erstwhile teachers in Winchester. Then he knew that he would have to see her again, and here he was.

Frances replenished the fire from the coal scuttle and poured tea from a chased silver pot, watching the straw-coloured liquid fill the fine bone-china cups. She offered him seed cake from the cake stand which he accepted. Then it was her turn to speak.

She spoke of her feelings of guilt at having neglected Millicent, of not having encouraged her to sing, of not acting more forcefully when she saw the condition that the poor girl was in.

No, he interrupted vehemently, she must not chastise herself.

He, Millicent's spiritual counsellor, should have done more. It was unseemly for a clergyman to apportion guilt, he said, but Millicent's father would, when found, be questioned; he would certainly appear before a Higher Court where his cruelty would weigh heavily in the scales against him. There were also those who bore false witness and they, too, would be punished.

Frances felt her heart beating wildly. False witness? Yes, he continued, there were those ignorant and vindictive enough to suspect that William Hennicker-Heaton was in some way involved. It was all nonsense. Yes, she said tonelessly, it was.

The clock chimed four. She drew the curtains against the darkness and rang for Mrs Lovell to remove the tray. After she had left the room and closed the door, Timothy looked at Frances awkwardly.

He had a request to make before the conveyance took him back to Codford St. Mary. What was it? she asked.

He would be so glad if she would allow him to take her around the cathedral in Salisbury. They could have tea there one afternoon. He could meet her at the station and they could have some three hours there together.

She gazed at him, this unhappy, unhappy soul, a man to whom she had taken an instant aversion, to his poise, his gait, his sanctimonious rejection of a sublime work of art, his priggishness... She thought of his tortured awareness of mutability, his inability to appreciate that which was lovely – but then remembered, blushing, how he had once spoken of her charms and had drunk, with her, a toast to her beauty. Well, Russalka, she thought impishly, you are now eclipsed!

Yes, she said, that would be very pleasant. She would be free on Friday. And his face, illumined by joy, struck her by its youthfulness and grace.

* * *

Frances, together with Mrs Lovell, caught the train at Codford St Mary on the Friday morning; the older woman, Frances sensed, had made the excuse that she wanted to shop in Salisbury in order to chaperone her, at least as far as the journey was concerned, and must have felt reassured by the Reverend Heywood's office that he was a respectable companion.

As they travelled through the December countryside Frances mischievously thought of the figurehead, the scurrilous rumours concerning Timothy's attention to it and Mrs Lovell's certain reaction if she had been apprised of them. She gazed out over the water meadows of the Avon and the view of the cathedral rising above them.

He was there to meet them; the look of muted disappointment at the sight of Mrs Lovell soon dissipated when the older woman took her leave, explaining that she would meet Frances at the station at four o' clock. Timothy offered Frances his arm and they walked through the mild moist air towards the Cathedral Church of St Mary.

He was agitated, eloquent. He waxed lyrical about the various bishops, the consecration in the presence of Henry the Third, the beautiful upper tower, the perpetual source of anxiety lest the light arches were not able to bear its weight, the addition of flying buttresses and the great internal girders, the strengthening of the whole structure by Sir Christopher Wren.

She gazed at him as he spoke: he spoke of desecration, the demolition of the sumptuous Perpendicular Beauchamp and Hungerford chantries flanking the Lady Chapel, the opening up of 'vistas', the wholesale destruction of the remaining stained glass.

He hated James Wyatt for this, he exclaimed passionately, also Sir George Scott, another stucco-Gothic mandarin with his elaborate programme of works that left the interior in its present state of encaustic floors, varnished marble and a quire bepainted and bedizened.

But then, he sighed, beauty is perhaps meretricious, and one should worship the Lord in a bleak, bare chapel. Yet he loved, she noticed, the close, the rambling bishop's palace and the little Mompesson house with its delicate ironwork screen.

They stood and gazed upwards. Look, he admonished her, on

the lofty pile of warm-hued, greyish stone, tinged with the green of lichen, look at the slender magnificence of the central tower and, poised above all, the tallest and loveliest medieval spire in England.

This man is intoxicated by beauty, thought Frances, but it is the beauty of stone and spirit, not of flesh. And yet, and yet, did he not once speak of my loveliness? What was the beauty to which we drank?

They walked across the stone flags of the long, lofty nave, the cool December light flooding and illuminating the lofty arches. He begged her to ignore the polychromatic horror imposed by Scott and drew her attention to the retro-quire and Lady Chapel, the attenuated shafts of Purbeck marble, the multiple vaulting. He seemed transported, invigorated.

I walk with him, she thought, and listen to his eloquence, but think of one who, on his sliver of rock, beguiled me. Yet there was also one for whom I danced and sang, and death it was that took him from me.

'But you must be tired,' he cried, 'and all I do is lecture you on grisaille glass and lierne-vaulted canopies. Let us take luncheon and rest!'

They walked through the town to the Salisbury Arms and sat in a comfortable room next to a cheerful fire.

'Thank you, Timothy,' she said, choosing not to tell him of her visits to the cathedral before, 'you are an excellent guide, and I am most indebted to your expertise.'

Over a light luncheon she asked him how it was that he had taken up the post on Heligoland, that bare, wind-whipped island. Surely a post in an English cathedral city would be more suitable for him? His face darkened and he sat in silence for several minutes before replying.

I would have liked, he said, high office in the Anglican church, but lacked the necessary connections; my background is humble and I struggled to escape it. He lapsed into silence.

The room grew dark, and the maid lit the oil lamp, suffusing the room with a mellow glow. And he suddenly reached for her hand.

'Frances,' he murmured, 'can you forgive me for my earlier churlishness? My awkwardness? My tormented soul?'

She withdrew her hand and lifted it to twist the bun of her hair back into shape.

'Please, Timothy, we are friends, there is nothing more to forgive.'

He sat upright, drank a glass of port wine, and his cheeks reddened.

'May I,' he asked, 'take the liberty of asking another favour?'

'What is it?' she asked.

'I wondered if we might see each other again, before Christmas.'

She gazed at him intently.

'I do not know how long I shall be staying here. I may well go back to Germany, to my father for Christmas.'

'Or to Heligoland?' he asked, running his index finger behind his clerical collar.

'I think not. Sir Edward doubtless has other plans and I do not wish to embarrass him with my presence.'

'I wonder if I shall ever return,' he murmured, his features strangely contorted. 'I have not been well, as you know, and Miss Freshet's suicide affected me deeply.'

'It affected us all,' she retorted.

He shifted uncomfortably in his chair, then looked at her.

'May I give you my mother's address in Finsbury Park? It would be so pleasant to see you if you are ever in London. I live very modestly, but we could go to the theatre, or, better, to the opera. There you could open my eyes and help me understand the things that you love.'

'And the proprieties?' she smiled.

'Mrs Lovell could accompany you. Or you could stay with friends in London. Your father must have many acquaintances there. But I must not presume too much, I am sorry.'

She gazed at the gathering dusk outside the window and listened to the clopping of a horse's hooves as it passed the hotel.

'It is very kind, Timothy, but I must get my house in order before going back to Germany. And you must spend as much time as possible with your mother. It has been a pleasant afternoon. I have learned much.'

He smiled wanly, and finished his glass of port.

They slowly walked back to the station, looking into the lighted shop windows and at the graceful spire dominating the wintry town. Mrs Lovell was waiting. He raised his hat at the two ladies, smiled at Frances and saw them into their carriage. He stood for a long time on the platform and watched as the train disappeared from view.

* * *

George was ebullient as he finished off his breakfast of a grilled chop and a glass of porter.

'I hear you've been gallivanting in Salisbury with an unmarried man,' he joked, lighting a Romeo y Julieta havana, 'I must see to it that Mrs Lovell keeps a closer eye on you, my girl.'

She playfully poked out her tongue at him and helped Mrs Lovell carry out the dishes. George looked through The Times and suddenly called to her.

'Something here for you, Fan. *Tannhäuser* at Her Majesty's Theatre. Sounds ghastly to me, but I know you like this stuff. Are you in it? No, it says Valleria, Burns, Schott, Ludwig, Pope. Conducted by Randegger. I'll take you if you're keen. Greater love hath no man for his dearest coz than to take her to hours of some purgatorial German noise. It's in English, thank God.'

She put down the dishes.

'I saw *The Flying Dutchman* at the Lyceum a few years ago,' he continued, 'it was dreadful. That Captain or whoever he was would run into deep insurance difficulties with his ship anchored next to those rocks in weather like that. Who would underwrite it? Certainly not my company. Give me Balfe any day. Saw *The Bohemian Girl* in Her Majesty's – splendid stuff. Come on, Fan, you can do "I dreamt that I dwelt in marble halls" for me for

Christmas.'

'I think I'll go for a walk,' she said, 'will you come too?'

'Lord no. I've got to ride my havana for a while yet.'

Mops pricked up his ears and jumped at her in excitement. She took down her beret, cloak and gloves and set forth.

The morning was fine and a still mist lay like milk over the plain. *Tannhäuser*! How violently agitated she was, distraught, discomposed at the mere mention of the name! Had he not spoken fervently of this, his earlier work, during their long walks in Bayreuth and Venice? He owed the world a performance of *Tannhäuser*, this he had insisted, a work which, more so even that Tristan, he longed to produce in his theatre.

In a late, last work the young hero had been lured by a castrated magician, gazing into his magic mirror, and by a tormented sorceress and penitent; in *Tannhäuser* it was Venus who had tempted the knight and lured him into her languorous realm. Had he not given her the score and the libretto to study? She recalled with great clarity her amazement at the opening scene: the wide, curving grotto, the greenish waterfall, the coral-like growths, the rosy half-light in which Venus rested, the bluish vapours, the moonlight, the fawning swan.

'Only my theatre can envisage this!' he had cried. 'The French in their perfidy ruined it in their Opéra. But the world will see what Bayreuth can do. Sing, and work. And then, one day, you can be my Venus.' And he had placed his hands on her shoulders and kissed her on the forehead.

She blushed crimson at the vision that had assailed her, striking the dead white grass with the lead, striding after Mops. Was it not William who had spoken flippantly, salaciously of the mons veneris, the mound of Venus? And you, Timothy Heywood, would you wish to take me to see this opera? You who rejected *Parsifal* – would *Tannhäuser* not offend you? But Elizabeth, of course, triumphs, and the Pope's staff blossoms.

Her boots swished through dead, sodden, matted leaves; Mops ran to left and right, then rolled energetically in putrefying matter. She stopped and looked out over the plain which stretched before her: the silver solar disk swam in thinning mist. There were grottos, yes, and in the grotto of love a young woman drowned herself, singing of death. She had no talent and sought solace in fantasies.

Is there another of whom this could be said? But this one was given beauty and was loved, was she not, by one who wished to redeem the world through art. Who had loved Millicent? No, no, do not think of it. There was much malicious gossip, prurient speculation.

The Rock! It suddenly came vividly to her mind, the red sandstone, the fissured, lacerated cliffs, the buffeting wind, the shrieking gulls, the steps, the Düne…

I must see him again, my Governor. We shall walk to the Nathuurnstak and gaze from the lighthouse to see the tower on Wangerooge. It is I who shall be on his arm, nobody else, and we shall dance in the ballroom at Government House. And I shall sing again.

She breathed deeply and filled her lungs – but then Mops was barking aggressively; she expelled the air and turned to look. A dogcart was approaching along the lane driven by a woman who suddenly reined in the horse; Mops jumped and snarled.

'Frances! Miss Prince! It's me, Dympna!'

Frances stared at the figure in the carriage, a woman of her own age, seated somehow awkwardly and wearing a long grey coat and old-fashioned poke-bonnet.

* * *

The horse, a brown cob, whinnied and pawed; Mops crouched growling. Dympna? The strange name eluded her, yet suddenly Frances remembered the crippled girl in St Etheldreda's school whose mother was a teacher there and who had been mocked and taunted because of her deformity, her strange name, her mother's position.

Had not she, Frances, once threatened to burn off all her hair? She also recalled the sunlit classroom, empty except for the two of them where Frances had bullied her and mocked her limping gait.

Dympna, Dympna…Had not Sophie and the others chanted her name in derision? Had they not once smeared her snow-white apron with ink? Had not Dympna, crimson with fury, reminded her attackers that Dympna was the patron saint of the insane and that she would never intercede for them, even when they were manacled and lying in straw?

'Frances! How lovely to meet you! Climb up and we'll ride together. My mother would love to see you!'

'I – I have a rather muddy dog with me, I'm afraid.'

'No matter, I have a rug and you can hold him on your lap.'

Dympna stowed her whip in the bracket and reached out a gloved hand. Frances hesitated, then, on an impulse, seized Mops and placed her foot in the rocking step, grabbing Dympna's hand. The two women sat close; Dympna passed over the rug, took out the whip, cracked it and the cob, a mare, started to trot.

The mist cleared; the air was still and warm; Frances gazed at her companion. Dympna's face was thinner, and her dark eyes more bird-like than Frances had remembered, her features harder. Yet her smile was sincere and bright, and genuine affection radiated from it. She chattered brightly as they trotted along the lane: how pleased she was that they had met; how her mother had thought that she had seen Frances in Salisbury in the company of a clergyman but that she, Dympna, had considered this to be unlikely as she believed that Frances was making herself a career as an opera singer in Germany; how she and her mother had so often thought of Frances's father, now a widower.

She, Dympna, had never married but lived with her mother and grandfather near Codford St Mary – they would soon see the house – and earned a modest income by embroidery and lace-making. Her mother remembered Frances well as a girl, also her friend Sophie.

With a light lick of the whip she urged on the flagging cob; Frances held the silent Mops on the rug spread across her knees. The road turned to the right between bare elms and Frances noticed the hamlet, a few scattered houses, from whose chimneys smoke rose perpendicularly in the still air.

Dympna guided the dogcart with skill and called the horse to whoa; it stopped, gently steaming, before the first house, a small brick-built residence set back from the road in a small garden.

Dympna smiled.

'I'd be glad if you'd alight first, Frances, then help me down. You may remember that I was born a cripple and have to wear my surgical boot.'

Frances stepped down and left Mops to run and lift his leg against a gatepost; she helped Dympna down and the two women, one hobbling, walked up a muddy path to the front door. Dympna rang the bell and then, as the door opened, she told her astonished mother who it was, and left to take Cassie the cob round to her stabling with the local farmer.

Frances was ushered into a dark, narrow hall, then into a small drawing room with a coal fire smouldering in the grate. Mrs Vernon welcomed her effusively, commenting on how well she looked and how delighted she was that Dympna had brought her.

Frances still felt slightly in awe of her erstwhile teacher who insisted that she sit by the fire and drink a glass of madeira. Frances suddenly remembered Mops, but Mrs Vernon reassured her: Dympna had given the dog a shin bone to gnaw and he was happily at work in a small enclosed yard at the back of the house (the thoughtful girl had also taken the dog's lead which Frances had left with her coat and hat in the hall and tied him to the pump handle).

Dympna entered, hobbling awkwardly but obviously delighted to see Frances talking to her mother. Mrs Vernon's hair was almost white; Frances recalled a tall, forbidding teacher who insisted that she learn her German grammar correctly, also her Greek verbs.

'You were always headstrong, Miss Prince!' laughed Mrs Vernon, enjoying her reminiscences and her madeira, 'and we on the staff used to call you our Proud Princess. It was always your voice we could hear on the stairs and in the corridor. Miss Stringer, the music teacher, was quite right when she said you would go far. Your voice, she said, was the voice of an angel.'

Frances blushed and moved restlessly in her chair.

'I did sing a little,' she said quietly, 'but was not good enough.'

'Your parents were so proud of you, especially your dear father. We later heard, after we'd moved away, that you had been invited to sing in Germany. But your knowledge of the subjunctive left much to be desired!'

'You always had a beautiful voice,' said Dympna, her eyes shining. 'I always remember that school concert when you sang "On the Wings of Song", I could have wept, it was so lovely.'

'Why don't you stay for luncheon?' said Mrs Vernon, getting up. 'It's only the remains of a pie, I'm afraid, with pickles and chutney, and stewed apples and cream for pudding. It would be so lovely to chat. My father will not bother us as he takes his meals upstairs in his room. He is an old man now and sits most of the day by his fire.'

Frances felt ill at ease. She suffered guilt at remembering how cruel she had been towards Dympna at school, and felt chastened by the latter's generosity of spirit and genuine affection; she could also not expect Dympna to take her back to Capewell House immediately. She also recalled that Mrs Lovell would not expect her back for luncheon as she was visiting her sister in Devizes; George would also not be back until evening. After lunch Dympna could take her back some of the way, and she and Mops could walk the rest before it got too dark. She smiled graciously and accepted the invitation.

During the meal she said very little about her life in Germany, and simply referred to her father's work as military attaché in Berlin and her brief sojourn on Heligoland.

Heligoland? Dympna was sure that her grandfather had been there as a young man – he had told her about it. Frances preferred not to speak more of the island and urged Dympna to show her her embroidery and lace-work: this, she said, was more important than aimless travel. And, indeed, the needlework was exquisite, as was the petit-point and the lace; Dympna also showed her a collection of collars, cuffs, handkerchiefs and shawls embroidered with delicate and intricate patterns.

'I shall do you a beautiful blouse, Frances,' she smiled, blushing, 'and when you are wearing it in Paris or Vienna you will think of me in my quiet house here.'

'It is you who have the true creative spark,' Frances replied, 'whereas I just posture and pretend.'

They drank their coffee and Dympna suggested, whilst Mrs Vernon cleared the table, that they should say a quick hello to grandfather before leaving. They walked upstairs, Dympna bobbing and holding the banisters. They entered the old man's room, a room that smelled of old age and tobacco; a fishtail burner hummed on the wall, for the day was dying.

Frances saw him sitting by the fire, a hunched figure with a rug over his knees, his sparse hair was white, his complexion mottled and lentiginous; his gnarled hands clutched an extinguished briar whose dottle lay in scattered crumbs before him.

'Grandpa,' said Dympna loudly, 'it's Miss Prince, Colonel Prince's daughter. She wanted to see you and wish you well. She's just back from Germany, also Heligoland. I said you'd been there once, in the navy.'

The old man turned his rheumy eyes on his visitor; he coughed and caught the phlegm in a large red handkerchief.

'Heligoland?' He wheezed and fumbled with the empty pipe, thrusting the spent dottle back into the bowl with his thumb. Dympna hobbled across to him and shovelled more coal onto his fire, replacing the fireguard.

'When you were young Midshipman Fallows with Captain Lavender? And you fell in love with his daughter? When you were dashing and handsome? And Miss Lavender turned you down and you were heartbroken till you met grandmother and knew that she was the one? You used to tell us about it, remember?'

The old man gazed into the fire and wiped the drooling saliva dribbling from his mouth. 'Heligoland?' He hawked and brought up a gob of catarrh which sizzled on the burning coals. Then, turning his sunken, blotchy face to Frances, he stared at her for a minute, then shook his head.

'No, it's not Euphemia. I married you, didn't I, Ada? Where's Robert? Did he die fighting Boney? Give an old sailor some rum, Ada, there's a good girl. Warm the bed for me, Ada, like a good wife.'

And, giggling, he gripped Frances's arm.

'You were a warm one, Ada, we had good sport, didn't we?'

A grey tongue rolled around cracked, pursed lips, and the rheumy eyes flickered.

A feeling of revulsion, of distress, of pity at the sight of doting decay, of disgust at such senile prurience overcame her, combined with amazement at the mention of Euphemia Lavender; a feeling also of bitter self-recrimination that she had not thought of Euphemia since hearing of her death.

Had this withered hawking husk once embraced the young girl whom she had met as an elderly spinster with faded blue eyes, who had taken her into her cottage and dozed before a fire, who now lay buried in a lonely churchyard? And she, fool that she was, dreams of Venus and voluptuousness whilst a lascivious old man grips her arm, gazes at her body and takes her for his wife.

She sought to extricate her arm; Dympna, acutely embarrassed, prised it from her grandfather's grasp.

'No, grandpa, it's Miss Prince. She must be going now.'

Frances wished the old man goodbye and followed Dympna from the room, from the smell of incontinence, from irremediable confusion and mumbling inanity; now she felt disgust above all, disgust which she sought to conceal, seeing Dympna's discomposure. Mrs Vernon was also apologetic when Dympna told her what had happened.

'He's very old, over ninety,' she sighed, 'and gets confused. I've noticed that with the very old, time telescopes, as it were, and they think their grandchildren are their daughters, or wives, or even mothers. You'd better be going, Dympna, it'll soon be dark.'

Dympna hobbled round to the farm to collect Cassie and the dogcart; Mops was encouraged to leave his desiccated bone and Frances took her leave of Mrs Vernon, thanking her profusely.

The dogcart trotted through the dark wood until reaching the point in the road where Dympna had stopped that morning, and Frances insisted that she walk the remaining three miles on foot. Dympna had held her tightly and, Frances noticed, wept.

'Dear, dear Frances, we must meet again soon, before Christmas.'

Frances stroked Dympna's hair and kissed her lightly on the cheek.

'Thank you, Dympna. God bless you.'

She jumped from the dogcart with Mops and stood waving as, with a crack of the whip, Dympna drove away. The memory of the strange, crippled girl remained long with Frances as she walked towards the lights of Capewell House in the distance, but so, intrusively, did the memory of the residual lechery in the rheum-caked eyes of her grandfather, Midshipman Fallows.

* * *

At dinner (George was absent, dining with friends in Codbury) she told Mrs Lovell what had happened, and the latter chided herself for not having alerted Frances to the fact that Mrs Vernon had moved back to the neighbourhood after the death of her husband, bringing her old father to live with them.

The family had lived for years in Portsmouth where Mr Vernon managed a small tobacconist shop; Dympna, poor child, had never married, her deformity probably being the reason. She used to walk with her leg in irons but now wore a special boot. The family lived very modestly on Mrs Vernon's small pension and the money Dympna earned from embroidery.

Did Frances not remember her from school? Oh yes, said Frances, I do. But Sophie became my best friend, Sophie Langton-Durham, who became Lady Berners.

She sat by the fire after the meal and drank a glass of brandy. The night was dark and still, and she put her feet on the footstool and gazed at Mops who was sleeping with his head between his paws.

When you were young Midshipman Fallows with Captain Lavender? And you fell in love with his daughter? When you were dashing and handsome? And she turned you down.

Now she lies buried on the Rock. She imagined the scene: a small knot of people around a lonely grave, Timothy Heywood's collapse and the service taken by Pastor Niep. You lie buried in British soil, Euphemia, but a Lutheran pastor conducts your obsequies. I should have been there, fool that I was to leave. I should have been at Millicent's grave, in hallowed ground which you, Timothy Heywood, would have denied her. But Edward stood firm. Two bodies lying there now.

She heard Mrs Lovell call goodnight and go up the creaking stairs. Two bodies lying in darkness, in wind and rain. Would the lighthouse illuminate them? Lay a silver finger across them? She stood up and went across to the bureau to find Beatrice's letter and then heard voices and the sounds of wheels outside, laughter, and exuberant male voices. She heard a whip crack, a horse neigh, and then George entered, flushed and vinous.

'Glad you waited up, Fan, I told Mrs Lovell I'd be out for the meal.'

He moved heavily to the fire and sat opposite her, taking out his cigar case.

'Have you a cigarette?' she asked, 'Mrs Lovell doesn't approve so I forwent the pleasure till you'd returned.'

'Sorry, old girl, only big ones. You should have asked me to bring you some.'

He saw her glass of brandy and rose to pour himself one from the decanter.

'How was it today?' he asked.

'Mixed. I met Dympna Vernon and she took me to her home.'

'Dympna, yes. Rum name. Hasn't she got one leg?'

'Not quite, coz, but she is crippled. We used to bully her awfully in school but she has forgiven me. She's a charitable, Christian soul.'

'Ah yes,' he smirked, 'absolution. I expect that clergyman of yours is working hard at it. But you'd better give up the foul weed, my girl, also the demon drink or you'll never become a bishop's wife.'

She kicked him on the ankle and he gave an exaggerated yelp of pain.

'Don't talk such nonsense, George! I met the Reverend Timothy Heywood on Heligoland and he kindly paid me a visit here.'

George groaned and drank more brandy.

'Yes, thank you I'm sure for reminding me of the blasted North Sea. I've got a difficult case to think about over the weekend, a ship called Pocahontas ran into trouble near Dogger Bank. Why are ships always women? It's the endless trouble they cause, I suppose. Enlighten me, Frances.'

She stared into the fire, then spoke:

'…At first indeed
Through many a fair sea-circle, day by day,
Scarce rocking, her full-busted figurehead
Stared o'er the ripples feathering from her bows.
Then followed calms, and then winds variable…
Storms, such as drove her under moonless heavens,
The crash of ruin, and the loss of all…'

He stared at her.

'Good Lord, Fan, I must remember that. Anyway, I'm off to bed now, and perhaps I'll dream of a full-busted figurehead keeping me afloat. Don't tell the Reverend Hayseed about this, he'll think we're beyond hope.'

He rose unsteadily.

'Dearest coz, I meant it when I said I'd take you to this German thing. Think about it. You could stay in the London house and we'll indulge in something cultured for a change. Or, rather, you can wallow in the howling and bellowing while I slip discreetly into the arms of Morpheus. Though whether I'd be able to sleep through all that din I'm not sure.' He yawned hugely, and a blast of stale brandy hit her.

* * *

She tossed and turned, unable to find sleep; she heard George snoring along the corridor and Mrs Lovell get up in the night and return to bed.

Why was it that Heligoland haunted her? She had been unable to forget the Rock ever since Beatrice's letter, bringing with it painful memories of the horror of October; then there had been the surprise visit of Timothy Heywood and the remarkable meeting with Dympna and the fortuitous, sudden recollection of Euphemia Lavender. And now George, insouciantly, innocently, had spoken of Timothy and figureheads: Russalka flashed through her mind, emerging into shrill light, then jumping back into darkness.

And *Tannhäuser*! A tangle of associations twisted through her mind – the grotto of love, the mons veneris, and she, she as the Master's future Venus. Yet what right have I to arrogate to myself such a role? I, whose voice is now a sad wraith. Yet I sang, did I not, on the road, and there was a creamy loveliness about it…

Edward, why have you not written? But why should he? He suffered much, and must now devote himself to official business, good works.

She saw herself walk up the steps, move on and pass beneath the ornate oil lamps hanging at the top. I shall count the steps…

A shallow sleep took her, but her nocturnal journey was confused and disagreeable. She was standing on the Düne, but Russalka had been replaced by a water-sprite, 'Lutine', and her cousin, in flowing robes, was seeking to dig in the sand for bullion lost in the North Sea.

'The bell!' he kept crying, 'ring the bell!'

She had then been in Dympna's house, terrified lest a toothless mumbling mouth, caked in filth, were to suck at her face; she had sought to find Sophie, now Lady Berners, in a cupboard, but William Hennicker-Heaton was hanging and twisting there. A hard-faced woman (the Priestess? Lady Augusta?) had flayed her face with nails that were crimson and serrated.

'You will never, never sing again,' was the insistent, throbbing message that had filled her head with a luminous intensity. Yet she knew she had to appear that minute in a public performance, she was naked, a cripple, bald…

At eight o' clock Mrs Lovell knocked and brought her tea, which she accepted gratefully; dishevelled, exhausted and pale she gazed from her bed at her reflection in the triptych mirror; a squall of rain beat against the windows.

George was devouring his breakfast with relish, swallowing eggs and bacon.

'You look a bit rough, Fan,' he chortled, 'any nightmares about the Reverend?'

She ignored his frivolity and asked him about 'Lutine', half-remembering that he had once told her about it.

'I'm glad you heed my words of wisdom, coz, but you should pay closer attention. The Lutine was a captured French warship which we recommissioned, and it left Yarmouth for Holland, about a hundred years ago it was now. Filled with bullion and specie, about half a million pounds.

'Well, she was wrecked on a sandbank that same night and sank off the Zuyder Zee with the loss of every soul on board except one, and he died as soon as he was rescued.

'It was a black day for Lloyds underwriters, as you can imagine. Some of the money was salvaged in the eighteen fifties as well as the bell and rudder. They made the rudder into a chair for the Lloyds chairman and a desk for his secretary. The bell still hangs in Lloyds and is rung once if a total wreck is reported and twice if a ship is overdue.'

'"Lutine" is a water-sprite in French,' said Frances, 'like Russalka and Undine. Melusine was a serpent from the waist down, and she screamed when her husband discovered her affliction. They call it "un cri de Melusine"'.

'I wonder he didn't scream,' laughed George, 'what was his name?'

'Raymond.'

'Not Timothy?'

She flung a bread roll at him, which he deftly caught.

'Now,' he continued, 'I'm taking Mrs L. to church this morning. You look as though you need some spiritual uplift, but I won't say by whom. Would you like to come?'

'No,' she said, 'I want to write letters.'

'Seriously, Fan,' he said, getting up from the table, 'have a think about Christmas. Mrs L. wants to know what our plans are. It's another two weeks, but tempus fugit as we know. And let me know about the opera – I'll get tickets in town tomorrow. Next Saturday would suit best. Let me know soon.'

He left the room in good spirits; Frances went up to her room to sort through her clothes for any sewing, darning or mending for Mrs Lovell to do. She sat by the window and watched the rain falling, seeing her cousin and the housekeeper walk away quickly beneath a large umbrella.

Why had she not gone with them? The reason was simple: to avoid a possible encounter with Dympna and Mrs Vernon, for the church lay half way between Capewell House and Codbury St Mary, and she dared not risk seeing the cripple again, being reminded of her earlier vindictiveness, of Dympna's Christian charity.

But she feared above all another invitation to Mrs Vernon's house, feared the revulsion she would feel at the proximity of the one who had embraced Miss Lavender and who now turned a milky, seeping eye in lust upon her.

But had she not overreacted? She shuddered at the memory of that knotted, gnarled hand upon her arm and began to brush her hair furiously before the mirror.

And *Tannhäuser*? George was solicitous and kind in his offer but, again, she feared that the work would be badly performed, never coming up to the impossibly high standards of its creator. And again, she feared meeting Timothy Heywood who would be cruelly disappointed if George took her. Dare she risk not telling him that she was going? Surely Her Majesty's was big enough to accommodate them both separately? She did not wish George to meet him lest the badinage become too irksome. It would be best to turn down George's offer.

And yet, and yet…To see the singer of Venus and to see how I would have sung it! Or would I not see, finally, that I am still good and can, one day, sing the role? She wandered around the empty house, ignoring the whining dog who looked at her from his basket in the kitchen. She went into the small study and fetched her writing case, but no thoughts came as she sat to write to her father, also to Beatrice, and her expressions, trite and fatuous, irritated her: she tore the sheets in half. She stood at the window, placed her hands on her hips, thumbs forward and thrust out her breasts; her head she tilted back and looked to the left. I should be wearing blue velvet, she thought, gazing through a medieval stained-glass window, then I would be Mariana indeed. But I am glad there is no mouse on the floor, nor dead leaves. She tried to find a volume of Tennyson but was unsuccessful, and thought long of the library in the Conversationshaus and her sitting there.

After returning from church Mrs Lovell busied herself in the kitchen and George lit a cigar, suggesting a game of Halma, the latest craze; they drank sherry and he won easily, getting her nineteen men into his yard without difficulty.

'Come on, Fan, you're miles away.'

Luncheon was a heavy meal of roast pork; George dozed afterwards on the sofa, a bleb of mucous glistening on the corner of his gaping mouth. The rain had stopped and she walked with Mops through squelching leaves down to the stream, now in spate.

This can't go on, she thought, I shall go mad here. A mad woman singing, floating down the river. She shuddered as she thought of Millicent, their first meeting in the hotel, the brown, billowing dress, the pale, sensuous mouth.

A singing head, severed, floating among the reeds, the head of Orpheus…

Mops barked and she froze, thinking of Dympna, but no wheels whirred through the damp afternoon, it was the crows that the dog was chasing, crows that flapped lazily in the bare trees.

On Sundays tea was substantial, taking the place of dinner, and Frances ate sandwiches and Battenburg cake decorated with glacé cherries and angelica. George sat in the study and considered the insurance implications of the sinking of the Pocahontas; she went upstairs and luxuriated in a hot bath full of aromatic essences and smiled when she remembered "Wellgunde". That was the night before the formal dinner when Dr Saphir gazed at me with lubricious eyes and Timothy bashfully complimented me on my looks. And Teddy....

She stepped from the bath, dried herself, putting on an old dressing gown of her father's and a pair of ancient slippers. She went down and knocked on the door of the study; a fug of tobacco smoke greeted her.

'Long live Virginia, long live Pocahontas!' cried George, in excellent spirits, having calculated the necessary amount of compensation.

'George, I'd love to see *Tannhäuser* with you, but - '

'No buts!' he chortled, 'I'll sort it all out tomorrow. I'll get a box for Saturday evening, so you can invite whomever you wish, Dympna, the Reverend Boxwood or the man in the moon if you like. It will be an honour for me to have you by my side, especially in that elegant outfit you have now.'

'Don't talk guano, George!' And she stepped forward and kissed him.

* * *

Next morning, after George had left for London, the postman brought a letter for Frances; it was from Timothy.

The letter, halting and hesitant, assured her that he had greatly enjoyed their afternoon in Salisbury and reaffirmed his desire to see more of her. He had tried to buy tickets for *Tannhäuser* (did she know that this opera was to be performed?) but without success: only boxes were left and these were unfortunately beyond his modest clergyman's stipend. He had had good reports, however, of Arthur Wing Pinero's play *The Schoolmistress* and repeated that it would be a great pleasure for him to take her. His mother had seen the latter's *Two Hundred a Year* and had spoken highly of it. It would bring him such happiness if she accepted his invitation to Pinero's play. He wished her well and finished the letter, uncharacteristically she thought, with a clumsy joke.

'If I were back on Heligoland I would say to one of the lads "Jacob, loop al wat dü kanst er bring de djààr Briààf na de Pöst"; here however, in Finsbury Park, I shall walk to the waiting letterbox and drop my missive into its red maw in the certain knowledge that, unlike Jonah, it will not reside in the belly for three days but be conveyed to you tomorrow.' He signed himself 'Your affectionate friend'.

She replied immediately, expressing her pleasure at receiving his letter and his kind attempts to buy tickets for *Tannhäuser*. Her cousin, she explained, had already noticed that *Tannhäuser* was to be performed and had hit upon the idea of a box. There would be ample room for the three of them, even four if he wanted to bring his mother with him.

She suggested the following: that he meet them at Her Majesty's at six o' clock. If he did not hear from her again he should assume that all was well; only if George were unable to get a box (but he was very persuasive, she added and, mischievously, very well off!) would she write again. She wished him well and looked forward to seeing him again and introducing him to George. She signed herself 'Your good friend Frances'.

She walked with Mops to the letterbox by the bridge and did not reprimand the dog when he jumped up at her with his muddy paws. When they got back, however, she became agitated about what she would wear for the opera. And for this opera! She spent many hours scrutinising her wardrobe, laying out dresses, rejecting, trying on, holding against her before mirrors. She had a small Gladstone bag for the toiletries necessary for two nights in George's London house in Eaton Square: she would also need to take a dress to change into for Sunday and the return on Monday. Should she wear her favourite cream silk gown, the one that had ravished the men in Government House? Would Timothy think that she was wearing it for him?

She saw herself sitting in the box, with many eyes and opera glasses trained upon her as she sat proudly, her hair beautifully coiffed, her long white gloves upon her arms, her throat and shoulders bare, her figure, her bust sculpted, moulded against the dark crimson of the tapestry. And the Venusberg, her Venusberg… The rosy light, the green of the waters, the silver clouds across an azure sky, Leda and the swan…

Mrs Lovell interrupted her by indicating that the cream gown had spots of wine upon the bodice. The tweeny from the village whom they had temporarily employed to help when Frances's trunks had arrived from Heligoland had said nothing, had probably not even noticed the stains when she hung the dresses in the wardrobe. But the spots were small, the housekeeper continued, were dots of faintest red that could easily be removed by salt and boiling water. A gentle application of bleach might also be necessary but she did not wish to discolour the silk. There was also a faint grubby mark on the left side of the bodice but this could easily be sponged out.

Frances, horrified, saw her dreams dashed but Mrs Lovell pacified her: she had removed worse stains than these. If they proved too obstinate then Frances should think about a second choice of gown.

Mrs Lovell had heard the 'Pilgrims' Chorus' from the opera and felt that it was in some way a religious work; she joked that Frances should go as a nun. Frances was not amused and scolded herself for not having taken better care of the dress. But her departure had been so precipitous, and they had both been glad of the tweeny's help.

On Wednesday morning a brief message came from George.

'Got the box, four seats. I invited Queen Victoria but she's off to *The Mikado* that night. So two seats are for us and two for whomever you like. Please go straight to the theatre on Saturday and leave your bag in the cloakroom (there's no time to come here first if I remember the trains). I'm assuming you'll stay for two nights? Your room's ready, and Mrs Dunn who "does" for me thinks you're my paramour so don't leave French lingerie scattered all over the room.

Seriously, I'm really looking forward to it, although I can't say why. I might slip out for a glass of two of Regent's Punch if it gets too awful and meet you when it's finished. Six o' clock then, on Saturday. Wear a sensible coat over your finery or the peasants will get excited. Love, George.'

Mrs Lovell, smiling with pride, showed her the dress: the stains were scarcely detectable.

'I should wear your stole across your front, then nobody can possibly see them. It might also be best, for modesty's sake, to cover your bust a little as that dress is rather revealing. But I suppose London society is full of mashers who are used to that kind of thing.'

Mrs Lovell had sponged the dress down very carefully, and the silk glowed and shimmered. Frances hugged her and checked shoes, gloves, reticule, jewellery. She would wear sensible shoes on the train and change at the theatre. She wondered what Timothy would say when he saw her and knew that George, beneath his flippant exterior, would be very proud. I shall dress, she thought, in his honour too, the genius who wrote this work and longed for me to sing in it. And Edward, Edward, you have held me, embraced me. All shall be honoured by my beauty.

On Friday a letter came, surprisingly, from Timothy.

'My dear Frances, how glad I am that I shall be able to see you tomorrow evening! It was kind of your cousin to invite me, and it was kind of you, for I know you were my champion. You know that I have difficulty with Wagner, but here a soul is redeemed by a woman's love. She is an intermediary and God, in his infinite goodness, causes the staff to blossom. I shall come alone; my mother, alas, is unwell but thanks you for thinking of her. I cannot wait till then! Your dear friend, Timothy.'

Frances breathed a sigh of relief at the news of Mrs Heywood's indisposition: nobody must be there but the two men. In absentia the third, the Governor. And, in spirit, the one who created the incomparable works, the one who enveloped her, adored her, transfigured her.

The Gladstone bag was packed, the jewellery chosen, night attire and toiletries selected. The hours passed like pallid sisters; she longed for dusk. She lay in the bath and, dreamily, caressed her breasts, her thighs, her damp, enfolded vagina. He knew of attar of roses, of silks, of perfumes and unguents, he saw the swan laying its head fawningly on Leda's bosom.

She rose, wiped the steam from the mirror and adored her pale pink loveliness, the rosebud nipples, the dark, moist tangle of hair on the pudenda. Venus!

She smiled and blushed at his comment on Kundry – that she should lie as naked as a Titian Venus. And she, Frances Prince, no longer a lowly flower-maiden but Venus herself…No Elizabeth can defeat me. I have no rival.

She lifted her arms and ran her hands through her hair, drawing the dark tresses down across her breasts. And she suddenly thought of Ingeborg Frostrup.

Silver-gold cannot compare with my rich colour. There is frigidity in her, coldness. To sleep now, and gather strength. She sought her nightgown and said goodnight to Mrs Lovell who was sewing a small satin button that had come loose on one of her long gloves.

* * *

A week later, sitting alone in her bedroom in the Conversationshaus, her back against the warm tiled stove, gazing at the sleet flying in the shrieking wind, silver, black, silver, she tried to make sense of what had happened, to bring order into the jostling turmoil of memories, sense into senselessness.

Or was it senselessness? There had been a crisis of some kind, a mass of confusion, yet a wedge of steely clarity had been driven into her mind, forcing a decision that she knew was right. A violent acceleration had occurred, propelling her forward; there had been no collapse, no disturbance, surely not; there had been no perversion of any moral or intellectual faculties, no hysteria.

Sophie had insisted that a doctor be called, but she knew that what had happened was necessary and not brought about by delusion.

She lit a Neptun cigarette from the candle and watched the smoke coil like ectoplasm around the flame. Remember, then, remember and trace the strand of inevitability which made this journey necessary.

She recalled how Mrs Lovell had dressed her that Saturday lunchtime, how incongruous the stout shoes had been, also the sensible coat and scarf that she had worn to conceal her evening gown, but Mops had known and seemed dazzled by her radiance.

A carriage had been hired to take them to Codbury, and thence the train had taken them to Salisbury. It had been early afternoon and it had been getting colder; she was glad of the winter coat and hat.

Then she had been stowed aboard the London train with her Gladstone bag, sharing a compartment with an elderly lady who had chattered and spoke of the days when skirts and petticoats had been so voluminous that it was difficult to enter such a compartment if two ladies were sitting there: Augustus Egg had portrayed it well.

The journey was dream-like, the metropolis approached, they had alighted at Waterloo; there had been teeming crowds, but she had caught the omnibus which dropped her close to Her Majesty's.

She recalled the flaring lights, the people milling outside the theatre, the crossing-keeper sweeping the ordure from the street so that she might pass across without soiling her skirts. Faces were illuminated by the glare; there were gentlemen in top hats, some smoking cigars, waiting. There were ladies alighting from carriages, dressed in furs. Was George here, florid and ebullient? Would Timothy appear, awkward and stiffly formal in his clerical garb?

Tannhäuser, or, The Minstrels' Contest on the Wartburg, there it stood for all to see, with Mme Valleria as Venus. There was a garish poster showing a voluptuous and vulgar Mme Valleria, empty of expression and swathed in scarlet draperies, staring at a bloated Tannhäuser, her hand upon his brow. Frances stood in the foyer, was jostled: 'Excuse me, excuse me…' Faces, flushed, impatient and disdainful swam around her, there was a smell of perfume, cigars, perspiration, moth-balls, a blur of animated voices, shrieks of delighted recognition.

She suddenly felt an utter aversion to this place, to the grotesque travesty of it all: this should have been my role. How could she tolerate the utter vulgarity of this theatre, the prostitution of his vision, a vision which I was to incorporate. He told me that it was for me, in my lap my lover's head would rest, his harp discarded at his side. Panic seized her, an inexplicable repugnance touched with terror.

She knew that she had run sobbing into the street, colliding with men in opera cloaks and crush hats who stared at her in consternation; an elegant dowager had scrutinised her through her lorgnette: a flower-girl shouted something; some ruffians guffawed.

How Sophie's name had occurred to her she did not know, also the address, the address of Lord Berners, his London house just off Mayfair.

She had run into the street, narrowly avoiding being run over; she hailed a conveyance, thrust money from her reticule into the jarvey's hand and momentarily fainted on the leather seats.

She recalled arriving, running up the steps with her bag, ringing the bell and collapsing into the arms of her friend who, amazed, brusquely dismissed the maid and accompanied the weeping intruder upstairs.

Had she made any sense at all? The following day, Sunday, was spent in perturbed oscillations of mood, attempts to explain to Sophie what had happened and what she must do. Sophie insisted on taking medical advice, but Frances had adamantly refused; she did, however, take a febrifuge which Sophie had prepared for her.

Throughout the afternoon she had lain in a semi-comatose state; the evening was quiet. Lord Berners had been informed of what had happened and knocked at her door. He was calm and sympathetic, and Frances had confided in him that she could not return to Wiltshire, that she must go to Heligoland and wait for her father there.

He assured her that she could spend Christmas with them, but she refused, thanking him. She explained that her father was on a delicate mission in Berlin and had suggested that he and Frances would travel after his return.

Why Heligoland? Because she had good friends there and had been invited to a birthday celebration on Christmas Day. She had contacts in Hamburg and the consul there, Sir Charles Dundas, would assist her. Lord Berners explained that he had friends in the Foreign Office and would see to it that a telegram be sent to Sir Charles tomorrow.

Sophie had a meal brought up to Frances and repeated that they would love her to stay, but Frances knew that she must leave as soon as possible. On the following day Lord Berners sent the telegram and Frances, much relieved, rose and put on the travelling dress that she had in her bag; she begged Sophie to help her shop for suitable dresses. Sophie relished the part of conspirator and eagerly accompanied Frances to the London shops; she lent her friend a generous sum of money and swore that she would say nothing about this escapade. Frances also bought gifts for Teddy and the other members of the family; Sophie encouraged her not to be parsimonious.

That evening Lord Berners told them that Sir Charles Dundas had been informed; it had been agreed that Frances should leave for Hamburg on the following day, that she should stay in the Hamburger Hof where a message from Sir Edward Hennicker-Heaton would be waiting for her. Sir Charles would see to it that she be met on the docks at Hamburg and any necessary papers provided.

Sophie entered the spirit of adventure with girlish excitement, yet Frances appeared composed and still. She scarcely thought of George, never of Timothy. Her belongings were packed and taken to Tilbury and, on the following day, a tearful Sophie bade her farewell and swore, again, to say nothing.

The sea was choppy but the crossing to Hamburg was

uneventful. At the docks a young man, Percy Tyrwhitt-Jones, met her and took her to the hotel. He explained that passports were sometimes demanded in Germany in towns and districts where the 'minor state of siege' existed, but that she would not need one here; had she been entering Germany from France she would have had to obtain a German visa in London.

Sir Charles, who regretted being unable to be present himself, suggested that the following document, bearing her name and nationality, would suffice. Heligoland was British anyway, and so she should have no difficulties about travel. He had, he confided in her, heard rumours, however, about the island's future status. She listened to him impatiently and hastened to her room after he had left: there stood the letter, written in familiar purple ink, propped against the heavy silver inkstand on the writing desk. She did not use the paperknife which lay next to it, but tore it open:

' Come in the evening, come in the morning,
Come when you're looked for and come without warning!'

Dearest girl, how lovely! We shall rantipole the year out! I've booked you into the Conversationshaus as G.H. will be swarming with relations celebrating Christmas and the birthday. But when the birds have flown you must come back to your old room here. It goes without saying that you'll dine with us whenever you wish. And on the Big Day, December the twenty-fifth, I shall personally come down the steps to escort you upwards, at midday sharp.

Dearest Fan, I have missed you. With fondest love, Teddy.'

A ticket had also been enclosed for the Kurland, sailing from Hamburg to Heligoland on December the twenty-third.

She remembered her distracted impatience, the desultory, last pieces of shopping in Hamburg as the wind rose and rain fell over the city; the barometer sank.

On the morning of the twenty-third she had her luggage sent to the ship and was driven to the docks. Her private cabin was comfortable and larger than the cabin on the Eitel-Friedrich; there were very few passengers. The crossing had been very rough;

the ship pitched and rolled and she lay with eyes closed, fighting against the feeling of sickness; her stomach churned, the cabin creaked and moved up and down, side to side. The porthole dipped and rose, a furious sea alternating with cloud-wrack and driving rain. They touched at Cuxhaven and Geestemünde where most of the passengers disembarked.

The waves grew mountainous; she retched frequently into the enamel basin, wiping the bitter puke from her lips. It was very dark when they arrived; she walked unsteadily onto the deck, holding the brass railing and avoiding the vomit that glistened in the fitful gleam of the ship's lantern. Few lights glimmered on the Rock: she made out the landing stage and the duckboards. She was guided down the steel steps into a bobbing boat; one man grabbed her round the knees to prevent her skirts blowing wildly in the wind, a second took her arms, and they settled her on a damp seat under a tarpaulin. She was helped onto the duckboards and saw her luggage being unloaded.

A young lad in oilskins, holding a lantern, had been sent by the hotel and would guide her there, collecting the luggage later. They hurried through the streaming rain and ran up the steps of the Conversationshaus; Herr Jensen was waiting to greet her. He had been deeply touched that she should wish to board with him again; her old room was waiting for her. And she had wept tears of joy when she saw it.

And now she was sitting there, quietly waiting, on Christmas Eve, on 'Greeter In' as Herr Jensen had called it, for the following day to dawn. The proprietor had invited her to join the small family gathering below; she had thanked him but declined. She heard the sound of singing from downstairs and saw that the sleet had given way to snow flurries.

I am here, she thought, I have arrived. And all will be well.

* * *

CHAPTER FIVE

She woke on Christmas morning; the wind, now from the north, had eased and she pulled back the heavy curtains to reveal a dead white world of softly spiralling snow, snow falling thickly over the sea and the Düne. The landing stage and the esplanade were blanketed in a white, soft integument.

A childish delight filled her, a delight in seeing snow, and snow on this day of all days. She put on the thick housecoat; the stove was tepid. A dark, plump young woman with jugs of hot water and a tray of breakfast knocked and entered; she was, she explained, Herr Jensen's daughter who was helping her father over the holiday period and would willingly be of any assistance to their English guest that she could.

She handed Frances a small box – a gift from her father. It was a bottle of Danziger Goldwasser, and Frances was delighted at the minute slivers of gold leaf which glinted in the colourless liqueur. Fräulein Jensen explained that the bedroom would be heated but the rest of the hotel would not, there being no other guests. Any meals that Miss Prince required would be brought up to her.

Frances thanked Fräulein Jensen who explained that the key to the hotel would be lying on a desk in the foyer downstairs: Miss Prince could come and go as she pleased. There were also capes, hats and galoshes at her disposal. She also reminded Miss Prince that Sir Edward would call at midday. She wished Frances a happy Christmas, and left.

As though she could forget! Yet she never gave a thought to her cousin's most certain alarm at her disappearance, neither did she attempt to imagine the equally certain bewilderment and concern that Timothy Heywood must have experienced: she was on the Rock, and preparing to meet Teddy, Major Sir Edward Hennicker-Heaton.

She took down a small valise and extracted the gifts she had bought for the family: for Lady Augusta she had chosen a small sardonyx cameo brooch, for Charlotte and Beatrice gold bracelets (their wrists were the size of hers, she had remembered), for William an elegant amethyst tie-pin, and for Teddy a heavy gold Albert-chain. These purchases had been made at Feinstein's of Bond Street, and Sophie had had them placed on her account.

'I give you a year to repay your debts, Fanny!' she had laughed, showing her beautiful teeth, 'so hurry up and find your German prince! Or Russian would be better. Then we could dress in furs and ride a troika with tinkling bells over crisp white snow beneath the Northern Lights. Feinstein's are discreet so Claud will never know what we've spent. Having a title does have its advantages, although I've never liked the name "Berners", it reminds me of manufactories and things like that. I'm sure you'll be something much grander. You're a "Prince" already, so why not Queen? Queen of Galizia and Lodomiria!'

They had laughed at such flights of fancy. Yet once, she thought, arranging the gifts carefully in her reticule, I did wear the star of the Bey of Tunis. Then suddenly a dark thought crossed her mind. Was there not another birthday on this day, commemorated outside a bedroom door at Tribschen? Forget it, forget it.

She took down a new blue velvet gown from the wardrobe and laid it out on the bed; she took an hour to wash herself, comb her hair, arrange it in a pleat, fastened by a silver comb, to dab perfume, and then to dress. She stood in front of the cheval glass and admired, adored herself. It was eleven o' clock.

One hour! One hour! She walked through the cold and deserted hotel to the library, pushing open the door and inhaling the smell of old leather books and tobacco smoke. She browsed without interest, wishing the time to pass. She suddenly thought of Herbert von Kroseck. They had dined here alone among the old maps of Heligoland. He had spoken of his sister Franziska, his love of the sea. He had been charming and had kissed her hand. She had been intrigued by him, she admitted this. Yet what had Ingeborg Frostrup called him? The word eluded her, and she frowned at Ingeborg's dubious aspersions. It was inconceivable to her that a man like Herbert should not love a woman.

There were, of course, Platonic friendships between men: of this there could be no doubt. But to imply – she stopped. Dympna, she felt, could love another woman deeply. But it was because no man wished to gaze upon her crippled body. She turned to the window; snow was blowing hither and thither. It is Christmas Day, she thought, and I must only think of him, now leaving Government House, soon approaching the steps. She left the library, returned to her room and completed her toilet, gathering up coat, hat and gloves, and descending the stairs. Should she wear galoshes? Vanity deterred her.

A clock chimed twelve. A figure of a man appeared outside the glass door of the Conversationshaus; Frances ran to open it. The figure quickly entered, stamping the snow from his shoes and beating it from a heavy overcoat. He removed a naval cap from his head and bowed. It was Herbert von Kroseck.

* * *

He kissed her hand.

'Well, Miss Prince, how delightful it is to see you! I wish you a very Merry Christmas! Today is the important feast-day for you, is it not? And it is a big day, too, for our young ladies.'

Frances felt her heart pounding; she felt shock at the appearance of one whose alien, putative inclinations had, a few seconds earlier, preoccupied her. She felt pleasure, also, at seeing him again, but acute disappointment, even annoyance that Teddy had not come. Herbert saw chagrin and bewilderment in her eyes.

'Yes, I am not, alas, Sir Edward! He is hopelessly entangled with guests and family and asked me to come in his stead. A poor substitute, I know, but a devoted and humble servant!'

'Herbert,' she stammered, 'I was just thinking of you! It's very remarkable!'

'Really? I am honoured, flattered.'

She had her coat over her arm and he helped her into it; she felt strong hands upon her shoulders.

'Will you need a pair of galoshes? It is very cold outside, also snowy. But I know that the daughters of Albion are of hardy stock.'

She laughed.

'I am not clumping up to Government House in things like that. I am not yet fat and forty and have no intention of looking like a frumpish Frau.'

Herbert wagged his finger in mock chastisement.

'Now, my lady, do not condemn German womanhood so dismissively! My sister Franziska is up at the House and she is slim and elegant.'

She blushed deeply.

'Forgive me, Herbert. How delightful to be able to see your sister! Where are you staying?'

'At Ingeborg Frostrup's. It is all very respectable. Franziska and Inge share a bedroom and I have a sort of hammock in the studio. I doze and swing surrounded by Ingeborg's visions.'

Suddenly Frances remembered the book that Ingeborg had shown her. Did Sicilian ephebes haunt his dreams? she wondered.

'Good,' she said, 'I am ready. Let us face the elements!'

He quickly opened the door and they stepped outside; she locked it and they walked into a whirling whiteness.

She took his arm and pressed close to his warmth; he held a large umbrella over them. The wind dropped and the snow now fell silently upon them, spiralling gently. The houses on the Unterland stood hunched, muffled in white siftings; to their right the cliffs rose, strangely alien, now, in pale draperies, their fissures like cracks through blinded glass. Their feet crunched through the white crisp dustings which grew thicker as they approached the steps.

'I am sorry, Herbert, about my stupid comment on frumpish Fraus. When I think of the dowdy, shapeless English women I've met, brrr…'

He laughed.

'It's Christmas Day and I shall forgive you everything. I'm sure your mother was the acme of beauty and good breeding. But where is your father? Are you not seeing him this Christmas?'

'I'm afraid he's in Berlin on some Foreign Office business. The ambassador needed him there.'

'Really? The Right Honourable Sir Edward Malet, Baronet? Yes, I have heard of him. But I move in illustrious circles too. I have on my arm the beautiful daughter of an important man who is indispensable in Berlin.'

She smiled at him and they stopped and looked down at the sea, scarcely visible behind the curtain of snow.

'I sometimes used to count these steps before going off to sleep,' she said, 'I never could remember exactly how many there were. Are there one hundred and eighty-four?'

'Sir Edward is thinking of building a lift,' said Herbert, 'I believe that Lindner and Treitel, Berlin engineers, are keen to build it. It would take ten passengers and one ton of goods. Sir Edward is a romantic and likes the old ways. But the times are changing.'

'Let them,' she said, keen to move on, 'I can't wait to see him.'

They climbed upwards, huddled beneath the umbrella.

'By the way,' said Herbert, 'I must tell you that Sir Edward and Lady Augusta have kept your arrival a secret from the girls, also from William. It will be a big surprise for them when you enter the room!'

They had reached midway and stood at the small vantage point. 'Would you like to rest here?'

'No,' she said.

The steps turned sharply to the right and they climbed up towards the ornamental arch with the lamp hanging beneath it.

'Why did he not come?' she mused, 'why did he not absent himself from his guests and come as he promised?'

They reached the top and caught the wind from the sea which blew the snow in wild gyrations; Herbert's umbrella flapped and tossed, and he freed his arm from hers to hold it.

'Time we were indoors!' he cried, 'I shall be delivering a Snow Queen to our Governor!'

She laughed and, holding her hat with one hand and her skirts and reticule with the other she ran over crunching snow towards the familiar garden wall, the cannon, the flagpole, all now capped and muffled in snow; she reached the solid front door, now decorated with an Advent wreath, and reached for the bell. But before she rang it the door opened: Teddy stood smiling before her and embraced her.

* * *

She was aware, as in a dream, of an impassive Frau Stoeven removing her coat and hat and laying her reticule on the sideboard, that a maid was bringing a warm towel for her to wipe the snow that sparkled in loose strands of hair, that a hand-mirror was provided for her to arrange the peccant wisps, that Teddy was smiling lovingly at her and, laying a finger on his lips, led her by the hand along the hall, past the dashing Hussar and the young Victoria to the drawing room. He drew open the door and ushered her in to the room.

It seemed as though she were entering a halo of soft luminescence, guided by the one who moved with effortless grace into the heart of light. A great fire burned in the hearth; Christmas candles shone on the massive tree; lights glittered and danced in the crystal ornaments. She saw faces turned towards her, expressions of interest, surprise, astonishment, delight. Beatrice had been conversing with a young man whom Frances did not know, then suddenly saw her and rushed towards her, her arms outstretched.

'Miss Prince! I cannot believe this! Is it you? Is it possible?'

Charlotte joined them, her eyes shining.

'How lovely to see you! What a marvellous present!'

'How could I miss such a special day?' smiled Frances.

She then saw William, dressed elegantly in pale grey, and wearing a monocle in his right eye.

'Well, Miss Prince,' he drawled, 'what a surprise!' And he gallantly kissed her hand.

His mother came across to Frances and kissed her on the forehead.

'It was a well-kept secret, was it not? Welcome, Miss Prince. Now, let me introduce you to those you do not know.'

A group of ladies, beautifully groomed, and attended by gentlemen in military uniform, stood by the fire and mustered her: Frances was introduced to Freiherr Detlev von Moltke, Gräfin von Strachwitz, Freifrau von Yorck, Generalmajor von Gneisenau, Oberstleutnant von Hechlingen, Leutnant Hyazinth von Keyserling. The latter was an exquisite young man in the uniform of an Uhlan who wore his dark green jacket, with its elaborate and flamboyant frogging, at a jaunty angle across one shoulder; he blushed as Frances smiled at him.

A slim young woman, wearing pale green silk, was summoned to the group and introduced by Lady Augusta as Franziska von Kroseck. Frances gazed at her.

'I know your brother,' she said, 'he kindly escorted me through the snow.'

Franziska von Kroseck was attractive, with handsome features; there was, however, a hectic, highly-strung nervousness about her.

'Herbert has told me about you,' she said quietly, 'and now I have the honour to meet you too.'

'You speak English well,' said Frances, smiling at the young woman.

'Not as well as Herbert.'

It was then that Frances noticed, to her discomfort, that the young woman's breath was rank: a smell of dead water, stale from a vase of flowers long rotted, struck her. From the corner of her eye she saw Herbert and Ingeborg Frostrup appear. She is beautiful, Frances thought, but I shall vanquish her.

Ingeborg wore a simple white dress and golden stole; her hair was loose and her eyes, eyes of smalt, glittered with delight.

'God Jul, Fröken Prince!'

At this moment Lady Augusta took Frances by the arm and led her to an aged and dignified woman sitting bolt upright by the Erard.

'Miss Prince, please meet my aunt, Fürstin von Hardenberg. Please speak German, she knows no English.'

Frances curtseyed low and stood with bent head before the princess; Fürstin von Hardenberg nodded.

'You are our English guest? It was kind of you to visit us.'

'It is an honour to be here,' Frances replied, 'I am very fond of Beatrice and Charlotte.'

'You came alone?'

'Yes, my father is in Berlin. He has meetings with our ambassador there.'

'Sir Edward Malet? A charming man. Bismarck's time will soon be over, we hear. He was an upstart, impoverished Altmark gentry. But he guided Germany well. The times will become uncertain under the new Hohenzollern.'

Frances nodded sagaciously, longing to move across to the Christmas tree where Teddy held court; Lady Augusta came to her rescue, and the Fürstin graciously dismissed her. She led Frances to a group standing near the buffet; a large man, florid, with a waxed moustache, introduced himself as Doctor Emil Graevenitz.

'I believe you met my locum, when I was on the mainland, a certain Dr Saphir,' he cried, shaking her hand vigorously, 'he was full of your praises, and I now see why!'

'Dr Saphir was too kind,' said Frances, recalling with distaste the lascivious gaze of the young doctor, 'is he no longer here?'

'No, back in harness,' explained Dr Graevenitz. 'He was talented, like his race usually are, but did not fit in here. There were complaints, especially from the female patients. But enough of that. You must love our island – I mean, your island – very much to come through wind, rain and snow all this long way!'

'I love it here,' she explained, 'and I am very fond of Sir Edward and his family.'

'But there is no culture here, no outlet for your gifts, apart from what our Governor arranges for us. Yes, I know, you are a singer, but will you be happy to sing just to the fishes?'

Frances smiled awkwardly and was glad when Lady Augusta took her to a squat, taciturn clergyman, Dr Martin Niep, wearing clerical garb and white bands. He is the one, she thought, who buried Miss Lavender after Timothy's collapse. She was also introduced to Mr Frederick Brass, a cadaverous young man, the new telegraph officer; Mr Brass stammered and was ill at ease; he broke wind. Servants suddenly appeared bearing trays of champagne glasses, and Frances was glad when her desultory attempts at conversation were cut short by Teddy who, tapping his glass with a knife, called for silence. Frances gazed at him, her eyes shining. The room was hushed; the fire crackled; the clatter from the servants' quarters was stilled. And he spoke.

* * *

He explained that he would speak in English, and that his wife would speak in German after him. This preference for English was not out of disrespect for his German friends and family, but for the simple reason that his grasp of the German language was still shaky. As a tribute to Herr Garer, however, who had gallantly attempted to teach him all the Frisian dialects, he would try the following Heligoland joke in the original. It was about a doctor who visited a patient and asked him how he was today. A little better, was the reply. Have you eaten anything for lunch? Yes, I ate a bit of beef. With appetite? No, with gravy.

There were loud guffaws from the back of the room where Frances spotted Herr Garer, who was nodding gleefully, and Dr Graevenitz; polite but restrained laughter was heard elsewhere; William, she noticed, winced in obvious embarrassment. Lady Augusta and her German relatives sat impassive.

It was difficult indeed, he admitted, to do full justice to the humour of Heligoland, Prussia, England and Denmark (here, Frances noticed, he nodded and smiled to Ingeborg, who smiled back) so he had better not try it. We peoples of the North Sea, he continued, of Frisia, Jutland, Schleswig and Holstein, of the German Bight, may appear saturnine and lumpish to those of southern blood, but we know how to drive out winter darkness by jollification: when the snow settles down on our Rock we can drink our grog, eat our Christmas cake, and have as good a time as any of them in the south.

Now, this Christmas Day was a very special one, for twenty-one years ago his dear wife gave him the finest present of all – two daughters. (Frances quickly looked at Beatrice and Charlotte who were standing holding hands and blushing.) It was before they came to the Rock, a very wild day, he remembered, and Augusta had punctually and efficiently given birth to Beatrice when, lo and behold, out popped Charlotte, quite unexpectedly. Any more? he had asked. No, Augusta had declared, two suffice. And then Willy had come in to see what all the fuss was about, and looked rather peeved. Send them back, he had said, he'd had enough. (There was laughter here; William looked out of the window and, Frances noticed, adjusted his monocle.)

But they had held on to the girls, and what a marvellous pair they had been. And now his fair damsels were fair young women, about to take on a stunned world. Beatrice he saw as Euterpe or Erato, Charlotte as Polyhymnia or Urania. They would all, as a family, be bereft when these two daughters chose to fly the nest and, selfishly, he and his wife would love to keep them there. So he had decided to commission portraits of the two of them, pictures that would hang in Government House until, well, Government House had a new tenant. But he and his wife had every intention of staying, so the girls would have to wait until they became their property. They did not know that the portraits were being painted for the artist had worked from photographs. Would Ingeborg mind?

Frances felt her blood run cold as she saw Ingeborg Frostrup leave the room and return with two oval pictures, one in each hand. Both were covered by a dark cloth. She handed them to Edward who bowed before her. Our artist, he explained. Ingeborg, would you please say a few words?

As Teddy placed the portraits on each end of the mantelpiece, leaning them against the wall, Ingeborg turned to the audience.

'When Sir Edward asked me to paint the portraits I was undecided, but he has persuasive ways, as we know. I do not see myself as a portrait painter, but use landscape to express the inner resonances of the soul. However, I agreed. Sir Edward showed me photographs of the twins and I used them to convey characteristic vibrations. They are not conventionally representational, but I hope they will bring joy to two remarkable young women.'

She turned back to the mantelpiece and removed the fabric: the assembled company craned their necks to look. And Frances saw the following: both portraits showed the girls' head and shoulders; both were posed against a viscous, coagulating sunset. That of Beatrice – and how well Ingeborg Frostrup had captured the likeness – showed the young woman gazing in profile, with parted lips, at a silver birch; the features were rapt, conveying a transport of some ill-defined emotion. The matt gold of the hair was expertly done, as were the flesh tints at the throat; a turquoise gown with soft white collar was also indicated.

The portrait of Charlotte was darker, the sun appearing as a damp kidney behind skeins of cloud. The girl gazed directly at the viewer; the mouth was closed, but a ghostly smile seemed to play about the lips. A hand lay along the side of the throat, touching the earlobe. The picture conveyed meditation, also resolve; the gown was blood red.

Frances heard the two girls gasp with delight and a low murmur of indeterminate response amongst the assembled company; a beaming father kissed the artist on the cheek before she stepped away.

'Now,' he said, 'I'll finish as we're all gasping for champagne.'

The servants filled the glasses and carried them around on silver trays.

'A toast, then, to Beatrice and Charlotte Hennicker-Heaton. A happy birthday to you both, and many more of them. Sie leben hoch!'

The glasses were raised in their honour, and the toast was drunk. Lady Augusta stepped forth and, in German, gave a brief résumé of her husband's speech, omitting the joke and the light-hearted reference to the birth of the twins. Again a toast was drunk, and Teddy led the guests into the ballroom where, on tables, the damask, the crystal and the silver were gleaming.

* * *

The family, together with the German relatives, sat at the high table, which stood on the dais; the other tables were arranged in an E shape below.

Frances entered, excited and agitated but displeased at the unexpected praise for Ingeborg, the latter's elevation and success; this displeasure increased when, to her great chagrin, she noticed that Ingeborg was sitting at the high table with the family.

The company stood, waiting for grace to be said; Teddy, in high spirits, leaned on the back of his chair and declaimed:

'God bless the bunch that munch this lunch.'

He then helped his daughters, one on each side of him, to sit. Ingeborg had been placed at one end of the high table, next to the blushing Uhlan; at least, thought Frances grimly as she took her place, she is a long way from the centre. She herself was sitting at the end of the middle bar of the E, close to the high table and almost opposite and below Teddy. He saw her and winked; she smiled weakly.

To her dismay she saw that she was sitting opposite a young man wearing a dog collar who must be Mr Eliot, the curate; she groaned inwardly at having to converse with yet another Anglican clergyman. There is no spunk in these creatures, she thought, no blood in their veins, only sugar-water. But on her right was Herbert and opposite him, to the left of the Reverend, sat Franziska. I hope she does not speak too much, she mused, her breath displeases me.

Mr Eliot, for it was he, smiled engagingly at her and introduced himself; he had seen Beatrice run towards her and call out her name and was glad to make her acquaintance.

'I have heard so much about you, and all of it is complimentary.'

'How kind,' she said.

'What do you think of the portraits?'

'Interesting.'

He laughed warmly.

'That means you don't like them.'

'And what do you think?' she asked.

'I think they're, well, idiosyncratic. I'm not a connoisseur but feel happier in the company of Alma Tadema's ladies.'

'Tut tut,' she said, mockingly, 'surely clergymen are not supposed to enjoy the depictions of pagan flesh?'

'I'm thinking of the marble,' he smiled, 'not the recumbent ladies of Amphissa.'

He ate his roast goose with obvious relish (three enormous geese had been carried in, carved, and served with mounds of vegetables), and his glass was refilled.

'How long are you staying on the Rock?'

'I'm not sure. I've come to celebrate the twins' birthday; I haven't made any Christmas plans other than that. My father is a widower, abroad, and I have neither siblings nor close friends.'

Mr Eliot turned to Franziska von Kroseck, Frances to Herbert.

'Your sister is charming,' she said, 'I'm so glad we have met.'

'I am very happy to be sitting between two such beautiful ladies. Look at Ingeborg,' he continued, 'she is enjoying every minute of being at high table amongst Prussian aristocrats. Our beautiful young Uhlan is captivated and will probably ride into battle with a lock of her golden hair close to his heart. But future battles,' he began – then stopped.

The great crystal chandelier above them was dimmed, and three enormous Christmas puddings, lapped by ghostly, pale blue flames, were carried into the room.

'Hurrah for Merrie Olde England!' cried Mr Eliot, 'the land of puddings and mince pies!'

'Don't forget our Plumtoort!' cried Herbert.

Sweet pudding wines were served; Frances gazed up at Teddy who was deep in conversation with Charlotte, whilst Beatrice flirted with the elderly Generalmajor von Gneisenau, throwing glances, however, at Frances and Herbert. William sat at the far end of the table close to Fürstin von Hardenberg who ate practically nothing. His movements were slow and yet strangely precise, giving the impression of one who had drunk a good deal.

Suddenly Frances heard a squeal of delight from Franziska von Kroseck who had taken a mouthful of pudding and bitten into a golden bean.

'Die Bohnenkönigin!' she cried, 'I am the Bean Queen! Now you must dance attendance on me!'

Teddy had overheard and raised his glass in her direction.

'To the Bean Queen!' he laughed, 'or let's say Queen Bee, sounds better!'

Franziska's health was proposed, also her elevation to the Queen of Forfeits. She laughed; again, that blast of rank breath, rotting lilies mixed with Sauterne, was all too noticeable. Frances turned away.

After the pudding port was served, wine of great vintage and sweetness. Mr Eliot, flushed and loquacious, held forth on Alma-Tadema, on how Frances should offer herself to this painter as a model. He saw her very much as Flora in the lovely 'Spring in the Gardens of the Villa Borghese', bending to pluck the flowers. He had been drinking copiously and his eyes gleamed brightly.

'There is also a painting called 'In the Tepidarium', he chortled, 'which is very naughty, I gather. It would be entirely inappropriate for me to imagine Miss Prince reclining with only a fan to conceal her modesty!'

'I think that the Bohnenkönigin should punish you for such impropriety. Anyway, does Alma-Tadema only paint young women? Are there no beautiful men in his work?'

Herbert had overheard and gazed at her intently.

'Indeed there are. Had she not - ?'

But here they were interrupted by Teddy who, on his feet, struck his glass.

'Fear not,' he said, 'I've no intention of making yet another speech, I'll spare you that. Nor will there be any formal toasts. Those who wish to smoke may do so now. I just want to say one thing more. We've all enjoyed good English fare; now I'd like to invite you to something of a more German nature, slightly more cultural. Don't worry,' he laughed, 'it won't last long! A small event is about to take place in the drawing room, and it is there that we should all repair. Those that is,' he joked, 'who haven't filled themselves too full of plum duff!'

There was a scraping of chairs, and servants rushed forward to help the elderly. Lady Augusta, Frances noticed, looked bewildered and whispered something to her husband, who smiled slyly. The guests moved back into the drawing room where, to Frances's surprise, chairs had been arranged in rows. Mr Eliot insisted on accompanying her; they sat next to Ingeborg and the young Hyazinth von Keyserling whose Uhlan uniform, worn with such panache, intrigued her. The Black Brunswicker, she thought, but Ingeborg is no modest maiden.

She looked for Beatrice and Charlotte, but they were nowhere to be seen; William had disappeared, as had Teddy. The guests sat quietly, murmuring amongst themselves.

And then Teddy entered, carrying his French horn, followed by William and Beatrice with violins and Charlotte with her flute. Teddy bowed and said the following:

'I am no musician, as you most certainly realize by now – I'm only a fumbling amateur. My children have far more talent, although I beg your indulgence for not having forced them to practise more in the past. It has not been easy to rehearse the piece that you are about to hear, for William has been in Copenhagen and Charlotte in Zurich and elsewhere; I've also had a mutinous Crown Colony to control! But Bea and I have somehow managed to reduce the score to manageable proportions, and when we were all together we scraped and blew and got the cacophony into some sort of shape. Now I, alas, did not write the piece. But the one who did write it had wished to thank his wife on her birthday, Christmas Day, for the birth of a son. The four of us now, on this

Christmas Day, thank my wife, Augusta, for all she has done, for the birth of a son and two daughters. The original was played on the landing and the stairs of Wagner's house in Switzerland. It was known as *The Siegfried Idyll.* Be tolerant, it only lasts about fifteen minutes. But it is meant as a tribute to my wife, from the girls, William and me.' He stepped back, looked at the children, nodded, and the music began.

It was William who led with the first theme, quiet, ardent and glowing; Beatrice joined in the development and the two wove and intertwined; Charlotte entered and the flute soared above.

Frances sat immovable. Yes, yes, eternal I was, eternal I am…The strings sang and the flute introduced the old lullaby 'Sleep, little one, sleep'. Teddy entered, fluffing the quiet horn passage yet coping manfully as the music swirled onwards. Yes, ever was I, ever am I, eternal to you, and ever new to you – the playing became agitated, despite its inevitable thinness, a flow of splendour rushed over them, a turbulent surge of love and joy, twisting and evolving. Teddy now reached his moment of crisis, playing the trumpet climax unsuccessfully on his horn; the players faltered, but regained their composure as Teddy skilfully played the Siegfried theme, whilst Charlotte excelled at the wood-bird, her fluttering flute notes intermingling with her father's muted brass.

Then the lullaby softly returned, and the passage gently ended. There was silence, then enthusiastic applause, and Frances saw Lady Augusta walk towards her husband, her eyes full of tears, and embrace him fervently.

* * *

Frances found herself standing outside the door, gazing into the darkness, a darkness intense and alleviated only by a pulsing beam and a few glimmering lights on the Unterland and the Düne; the snow had stopped, and a wind moaned from the sea. She scarcely noticed the cold, nor the tears welling in her eyes, tears of anger, of guilt, of disappointment.

Why am I here? Am I not an intruder? What right had I to come? She thought of her father, of George, of Timothy Heywood, of Sophie – and a strange picture of Dympna arose within her, in a white muslin dress with a rose in her hair. George and Mrs Lovell, she felt sure, would have informed the police and also her father of her disappearance; she, in her selfishness, had caused pain to those who loved her. Why, why had she not stayed in Capewell House? Why had she fled from the performance of *Tannhäuser*? Why had she not sat between George and Timothy? Because…

The door opened and William stepped out into the night, putting a light to his cheroot; he started, and came towards her.

'Come in, Miss Prince, you'll catch your death out there. Trying to expunge the memory of that hideous concert, I expect. Ghastly, wasn't it?'

His speaking was slightly slurred; he leaned back against the wall for support.

'Pa made a mess of it, but the girls were passable. I don't know how I got through it after Pa's excellent vintages. Pa says that his attitude to the grape is one of blithe and grateful acceptance – mine too!'

He giggled, nervously, and his hands shook.

'Let's go into Pa's study, he won't mind. I can't stand all these German relations – imagine trying to talk to Gräfin von und zu Kackenscheidt about Herman Bang's novel *Families Without Hope!*'

'Tell me about Copenhagen,' she said listlessly as they walked through the hall and reached the door of the study; suddenly there was a burst of laughter from behind them. It was Franziska von Kroseck, waving a brass poker.

'Now, do not run away! The Bohnenkönigin commands you to join us in the drawing room!' Mr Eliot ran up and seized them both by the arm.

'Now, no French leave! Come on, Miss Prince, don't disappoint us. We're going to play parlour games – great fun! The Prussians have been defeated and left the field to us and the younger colleagues. Save me, my Princess, from this Queen Bee or whatever she is!'

William, scowling pulled his arm free and swayed towards the study, but Frances felt herself propelled into the drawing room, its warmth, light and laughter.

Mr McBride, perspiring and obviously ill at ease was suggesting a game concerning the devil with his wooden spade and shovel, which met with loud groans of good-humoured ridicule.

'Sounds jolly daft to me,' said Mr Osborne. He was wearing a mustard-coloured suit with pink cravat; he had just returned from a holiday in Southampton and felt very sure of himself.

'Er ist dumm,' he said to the young lieutenant, pointing to Mr McBride; Hyazinth von Keyserling blushed, smiled and smoothed his golden moustache.

'I suggest musical chairs,' Mr Osborne continued, 'although we don't have enough ladies.'

He counted: Ingeborg, Miss Prince, the Queen Bee.

'Where are Miss Beatrice and Miss Charlotte?' he cried, 'let's have some warm, plump posteriors to bounce on our bony knees!'

'You are naughty,' cried the Queen Bee, tapping him on the cheek with her poker, 'now you must pay a forfeit.'

'Yes, please!' he riposted, kneeling before her, 'your wish is my command.'

'You are an Esel,' she said, 'a donkey. Now talk like one!' 'Ee-or, ee-or!' he brayed, 'Ee-or!'

Mr Strang stepped forward.

'I think it's time we played a different game,' he announced, primly. 'Miss Frostrup can draw a donkey for us and we'll try to pin its tail on.'

'Yes!' cried Mr Eliot, 'please draw us a donkey, Miss Frostrup.'

Ingeborg had been sitting by the fire, nonchalantly smoking a slim cigar; this she threw into the flames and joined them. Frances noticed that the portraits of the girls had been removed, doubtless for critical or acclamatory scrutiny by the family in the ballroom or the dining room.

'Donkeys I do not like,' she said, 'but I shall draw you a centaur if you wish.'

This suggestion was greeted with delight; Frau Stoeven was summoned and reproachfully brought scissors, a piece of cartridge paper, a thick pencil, some pins and a piece of hardboard. Ingeborg deftly drew the outline of a centaur, a rearing horse whose torso became that of a man; this creature raised its fists in a belligerent fashion and stood against a background of churning clouds. This was pinned to the board and stood upon a table against the wall. Attempts at making a tail out of strands of lametta from the Christmas tree failed, and Ingeborg improvised, cutting out a sausage-shaped strip of card from her cigar packet. A pin was thrust through the end; Herbert produced an immaculate white silk handkerchief which was bound over the face of Mr Brass who had been nervously watching.

'Vorwärts!' cried Herbert, and the thin young man was pushed in the right direction; after much fumbling he stuck the tail in the centaur's eye. There was much mirth at the hapless telegraphist's attempt, as there was when Frances succeeded in pinning the tail to a cloud, Mr Eliot to a hoof and the Queen Bee to the table.

'Now,' said Herbert to the young lieutenant, 'it is your turn.'

He gently tied the handkerchief around the young man's eyes and led him to the board. Hyazinth von Keyserling hesitated, then applied the tail to the rearing centaur's lower belly, where it gave the appearance of an erect phallus. This was greeted by shrieks of laughter, an admonition from the Queen Bee and applause from Ingeborg; when the young Uhlan saw what he had done he blushed deep crimson.

'Well,' said Herbert, 'our centaur is now complete.'

Mr Strang removed the errant tail and suggested that a new game be played. It was Mr Eliot who suggested charades. He moved to the centre of the room and ebulliently held court, much to the bewilderment of the German guests. After an interminable rigmarole had produced the word 'Sin-gap-ore' he turned to Frances.

'Now you tell us one, Miss Prince,' he cried. Frances's heart sank. She remembered with displeasure her mother's delight in charades, how she had forced her daughter to memorise them and entertain assembled aunts and uncles. How inane these games seemed!

'I think,' she murmured, 'that this is unfair on our German friends. They may find our puns incomprehensible.'

'And your Danish friend too,' smiled Ingeborg archly. 'Would you like to hear some tongue-twisters from Zealand?'

'Do you know "Buried Birds"?' asked Mr Strang, who had turned over the centaur and wrote the following on the blank paper: "Roll in nets and if you see a fish with a gold fin, chase it. Clasp arrows in your hand; her robe is black; capture her. Yes, nip each of them." This was greeted by silence.

'Or rivers?' he continued, hopefully, ' some of them are German. "The broom is here. The kettle, Gerald, is boiling. Your allowance is due. He sang the ode rightly. Ethel began to cry."'

To Frances's surprise Mr Brass got to his feet and underlined the rivers correctly, to exaggerated applause.

Please God, no more, groaned Frances, please. She saw Mr Eliot giggling with Mr Osborne; he came across to her.

'We've got a topping game called "Nelson's Eye" he whispered, 'Mr Osborne will go upstairs and lie down on a bed - no matter which, as long as there's not a German dowager in it – and pretend to be Nelson on his death bed. He'll take his arm out of one of his sleeves and lie there. We'll blindfold one of the girls and take her upstairs to touch the corpse – quite decorous, fear not! He's no centaur! She touches his leg, chest, and so on, we can use the poker as his sword. And then she touches the empty sleeve. But then, think of this! I noticed that there was a rotten orange in one of the fruit bowls, mouldy, you know, squishy. Then we'll get her index finger and make her shove it into the slimy orange. And that's Nelson's eye!'

Frances shuddered. 'No thank you, it sounds awful.'

'Very well, we'll play it without you. We'll blindfold the Queen Bee, or Bohnenkönigin, you know, Franziska, and see what happens!'

Frances turned her back and sat next to the fire, staring into the crimson glow. She saw Mr Osborne leave the room and, after five minutes, Mr Eliot made the following announcement: at great expense Sir Edward had managed to borrow Lord Nelson's body which was lying in state upstairs. It was the highest honour to be allowed to stand before the catafalque of this great hero who had destroyed the French and driven them from the seas. But visitors would have to be blindfolded lest the sight of the dead man prove too overwhelming.

'But how does our visitor then see Lord Nelson?' asked Herbert. Mr Eliot explained that the visitor may not see him, but may touch him. And this signal honour had fallen on Franziska von Kroseck, sister of the one who understood the glories of naval tradition! (Herbert bowed.) The Queen Bee, standing close to Frances, smiled nervously as Mr Eliot blindfolded her and led her upstairs. Frances sat alone, waiting. She did not wait long, but was not prepared for the dreadful scream, the hysterical laughter, the running footsteps and the appalling crash as Franziska, catching her foot in her gown, fell headlong down the stairs.

* * *

A small gathering sat in the dining room at nine o' clock, enjoying a cold collation of ham, tongue, pheasant and slices of goose; there was black bread, rollmops, beer and bottles of wine and port. Teddy sat with Frances, William and the twins, Mr Eliot (now contrite) and the young Uhlan. The elderly relatives had retired, as had Lady Augusta who, exhausted and happy, longed to gather in and relive the impressions of the day in a peaceful moment before sleep.

'What a shame the poor girl fell downstairs,' said Teddy, cutting himself some cold tongue and pouring a glass of claret, 'probably having too good a time. Shorter skirts, that's what we need. She's a funny child, highly intelligent, but overwrought. Hysterical too, I should think. Must ask Graevenitz. Where is he, by the way?' Dr Graevenitz had left, Charlotte explained, after luncheon, with Pastor Niep. Many of the other guests had gone, too, Herbert with his sister, pushing her on a rudimentary sledge, and Ingeborg; Mr Brass had returned to the telegraph station, together with Hamish McBride; Mr Strang had led Mr Osborne back to the Rathaus.

'Do you think that Herbert will come back?' asked Beatrice of her father.

'Unlikely,' he replied, 'he's probably drinking grog with Ingeborg Frostrup.' Beatrice frowned at William who, somewhat dishevelled, was drinking brandy.

'Silly thing to do,' he muttered, 'falling down the stairs. I expect Oberstleutnant von Hechlingen was in hot pursuit with dishonourable intent.'

Hyazinth blushed, and Mr Eliot looked down at his plate.

'It was a lovely day,' said Frances, 'and I was so moved by your playing. It was such a nice idea.'

'It was Bea's,' said Teddy, grinning broadly.

'But we couldn't have done it without Charlie and Willy,' Beatrice interjected, 'or without Pa. We played before the Kaiser once, Willy, do you remember?'

'Lord yes,' he drawled, 'he must have thought it was bloody awful, a casus belli.'

'At least he didn't hear me,' said Teddy, lighting a small cigar, 'that really would have caused war between the nations. Thank the Lord, Fanny that you'd never heard my playing before!'

But she had, and she remembered it vividly – a moonlight night two months ago, an excited crowd on the landing stage, bursting flares and fireworks, and the clear call on a horn, Siegfried's horn…She shivered involuntarily. Was she cold?

'Let's move closer to the fire in the drawing room' she said. But Mr Eliot rose to take his leave, to thank his host and congratulate the girls once more. Young women now, having reached their majority. 'God bless you', he said, and discreetly retired. Charlotte and Hyazinth remained seated; Beatrice, William, Teddy and Frances walked through to the fire.

'Charlotte looks well,' said Frances, 'less intense, more mature, more at ease.' She turned to Beatrice. 'Tell me, what do you think of the portraits?' she asked.

'Charlie likes hers but I'm not sure of mine, it makes me look, well, dippy.'

'You look,' announced William, 'as though you were about to wet yourself.'

Beatrice screamed and hit her brother; Teddy grinned.

'Could we see them again?' asked Frances.

'Sorry, Lady Augusta's taken them upstairs to examine them thoroughly,' Teddy explained. 'I think she doesn't really like them, she would have preferred something by Winterhalter. But Ingeborg has talent.'

'I should say she has,' said William, 'Copenhagen's full of her stuff. Mr Innis dragged me round the art galleries there and she's everywhere. But give me the Tivoli any day!' He gave a braying laugh and slumped in the chair. A unsteady hand lifted a glass to his lips. Yet this arm, she thought, drew a bow with great sensitivity over the strings…

Teddy, looking tired, stifled a yawn; she too felt exhausted. The day had brought a variety of bewildering emotions: excitement, exhilaration, resentment at Ingeborg's success, at Teddy's lack of attentiveness, at the tribute to his wife, dedicated to his wife. And she, this wife…She felt angry with herself at feeling such resentment, vexed by the parlour games, the silliness of Mr Eliot, the puerile antics of Franziska. Yet I, too, stumbled down those stairs once…

'It's time that I went,' she smiled, rising to her feet.

'Stay a bit longer,' murmured William, 'it's too early to go to bed. Pa's got out the special brandy for today.'

'No, I am very tired.'

Teddy rose too. 'I'll take you down the steps,' he said, smiling tenderly, 'to make up for dereliction of duty this morning.'

They walked beneath glittering stars over crunching snow; it had grown very cold; he placed his left arm across her back and round her waist; she laid her head upon his shoulder. They approached the oil lamp which hung above the steps and stopped, looking down at the Unterland, at the scattered lights; then they walked down the steps to the vantage point.

'Bless you, Fan, I'm so glad you came. What a kind gift that was.'

She suddenly stopped and turned to face him.

'Teddy, what I fool I am, I forgot to give your family my presents. They must still be in my reticule – Frau Stoeven must have them. I chose them in London on my last day there. How stupid of me…'

He stopped her by laying his finger on her lips.

'Shshsh, Fanny, you shouldn't have brought anything. We'll open them tomorrow and I'll come to the Conversationshaus at six for a quiet drink. Sorry I can't invite you tomorrow, it's strictly a family beano I'm told. I'll tell Herr Jensen to heat the library so we can have a gemütlich tête-à–tête before the tribe claims me. They'll be leaving before Sylvester, so I'll have more time for you then.'

They continued down the steps; the sea groaned in the darkness and the lighthouse pulsed behind them. They crossed the deserted Marcusplatz, ghostly in its shroud of snow.

'Have you the key?' he whispered. She nodded. 'Till tomorrow, then.'

But there was no kiss on her mouth, only the gently touch of his wet glove laid upon her cheek, and across her parted lips.

* * *

She slept soundly; towards dawn a strange dream visited her, a dream of Franziska from whose mouth ectoplasm bubbled, congealing into a gelatinous mass which formed itself into Nelson's eye. Mr Eliot was also present, laughing and weeping. At eight o' clock Fräulein Jensen entered and brought her breakfast tray with hot water; she ordered the commode, drew back the curtains and wished her good morning. She announced that the day was bright and clear; she had heated the stove. After she had withdrawn Frances quickly performed her ablutions and dressed.

From her window she saw again a white, silent world and a sea of obsidian.

After breakfast she put on her coat, tammy, gloves and stout shoes and went downstairs, shivering as she passed through the unheated vestibule; Lambrecht's Wettertelegraph predicted change. She stepped into a clear, cold world and walked to the steps. She climbed upwards, brushing the snow from the wrought-iron railing with her gloved hand. She stopped half way and gazed down at the Unterland and across at the Düne, a white shell floating on the sea.

' "Thy snowy breasts of milky alabaster…",' she murmured. Yes, Russalka, frozen now in snow, petrified, silent. Where is your lover now? She frowned as she remembered Timothy Heywood, George, *Tannhäuser*, the disturbance, the agitation. I shall give myself up soon, she thought, but have things to do here. She continued to climb and reached the top; the lamp hung suspended from its iron arch, capped, bell-like, in snow.

The snow was still firm underfoot; she left the settlement to the right and strode across the frozen earth to the church. She prayed that Mr Eliot might be elsewhere, being in the mood neither for good-natured platitudes nor contrite apologies. The rusty iron gate creaked as she entered the churchyard; the church stood, like an upturned blade, embedded in the firm grey sky. The new graves were not difficult to find, yet she was drawn also to a more venerable stone commemorating Malwine Erk, actress, who had died in eighteen fifty-three, struck by lightning.

Yes, she thought, you fled from danger to be incinerated here, blighted, blasted like Semele. Did you long to see God? Did Zeus appear in a flash of emerald fire? Was this your punishment?

The stone was wet, dank, fissured; the grave neglected. Next was one of the newer ones and here she stopped, her heart beating. It was the grave of Millicent Freshet, a simple stone with name, and date of birth and death. Here she lay, the suicide, the one who had wished to sing, to let her voice ring forth, the afflicted one, abused, beaten, struck down, the one who, at the end, sang of release. The one whom Timothy Heywood had sought to banish to unconsecrated ground, but who lay here now. The brown, billowing dress, the diamonds of rain in her hair, her gloves… Then people started to say afterwards that Willy had had an affaire with Millicent…It's scandalous, saying Willy drove her to it. Stop, stop. Pa really suffered… Who has not suffered? "And from her fair and unpolluted flesh, May violets spring…" Unpolluted? And two months now, in the damp earth here. She shivered and drew her coat more closely about her.

There was one more grave for her to visit, to stand before. The new headstone was easy to find: Euphemia Lavender. A young midshipman once loved you and you rejected him; now he sits dribbling in front of his fire, lost in a crazy world of phantoms. His granddaughter Dympna I mocked and teased because of her deformity. Did you die a virgin, Euphemia, on this bleak rock? Yet your sister knew the one who – touched me. I think he was quite fond of her from what she said…Fond of her…Did she look like you, Euphemia? *My* lips he kissed, *I* was to be his Venus. What are you now, Selena? Faded? Withered? Miss Lavender left you a few bits and pieces in a sealed box…Did Selena predecease you? The lips that he kissed now soft viscous mud, rancid worm-casts, ooze…

A wave of nausea passed over her, she felt the blood drain from her cheeks. Three women lie buried here, the first struck by lightning, the second drowned, the third dying in the ripeness of years after a fall. And I? A wind suddenly gusted from the west, and a few flakes of snow whirled about her. She turned to retrace her steps, lifted the rusty iron latch, then burst into tears; convulsive sobs shook her body as she hung on to the flaking ironwork. The sobs receded and she wiped her eyes and nose upon her sleeve; her teeth chattered and the damp cold crept up her legs.

Then a figure suddenly appeared in the thickening snow, and a gnarled hand was placed upon her shoulder.

'Come away, lassie, the kirkyard is no place for a young woman on a day like this.'

It was Hamish McBride. He took her by the arm and they walked along the Falm, turning off towards the lighthouse.

'I'll be all right, Mr McBride,' she murmured.

'Nonsense. Come in for a warm drink at least. The weather's changing, and there'll be more snow before it thaws. Are you staying up at the big House?'

'No, I'm in a hotel down below.'

'It's no very comfortable for a lady in the lighthouse but I've got a good fire burning. And some soup if you want it.'

She smiled gratefully. 'Thank you.'

They hurried towards the squat red building with its large white dome and thick glass windows and entered. She took off her wet coat and tammy and he told her to kick off her shoes. A fire glowed in the hearth and he heaped more wood onto it.

I was here, she remembered, on my first Sunday, when Teddy proudly talked of his electric clock-machinery. Then we were in the church and I felt his warmth against me. Then the telegraph station…

Hamish pulled up two chairs and thrust a small glass of amber-coloured liquid into her hand.

'It's a wee dram. Nothing better to keep out the chill.'

She sipped it and the whisky glowed within her; she smiled across at him.

'Did you enjoy the party yesterday, Mr McBride?'

'I did not. The luncheon was generous, I admit, but I did not like their foolish games. I never could see the point of charades.'

'Neither could I.'

'There was great silliness. That young minister should be more grave, more sober. I don't hold with the Wee Frees, but Mr Eliot could learn a lesson from them. I was glad to leave. Now,' he continued, 'I'll make you something to eat and we'll have a chin-wag.'

He busied himself in his kitchen; Frances sat at ease, her stockinged feet before the fire; snow blew past the window. She heard voices above, and Hamish McBride shouting instructions in a gruff tone. He returned with two steaming bowls and a hunk of bread.

'It's rough and ready here, but it'll warm the cockles of yer heart. Do you want to sit at table?'

'No,' she said, 'it's cosy here.'

Heavy spoons were produced from a drawer; the two sat on either side of the fire and enjoyed the rabbit stew. After they had finished he offered her more whisky, which she accepted. He lit a pipe and gazed into the fire. She felt a great need to speak to him.

'It was so kind of you to bring me in here,' she murmured, 'but I felt I had to go to the churchyard to pay my respects. I was very fond of Millicent and wished I had helped her more. I was fond, too, of Miss Lavender – I met someone recently who remembered her when she was young. Then there was that actress. She's always fascinated me. She came here to avoid her fate, and was killed.'

'Aye, that was long before my time.'

He lapsed into silence.

'There's fatalism in things,' he continued after five minutes, 'ye can't run away from it. Ye think ye can come here to escape the plague, but ye'll run into something worse. What did she call herself?'

'Malwine Erk.'

'Erk, aye, that's the one. Ye never get lightning here, very rare anyway. But it killed her. Not the sea. The sea killed so many, and will do so till the end of time. She reached dry land after coming from Russia. But the electricity destroyed her.'

The sea took Millicent, thought Frances, staring at the flames which roared up the chimney, a cold, glaucous embrace, the salt slap in the throat, the nose, the eyes, the lungs filling up with quenching, icy water, the panic, the terror.

And yet there was one who knew of drowning, of oceanic ecstasy, of dissolution. He died by water, was carried over it on a gondola.

Have I the courage to emulate Millicent? 'Unbewusst… Höchste Lust'…

An absurd, blasphemous image of her and Teddy, locked in passionate embrace, presented itself, a plunge from the Nathuurnstak into the churning foam beneath. She pulled herself together.

‘I often think of Millicent. It was a tragic case. I am glad she lies where she does, at peace. What did become of her father? Was he ever found?’

‘They reckon he fled on a fishing boat the night ye were all fooling about on the water by the grotto,’ said Hamish sternly, ‘there were a couple of Dutch boats in the area. He was a strange man, a violent man when the mood was on him. He loved her too much, and punished her too much. He knew the lassie was demented, terrified.’

‘But how could he love her, doing what he did?’ ‘He was no right after the death of his wife. He didn’t want the girl contaminated with all the thoughts of music and art and such like. He also thought, well, that she might be getting ideas above her station. He wanted her all for himself. He feared he might lose her. And now he has.’

He lapsed again into silence; the room darkened; the fire collapsed into a cloud of sparks.

‘I must see to the lights. Henk will take you down the steps.’

She started. ‘No, I can easily find my way.’

‘Ye will not go on yer own. The steps can be icy, and we don’t want any limbs broken. It’s time our Governor built that lift he’s always supposed to be doing instead of dancing and turning ladies’ heads.’

An expression almost of pain crossed his features; he knocked out his pipe and helped her into her coat, crossing to the spiral staircase and shouting for Henk, one of his crew.

‘Thank you,’ said Frances, shaking his hand warmly, ‘it was a pleasure sitting by your fire.’

‘Straight home now,’ he admonished her, ‘and no more brooding in the kirkyard.’

Henk appeared, a tousle-headed young man in oilskins; they stepped into the wintry dusk and she was glad of his strong arm as they descended the steps. Henk walked with her to the Conversationshaus, bowed awkwardly, and took his leave.

* * *

Her room was agreeably warm; she took off her wet shoes and lay on the bed, gazing at the window. The snow was wetter, the flakes bigger, gyrating in the rising wind. Strange that she should have wept in that uncontrollable manner, she was normally not lachrymose. Grief at Millicent's tragic life, at Euphemia Lavender's end, the cold damp transience of things. A man loved his daughter too much, chastised her lest she fall for another. She must not be contaminated by music and art, must not rise above her station. Had William, had Teddy…? – no, no. What were those words? Dancing and turning ladies' heads…But this was absurd. She thought of Euphemia and her faded blue eyes, her skin like parchment, her silvery hair, her upright bearing. She dozed and woke with a start at five; the room was dark and she lit the candles and a new oil lamp which stood on the writing desk. It was pitch-black outside and the sea was grinding and sucking back over the pebbles beneath the esplanade. But there, there, a pulsing stab of light from behind, from the lighthouse.

She rang the bell for hot water and Fräulein Jensen promptly arrived. The library was heated, and Miss Prince may eat there with Sir Edward if she wished. She would be dining alone, she explained, the Governor could only stay half an hour. Fräulein Jensen added that the hotel would be back to normal on the following day when the staff would be returning before the arrival of the winter visitors.

Frances washed and dressed carefully, choosing the leg-of-mutton blouse and grey skirt; her hair she would wear in a bun. Just after six she went downstairs and stood by the glass door, peering into the gloom. She placed her hands upon her hips and breathed deeply, pulling in her waist; suddenly her hands and her waist were seized from behind and she heard Teddy's laughing voice declaim:

' "No sacred bard did e'er invent, With such wild wit as placed, Betwixt love's either continent, The isthmus of your waist." Sorry, Fanny, I couldn't resist!'

She turned quickly to face him, blushing.

'I love "The Rosy Bosom'd Hours",' he laughed, 'and when I

saw your beguiling isthmus I couldn't resist. Do forgive me. Have I upset you?'

'You startled me,' she murmured as they walked towards the library. Had he been drinking? He presumed too much, took too many liberties. He walked to a small table where bottles of wine and spirits were standing and poured himself a generous brandy.

'What can I offer you, Fanny?'

She took a small glass of whisky and soda, and then she noticed a cardboard box standing on the table next to the glasses. It was tied with ribbon and sealed with red wax.

'From dear Euphemia,' he explained, 'her few remaining treasures that she wanted to leave to you. I took it upon myself to place it in your hands. I don't think we have to summon the entire episcopate, it's not Joanna Southcott's box! So open it at leisure, in a quiet moment.'

'Thank you, Teddy.'

'And do please forgive my quoting Coventry Patmore, the business about the isthmus. I felt so pleased to see you and got carried away.'

'I think I have a rather thick waist,' she replied, 'it's not one of my best features.'

'Now,' he continued, putting down his glass, 'how about this? No isthmus here nor (yet!) a corporation, but a manly trunk, virile and adorned!'

He thrust out his abdomen, pointing to a handsome waistcoat from which depended an elegant watch-chain with fob.

'A thousand thanks, Fanny! And a thousand thanks from Augusta for the brooch, from the girls for their bangles and from Willy for the splendid tie-pin which I shall appropriate when his back is turned. How you have spoiled us! The family, I warn you, will overwhelm you with gratitude when you next meet them, which must be soon. You were much too generous – Feinstein is the best jeweller in Bond Street. You give us gold, Miss Lavender gives you her box and I come empty-handed.'

'You tolerated my being here,' she replied, 'you made

arrangements at the last moment. I arrived like a lost soul and you kindly took me in.'

He looked at her intently.

'I cannot say how much it means to have you here,' he said, quietly. 'This must be your home now. This is where you belong.'

He held out his arms, but Fräulein Jensen coughed and entered. Was the Governor quite sure that he would not be able to dine here? It was a selection of cold cuts and salmon; lobsters could be provided. The Chablis was on ice. Teddy smiled.

'Alas, duty, that sublimely Prussian virtue, must be obeyed, and I must forgo the delights of this pleasure-dome.'

He picked up his coat, hat and gloves and walked to the door, Frances beside him.

'I still have your lovely umbrella,' he laughed, 'which Beatrice covets but which I shall keep as a pledge that you will come back soon to the Bopperlun and brighten our lives again. Bless you, Fan.'

He kissed her on the cheek; his breath smelled of brandy and cigars.

'By the way, I almost forgot, William invites you to a New Year's Eve party in a new establishment he's found, the Grünes Wasser. That's where the young gather now, sounds delightfully disreputable. But we must see you before then.'

'Do thank William,' she said, abstractedly, 'I shall let him know.'

Fräulein Jensen brought the Governor's lantern and, blowing a kiss, he opened the door and disappeared into the night.

* * *

After finishing supper she took the box upstairs. Her mood was complex: delight at seeing Teddy was somehow attenuated by vexation that he should have seized her waist from behind, indifferent to what Fräulein Jensen might see. His expression of gratitude for the gifts seemed shallow – but what had she expected? William's invitation to the New Year's party had also incommoded her, yet she felt guilt at appearing to be less than enthusiastic. A stupid word, 'isthmus', she thought; supposing she lisped? She also held little interest in what might be in the box: an old woman's trinkets, some rings, perhaps, that would not fit, a heavy brooch, gold, with twists of marmalade-like chalcedony held beneath glass. On the washstand stood a huswife containing a small pair of sharp scissors. Frances cut the string, opened the box and gazed at the contents. There was a letter tied with pink ribbon, a large envelope and a twist of tissue paper. She opened the envelope in which she found a piece of thick paper, lightly foxed on which musical staves had been drawn in brown ink: the notation on them was bold, yet elegant, and superscribed 'The London Waltz'. She knew this hand, of this she felt sure. She opened the twist of paper and saw a thin lock of brown hair, tied with pale blue ribbon. In a trance she undid the ribbon around the letter, a letter written in bold copperplate, and read the following:

'My dear Frances,

We agreed, some months ago, that we were friends and would use our Christian names. You are now far away, but I feel that there is a bond between us, a bond which encourages me to write to you. For I am dying and long to speak before the good Lord closes my mouth and my eyes for ever. Do I need to speak? I feel that the truth should be known and you are the one who must listen. I impose this burden on you, yet also give small gifts, tokens that I know will bring you joy. When that dear, dear girl, my granddaughter, drowned herself I knew that I too, would die, and the fall that frosty morning was but an outward sign.

You know, I think, that my father was Captain James Lavender who settled here after the end of the Napoleonic wars. I was born here. As a very young girl I remember being introduced to the then Governor, Lt. Col. Sir Henry King. My father died when my sister Selena and I were still young, and my mother moved back to London, to Portland Terrace. We went to school in London, it was a happy time. We had always kept in touch with Sir Henry

King and one summer he invited my sister and me to the Rock for the summer. Selena was ill at the time so I went alone, quite an adventure for a young maiden who had not reached her majority! It was a glorious summer and I met a young midshipman who was visiting the island, a Mr John Fallows. We fell in love, it was a brief, passionate affaire; I remember lying with him in a hollow on the Düne, gazing at the stars. He rejoined the fleet and sailed to the New World, promising to return.

I discovered that I was with child by him. I need not tell you of my feelings of helplessness and shame. I confided in my mother who was furious and refused to help me, telling me to return to Heligoland for I was not welcome in her house. I had befriended Sir Henry King's daughter Rose, but soon after I returned to the Rock the Kings left the island, the new Governor, Sir John Hindmarsh, arrived, and I felt isolated. I lived alone, supported by money that Selena was able to send me; I hoped in vain that John would return. When it was no longer possible to conceal my condition I decided to return to London and throw myself on my mother's mercy; I also had the notion that I could trace John Fallows through the Admiralty. I sailed on the Aurora, I remember, and disembarked at Gravesend, where I took lodgings. But my mother had utterly rejected me and forbade Selena to have anything to do with me.

When my accouchement approached I even thought of drowning myself in the Thames: if I had, my granddaughter would have been spared that fate. I was delivered of a son whom I called William. I had very little money but the people I lodged with were kind, despite their poverty. I gave up the idea of seeking John; it was demeaning and fruitless. I was introduced by my landlady to a childless couple who were desperate to adopt a son; the husband's name was Freshet, he was an engineer with good prospects, I was told, in the railways. I gave up my son to the Freshets with the proviso that, should John Fallows return within two years, my child should be returned to me. I never saw my baby again. Perhaps I lacked maternal warmth, but the separation was not as hard as it is so often described as being.

I returned to the Rock and lived quietly; Selena later married well and sent me money. I also had a small annuity from my grandfather's will. When she had her London house I paid her clandestine visits; I never saw my mother again. Selena's husband had relations in Hannover which was pleasant, and I often went there. My life, I thought, would pass peacefully, uneventfully – but it was not to be. Some twenty-five years ago, when Sir Edward was Governor, the post of telegraphist was advertised, and a Mr William Freshet and his wife and daughter joined us. Immediately I saw him I knew that this must be my son. Yet I said absolutely nothing. He told me once of his childhood in Gravesend, of a father who had been a railway engineer. I saw John Fallows in him, there could be no doubt. They had a daughter, Millicent, whom I adored; I took every opportunity to look at her when she ran and played, when she grew to womanhood; she was gifted musically too, but her parents had very little interest, although Sir Edward tried to help.

Mrs Freshet was not robust and caught pneumonia. She died, leaving him a widower; things then got very unpleasant, and I was heartbroken. He grew embittered and violent, that I heard. And Millicent? Poor, dear Millicent. The rest you know. When I saw her coffin lowered into consecrated earth – and I thank Sir Edward from the bottom of my heart for insisting that it should – I felt the cold hand of death grip my heart. I knew that I would soon follow her.

My dear girl, I am imposing this heavy burden of knowledge on your young shoulders. I give you permission to divulge this knowledge to whomsoever you wish. I shall never see my son again; Millicent has gone to a better place where I shall soon join her. Perhaps Sir Edward should be told? He took a keen interest in Millicent and may like to think that a faded old woman knew, briefly, of love.

But now you must be rewarded for your forbearance. I told you that Selena once got to know Richard Wagner when she and my mother were living in Portland Terrace, and that there was a tendresse. She predeceased me and left me the little waltz that he wrote for her, also the lock of hair. She gave him a lock of hers in return. It was a beautiful auburn, as mine once was. These little gifts may bring you pleasure.

Forgive me, Frances, for imposing on you thus. But you are a sensitive young woman, also strong and resilient. I hope you will cherish my granddaughter's memory and gain inspiration from the little manuscript and the physical presence of a very great Master. May your life, and your art, take wings.

Your dear friend,

Euphemia Lavender.'

* * *

She scarcely slept: how could she? She read and re-read the letter; she held the precious lock of hair to the light; she gazed at the The London Waltz; she paced the room. The wind boomed in the chimney and moaned at the window; the sea ran high.

How is this possible? How is it possible that Euphemia was Millicent's grandmother? But why doubt the old woman's letter? Why doubt that she, as a young girl, had had an affaire with a Midshipman Fallows. She suddenly stopped, amazed. But Fallows was the name of Dympna's grandfather, was it not? Midshipman Fallows, the old grandfather, coughing up phlegm, mumbling, confused. When you were young Midshipman Fallows with Captain Lavender? And you fell in love with his daughter? And Miss Lavender turned you down and you were heartbroken till you met grandmother and knew that she was the one? But she did not turn you down. You deserted her. Then she was ostracised and banished to the Rock. Your son was Millicent's father. And Dympna, poor, crippled Dympna, is Millicent's distant cousin.

Wild and whirling phantoms filled the room, Millicent Fallows, Bill Freshet, Mrs Vernon, Millicent as a corpse. A ghostly Selena, whom she had never met, stepped up to her in silver effulgence and gave her a lock of hair. A lock of brown hair given as a token of love, in a quiet pavilion, perhaps, in Regent's Park. (His hair was grey when she had known him, had loved him.) A lock for

Proserpina that the dead soul may be freed. May your life, and your art, take wings…

The stove grew cold and she lay beneath the eiderdown, listening to the wind. Some ten weeks ago I came to this island to rest, to escape, to forget what I had done. And one came here to escape sickness and was incinerated. She gazed at the candle, its flame moving slowly in the draught; strange shadows haunted the walls. Father, she moaned, father, take me away from here.

Sleet battered against the panes and the day passed before her – the graveyard, the lighthouse, the descent of the steps, the opening of the box, the lock of his hair, his handwriting. She prepared herself for a bad night and tossed and turned in restless agitation; after many hours the little gold watch told her it was five fifteen and she sank into a deep sleep, drowning, drifting into deep, cave-like hollows, devoid of puny recollection, recrimination, resolution; she did not see the dead candle at dawn, nor the lurid orange light over the sea.

After breakfast, brought this morning by a maid, she looked in her jewellery box for the gold locket which contained a portrait of her mother. She had always disliked it: Dulcie Prince looked with cold eyes at the observer, a half-smile frozen on her lips. Frances removed it and destroyed it; she twisted the lock of hair into a tight curl and inserted it.

I shall wear it on my breast, she thought, where he rested his head that wet afternoon in Venice, when his hair was grey. What was given to Selena is now mine.

She washed, dressed and went down to the library; a few guests were noticeable, some naval officers; Herr Jensen greeted her politely. The day was raw, he said, the wind had dropped and the rain had ceased, but the snow was turning to slush. He did not recommend that she walk too far. The newspapers had arrived from Hamburg; they were out of date, of course, but informative. He would spare her, he smiled, the Stock Market Gazette. Ah, how foolish, he had almost forgotten: a letter had been delivered for her, early that morning. She took it into the library and read it; it was from William Hennicker-Heaton.

'Dear Miss Prince, I thought I'd better scrawl these few lines in case Pa forgot, which he probably did. A crowd of us are going up to the Grünes Wasser for a hoolee on New Year's Eve and I'd greatly appreciate it if you came too. It's up here on what they call the Leuchtturmstrasse (some 'Strasse' I must say). It's a lively place where we can have a jig if we're feeling up to it. The girls are coming, plus Herbert (of course! Why is he always sniffing about?) and Ingeborg and Hyazinth von Keyserling (a divine name, don't you think!). I've got a couple of chums over from Copenhagen so it won't be only fishermen clumping about in heavy boots. Pa will doubtless look in sometime, Ma certainly won't as she's got a touch of the grippe and is exhausted after the Christmas invasion. The hordes, thank God, are returning to their estates in Pomerania and all points East. (You'd never guess I'm half German, would you?!) Hyazinth will stay a bit longer. Such a charming young man! I'll pick you up at the Con. and walk with you up the steps. It's time my father built that lift instead of drooling over Paul de Kock. (I'll purloin *The Lady with the Three Pairs of Stays* for you to read.) Be warned: as soon as New Year's over he'll be planning the next theatrical extravaganza and you're bound to be the star! Do come. Just send old Jensen running up the steps with the answer. Yours, William H-H.'

Well, she thought, perhaps, perhaps not. She felt in need of exercise, despite Herr Jensen's advice and asked him if there were any oilskins she might borrow. Indeed there were, also a sou'wester and rubber boots that belonged to his daughter and which might well fit her. They did, and she set forth, much to his amusement.

'Now you look like a real fisherman! Bring me some delicious cod for our table tonight!'

She briskly walked up the wet steps and gazed down at the Unterland; there was more activity than the day before, a few fishing smacks bobbed on the water. She was determined to count the steps but feared that she may have miscalculated; she reached a total of one hundred and eighty-four. The Falm was muddy, the settlement was silent, closed in upon itself; she passed the cottage where Euphemia had lived, now silent and dilapidated.

She struck off across the wet turf towards the church which she left to one side. No graveyards today, she muttered. She waved to Henk and another man who were carrying a ladder behind the lighthouse; a gruff 'Gu'n Morgen' floated in the wet air. The sea, on her left, at the bottom of the cliffs, was restless, grey heaving mercury; on the horizon a large ship hung suspended. The cliff path was rutted and strewn with pools of rainwater which reflected an ashen sky; a few sodden sheep cropped the turf. The snow had completely vanished now; the temperature had risen in the night. She was grateful for the rubber boots and decided to walk to the Nathuurnstak, the battered head of which she saw rearing before her; a shrieking clamour became more audible. She kept well away from the cliff edge, but suddenly stopped.

A deep fissure opened before her, an inlet, as it were, a crack running inland from the cliff, an indentation whose edges were overgrown with long sodden grass. She noticed that rough steps had been cut within the cleft, steps that led downwards. Her heart beat wildly. This must be the entrance to the Grotto of Love, the way Millicent had taken on that night of horror to sing her swan song below. A damp rope, fixed to a post, hung limply downwards, a rudimentary support. Two months, two little months ago a distracted woman had chosen to climb down this fissure to die, Euphemia's granddaughter, Dympna's distant cousin…

Without thinking she gingerly put her foot onto the first wet step, holding the rope. She turned and backed down the steps, into the clammy crumbling fissure, dislodging pebbles and clods of earth as she went; she lowered her right foot onto the step below, but this step, little more than mud, had been virtually washed away by the snow and the rain. She pulled herself upwards, but the rope and the rotten post came away and fell upon her; she screamed and slithered, slipped, fell in a shower of stones, marl, earth, mud and bracken onto the wet sand of the cave, some twenty feet below.

She lay there bruised, shaken, crying, her sou'wester lying at the water's edge. The cave stank of weed and slime; a greyish-green light suffused it. She pulled herself to her feet, gripping those boulders that had, when illuminated from behind, formed the pair of lovers, but in the sickly gloom little could be seen of any erotic demonstration. She walked, hobbled to the back of the dripping cave; one foot was painful to walk on and there was a dull ache in the back of her right shoulder. The wet rope and rotted post lay coiled before her. Fool, fool that I was to climb down here. The sea slopped into the mouth of the cave, ran towards her, receded. There was no possibility of climbing back up the cleft – and suddenly a fearful thought struck her. If the tide were coming in, she was trapped. Nobody knew she was here. The sea glooped, ran across the sand, caught the rope, carried it towards her, withdrew; her feet sank into the sludge of sand, seashells and bladderwrack.

Back, she thought, as far back into the cave as I can go. But the cave, although broad, was not deep. She climbed with difficulty onto the rocks which lay tumbled against the back of the cave and sat trembling against the slimy wall; her shoulder ached and she noticed that the wrist and palm of her right hand were bleeding from a deep graze. I shall die here, she murmured, as Millicent did. Her gold watch had not been damaged and told her that it was midday; feverishly she tried to envisage, to remember the tide charts that hung in the lobby of the Conversationshaus, but to no avail. She had scarcely looked at them, let alone memorised them. Was the tide coming in? Should she attempt to swim? To divest herself of clothes and swim naked in the bleak waters? But she swam badly and shuddered at the prospect of inundation. She desperately tried to convince herself that the tide had not reached a certain point in the sand, but knew that it had, and a rushing wave superseded the erstwhile tidemark, almost reaching the rocks on which she was crouching. Wet and terrified she stared at the sea spurting coldly into the mouth of the cave; she felt her tears on her frozen face.

'Help!' she screamed – but who could hear? The horror of dying overwhelmed her, the dreadful awareness of finality. Millicent, she moaned, Millicent. But Millicent had sought death, whereas she was terrified of it, terrified of the horror of drowning, the salt invasion, the helpless flailing, the panic. Frozen, stiff, aching and sick with dread she waited for the inevitable surge of icy, indifferent water that would overwhelm her. But there was no inevitability: the tide had turned and the sea, after spiteful, dashing forays which soaked her to the skin, advanced no further. Glaucous-grey tongues of seawater licked, raked the floor of the cave, then were gulped back.

She crouched, petrified, hoping, yet not daring to hope, distrustful, expecting a savage aquamarine ravishment after the deceptive lull. But none came; the sea entered, yet did not rush, entered, but did not reach the tidemark, withdrew. She stretched a stiff and sodden leg from the rock and sank into the wet sand, her feet in squelching sediment. How long she stood she did not know, reclining back against the rocks, the wet slime, gazing numbly at the stony figures, at breast and phallus, ostensibly, at arm and thigh. The golden ticking pressed against her ear revived her, told her it was mid afternoon. And it was growing dark.

She dared not venture to the mouth of the cave where the sea was still sovereign, but she now felt that she had a chance. But could she survive in the cave till the tide attacked again? Never. She must shout, sing, scream in the hope, the faint hope, that her voice be heard. Her cracked lips, caked in salt water and dirt, scarcely opened, and only a grating croak issued from her mouth. But she persevered. She sang 'Ah-ah-ah,' she filled her lungs, lungs which the water had spared, and shouted. And the noise reverberated in the cave. She crooned, shouted, yelled, sang: 'Oh would I were but that sweet linnet...They bid me slight my Dermot dear...She never told her love...Nachtviolen...Ich wollt', meine Liebe ergösse sich...' a febrile, strange and haunting pot pourri. An immense tiredness overwhelmed her, but she cried for help and sang, sang. Her voice cracked, her throat closed, but she knew that she had to express sound, for that was her only salvation. 'Blow the wind southerly, southerly, southerly...Lost is my quiet...I loved thee once, Atthis, long ago...' But darkness fell, and she slithered down onto the wet, stinking sand. It was Millicent's final song that drained from her lips, 'Auf dem Wasser zu singen', to sing on the water...She lay, her face sinking into the wet, cold mass, the booming sea waiting, waiting. 'Till on a high – and gleaming wing – I too shall vanish from change and from time…'

But it was Rasmussen's strong arms that lifted her up, not Death, carried her through the water to the boat bobbing outside the cave, Rasmussen who, alerted by Pastor Niep, had come with two lads to see what was happening. For Pastor Niep, walking along the cliffs in the dusk after visiting the church, had heard strange sounds emanating from the earth, from the cave below. He had run back to the landing stage to find Rasmussen. And it was, as the pastor would say later in his halting English, 'as when mermaidens were singing in the sea, with sweet beguilement.'

* * *

CHAPTER SIX

Dr Graevenitz arrived early next morning. It was, he said, a miracle that she was still alive. She recounted what had happened; he ascertained that her left heel was bruised and swollen, that she had badly pulled a muscle in her back and that there was a deep contusive graze along her right wrist. 'You were saved,' he cried gleefully, 'by German theology and German music. If Pastor Niep had not walked in meditation in the dusk, preparing his sermon, and if you had not sung Beethoven, Haydn and Schubert you would not be lying in this bed now, your body would be floating in the North Sea, past the Dogger Bank.'

He produced a small dose of morphine to alleviate any pain that she might feel. On no account should she leave her bed till the following day. Rest, rest. And not too much Hüllihait on Sylvester's Eve! He left, shutting the door vigorously behind him.

She dozed, drinking the broth brought to her at midday, then lay reliving the sickening, slithery fall, the wet sediment, the inroads of the predatory sea, the turn of the tide, the terror of isolation, the song, song bursting forth from her mouth (for this mouth was not to be invaded by stifling terror), then vertigo, the rough rubbing of Rasmussen's jacket, the kicking boat, the arrival at the landing stage and the dream-like passage to the hotel steps and oblivion.

She shuddered beneath her quilt, although the room was warm; Herr Jensen had given strict instructions that she be cosseted. A bottle of brandy stood, with glasses, on her bedside table; brandy, he had let it be known, would warm the heart and bring a sense of wellbeing.

So this, she mused, is how the year would end: a convalescent lies in a lonely room, a convalescent who had arrived a few days ago full of joy and longing. Longing for what? She wondered how long it would take her father to find her here; she remembered the last time she had seen him, in Cuxhaven. She had walked at his side with her elegant black umbrella and its beads of jet. Her Venetian umbrella. Strange that I should think of this, after the brush with death.

She suddenly felt for her locket; it lay safe and warm upon her skin. The North Sea shall not have it. It nearly took him once, though, he had told her, when he was young. The Thetis almost foundered, driven into a reef before taking shelter at Sandwike. His wife, he told her, longed for death by lightning rather than drowning. Three and a half weeks of storm and wild weather in the Baltic, the Skagerrak, the North Sea. Then there was the glimpse of the English coast at Southwold, then the river steamer up the Thames from Gravesend. George, she thought, Pocahontas. She drifted into an uneven sleep but suddenly, towards four, when the room was already dim, she was wakened by a gently knock at the door.

'Wait, please.' She lit a candle, smoothed her hair and drew up the quilt, adjusting the blue ribbon that passed through the lace of her nightdress. 'Who is it? Please come in.'

The door opened, and he entered quietly. 'I hope I'm not disturbing you.'

It was Teddy, carrying a large bouquet of roses and lilies. He came towards her and laid the flowers on the bed, bringing a chair to sit on. He looks tired, she thought, and she noticed the thinning of his hair at his scalp, the flecks of grey in his mutton-chop whiskers. His suit was crumpled and his cuffs were grubby.

'Purloined from the girls' bouquets, I'm afraid. Not many roses or lilies growing on the old Rock at this time of year, nor any other, come to think of it.'

He held out his hand, which she took.

'I hear you've been swooning in Rasmussen's muscular arms. Seriously, Fan, what a shocking thing to have happened. Thank

God Martin Niep heard you and they fished you out. I can't help reprimanding myself for not fencing off that wretched fissure. I might have been responsible for your death.'

'No, Teddy, it was my fault. I tried to get down into the cave but everything gave way and down I went. For some reason I wanted to see where poor Millicent…'

'Don't talk of her,' he said abruptly. Then he stood up.

'I'll get a vase for these. Is there one in the room?'

'I don't think so.'

'Well, I'll fetch one.'

He left the room and she quickly got out of bed, slipping into her Turkish slippers and her negligé. She brushed her hair and dabbed herself with eau de cologne; he returned with a vase and started to arrange the flowers.

'Let me do that,' she said.

She grouped the flowers casually; the vase was narrow and three lilies did not fit in. She carried them across the room to place them in her water jug.

' "And the lilies lay as if asleep along her bended arm",' said Teddy.

'I am hardly the blessed damozel,' she retorted, 'I do not have seven stars in my hair which is, anyway, hardly yellow like ripe corn.'

'Wear this, then, in your dark tresses.'

He had plucked a rose from the vase and placed it in her hair; she stood, blushing. The golden locket, she noticed, was hanging outside her negligé, and he put out his hand and touched it.

'Well, is there a rival here?' he joked, 'I'm quite jealous!'

'No,' she stammered, 'it's – it's – my father.'

He withdrew his hand, and a strange expression passed over his face.

'Lucky Jack, between the two roes grazing among the lilies.'

He took a Manoli from his cigar case, lit it at the candle and moved towards the windows; rain dashed against the panes. He twisted his bottom lip and blew the smoke sideways. She sat close to the stove, wishing that there were noises outside, laughter, the clattering of crockery, but the corridor was quiet. Or did she long for this silence? She gazed down at her Turkish slippers, frowning. Why had she lied about the locket? Had it been to deter him? And yet, and yet…

He walked to the table and poured himself a glass of brandy. Then he turned to her.

'Does Jack know you're here?'

'No, nobody does. I came on an impulse, a whim, that's all.'

He sat opposite her; she drew her negligé tightly around her, pulling her slippered feet back under the chair. The rose slipped from her hair, but he deftly caught it in his left hand, smiling. He lifted it to his nose and inhaled its perfume. They sat in silence; the only sound she could hear was her heart, beating wildly. Then he spoke.

'Let me tell you a story, Fan. There was once a young officer cadet, not much older than the blushing Hyazinth, our blooming Cornet or whatever he is, who fell in love with a general's daughter who was very beautiful and very proud.

He fought bravely in the wars against Her Majesty's enemies the Russians, he was gallant and dashing. He fought with panache, won medals, was mentioned in dispatches. But still the general's daughter rejected him. Slanderous tongues said she loved another, that he was not good enough for her, but he ignored them. He worshipped the proud and beautiful lady, let us call her Lucinda.

Our officer was held in high esteem by his men, he was also popular and cultivated. He courted Lucinda, hoping against hope that she would give him her hand, but to no avail. Did he have a rival? He could not believe that he had; he loved her coolness, her repose. But with time he grew discouraged, became dissipated, contemplated suicide. But he pulled himself together, and got a position abroad. He kept close ties with Germany and spent much time there, speaking the language well. And finally, after much devoted wooing, Lucinda did give him her hand.

He married, then, the woman of high standing who, it had been said, loved another. And he is happy now. Do you know of whom I am speaking, Fan?'

‘Of course,’ she whispered, almost inaudibly, ‘you are the young officer. But Lucinda is my mother Dulcie, is she not? You have made a mistake. You married the lady of high standing, Augusta.’

He smiled. ‘No. The young officer is your father. How could Lucinda love another if your father loved her?’

‘You loved my mother,’ she murmured, ‘I know you did.’

‘But she chose Jack after all. And now her beautiful daughter sits opposite me.’ He leaned forward and gently opened her negligé, placing the rose in her nightdress between her breasts, next to the locket. ‘At least one rose,’ he whispered, ‘grazing among the lilies. A rose for Dulcie, Jack.’

He rose to his feet, kissed her on the forehead, and left the room.

* * *

That evening the maid brought a note from William: he quite understood if she preferred not to come tomorrow after her accident, but he nevertheless hoped that she would. He would come at eight o’ clock anyway, but she must feel under no obligation.

Ignoring Dr Graevenitz’s instructions she dressed and went down to the library, her thoughts in turmoil. She was furious at Teddy’s impudence, shocked at the inference that there was more than a tendresse between him and her mother and upset that her father had been called dissipated, and had even contemplated suicide. A temporary aberration, of course, but nevertheless…

She had torn the rose from her nightdress and flung it out of the window into a dark, wet world. Why had she not forced him away when he had tampered with her clothes? She knew one thing for certain: that she must contact her father and leave this island for ever. The thought of slinking back to Capewell House, however, appalled her: how could she explain what she had done? Offer excuses to George and Mrs Lovell? And Timothy Heywood? Her father must come to Heligoland, and they would go away together. Had he not spoken of the Riviera?

The hotel was filling noticeably with guests who had presumably come for the New Year's revels, the Pottensmitter-In as Herr Jensen had called it, when crockery was smashed to greet the Wenskerdai, or New Year's Day. He had entered the library and was surprised to find her there, alone. He exhorted her to join in the coming festivities: Herr Garer would be there with other dignitaries who would be honoured by her presence. Dr Graevenitz could also keep an eye on her, he said. Dr Saphir would also be over for a few days.

She shuddered inwardly. Thank you, she replied, but she was contemplating spending a quiet evening in her room.

Impossible! he cried. He would send the two doctors up at midnight to carry her down to drink champagne and greet the new decade! There could be no escape! I shall see to it my door is locked, she retorted. But he had a master key! But I shall leave my key in the lock from the inside! But we shall bring ladders to the window!

He was in good spirits, amused and emboldened by his ability to make louche suggestions. She changed the conversation, taking Wilhelm Jensen's *Ebb and Flow* from the shelves.

'Is he a relation of yours?'

' Yes indeed, a cousin of whom I am very proud. Wilhelm often visited us to gain background knowledge for his new novel *Lee and Windward.* The Frisians are a cultured people and read many books.'

She was glad to have deflected the conversation from Dr Saphir and the prospect of being abducted by him, and smiled at Herr Jensen, taking the book with her as she went up to her room.

But how could she read? She heard sounds from below, distant laughter, doors being opened and shut, footsteps. Wilhelm Jensen failed to engage her interest; her thoughts wandered; she twisted the locket. She thought of Euphemia, of the unknown Selena, one sister of good report, the other of the moon. She thought of Euphemia's tribulations, her son, of Dympna and Millicent. *Ebb and Flow* was tossed to one side; she stood with her back to the stove.

He shall not touch me again, she murmured, never. A rose for Dulcie, Jack…Never. That rose now lies in darkness and mud, crushed, trodden. It is not my father I have here on my breast but one who - . She stopped, remembering *The Siegfried Idyll.* Teddy, Teddy, what are you doing to me?

She noticed the morphine and gratefully swallowed a small dose; she undressed and noticed a small red scratch on her skin where the stem of the rose had been pushed against her.

You took liberties, sir. What would my father say? *Ebb and Flow* was retrieved from the floor, its tedium casting a spell over her eyes which grew heavy, and closed. The year dies, she thought; where was I a year ago? Not here, not here, not anywhere…The book slipped from her hands and Morpheus claimed her. And her dreams, when she tried to remember them the following morning, when drizzling rain drenched the Rock, had been of the sister she had never known, who had died so young, walking as a young ghost across a long beach of shingle.

* * *

Her bruised heel was now cured, the ache in her back a mere twinge, her grazed wrist, although unsightly, was not painful. After breakfast she walked up the steps through the dull morning. She counted, miscounted, counted; she walked beyond the curved ironwork arch, she walked past the settlement, noticing the Leuchtturmstrasse, indicated by its wooden signpost, and saw the Grünes Wasser, a barn-like structure at whose entrance barrels and crates of bottles were stacked in waiting.

She walked on; a wind from the west blew a fine rain across her path. There was a swell on the sea; immense breakers rolled lazily, booming amongst the shattered fragments of rock which had tumbled down the cliffs; the gulls and guillemots rode and cackled above. She saw the telegraph station on the cliffs, but also noticed that two figures were approaching; both were in cloaks, the taller, a man, wore a military kepi, the smaller, a woman, wore a poke-bonnet. They were arm in arm and deep in conversation. It was, she realised, Charlotte Hennicker-Heaton and Hyazinth von Keyserling and, although she longed to talk to Charlotte about the young woman's travels and mental development, she felt reluctant to meet them and turned instead into the Bindfadenallee, passing the rope-maker's shop, then into the narrower Nelsonstrasse, a row of sullen, one-storey dwellings, hunched against the rain.

What lives are lived here? she wondered; greasy smoke tugged at the chimneys and blew low across the muddy road. A weather-beaten signpost, crooked and mildewed, pointed to the Viktoriastrasse and she turned into it; a stench of rotting fish hung in the air. She had not visited this quarter of the settlement before; the houses were mere hovels, put together from variegated flotsam and jetsam, their roofs of tarpaulin and compacted turf. The last house, standing on the edge of the common ground, was especially low and cramped; its rotten door had broken away from the rusty hinges and stood propped against the wall to cover the aperture; its one window was an irregular piece of filthy glass which, she surmised, had been salvaged from a wrecked vessel and carried up here, miraculously intact.

The door was suddenly pushed to one side and a woman emerged into the rain, a gaunt young woman carrying something in her right hand. Frances only glimpsed her in profile, but the pale, angular features she recognised: it was Stine. Wisps of lank hair escaped from a coarse scarf thrown over her head, and she moved as in a trance, gazing fixedly ahead. It is a wreath, thought Frances, she is carrying a wreath.

She held back and stood stock still; Stine had not seen her, she was sure of this. The girl wore a shabby black cloak which only just covered a dark dress with a ripped hem; her dirty feet were thrust into clogs. A sense of hopeless depression, of abject misery emanated from her. She had now left the settlement and was walking in the direction of the telegraph station, but veered to the right, towards Hamilton point, a rocky, boulder-strewn promontory, a desolate corner of the Rock, of little interest to the summer visitors coming to gaze through telescopes at sunsets for it looked east; a few goats, whiskered and with amber eyes, cropped the sparse turf.

Stine moved out of view behind a rough knoll; Frances quietly followed, feeling increasingly uneasy. What right have I to spy on her? But why was she carrying a wreath to such a place? The graveyard and the church are on the other side, not here. Her unease turned to fear: the girl might attempt some desperate act – had she not once before? Frances now moved quickly, buttoning her warm coat against a rising wind.

The rain had ceased, but the day's damp desolation filled her with foreboding. Had Stine - ? But then a low moan, quickening to an anguished keening, told her where the girl was. Frances ran now, stumbling over the wet glistening boulders, scattering the bleating goats, and came to a small patch of marl-grass surrounded by scree and shattered sandstone. And then she stopped.

Stine was crouched on the turf, crying and rocking back and forth. She had laid her wreath against a dark, smooth rock on which a name had been scratched; Frances could not read it. She gently climbed down and knelt beside the unhappy girl who made no response, but continued to weep uncontrollably. Frances looked at the wreath: it had been roughly made of pieces of bracken, fronds of spruce from a Christmas tree, strands of marram grass. Cheap glass beads had been threaded in it. But her gaze was fixed on a sodden dark rose, limp, black-red, with a twist of dirty silver foil around its stem.

A rose, she thought, on Heligoland, on the last day of the year. And this rose she recognised. It must be the one – and she knew it was – that she had thrown into the night, and this poor, distracted girl had found it on the wet esplanade and put it in her wreath. She put her right arm around the sobbing Stine who buried her face in her breast. The name on the stone, streaked with bird droppings and crudely scratched, was "Wilhelmina".

The rose you stole from your daughters for me, thought Frances, now lies here for *her* daughter. For this must be she, the sad fruit of an illicit liaison. She gently lifted Stine's tear-streaked face upwards and kissed her; they staggered to their feet, but Stine then thrust Frances from her and stumbled awkwardly through the boulders back to the path. Frances ran after her but the girl raised her arm and pushed her away. I have intruded, thought Frances, leaning against a boulder, defiled her sanctuary. But I shall help her. Was the perpetrator duly punished, the father of Wilhelmina? She shuddered and scrambled back the way she had come, walking vigorously towards the telegraph station. But Stine was nowhere to be seen.

* * *

Mr Brass lived alone in the station; Mrs Wilson cooked, cleaned and did his laundry. Mr Brass opened the door, blushed, and stammered that she could come in. She explained, sitting on the threadbare couch where poor Millicent had lain, cold and in anguish, that she wished to send a telegraphic communication to her father. This could be sent to the British consul in Hamburg, Sir Charles Dundas.

Mr Brass brought pen and paper for her to write her message.

'Dearest Papa,' she wrote, 'do not worry about me. I am on deät Lun again and long to see you. Please come as soon as you can. I shall wait here. Your ever-loving daughter, Frances.'

Mr Brass, stammering furiously, asked her if Sir Edward had given her permission to send this message as the telegraph station could only send official messages, not private ones. She expressed annoyance. Sir Edward and her father were old friends; her father was on official business; the message was not trivial. She had assumed that letter post would not be collected until after the New Year break: that would cause a delay.

Mr Brass broke wind and, deeply embarrassed, agreed to send the message forthwith. Here, Frances thought, Millicent suffered at the hands of a brutal father who, it is said, loved her too much. He was Euphemia's son. I wrestle with an officious functionary. The room, although bleak, was spotless; a green canary-bird chirruped in a cage by the window. 'O would I were but that sweet linnet…' She wished Mr Brass a Happy New Year, and left.

The Conversationshaus was rapidly filling; a steamer had been hired, she learnt, to bring guests from Hamburg for a few days of revelry on the Rock.

'They come from St Pauli,' cried Herr Jensen excitedly, 'from Ottersen, Süllberg, from Rainville's Garten, from Blankenese to come to my humble house. Be careful, Miss Prince! No hiding away at midnight!' She smiled and frowned.

'I shall play billiards with Mr Strang,' she explained, 'and we shall finish your splendid Danziger Goldwasser. Then I shall retire.'

He burst out laughing. 'Billiards? What sort of game will you play?'

'Cannon, with five balls' she retorted. He doubled over and clutched his knees in mirth, his face turned scarlet.

'Cannon, with five balls? Miss Prince, Miss Prince! You will certainly win if you make a cannon!'

She turned away: Oelrich's dictionary of the Heligoland dialect had been put to frivolous use, and she tired of the joke. She saw him wiping the tears from his eyes before greeting other guests. Of billiards she knew nothing, despite her cousin's attempts to teach her. 'Come, let's to billiards,' she muttered, and went up to her room.

But Stine, Stine…She thought constantly of the girl, the tear-streaked face, pale and emaciated, the wretched grave, the tawdry wreath and rose.

Her rose, that he had placed between her breasts, the rose for Dulcie, Jack, to lie, however, beside his hair, a lock once given in love, now lying on my heart. Let me blossom for thee, stroke thy cheeks, kiss thy mouth…I am fairest! Nay, I! I smell sweetest! Nay, I! Yes, I! And Kundry as a rose of hell, lying naked as a Venus by Titian…

She rang for tea and drank it, gazing into the gathering dusk. Lights were visible below; people walked the esplanade in groups; lights also flickered on the Düne. Russalka, Timothy, George… When will my father arrive? A rose for Dulcie, Jack. No, no.

She suddenly spotted a dark man in an astrakhan coat standing laughing on the esplanade, talking to an attractive woman she did not recognise. It was Dr Saphir; he was gesticulating extravagantly, flicking a limp left hand back from his wrist; his other hand held a cigarette.

From all corners they come as well, to let their eyes cover me in lubricious slime. The eyes rheumy, a foetus, an embryo of an angel, perhaps. Or an oyster, an oyster swallowed by a gluttonous sybarite. A foetus, a sad fragment of flesh, aborted, viscous, putrefying. Her gorge rose; she rushed to the commode, gagging and retching; nauseous bile filled her mouth. The attack passed; she drank water and gazed at the mirror: a pale woman gazed back, eyes glittering.

I should have stayed in Capewell House, played halma with George. Or Dympna could be with us to play Decapitation. 'Rubbish, rubbish, just behead, Precipitate you'll have instead. Behead again and you will see, You'll have at once a well-known tree.' Trash, rash, ash. A quiet room at midnight, the bells of Codbury St Mary sounding across the plain. Then my dear father will enter and fold me in his arms. Then no one can touch me.

She poured herself a glass of Danziger Goldwasser; the strong liqueur took her breath away. Come, she said to herself, we shall get over this. It had grown dark outside and she saw that a fire was burning on the Düne, the Hallem. Burn her, she said out loud, burn her. Then we shall be free.

* * *

At seven, after dozing, she heard music from below, also singing. She knew that the hotel would stay open all night, that she could accept William's invitation to join the party in the Grünes Wasser and stay with them till well after midnight, then return and, with luck, avoid the attentions of Dr Saphir and get back to her room. The thought of staying in the Conversationshaus was impossible and there was no alternative. To beg ingress into Government House was out of the question and, besides, she feared meeting Teddy, displeased as she was with the account of her father, his love for Dulcie, his clever, improper punning (the rose, yes, the roes: had not she and Sophie giggled at this when girls?), his arrogant assumption that she would submit to him whensoever he desired it.

She felt that things were coming to a head, that she must bring to the light the dark and sordid secrets surrounding the death of Millicent and the raping (for this is what it must have been) of Stine. She racked her brains, trying to muster evidence: Teddy's evasions, Millicent's awkwardness in his company, Charlotte's concern for Stine and her determination to help the girl, implying that she knew things that were not complimentary towards her father and brother, that Teddy had punished a sailor to save his own skin – or his son's? Had not Bill Freshet implied that his daughter had been in thrall to Teddy? And William?

'But Ma knew about Silly Milly, didn't she?' Knew what? Her brain reeled as she tried to remember innuendoes, aspersions, half-truths, evasions. 'There were those ignorant and vindictive enough to suspect that William Hennicker-Heaton was in some way involved.' His involvement in the death of Millicent and the rape of Stine? Was Teddy guilty of gross irresponsibility? Dancing and turning ladies' heads...Yes, mine, mine! And my mother's! Did he clasp her waist? Place roses in her bodice? My father, my poor father a cuckold. I, Frances Prince, shall punish the Governor and his wayward son.

A picture of Judith flashed through her mind, holding the severed head of Holofernes; she severed it as a fishwife cuts the head from the cod on a table by the landing stage, the knife slicing through flakes of flesh, crunching through bone, the glassy eye gazing whitely upwards as the head lay in scales, blood, slime.

Take care, my Governor. An avenging angel approaches, a Brünnhilde bent upon the annihilation of a noble house....

A sense of ecstatic wellbeing surged through her; she drank another small glass of Goldwasser and set about deciding what she should wear. Nothing sensational, nothing seductive. The youth of the Rock would be gathered there. Am I young? Yes. I do not wish to play charades, nor retire at nine o' clock. I can still compete with Ingeborg Frostrup.

She pulled out gowns, blouses, skirts. My burgundy gown, yes, with a stole, and my hair in a chignon. And if blood be spilt, mine or his, so let it be. She stepped before the cheval glass in camisole, stays and petticoats. Beware, she murmured, I am coming. And her ablutions began.

* * *

At eight o' clock she descended the stairs, pushing her way through a crowd of revellers wearing paper hats and throwing streamers. She walked to the door; the night was overcast and still. She had glimpsed Dr Saphir in the dining room and was glad to have given him the slip; Herr Jensen, however, had spotted her. He advanced wearing a dark cut-away and wagged his finger.

'Now now, Miss Prince, where are you going?'

'To the Düne,' she said, hardly knowing why.

'To Russalka? Is she leading the revels? Stay here, Miss Prince, the evening will be very jolly, we shall dance the night away. There are many here who wish you well.'

'I shall come later,' she cried, 'don't forget the billiards.'

'Let's have a game,' he laughed.

'I wouldn't mind having one sometime,' she riposted saucily and stepped outside; to her great relief William was coming up the steps. He offered his arm and they set off.

'Top-hole, Miss Prince, I'm so glad you could make it.' She noticed immediately that he had been drinking; his speech was curiously precise and his eyes preternaturally bright. Good, good, she thought, I can get the better of him. They walked towards the steps; there were many people on the esplanade, jostling and laughing. They made their way upwards; William slipped and grabbed the railings.

'Should be a lively crowd up there,' he cried, 'I've invited a couple of Danish chaps. Hope they don't give away too many secrets of life in the Tivoli! Mustn't shock Miss van Egmond! Bea and Charlie will be there. Bit more entertaining than the Con. anyway. Pa'll be in later. He's on about 'The Fair Toxophilites', so beware! Bows and arrows, but he draws the line at the Amazons! Beware, Miss Prince, the dreaded mutilation! *Multatuli*, did I mean him? Eduard Douwes Dekker – he's my man! Perhaps I'll be the big Tuan one day, the boss in Batavia.'

'Not the Danish West Indies, then?'

He did not grasp her meaning and walked unsteadily up the steps, holding the railing.

'I mean Miss Frostrup,' she continued. He giggled.

'Ingeborg – Pa warned me she was a cock-teaser. Honour thy father and – hey! They've started early!' A rocket whistled up from the Düne and burst above them in a cascade of scarlet sequins; the sea, oily-black and restless in the moonless night, threw back a dull reflection.

'Hope the squibs ain't too loud, I can't stand it when they go off! Hey, do you think I'm a squib, Miss Prince, a battered unmarried beast, squibbing about from place to place? Perhaps you and I should make a go of it – Pa would be pleased, he's obviously taken a shine to you as our American friends would say. Ma wants me to settle down with Florike, though. A big, comfortable eiderdown for me to sink into.'

Frances said nothing; they turned into the street and approached the Grünes Wasser from which laughter, singing and shouting resounded. They entered the open doors; a greenish light from tinted oil lamps greeted them as they stepped into an aquamarine gloom.

A dance was in progress; there was much clumping and shouting. Six couples were twisting and turning, the women dressed in national costume, the familiar red skirts, green scarves and white blouses, the men in dark blue trousers and light grey smocks. The fiddlers played vigorously and with great skill.

'Chaps from Hardanger,' yelled William, pushing Frances to one of the tables which had been reserved for his party, 'brought over especially.'

Benches ran along the sides of the walls; here most of the young were sitting whilst the tables were occupied by the wealthier clientele. William introduced his two friends from Copenhagen,

Herre Torsten Helvsted and Herre Jens Brøvik; they were dressed stylishly, foppishly even, and bowed, kissing her hand.

'And you have met Florike, haven't you?' he drawled. 'May I introduce Miss Florike van Egmond.'

Frances looked at the stout young woman who sat blushing, looking at the floor; she was dressed in a pink taffeta gown which ill suited her.

'I think I saw you last October in the Princess Alexandra. I am pleased to meet you here.'

William ordered grog, red wine and bottles of porter; Florike sat in silence.

'You are from Copenhagen?' asked Frances, turning to Herre Helvsted, knowing that her question was empty, otiose; Herre Helvsted exuded a strong scent of pomade and smiled behind his gold-rimmed pince-nez.

'Indeed I do, as does Herre Brøvik. We live in the St Annae Plads, near the Kongens Nytorv. It is a fine city.'

Herre Brøvik gave a whinnying laugh, pushing back his beautiful lace cuffs which protruded too far from his tailored jacket.

'I believe you are a friend of one of our most talented artists,' he purred, 'a woman of whom Denmark can be justly proud.'

'Really?' Frances asked, sipping her wine.

'I think he means Ingeborg Frostrup,' whispered Florike.

'I have seen her work, I think, but am unable to pass judgement,' Frances continued, irked by the praise of her rival and determined not to think of her; William lit a Manoli and offered her a Neptun which she accepted, inhaling the smoke gratefully.

'We are making a civilised man of William,' continued Herre Helvsted, lifting his grog and smiling. 'Copenhagen suits him, he has been too long amongst these German clodhoppers.'

The fiddlers, who had been resting, drinking their beer, struck up. It was a waltz. Herre Helvsted stood up, bowed, and asked Frances for the pleasure of her company. He danced well, but his touch was repellent, cool and yet wilting; the scent of macassar oil and rose water she also found disagreeable. He held her right arm high in the air; the light caught in his pince-nez and turned his eyes into glittering, green-gold disks. His teeth, she also noticed, were discoloured.

'Come to visit us,' he murmured, tightening his hold on her waist. She smiled past him at the fiddlers, saying nothing. And then she noticed Herbert and Hyazinth von Keyserling enter the room. The waltz stopped; she thanked Herre Helvsted, who had accompanied her back to their table. Herbert, she noticed, had made no attempt to join them but had sought a small table in the furthest corner.

Herre Brøvik was asking Florike her opinion of the novel *Max Havelaar*; she had not read it. This he found difficult to believe.

'It is a masterpiece of Dutch prose!' he cried.

'*Multatuli!*' crowed William, '*Multatuli!* I have suffered much, yes!'

Had Florike read Louis Couperus's *Eline Vere*, which had come out recently? She mumbled with downcast gaze that she had not: she read very little. But at last the literature of Holland was catching up! It would, however, be a long time for the Dutch to reach the genius of Herman Bang.

'*Families without Hope!*' cried William again, 'yes, that's us! Me, I'm finished. Ibsen knew all about it. Think about poor old Osvald, what did the doctor call him? "Vermoulu", was it? Softening of the brain, yes, made him think of cherry-coloured velvet curtains, something soft to stroke.'

'Stop talking like this, please,' Florike implored.

'You enjoy the role of degenerate, don't you?' said Frances sharply. She remembered a similar conversation with Ingeborg Frostrup in the Stadt London.

'Mr Hennicker-Heaton is a man of refined sensibilities, a neurasthenic,' explained Herre Brøvik, stroking his right eyebrow with the beautifully polished nail of the little finger of his right hand.

'Do you know what?' said William, slumped in his chair, 'I'll get so limp and thin that Florike can use me as a boa and wear me round her neck.'

His maunderings were interrupted by a gale of laughter from the adjoining table where a young man had placed a carafe of wine upon his head and was swaying to the tune of 'O, du lieber Augustin'.

The Hardanger fiddlers were now resting again, replaced by a contingent of clarinets, trumpets, drums, a zither and, impressively, a glockenspiel or jingling johnny; many couples took to the floor for a Schieber, an energetic dance which involved much striding, turning, marching, spinning. Frances, to her surprise, was invited to dance by a complete stranger, a middle-aged man with a ruddy countenance who shoved her, pulled her, spun her round the floor with great panache. Gone were the thoughts of William's lassitude as she exulted in rapid motion; from the corner of her eye she saw Herbert, who nodded as she flashed past.

The dance finished and, out of breath, she thanked her partner, but a form of military two-step followed and he seized her round the waist and flew with her around the floor. The jingling johnny was raised and lowered, raised and lowered with verve and skill, and the dance became more march-like. Janissaries, she thought, as she whirled and strode, marches alla turca! How well Turkish pantaloons would suit her, a jacket, a veil!

The military two-step ended and spontaneous applause resounded throughout the room. Her partner, florid and perspiring, bowed and returned her to her table.

'We must dance again,' he said in English. She smiled and nodded graciously. The next dance was a polka and, to her chagrin, she saw Mr Osborne approach. He asked her to dance but she refused, claiming that she had twisted her ankle somewhat and would prefer to rest it. With ill grace he asked Florike, who, to Frances's surprise, accepted. William was sitting alone; his Danish friends had moved to a table where a cold buffet was displayed, and were eating rollmops. William's face was blotchy, his gaze unsteady and flickering, and he drank grog.

'She is fond of you, William,' Frances said, holding his hand.

'Well, yes. What it is to be young, eh!'

'I saw a young man once dive into the sea and swim strongly,'

Frances continued boldly, 'trying to save a desperate woman. You tried to save her. You were brave, foolhardy perhaps.'

He thrust out his lower jaw and grimaced. 'Silly Milly, yes. She never learned. Pa had the devil's own job getting rid of her. She clung like a limpet. Made Pa's life difficult. I tried to take her off his back, but it didn't work. Ma knew this, and behaved like a brick, but, well, you know…'

Emboldened by wine, by the exhilaration of dancing, she leaned forward.

'Was there anything between Millicent and your father?'

'Good Lord, no,' he sniggered, 'Pa likes women and has a good time, but would never do anything like that. She went after him.'

'And Stine?'

'Stine? That wretched piece of miserable flesh? Pa punished the perpetrator, sent him away.' He rose unsteadily to his feet. 'Must go outside. Don't feel too good. Think I must - ' He fled from the room.

What credence to give to these febrile utterances? She noticed that Herbert and Hyazinth were in deep conversation. Where were Beatrice and Charlotte? Suddenly there was a roll on the drum and a figure stepped into the middle of the floor. It was Mr Osborne who had perfunctorily taken Florike back to her chair and was now addressing the assembled company. He spoke in English and then, with remarkable facility, translated this as he went along into the local tongue.

'It is splendid,' he said, 'to be gathered together on this last night of the year, of the decade, and it is appropriate that all should enjoy friendship and conviviality. Let them revel elsewhere if they wish; only here in the Grünes Wasser do we know the true meaning of having fun! But there is one guest who is welcome above all, a guest who is about to make an appearance. This guest is no stranger but has only been able to come at the very last minute. The journey has been difficult, but where there is a will there is a way. The honoured guest was now waiting outside the door, ready to enter. Please fill your glasses and prepare to drink a toast. 'One, two, three!' he counted. The doors at the end of the hall were opened – and Russalka was carried into the room.

There was a moment's silence, then an explosion of laughter, a clinking of glasses and stamping of feet in approval. Frances gazed in amazement at the figurehead which, reclining in a boat carried by four strong young men, was now a fully fledged mermaid whose torso now merged from a moist, scaly tail of pale green silk, cunningly bifurcated at the end and draped in dried seaweed. The turquoise eyes gazed upwards; the wooden hair gleamed in the light, the cream arms were close to her sides. The lads carried her from table to table where there was much toasting, badinage, salutation. But the greatest paroxysm of mirth was caused when a young reveller, his napkin twisted round his neck to simulate clerical bands, jumped into the boat and lay beneath Russalka's breasts, his mouth encircling an emerald nipple, his hands pressed together in prayer, his eyes rolling heavenward in ecstatic devotion.

'Reverend Heywood!' went up the cry. Another lad sought to drink from the second nipple but was dragged from the boat by his dancing partner, a young woman; the boat rocked alarmingly. "Pastor Heywood" was also tipped onto the floor, and Russalka and her barque were carefully carried to the front of the hall and placed next to the band on an elevated table; here the boat was tipped at an angle and held with wedges so that the mermaid could gaze down at the revellers with her turquoise eyes and they could admire her loveliness. The band struck up another Schieber and the dancing continued.

Frances sat in silence, her thoughts in turmoil. Who had thought up this dreadful joke, bringing Timothy Heywood forcibly to mind? And was there truth, then, in the scurrilous rumours of the clergyman's hapless devotion to this figure of wood? A jest, only a jest, that was all. And she saw the pale young curate standing helplessly in Her Majesty's Theatre, disorientated, looking for her, hesitating, torn between taking his seat and waiting, waiting. Then the journey back to his mother in Finsbury Park, for he would never have seen *Tannhäuser* without her, this she knew. He would have written to Capewell House for news of what had happened. Would George and he join forces? George, she felt sure, would know what to do, know how to find her. Russalka, what have you done to me?

She was aware that Mr Osborne, flushed and excited, was sitting next to her, talking to William and Florike; the Danish gentlemen had now joined Herbert and Hyazinth.

'Wasn't it a wheeze!' he cried, drinking greedily. 'It was the very devil of a job getting her up those steps, I can tell you! We managed to detach her from the wall on Düne all right and row her across but then we had to hide somewhere and touch up the paintwork. Didn't mind doing that, though! We hid her in the Rathaus, much to old Strangy's annoyance, old Strangury I call him. Then we got a boat, no difficulty there, and put her into it. Miss Frostrup did the tail for us, then we were home and dry. Wasn't it a lark when that young nipper jumped in and had a suck!'

Florike turned away, and William smiled wanly, his trembling fingers holding a cigar to his lips.

'Was it your idea, then?' asked Frances, looking coldly at Mr Osborne.

'Well, in a way it was. But what started me thinking about it was when Sir Edward mentioned getting her over for some sort of masque he's thinking of, something with you in it as well, Miss Prince. It's a pity to waste her on the Düne, he said. But the rest of the idea was mine, so I got Peter Eliot to help me, and a couple of local lads. I didn't plan that whipper-snapper pretending to be the Reverend, though! Fancy a dance, Miss P?'

'No,' she said. And then she saw Ingeborg enter with Charlotte and Beatrice.

Ingeborg was indeed striking in a dress of pale green moiré silk; her arms were bare and her hair was loose, coiling downwards across her ivory shoulders. She smiled when she saw Russalka gazing down at the dancers, then looked serious and took Frances to one side.

'I am concerned about Beatrice,' she whispered, 'who is

deeply in love with Herbert and cannot understand his coolness towards her. I told you of his predilection for young men, but a young girl like Beatrice – or a young woman, I should now say – cannot grasp these things.'

'And Charlotte?'

'Charlotte is drawn to our young Uhlan but has a keen intellect and does not let her heart rule her head. Herbert has been – what do you say? – a cad. He has been playing with Beatrice, and this will break her heart. Let us join your table.'

Frances turned to Beatrice who had removed her cloak and bonnet and was looking around the room; Charlotte took her sister by the arm and followed Frances to the table where William and Florike were sitting. He gazed at his sisters uncertainly.

'Fancy seeing you here! Is Pa at an orgy somewhere? You've missed the fun – Ingeborg, I mean, Russalka, carried about in a boat! What does mermaid's milk taste of? Pa's rancid Pouilly-Fuissé I expect. Poowee Fweesay.'

He giggled nervously; Florike put her arm about him.

'Don't drink any more, William, please. At midnight one small toast, then we shall go back to Government House.'

'She's right,' said Charlotte, sipping her wine, 'don't let Pa see you like this. He'll be dropping in here sometime.'

'Why didn't Herbert come for us?' asked Beatrice, her skin puffy, her eyes lustrous, 'he promised to look in and wish us a happy New Year, but he's sitting over there with Hyazinth.'

'They're talking about something,' said Charlotte, 'they'll come over when they see us.'

'Let's go over now.'

'Let them come here,' her sister retorted, 'we don't want to give the impression that we can't live without them.'

'But supposing it's true?' Beatrice cried, 'I can't understand this, he seemed so attentive once, so loving.'

Frances got to her feet and walked around the floor where the Schieber had given way to a country dance which involved much stamping and waving of feet and hands; she beckoned to the Danish gentlemen who obligingly came across to her.

'There are two charming young ladies in need of diversion,' she explained, 'please show them how gallant you can be.'

'With pleasure.' They walked across to the two twin sisters and joined their table.

'Well,' Frances said to Herbert von Kroseck, 'may I sit?'

A strange look passed across his face, part arrogance, part resignation; the young lieutenant rose to his feet and fetched her a chair.

'At least there is one gentleman here,' she said, turning to Hyazinth von Keyserling. 'Are you staying long here, Herr Leutnant?'

He replied in a surprisingly mellifluous voice that he would be leaving in three days to rejoin his regiment. He blushed and played with an elegant skin-tight kid glove that lay on the table.

'Where is your regiment? I am a soldier's daughter and understand such things.'

'Tut tut,' interrupted Herbert, 'state secrets! Perhaps Miss Prince is a spy, working for her father in Berlin.'

'I see it now,' said Frances, looking at him. 'You played with Beatrice because you thought you might get access to Government House.'

'I hardly think Sir Edward is a man from whom one could learn anything of use,' came the reply, 'apart from seduction and irresponsibility.'

'You speak in very ungrateful terms of our – of your – Governor,' she retorted, scarcely able to conceal her agitation, 'you abuse his hospitality and give Beatrice reason to believe that you are fond of her.'

'I gave her no reason to assume anything. Besides, I'm sure that Ingeborg has told you that I have, shall we say, other interests.' He picked up the kid glove and inserted his fingers.

'Oh dear,' he grimaced, 'a bad fit. A little widening will be necessary, I think.'

He looked at Frances and slyly smiled. 'Very well, I shall talk to the maiden for a few minutes if you think it will make her evening. Then Hyazinth and I will leave this vulgar establishment and amuse ourselves elsewhere.'

He rose to his feet and sauntered across to William's table; Frances saw Beatrice look up, startled, then smile. He will destroy her, she thought, he will play with her, then cast her aside. No, Teddy was not like this. The avenging angel will become a supplicant, begging for mercy. She smiled at Hyazinth von Keyserling; the band had retired, and the Hardanger fiddles had returned. 'Let us waltz, Herr Leutnant.' And he took her onto the floor where they danced with great skill and aplomb. She noticed that Charlotte was dancing with Herre Helvsted, and Florike with Herre Brøvik; William, Beatrice and Herbert sat in silence.

Suddenly a ship's bell, hanging from the ceiling, was rung vigorously. Supper! Waiters and waitresses rushed in and advanced to the tables carrying oysters, lobsters, salmon and other delicacies; this was the last meal of the year, of the decade, and there was an hour to go until midnight. William ate very little, but demanded that the waitress bring him more wine despite Florike's attempts to dissuade him. He seized the waitress's arm who pushed him away contemptuously. Frances looked at her: it was Elke, Stine's half-sister, a pallid, resentful Doppelgänger.

'Elke,' she said, 'Elke, let me talk to you later.' The girl ignored her and hurried back to the kitchen.

'The lobster is excellent,' said Herre Helvsted, breaking open a claw with a dainty hammer.

'The best in Germany,' said Herbert, who had approached, 'or do I mean Great Britain?'

'The island was once ours,' said Herre Brøvik, 'but we transgressed, and Nelson bombarded Copenhagen.'

'But an island so close to Germany should be German, don't you think, Miss Hennicker-Heaton?' asked Herbert, staring at Beatrice.

'I don't know. I don't care,' she murmured, twisting a handkerchief.

'But your mother is German, is she not? You must feel some affinity with the aspirations of modern Germany?'

'I couldn't care,' she whispered, 'I'm not interested in politics. I leave that to Charlie.'

He is deliberately tormenting her, thought Frances, he knows she cares nothing about such things, knows all she wants to do is fall into his arms. But he despises her, despises us. She glimpsed Russalka, and the image of Ingeborg Frostrup passed through her mind.

'Where is Ingeborg?' she asked. Nobody had seen her.

'I expect the Governor has invited her to a private function,' said Herbert, looking at her, 'an exclusive tête-à-tête, to see the old year out, the new year in.'

'Well done, Pa, well done Pa!' crowed William; it was Charlotte who took him by the hand.

'Come on, Willy, it'll soon be time to go.'

'I don't think,' said Herbert, 'that Master Hennicker-Heaton is able to go anywhere.' He turned to Hyazinth. 'Like father, like son…' he murmured, but Frances had overheard him. Her senses, despite the wine she had been drinking, were alert, and she was determined to strike back.

'How is your sister?' she parried, 'I am sorry that she was unable to join in the games, despite being Queen of the Revels. Is she often hysterical?'

'The English sense of humour bewildered her,' he replied, 'and our Governor should make the treads on his flight of stairs more shallow. Goethe did this in Weimar. We Germans have an understanding of such things.'

The dishes were cleared away with great speed, lest the time before midnight be wasted; Frances saw Elke, but the girl avoided her. Was Stine alone, sitting in her gloomy hovel whilst they sat here? She drank a glass of Hollands geneva that William had ordered for her; he lay dozing, his head lolling back in his chair. Hyazinth had invited Charlotte to dance, and they moved energetically across the floor in a polka.

A strange young woman, thought Frances, intense, intelligent, mature beyond her years. But her lieutenant? Is he in thrall to Herbert? She saw Beatrice gazing at Herbert, her eyes filling with tears, her lips tremulous; the naval officer, however, had procured a pack of cards and ostentatiously avoided looking at her.

No, he is an Urning, she thought, a man who captivated me when I first met him, who seemed to be solicitous and charming. But there is ruthlessness in him, also perversion.

What is sodomy? An unnatural act of sexual intercourse, of one male with another, George had told her this. George, was he coming now, with her father, to rescue her? From what? Was she in thrall to a man, a man old enough to be her father, a man who had taken liberties, had seized her waist, unfastened her negligé, kissed her on the mouth? To a man who had loved her mother? To a man who was frivolous, irresponsible, yet loveable, humorous, life-enhancing? Did he love her? Hardly, for he brought a moving tribute to his wife, displayed it, performed it. The music of the one who had composed it for his wife on Christmas Day. Yes, I was in thrall to him. And this brought death. He told his wife that he had invited me to the Palazzo Vendramin-Callergi, and the servants later told me of the dreadful scene. The hand of death crushed his heart that February afternoon in Venice.

It seemed as though the room had become oppressively hot; the stench of sweat, alcohol and cigar smoke overwhelmed her. She gazed at Herbert and Beatrice, at William and Florike; she saw that a wag had thrust a pipe between Russalka's lips and that a sailor's cap had been jammed on her head. The dancing stopped, and bottles of champagne were brought to the tables for the stroke of midnight. Piles of plates, she noticed, were stacked for the Pottensmitter-In, the breaking of crockery to celebrate the arrival of the Wenskerdai, the beginning of the year. All eyes turned to the large ship's clock in its brass casing which adorned the far wall; it was shortly before twelve.

Then, suddenly, she heard a flourish on the trumpet – Teddy entered with Ingeborg to a burst of applause. He was wreathed in smiles and walked towards Russalka where, in much mock disapprobation, he removed the accoutrements and, to screams of delight, he lovingly encircled her wooden breasts, winking over his shoulder. He then turned to face his audience and rubbed his hands.

'Well,' he cried, 'I told you I'd be here! No better place to be for the Ooldjooars-In! Champagne!'

He moved with alacrity through the hall, shaking hands, kissing cheeks, patting backs, laughing, jesting. Was he timing it, she wondered, to come to me on the stroke of midnight? The countdown began, with increasing volume: Teien, negen, acht, söben, sös, fiev, schtjuur, tree, tau, iaan! – and he was standing before her, placing his hands on her shoulders. De klok slààt twalw! An uproar deafened her, a chaos of smashing crockery, shouting, popping champagne corks, fanfares, squibs, fire-crackers.

'Well, Fan,' he smiled, 'Happy New Year!' And he kissed her mouth, and put his arms around her. She pulled her lips from his, and swooned against him.

'Teddy, Teddy.' He gently lifted her face towards his, and kissed her again.

* * *

What would she remember of that night, a night that ended in such horror? She knew above all of Teddy's kiss, her weakness at the knees, her pounding heart, a kiss yielding yet firm, with parted lips. His breath was not redolent of the warm sea wind, rather of tobacco and brandy, but what of it? She had scarcely been aware of the revellers around her, and longed only for him, but her hand had been seized, she remembered, by Rasmussen who dragged her into the chain dance, pulling her out into the night air where a large circle of dancers held hands and ran, skipped, hopped, turned. Fires had been lit outside, and the sandstone cliffs threw back dull ruddiness; fireworks fizzed around her, Catherine wheels spinning and frothing while rockets burst overhead.

A great fire had been lit on the Düne, now bereft, she thought, bereft – but where was Teddy? She saw him in another chain, dancing down the Leuchtturmstrasse; a loud booming came from the sea below as the Prinz Eitel-Friedrich sounded its sirens in full blast. Her chain danced and snaked its way along the Falm, where it was met by revellers from the Stadt London and the Princess

Alexandra; fireworks roared up from the Conversationshaus below. The Hardanger fiddlers followed, playing like men possessed. The chains had broken and the musicians were joined by clarinets; dance melodies now resounded beneath the oil lamp hanging at the top of the steps. 'Play "Papen van Istrup!"' shouted Jörg, who towered head and shoulders above the rest; he seized Elke, Frances noticed, and lifted her high in the air; another figure (Henk, was it?) glowered in the darkness. She was seized in turn by the young lad who had enjoyed Russalka's mammary nourishment and, despite her breathless, laughing insistence that she did not know the dance, she was swung, twisted and spun in elaborate configurations. She thanked the young man when the dance was ended and leaned back against the wall, flushed and out of breath, longing for Teddy.

She saw the lights of the Stadt London and a crowd of people standing at the door; a gentleman she did not recognise beckoned her; she approached and saw that it was the owner, Mr Russell.

'Happy New Year, Miss Prince! Enjoying the country dancing?' He was talking to Mr Eliot, who smiled when he saw her.

'Do come and join us, Miss Prince! We're doing quadrilles in here, not quite as energetic as what you're doing but fun nevertheless!'

She did not relish his company but reminded herself that it was he who had devised 'Nelson's Eye', a game which had caused much distress to the foolish Franziska. And perhaps she would find Teddy here? She returned his smile and went in to the hotel; the dining room had been cleared and groups of ladies and gentlemen were performing cotillons: a lady danced between two gentlemen who held her left and right hands with theirs, their free arms reaching overhead to form an arch for her to dance under.

'A drink on the house, Miss Prince!' cried Mr Russell, offering her champagne. 'You've been in the Grünes Wasser I hear! Quite lively there, I'm sure. What's happening in the Conversationshaus tonight, then?'

She shook her head and shrugged her shoulders, smiling; she looked at the dancers but Teddy was not there.

'I wondered if you'd seen Sir Edward?' she asked.

'Oh, he's doing his rounds, I expect. Droit de seigneur, you know!'

'I'm sorry?'

'He likes his bit of fun. His wife lets him get on with it. That son of his ain't too bright, is he? Too much of this, I expect.' He jerked his right hand upwards towards his mouth, repeatedly. Frances found his vulgarity distasteful.

'We thought you'd gone back home for good, Miss Prince, after you know what. The boss sent you back, did he? He has his fling, as they say. Unrestrained indulgence the gentry calls it.' And he winked at her.

She turned away in disgust; Mr Eliot approached.

'Do join the quadrilles, Miss Prince! We need another man. I think Mr Strang's here somewhere. I'm sure you can dance like Terpsichore herself!'

'You are very kind,' she replied, 'but I'm being very rude, I'm neglecting my party. My dress is not appropriate and my shoes are damp and muddy.'

'Well,' he sighed, 'I shall have to seek another. The Danish mermaid, not the English rose.'

'Do you mean Miss Frostrup?'

'Yes, look, she's sitting over there.' He pointed to Ingeborg and an elderly man sitting smoking and drinking by a container of potted palms; Frances, her mood compounded of exhilaration, annoyance at Mr Russell's innuendoes, desire for Teddy and curiosity to learn of Ingeborg's activities, joined them.

* * *

'Miss Prince! How delightful! Glædeligt Nytår! Do join us! May I introduce my husband, Herre Julius Bregendahl. I see you are surprised! But we emancipated women also have our weaknesses.'

Herre Bregendahl was stout and bald with grey whiskers; he kissed Frances's hand gallantly and bade her sit with them.

Frances sat and drank the proffered champagne as though she were in a dream. Ingeborg Frostrup married! Had there ever, then, been any amorous relationship between her and Teddy, as she had suspected? Had this predated Ingeborg's marriage? Herre Bregendahl was much older and made the impression of unimpeachable respectability. Was Miss Prince also an artist? he enquired. No, no, she was entirely ignorant of painting. But she greatly esteemed Miss Frostrup's – his wife's – work. His wife had exhibited in the new Art Gallery in Copenhagen he asserted proudly.

'What do you think of my portraits of the twins?' Ingeborg asked quizzically, screwing up her eyes against the cigar smoke.

'I found them impressive,' Frances said.

'They were poor,' retorted Ingeborg, flicking cigar ash onto the floor. 'I did them simply for Teddy. I shall do nothing more in that line. I am soon to move to Berlin in the footsteps of a young Norwegian, Edvard Munch, who has exhibited remarkable work in Oslo.'

'Berlin,' said Herre Bregendahl, 'would soon become the most important city in Europe, even the world. I am a businessman and am amazed at Prussian energy and inventiveness. The Germans will soon overtake us all. I am also a collector, and encourage my wife in her work.'

'Miss Prince is a singer,' said Ingeborg, 'she has sung in Bayreuth.' Herre Bregendahl congratulated her.

'Wagner is a genius', he exclaimed, drinking champagne and demanding more. 'A Nordic spirit is abroad, the Latin races have had their day. Paris is meaningless, a meretricious excrescence. I greatly admire Axel Gallén's illustrations to the Kalevala. Do you know Grieg's articles on Wagner and the eighteen seventy-six festival in the Bergen Post?'

Frances admitted she did not, and longed to return to her quest for Teddy.

'Have you seen our Governor?' she asked Ingeborg, 'I was in the Grünes Wasser and saw you both come in.'

'My husband wished to pay his respects to Lady Augusta,'

explained Ingeborg, 'so we spent two hours in Government House. Then I knew where you would be and suggested that Teddy seek you there. Then, at midnight, I met Julius here.'

A feeling of irrational joy surged through Frances, joy in the memory of Teddy's kiss and also in the conviction that Ingeborg was not a rival, that she owed allegiance to her husband and her art. A dalliance, perhaps. But she, Frances, was stronger, was free. She was aware that she had drunk a considerable amount of champagne on top of Hollands geneva.

'I wish you well, Ingeborg,' she said, rising unsteadily.

'Might I accompany you?' Herre Bregendahl enquired.

'No, no, I'll just step outside, the night air will do me good.'

Ingeborg rose and kissed her. 'Be happy,' she murmured, 'and take care of Beatrice. I must now dance a cotillon.'

Frances crossed the dance floor, avoiding the four couples dancing a quadrille; she evaded the lubricious leer of Mr Russell and stepped out into the acrid smoke of fire-crackers and Roman candles that were turning the night into phantasmagoria.

* * *

Was she inebriate? It seemed as though she were walking high above the ground, that people were at a great distance from her. She turned in the direction of the Grünes Wasser; the steamer sounded its siren down below; figures carrying sparklers ran before her, then went bobbing down the steps to the Unterland. The night crackled and fizzed, boomed and split. Suddenly a cart careered towards her; Russalka rode high upon it, her boat having been lifted on to it; her scooping breasts were garishly illuminated by phosphorous, her backward-thrusting arms were livid, her wooden hair ghastly in the light. Russalka, Russalka! Several young men were pushing the cart, were slipping, slithering, staggering, laughing; Frances stepped back to avoid the wild stampede.

'Ik ben ferleeft!' screamed one of the revellers, 'I am in love!' He sprang onto the cart to violate the mermaid; two of the lads stumbled, the others lost control and the cart with its ill-matched couple rolled towards the steps. It struck the base of the wrought-iron arch and threw the amorous young man free, but then bounced jerkily down the steps, gathering momentum; horrified, Frances saw it careen against the railings of the vantage point halfway down, tip and send both boat and figurehead hurtling over the railings down through the darkness. She heard them land at the foot of the steps on the Marcusplatz, scattering the terrified dancers who were performing a chain dance below.

A crowd had run out of the Grünes Wasser after the cart, and there was a great shout of laugher at the top of the steps and down below. Frances forced her way into the dancehall to seek Teddy and tell him what had happened. The word 'masque' floated in her febrile mind, a masque is being planned, but she lies shattered and I am ready. The fair toxophilite, was it? Diana and the hunt? What revels do you plan, my Lord?

He was overjoyed when I danced and sang for him, on my breast he pinned the star, not on Fräulein Lorenz. And Venus I shall sing for him, not Madame Valleria, who is as ugly, chaste and cold as Elizabeth. Frances was buffeted by a crowd of sailors and entered the dance floor where couples surged past her in an energetic polka. But where is my Master? 'The master plucked us in springtime', ah, yes. But it is winter now, is it not? New Year's Eve is upon us.

She was suddenly aware of a young woman seizing her arm; it was Charlotte.

'Miss Prince, thank God you've come. There's been a dreadful scene: Beatrice flew at Captain von Kroseck and said some terrible things; William woke up and tried to intervene, but Captain von Kroseck struck him. He's left with Hyazinth. Fool that I was, I should have realised.'

'Realised?'

'That Captain von Kroseck is obsessed with Hyazinth. I had thought – well, it doesn't matter now.'

Charlotte was flushed; her birthmark was a dark mulberry claret on the left side of her throat.

'Where is she?' asked Frances, suddenly alert and attentive.

'In a small room off the corridor – we're in there.'

The two made their way through the couples, passed the trilling, shrieking clarinets, the jingling johnny, the trumpets and the fiddles and pushed open a narrow door, closing it rapidly to shut out the stamping, raucous din. Frances went across to Beatrice, who was sobbing uncontrollably, her hair dishevelled, her face ugly in its grief, her cheeks streaked with tears; William sat on a shabby sofa, with Florike's left arm around him; he was smoking in great agitation. His right cheek was bruised, his bottom lip was split and puffy.

'Another tooth gone,' he whispered, 'soon be the last of the Mohicans, eh, Florry?'

Florike gazed at Frances.

'He was brave. He tried to defend his sister's honour. The German was a brute.'

'Where are your Danish friends?' Frances asked, 'didn't they come to your assistance?'

'Gone. Done a bunk. "Excuse me, please tell me the way to the railway station?" But there ain't no bloody railway station here, chaps! You'll have to wait for the steamer, the Dampskib! Damp squib, yes, that's me! *Multatuli*, Florry, *Multatuli*!'

Beatrice stood up and hugged Frances, burying her face in her breast.

'Miss Prince, oh Miss Prince! I loved him so! He was so kind! But then, what did I do? It was Ingeborg, I thought, Ingeborg who wanted him. But no, it was all so awful, so furtive, so – unnatural. Why did he pretend it was me he wanted?'

Frances smoothed her hair and kissed her.

'He wanted information,' said Charlotte, 'he curried favour with us. He's some sort of spy. He knew that Pa was careless and thought he might learn something.'

'But what?'

'I don't know. But I should have been more vigilant. I fell for the charms of a young lieutenant who, well, fell under the spell of another.'

'But another man!' sobbed Beatrice, 'do they kiss? It's so awful.'

His sister had rank breath, thought Frances, and became hysterical, and fell down the stairs.

'Come,' she said, 'we must find your father.'

'Perhaps we should go back to Government House,' said Florike, 'and wait for him there.'

'No, we'll find Sir Edward first and tell him what has happened.'

'I think you're right,' said Charlotte, 'we don't want to wait until dawn and find out that some garbled report has made things worse. He should be told that a German naval officer has behaved disgracefully and should be banished from the island.'

'I should tell him, too,' said Frances, 'about Russalka.'

'But where is Pa?' asked Beatrice, wiping her tears away.

'I've just come from the Stadt London and he's not there,' Frances explained, 'unless I've just missed him.'

'He'll be in the Princess Alexandra,' said Charlotte, 'he always starts in the Stadt London, comes here about midnight, then moves across to the Princess Alexandra, ending up at the Conversationshaus.'

Always, thought Frances, always...? It was not me he wanted to see at midnight, then. With heavy heart she assisted Florike in helping William stand, and the five moved silently to the door.

* * *

They walked across this sliver of rock surrounded by inky darkness, a darkness pricked out by the lights of solitary ships and interrupted by a pulsing beam, a darkness smudged by lurid green and phosphorescent white, by crimson pyrotechnic display; the sea rolled restlessly, reflecting, swallowing. Fragments of sound blew upwards, glass shattered, voices beat against a rising wind. They moved through faces garishly illuminated by fire and fireworks, through flailing hands and tossing hair, to the Princess Alexandra, a sedate establishment outside which a burly figure stood to discourage undesirables; he saluted when he saw the Governor's children and their companions.

They entered, and Frances vividly recalled meeting Florike here, and William brandishing *Persephone*. She was light-headed, buoyed up by wine, by ardent spirits, longing to see, yet fearing to encounter. A pomegranate, she thought, I have eaten a seed of pomegranate and the Lord of Hades has me in thrall. But my father will persuade him to release me.

She looked in the ballroom and saw him; he was dancing a polonaise with a middle-aged lady she half recognised: was it one of the Misses Payne? The dance was elaborate, an intricate march in triple time, a procession, a promenade of couples. It ended, and there was polite applause and the orchestra bowed. He escorted his partner to her chair and looked around the room; he saw her and came towards her.

'Well, Fanny, what happened to you? I saw Rasmussen bear you off into the night and feared the worst! He pulled you from the water once, I thought, and now demands his tribute! My Heligolanders certainly know how to celebrate, you must give them that. There won't be much work done tomorrow with all those sore heads and aching limbs! Or do I mean today? What time is it?'

'Nearly three,' she replied. The orchestra struck up a popular waltz.

'Dance with me, please,' he said, 'they'll be doing a Halling in the Grünes Wasser, you know, kicking the rafters and doing somersaults in the air, but I'm not up to that at my age!'

'I hoped you'd come to look for me there at midnight,' she murmured, 'but I'm sure it's your annual ritual.'

'You're angry with me,' he said, taking her hand.

'I must tell you what's happened,' she replied.

'Later.'

'No, now. Beatrice has had a bad time with Herbert von Kroseck, who argued with William and struck him. She's very unhappy, I think you should take her home.'

'Charlie can look after her, and William has his Dutch beauty. Please, Fanny, dance with me.'

'There's been an accident with Russalka, who ended up at the bottom of the steps.'

He laughed out loud. 'Tim Heywood can restore her loveliness, we'll get her back home in one piece. Ah, love's artillery! Close couched in your white bosom! Perhaps she's a danger to the morals of our young fisherfolk. I'll hand her over to the Russian ambassador when next I see him in London. But not before I'm finished with her! I have plans! Please, Miss Prince, do me the honour.'

'I have eaten the pomegranate,' she said. He put his finger on her lips.

'Ssh. Let's dance.'

She felt no tiredness, felt as though she were a disembodied spirit, saw crystal chandeliers, mirrors, musicians, dancers revolve around her and his face, his face smiling at her. Her hair tumbled about her shoulders; she tossed her head, feeling the weight of Mariana's tresses. But there was no weariness, her limbs were free, there was felicity, movement, circumfluence. His thighs were pressed close to hers; he held her tight against him; her breast was against his chest, her golden chain. They waltzed, reversed, waltzed; their feet wove interlocking patterns.

One claimed that he was the best dancer in Saxony, I have his waltz, his hair. The other dances with me now, he has my chain upon his breast. Waltz, rock, reverse, rock, waltz. My London Waltz, my gift from Euphemia, crystals, mirrors, skirts, waistcoats revolving around me, his hair in my locket, his arm round my waist, I danced as a flower, he praised me, applauded, he gave me the medal, he kissed me at midnight, waltz, reverse, waltz.

'Dreamer!' he whispered, 'come back to this planet!' And then the waltz stopped.

There was polite, muffled applause. There would now be a break.

'Let's eat ice,' he said, 'it's excellent here. Ice and maraschino cherries, irresistible!'

She saw, as through a skin of water, Charlotte in deep conversation with her sister and Florike sitting with William: what had she to do with them? She saw Teddy summon a waiter and order the ice and liqueur; he also turned to a tall, dark man with a heavy moustache.

'Fanny, this is Mr Taylor, an excellent photographer. How about a fine photograph to commemorate the new decade? You've got your Ensign studio camera in the corner, I can see it, Harry.'

Mr Taylor bowed to Frances.

'I've taken some earlier this evening but people don't want one at this time in the morning – too tired I expect!'

'Let's have one,' said Teddy, impetuously, 'Frances, me, Willy, Florike and the girls.'

'Or you and me, Teddy. Is it wise to take the group?'

'We'll have the group first.'

'I'll have to tidy my hair, it is loose and disordered.'

'Your beauty,' he smiled, 'is unimpaired! I want a wild woman at my side!'

He led her across to where the others were sitting.

'Harry wants to photograph us,' he cried, 'away we go.'

'We're too crumpled,' said Charlotte, 'and Beatrice is tired.'

'Might be fun,' drawled William hoarsely, 'a dangling fag can conceal my battered lip. The exhausted courtesans with Nero and his catamite. Oops, no ciggies in Rome!'

'No,' begged Florike, 'we are not well.'

'Oh, come on,' said Teddy, moving across to a long chesterfield, 'you can sit here, the four of you, and Fanny and I will stand behind. Your Governor insists.'

'Pa, please,' whispered Beatrice, 'I am not up to this.'

'What? Can you not watch with me for one hour? O ye of little faith!'

Mr Taylor was standing behind his Ensign camera; it rested upon a substantial adjustable tripod. The four sat upon the chesterfield, the women distraught and ill at ease, William simpering.

'I faithfully promise,' said Teddy, 'that if we do look awful I'll get Harry to smash the plates. I would not wish to bestow a photograph of ravaged debauchees to posterity!'

Mr Taylor looked under his black cape, took a slide from his box and inserted it. Frances saw his hand move towards the rubber ball and waited for the familiar exhortation to watch the birdie and then the flash – but it was not the explosion of magnesium which transfigured the room. There was a sudden uproar at the door, commotion, disturbance, shouting; she saw with great clarity a man in a heavy coat run across the floor, his face covered by a black wide-awake. He drew two pistols from his pockets, and the flat detonations cracked and reverberated around her as Florike's head burst into blood, Charlotte jerked back screaming and Teddy, the blood pumping from his neck, fell across her with a ghastly smile.

* * *

CHAPTER SEVEN

Tetchy and irritable, George waited until the last bell had been rung and the foyer emptied. He sought an usher: had he not seen a tall, attractive young woman with dark hair about to enter a box? Had any message been left? The usher was sorry: there had been no message and the box in question was empty; he also begged the gentleman's pardon as the music was about to begin and he must close the doors. That gentleman in the corner had also been making enquiries; George looked and saw a pale, round-shouldered man frowning and obviously ill at ease.

'Reverend Heywood?' asked George, moving rapidly towards him, 'have you seen my cousin?' The Reverend Heywood introduced himself in great agitation: no, he had not seen her and had been waiting over half an hour. The muffled strains of the Pilgrims' Chorus reached them; George impetuously thrust his card into the clergyman's hand.

'There may have been an accident. You wait here a bit longer, and let me know if she turns up.' He hurriedly took his top hat and cloak from the cloakroom and hailed a cab for Eaton Square.

The night was restless, he was tormented by irrational fears. Had she been robbed? abducted? murdered? He had visions of his cousin gagged and bound in an opium den in Limehouse whilst furtive Chinese coolies sought her extradition hellwards to Shanghai. The following morning, Sunday, he informed the police that his cousin had not appeared the previous evening and that he was concerned. The rest of the day was spent wandering under a slate-grey sky, kicking the dead leaves that remained in Regent's Park and drinking porter as he listened to the chimes of the Swiss clock in his Eaton Square drawing room. In the evening he played Patience and retired early. Frances, where are you? His affection for her had deepened to something which, he felt, must be love; her dark hair, winning smile and generous figure hovered before him. I love you, Fan, he said out loud. Don't talk guano, George, he replied.

On the following morning he decided to absent himself from his office and take an extended Christmas and New Year holiday. The police reported nothing. He caught a train to Salisbury and, at Codbury St Mary, made enquiries. The clerk in the ticket office haughtily explained that he could not be expected to remember every young woman who had bought a ticket to London, but suggested that a recent photo be displayed which might jog the memory of passengers. The police had also suggested a similar ruse, that a photograph be hung in Her Majesty's Theatre. He arrived at Capewell House in the middle of the afternoon and informed an alarmed Mrs Lovell what had happened. Perhaps she had been knocked down and was lying in hospital? The police had no information, he explained, and walked with Mops in the gathering dusk.

That evening Mrs Lovell suggested that Dympna might know of a possible friend with whom Frances was inexplicably staying. Dympna the cripple? It was a long shot, Mrs Lovell agreed, but worth trying. They also looked at photographs to select the best to display at the station and the theatre. There was Frances in a group of young maidens in diaphanous draperies, looking amorous; Frances looking stern as the Valkyrie Sieba; Frances wearing a mantilla and looking seductively over a fan: this intrigued him.

'She looks too Spanish', said Mrs Lovell sagaciously. He finally chose one of her in profile, her hair twisted on top of her head, with one curl curved above her right cheek; she was wearing a choker or scarf tied high across her throat, decorated with arabesques twining on a light material; her dark blouse had high puffed sleeves. She looks very lovely, he thought, but reprimanded himself for talking guano. This photograph was to be displayed at the station and a similar one, with shoulders bare, would adorn the foyer of Her Majesty's Theatre.

He had never seen Dympna and shied away from making her acquaintance, having an instinctive reluctance to see deformity. The day was damp, ashen; he took the dogcart and approached the house with trepidation, fearing the prospect of taking tea with an ailing widow living in bleak viduity with a crippled, lachrymose daughter. Mrs Vernon, astonished, led him through the dark hall to a small parlour where Dympna sat embroidering by the window. He explained who he was and the reason for his visit. He was very concerned about his cousin, Miss Frances Prince, who had disappeared on Saturday night. He believed that Dympna and Frances had recently met: had his cousin seemed distraught in any way? Dympna, disturbed, took her steel spectacles from her nose; he heard the clattering of crockery as Mrs Vernon made tea, and wheezing expectoration upstairs.

Miss Prince had been charming, Dympna said, and they had had a delightful afternoon. Had she given the impression that she was concealing something, or planning something? Not at all, she had been open and frank, there had been nothing duplicitous in her manner. They had had lunch and Miss Prince had graciously talked to her grandfather before leaving. Mrs Vernon entered with madeira and slab cake; a tinny clock chimed three. Perhaps Miss Prince had been suddenly taken ill and was resting with friends in London? I am her only friend in London, retorted George sharply, and she would have come to my house in Eaton Square. There is, said Dympna shyly, another friend in London, a Sophie Langton-Durham, now Lady Berners. The three of them had been in school together, explained Mrs Vernon, where I had been a teacher, but Miss Sophie had been far too hoity-toity and had wanted nothing to do with the likes of us. Dympna felt sure that Frances had no contact with Sophie. George stayed until four, then fled into the wintry dusk, reassuring Mrs and Miss Vernon that he would keep them informed of any developments.

The following day was passed in emptiness, frustration, annoyance; Mops was cowed, sensing that all was not well; George went up to Frances's bedroom, standing staring at her underwear and running his fingers through her dresses, inhaling a faint odour of stale frangipane. He drank much heavy wine and brandy, sensing but ignoring Mrs Lovell's disapproval.

Where was she? Perhaps Heywood had raped her, dismembered her. The thought of Jack the Ripper crossed his mind, to be queasily expunged. The afternoon post brought a letter from the clergyman, whose distress was plain to see in the overwrought prose. He had waited long, but to no avail; he had made enquiries, which were fruitless. He had prayed long and fervently, he explained, for Miss Prince to return to them safely, a young woman of beauty and talent whom he esteemed highly. George threw the letter aside and stared gloomily at the Christmas tree which Mrs Lovell had lovingly decorated. Carol singers from the village were brusquely dispatched with a few pennies. He slept little and rose at dawn; a dark mist hung in the blackness and cocooned him in shrouds of sullen despair.

After breakfast, however, a fly drew up outside the house and two figures emerged, a young man and an elderly woman. They were admitted: the young man explained that he was bringing his aunt, a Miss Crampton, who had seen the photograph of Mr Havelock's cousin at Codbury St Mary railway station. Miss Crampton, an alert woman in her early seventies, confirmed that she had travelled up to London with Miss Prince on Saturday December the eighteenth; she distinctly remembered having shared a carriage with the young woman and that they had discussed the voluminous dresses of Miss Crampton's youth, referring to Augustus Egg's 'The Travelling Companions'; the young lady had astutely commented that they, alas, could not see Menton from their carriage window. Augustus Egg, explained Miss Crampton, had gone to Menton for his asthma. George thanked the lady and her nephew profusely and offered a twenty guinea reward for information; this was laughingly refused, and he waved as he watched them drive away.

He was stirred into action: he would go up to town and seek out Lady Berners. He was clutching at straws, he knew, but Miss Crampton's visit had invigorated him. He caught an early train from Salisbury and went first to Her Majesty's Theatre where his cousin's photograph smiled at him; alas, there had been no information. He enquired at the nearest police station if they were able to give him Lord Berners' London address as this might have a bearing on the disappearance; he took a cab to Regent Street and rang the bell at an imposing residence. A maid showed him into a room decorated tastefully with holly and ivy. Lady Berners saw him and enquired, coolly, whether she could be of assistance. He explained, but she replied quite firmly that she had not seen Miss Prince since they were schoolgirls. She expressed surprise at her disappearance, but felt sure that Miss Prince would soon return. Her sang-froid displeased him and he left downhearted; he walked through festive streets, past costermongers, hawkers, barrel organs.

He would give it till Boxing Day and if there were no developments he would, if necessary, go to Berlin and seek out his uncle to tell him what had happened. He spent the night in Eaton Square and went to bed disgruntled and apprehensive; an excess of claret and whisky brought a pounding head towards dawn, dehydration and a sense of futility. He breakfasted on porter and mutton in his favourite chop-house and followed the crowds doing their late Christmas shopping, for it was Christmas Eve.

Should he try once more at Her Majesty's? He entered, despondent, but was welcomed by an excited manager who explained that a young woman wanted to see him. Her name was Alice Stokes, she was a flower-seller and was waiting in his office. She was interested in claiming the generous twenty guinea reward. George met a neat person in a red shawl and black straw bonnet: she distinctly remembered seeing the lady like the one on the photograph who had rushed past her a week ago at about seven in the evening, just as the show was about to start, and had hailed a cab. Did she know the cab driver? Yes, and his horse and cart were out there now. George thanked her and spoke to the cabby who remembered his fare: she had wanted to go to Regent Street. The flower-girl, amazed, received five gold sovereigns, George's card and the promise of the rest of the money later; the cabby, when he deposited the gentleman at the Regent Street address, was delighted with a most generous tip. He rang the doorbell forcefully, determined to get to the bottom of the matter: had Lady Berners deliberately misled him? Was she involved in some nefarious practices? He rang the bell again and again, but there was no reply; the windows were curtained, the house was silent.

He returned to Eaton Square deflated and bitterly disappointed at meeting this blank wall, yet also somehow convinced that the trail was leading to her. Fanny, Fanny, I love you. Guano, George, guano. A bread roll thrown at him, deftly caught. Halma, a bent head, a wisp of hair pushed back behind the ears. Her Neptun cigarettes, smoked defiantly in spite of Mrs Lovell's strictures. Her corsets and drawers, discreetly carried by the latter to be washed in the boiler down in the cellar. Where are you, why have you fled from us?

He walked to mass at St Stephen's, returned to an empty house. On Christmas Day he dozed, smoked, and thumbed through his collection of Alexander Gibson's shipwreck plates. London slept in gross somnolence, induced, he thought, by over-indulgence; I read of the Stirling Castle and fear that something dreadful has befallen a lovely woman. Did she fall in the river? Is her body now stuck in the squelching mud of the Thames estuary? Stop this, stop.

He walked through deserted streets, caught glimpses of Christmas cheer as he looked through windows. It had grown colder; the sky was ashen grey. He dined at his club, The Travellers, which was well attended and caught up with his reading of The Times. What are you doing, Fan? I shall find you. He was glad when darkness began to fall and made his way slowly back to Eaton Square. His feet were swollen and tired with the miles he had walked. At home, beneath the flaring gas fishtail, he thought of his life with her and of what his life with her could be. They were both unattached, his uncle was fond of him, he had an adequate competency. He thought, guiltily, of her nakedness, glimpsed once or twice. They could live in Capewell House with Mrs Lovell as housekeeper. A horse clip-clopped in the Square; the gas hissed. His loneliest Christmas Day came and went.

On Boxing Day he felt driven again, out of despair, to the Regent Street residence. He rang the bell and, surprisingly, a maid appeared who immediately called the butler. What was the gentleman's business? He wished to speak to Lady Berners. Lord and Lady Berners left shortly before Christmas to spend the winter in Lausanne, as was their wont. Might he ask what the gentleman wanted of Lady Berners? The gentleman wanted to ask Lady Berners what had happened to his cousin who had called a week ago. There seemed to be a misunderstanding. The matter was grave and the police were involved.

'Yes,' blurted out the maid, 'a lady did call here a week ago in a very upset state.'

The butler bade her be silent. George gave him his card and the butler led him into the house. Kitty was right, he said, a lady did arrive. And where was she now? The maid remembered talk of foreign parts, Germany she thought, Hamburg maybe. The butler confirmed that luggage had been taken to Tilbury for shipment. George, normally a phlegmatic man, was overjoyed. Hamburg? Yes. Was the visitor tall, dark and attractive? The butler winked. George pressed a golden sovereign into the hand of each and, imploring them to keep his visit a secret, ran from the house.

The following day was a frenzy of activity; a letter to Capewell House informing Mrs Lovell of the developments; enquiries as to the address of the British consul in Hamburg who might know of her whereabouts and who could certainly seek to contact Colonel John Prince in Berlin. The British consul was telegraphed by a secretary in the Foreign Office whom George had once advised on an insurance matter and the reply, when it came, confirmed that a Miss Frances Prince had recently arrived and had been met by Mr Percy Tyrwhitt-Jones who had stood in for the Honourable Charles Dundas. Miss Prince had spent a night in the Hamburger Hof and had left for Heligoland the following day.

Heligoland! Fool that he was, why had he not thought of this! He enquired after Colonel John Prince but was informed that the colonel was on a delicate matter and that no information as to his whereabouts could be given. No matter! Fanny, I love you!

He returned to Eaton Square, put his house in order and drew a large sum of money from his bank; he ate a heavy meal in his club. He imagined stepping before her and taking her in his arms; Heligoland, he imagined, was something like the Isle of Lewis which he had visited as a boy. He drank too much and slept fitfully: he was playing cricket on the Dogger Bank and Frances was bowling; the ball was a bread roll which he clouted straight at her, but she swallowed it, laughing. Next day he went to a Turkish bath and luxuriated in the hot, heavy steam. Regent's Park Zoo in the afternoon, then the evening steamer to Hamburg.

* * *

The hotel Hamburger Hof, on the Jungfernstieg, overlooking the Alster-Bassin, was a large edifice in the Renaissance style boasting elevators, baths and electric light. George alighted from his droshky; the water was steely grey beneath the morning sky. He rested in his spacious room and checked on the times of sailings to Heligoland; dinner, he noticed to his slight annoyance, would be served at five in the evening. He walked around the Binnen-Alster, thinking of Frances and wondering if he could get across to celebrate New Year with her. There was one sailing on the following afternoon, the thirty-first of December, and after that sailings would recommence on January the third.

He walked to the British consulate on the Hohe Bleichen; the office was, however, closed. No matter. Back in the Hamburger Hof he was surprised, in the lift, to bump into Mr Samuel Dawson, a broker whom he frequently met in the city. Mr Dawson explained that he was en route for Königsberg to visit his sister who was married there. It's a barracks of a place, he continued, headquarters of the First Corps d'Armée, a garrison of seven thousand armed men. His sister was married to an army chaplain there. He suggested, and George willingly agreed, that they dine in one of the restaurants close by. Did George like oysters? He did indeed. Very well, they could eat a dozen or more at Heuers on the Alsterdamm, an excellent restaurant where they could get sherry and English ale.

They agreed to meet at seven; a thin drizzle hung in the air, making the street lamps blurred and furry. The Alsterdamm ran along the Binnen-Alster at right-angles to the Jungfernstieg; there were few people about. Heuers was cheerful; they hung their damp coats in a small cloakroom and sat by a large wrought-iron stove. They drank sweet sherry and puffed Manolis. Mr Dawson was not looking forward to the long journey, changing trains at Berlin; there was, however, an express train to Königsberg and he would probably arrive during a cannonade of rockets celebrating Sylvesterabend.

George had little idea where Königsberg was and even less interest; he awaited the arrival of the oysters with impatient anticipation. The waiter brought them on a large silver platter together with Tabasco pepper sauce. They both ate with relish and drank English ale.

'I sometimes think,' said Mr Dawson, 'that Hamburg is a piece of England that became detached and floated across the North Sea.'

'Perhaps we could swap it for Heligoland,' said George, swallowing a briny twist of slime; the Tabasco was pungent and sharp.

Mr Dawson described the harbour with its numerous vessels from all quarters of the globe; the quays had been recently expanded and now stretched some five miles along the Elbe; they could accommodate upwards of four hundred sea-going vessels and a large number of barges and river craft. There was a steam-crane on the Asia quay with a lifting capacity of a hundred and fifty tons.

George ordered more huîtres au naturel and listened with half an ear; he imagined his cousin sitting alone in a small room on Heligoland, gazing into darkness. What a surprise for her! The reasons for her flight would become apparent; he would understand and condone them. They would walk the cliffs together. Dare he hope for her hand? Propinquity, blood relationship, need not be a difficulty, far from it. They were the dearest of friends. Perhaps Heywood would marry them?

He ate distractedly, drank English ale, let Samuel Dawson talk. The windows looked out onto a dark, damp world, lights twisting sluggishly on the Binnen-Alster. Did the oysters have a greenish tinge? He scarcely noticed. Mr Dawson spoke of the Bonded Warehouse district, the canals or Fleete. Mr Havelock should visit them if he had time. He, Mr Dawson, had to get up at five thirty tomorrow to catch the Berlin train. They finished eating at ten, drank ice-cold schnapps and sauntered back to the hotel. George wished him a pleasant journey and all the best for the New Year.

In the night he had violent diarrhoea accompanied by spewing; his dreams had been distressful, of Frances with oysters for breasts, her nipples dabs of orange Tabasco. The sheets were stained with excrement, the carpet with vomit. At eight he rang for room service and described in halting German to an impassive maid what had happened; the under-manager arrived later with a local doctor.

Had he eaten in the hotel restaurant? No, groaned George, at an establishment on the Alsterdamm. The doctor examined him when the bed was changed and the carpet scrubbed; water closet and bath were also disinfected. An obvious case of food poisoning brought on by the consumption of oysters contaminated by sewage. Rest was necessary, and he must fast for a day. But, the invalid protested, he was due to sail for Heligoland that afternoon. Impossible. He was in no fit state to climb up and down gangplanks and the prospect of seasickness was, the patient must admit, undesirable. The journey must be postponed: acute food poisoning could develop into enteritis if not properly treated. If Herr Havelock felt better on January the second the journey might be allowed; January the third would be preferable.

George weakly concurred, knowing full well that the doctor was right: the prospect of a heaving deck or cabin was appalling. He, who exulted in shipwreck and foundering, was not a good sailor. He felt weak, sick and debilitated, and lay back on his reconstructed bed, gently moaning. In the afternoon he drank a weak infusion and in the evening attempted to eat a light gruel, which he promptly voided. He heard the New Year revels from afar. His strength slowly returned on the first day of the new decade, but he knew that there would be no sailings until January the third. And on that day, as he made his happy, unsteady way to the steamer, he heard of the attempt on the life of the Governor of Heligoland.

* * *

Lady Augusta had been woken by a demented Frau Stoeven bringing the dreadful news; the grim cortège waited below. She rose instantly and dressed, sweeping past the gasping housekeeper and striding to the door. Her husband, bleeding profusely, was lying on Russalka's cart which had been retrieved from the steps; his throat was bandaged by a scarf and he breathed stertorously. Charlotte, shot through the shoulder, was slumped on a chair; Beatrice was screaming hysterically and William, ghastly beneath the electric light of the hall, was shuddering convulsively. Florike van Egmond, Lady Augusta was informed, was lying dead in the Grünes Wasser, shot through the head. The perpetrator of these dreadful crimes, Bill Freshet, had turned the gun upon himself and blown his brains out.

Lady Augusta immediately gave orders that Dr Graevenitz be summoned; her husband was carried upstairs and laid in the bedroom that Frances had once occupied. She ripped her daughter's blood-soaked gown from her shoulder and saw that the bullet was still lodged there; she gave orders to William to attend to the hysterical Beatrice and, shaking Frau Stoeven vigorously, told her to take Charlotte to her room where she would attend her. She utterly ignored the hapless Englishwoman who stood, transfixed by horror, beneath The Dashing Hussar.

The blood-soaked ghastliness of the chesterfield, her blood-sticky burgundy gown, the brain-spattered horror of the wall against which the murderer had fallen (she had seen, too, his eyes, staring in hatred and shrieking insanity as the wide-awake fell to the floor when he put the gun into his mouth): this flashed before her, frozen as though a memory of Mme Tussaud's Grand Guignol, a scene of appalling immediacy and drama – Teddy stumbling against her, a rictus of glazed incomprehension on his features, Florike's head a head no more but a turmoil of scarlet.

The cracking reverberation of the bullets, then silence, then pandemonium, the stampede to the door, doors slamming and banging in the wind, then shouts, screams, the rush to save the Governor. She had stood petrified in the midst of the frenzy, slowly wiping his blood from her breast, cupping and caressing it, gazing at his blood on her hand, kissing it, touching it with her tongue. Then the procession through the windy night of darkness, where fireworks crackled incongruously below, and fires blazed on the Düne. They did not know, did not know – until figures were running down the steps and she heard shouts, cries: the fizzing sparkling stopped.

Now standing in the hall, otiose, sterile, nugatory. She fell sobbing upon an ottoman, cupped her left breast automatically, withdrew her hand, lifted it to her lips, touched it with her tongue. Sat there oblivious while servants rushed past, Dr Graevenitz, Dr Saphir. His rose. His blood. The wound. Die Wunde. At dawn she was led away.

* * *

The island was in uproar. The Governor was dead, was alive; his son was dead, as was Charlotte Hennicker-Heaton. Miss Prince had attempted suicide, and had succeeded. Beatrice Hennicker-Heaton had been shot in the stomach; Florike van Egmond had died trying to save the life of the Governor. Bill Freshet was in the pay of the anarchists; a British fleet was on its way. The Reverend Heywood was behind it all, he was a Freemason. Mr Strang had planned it all, he wished to seize power. The German Emperor, Wilhelm the Second, was about to occupy the island, making it his capital. There were signs and portents.

Frances lay supine upon her bed, closing her ears to the gossip of the maids, the wild speculations swirling about her in the Conversationshaus. One thing she knew to be true: that Florike had thrown herself across the Governor's son, and had been killed. Teddy, Herr Jensen told her, was hovering between life and death. Florike, she moaned, Florike. You saw the pistol before any of us, you acted, threw yourself sideways. I, I should have done this, then Teddy would have been spared. Blessed, divine girl, you saved the man you loved. What did I do? Stand like a pillar of salt whilst my lover fell across me, dying.

The day passed, grey, cankerous, crumbling; evening dusk appeared; news came that Teddy was still living. She ate nothing, gazed at the light, the stabbing finger of light. The Dutch consul, she heard, had been informed and would come in person to organise the shipment of Florike's body to Amsterdam; her parents would be sailing from Batavia. A lovely townhouse on the Keizergracht, a summer residence at Scheveningen. No, no, a family mausoleum, a sombre internment, exequies solemnised with dignified pomp. And forever remembered as a heroine who died to save him, whereas she…

She gazed into the darkness, drank brandy, smoked several Neptun cigarettes. You in your ill-fitting pink taffeta gown, now transfigured. She heard the doleful foghorn; a thick mist hung in the darkness. Teddy, Teddy, let your Isolde come to you with life-giving potions. Or to die with you.

The hotel was hushed, voices were lowered. She took the morphine that Dr Graevenitz had given her a lifetime ago and drifted into an uneasy sleep where ghostly figures moved through blood and lay upon her bed; Florike, with half a face, crooned and gibbered. When she woke the Rock was covered in a damp mist which hung like a smoky waterfall down over the cliffs; the esplanade was almost deserted.

Dare she walk up the steps to Government House? She feared the worst: a flag flying at half-mast, a housekeeper in black, Lady Augusta in widow's weeds. What meaning would her life have then? Another death, another death…She walked by a sullen sea, spurting and chattering over stones and loose shingle. 'Come,' he had said, 'unto these yellow sands.' He had put his hand under my arm.

She walked now as a revenant, a damp mist glistening in her hair, her boots soaked as the sea dashed at her on the beach. I followed Stine, did I not, now I walk alone. But my father will come, will take me away. The air was raw; she gazed across at the silent Düne, muffled in mist. And she thought of Russalka. Where was she lying? Shattered, perhaps, at the bottom of the steps? She turned and walked back across the Marcusplatz, avoiding the mementoes of that terrible night (vomit, charred fireworks, broken glass) and found her. She was lying not on the square but amongst the rocks, the sparse vegetation and sundry detritus lying at the foot of the fissured cliff; her tail had come away in her fall and lay limp and sodden beside her; part of her hair was missing, her left breast was badly scuffed and the fingers of her right hand were missing. I too had my fall, she thought, we are both sisters, you and I, both pulled from the sea.

The mist had grown more dense; she touched the damp wood of the figurehead, her cheek and mouth. She walked back past the shuttered, silent Strandbazar to the esplanade. Here she sat, upon a damp wooden bench, listening to the dull booming of the foghorn. Gog and Magog, she thought, there were giants on the earth in those days. She felt for her golden locket.

* * *

She was sleeping fully clothed on the bed, a leaden sleep of exhaustion, when, unexpectedly, Herr Jensen knocked at the door and entered. He was deeply concerned for her after the appalling incident in the Princess Alexandra; she was not simply a client but a friend, the daughter of a great father. She smiled weakly and swung her feet onto the floor; he brought her a chair and stood beside her. He had heard from a maid in Government House that Lady Augusta had stanched the wound, that the doctors were in constant attendance, taking turns, and that a surgeon had been summoned from Germany. Sir Edward, although gravely ill, for the bullet had pierced his windpipe, was fighting valiantly for his life. Miss Charlotte was in considerable pain, but resting; Miss

Beatrice was heavily sedated. And William? she asked. The young Herr Hennicker-Heaton was distraught, inconsolable at the tragic death of Júfvrouw van Egmond. Mr Strang was Acting Governor and had ordered that the body of the murderer be deposited in the Rathaus. It was the act of a madman, he sighed, a maniac, a man unhinged by the death of his daughter – a death for which he was responsible.

He looked paternally at Frances.

'You are in shock, Miss Prince, but you must eat something. You have seen terrible things: you must build up your strength.'

'What shall I eat then?' she asked, light-heartedly, almost flippantly.

' Barley broth and porridge!' he replied, smiling. 'I'll have some port wine sent up, this will thicken the blood.'

He put a plump hand on her shoulder. The 'barley broth' was a joke, they had excellent haddock in the kitchen, also skate. There was almost nobody in the dining room; she need not dress for dinner; she could sit quietly in the corner. But she must not brood: distraction would help to drive away those pictures of horror. But if she did prefer to dine here in her room he would see to it.

'I have a blood-soaked gown,' she murmured, 'it is lying over there by the washstand'.

He turned pale. A maid would collect it immediately and give it to the Waskwüf.

'Miss Prince,' he cried, 'dear Miss Prince, you are young, you will forget'.

There had been spots of red wine on another gown, she remembered, the night that Teddy….

'Thank you, Herr Jensen, for your solicitous concern. Yes, I'll come down for dinner, but not in this,' she smiled, gazing at her creased grey skirt, her crumpled blouse.

'Your beauty,' he cried gallantly, 'will shine through these humble garments and illuminate the room! Be of good cheer, Miss Prince, he will live, he is strong.'

Then, checking himself and clearing his throat, he mopped his brow and left the room.

She descended the stairs an hour later in her pale blue gown and lace stole, her hair in a French pleat. There were very few people in the foyer; she gazed through the glass door at a thick mist pressing like dull wadding against the panes. Her father had told her of Morell Mackenzie's account of the fatal illness of the last German Emperor, the cancerous larynx, the insertion of the canula, the blunt hooks; she felt weak and sought the library to rest for a while.

How can I eat when he fights for breath? Strength, they tell me, I must build up my strength. She forced herself into the dining room, sitting at a small table at the back. She had armed herself with *Ebb and Flow* as a shield against importunate intruders; she ate steamed fish and sipped some Chablis. She read without recalling, when she turned the page, what it was she had read; she would climb the steps tomorrow, seek entrance to Government House, beg to be allowed to see him. No news of his death had reached them here; no news was, then, good news. What was *Ebb and Flow* to her? She pushed her plate away, finished her carafe of wine and rose to enjoy a Neptun in the library.

As she crossed the foyer she saw that Herr Jensen was talking to Mr Strang; the latter, when he saw her, excused himself and came to speak to her.

'How are you, Miss Prince? What a ghastly business, ghastly.'

'Have you any news of Sir Edward?' she asked.

'There has been a slight improvement, and the doctors are hopeful. Thank God the spine wasn't damaged. But I can't see a surgeon getting over here in this fog: all sailings will be delayed.'

He also added, grimly, that the murderer's body would have to stay in the Rathaus. He was desperate to hand it over to the police in Hamburg. It was not a pretty sight. He did not want to distress her unduly with these matters: she had already experienced the horror at first hand. But she was her father's daughter, he knew that, brave and strong. He wondered if she would join him in a nightcap. She hesitated, then agreed.

They sat in the lounge where he drank whisky and she a cognac; she sat where Millicent had sat, her brown silk dress billowing around her. Now she, and her father, Miss Lavender's son, were no more. John Fallow's son violently took his own life; his daughter slips into the cold black embrace of water. And John Fallows sits waiting for death, rheumatic, addled, goatish.

She gazed at Mr Strang.

'Why? Why did Bill Freshet do this terrible thing?'

'He was crazed, demented,' was the reply. Plucking up courage she asked:

'Had there been any suggestion of a clandestine affaire between the Governor and Miss Freshet?'

Mr Strang was silent, then spoke gravely. There was no question of an impropriety between the Governor and the lady in question. What he could say was that she had made the Governor's life difficult. The Governor had acted with decorum in a delicate situation. This was all he wished to say on the matter.

'But why,' urged Frances, 'did Bill Freshet also shoot at William?'

'He would have killed them all,' said Mr Strang darkly, 'but that dear, brave young woman saved his life'.

'Was it,' blurted Frances, 'because William had had an affaire with Millicent?'

Mr Strang looked at her intently. That had never entered his head. There could be no question of it. The young man, to his certain knowledge, had never behaved improperly towards Miss Freshet.

'And Stine?' cried Frances, wildly agitated, her eyes glittering.

'Stine?' Mr Strang looked puzzled.

'The girl who tried to kill herself!'

Mr Strang still failed to understand.

'Please,' she cried, 'I wish to know'.

Mr Strang ordered another whisky.

'Know what?'

'Was there any – dalliance – between William and Stine? Was the Governor's son guilty of dishonest behaviour?'

Mr Strang asked for permission to light his pipe; she gratefully gave it and drew out a Neptun cigarette; he offered a friction match. An era was probably coming to an end, he said quietly, and our Governor, were he to be restored to health, might not necessarily remain in post on the island. It was not even certain what the status of the island would be. He felt it was therefore not inappropriate or indelicate to mention what had happened. Who, now, would think of it anyway?

Mr William Hennicker-Heaton had been involved in an unsavoury incident: the girl Stine was with child and had insisted that he was responsible. He swore on oath he had no carnal knowledge of the girl; he did, however, admit to an unseemly dalliance. The evidence pointed to the girl's having had an affaire with a German sailor from Bremen called Wilhelm Rank who had visited the island. This Rank was a thoroughly unpleasant sort by all accounts and was most certainly the father. He saw that he had a golden opportunity to blackmail Mr Hennicker-Heaton and forced Stine to deceive the young gentleman into giving her money.

Mr William foolishly gave her a generous sum, but Rank demanded more. The girl became more and more frantic and finally, in an act of desperation, tried to kill herself. She did not succeed, but lost the child. Mr William confided in his father who punished Rank very severely. But it was felt in some quarters that Sir Edward was simply defending his son's honour and that Rank was innocent; Stine went into a cataleptic trance and could say nothing.

There was much bad blood at the time, and much anti-British feeling, which is rare here. Lady Augusta supported her husband and son, as did Miss Beatrice, but Miss Charlotte grew rebellious and felt that some wrong had been done: she tried to help Stine.

'It is all past history, Miss Prince. I was convinced of Mr William's innocence; he was weak and foolish. But we must support this family in their hour of darkness and pray that Sir Edward may pull through. He has his failings, but he has been the best Governor that this island has ever had. Let us hope that he will remain so.' He rose to his feet, bowed, and left the room.

* * *

A bank of dense fog lay over the Heligoland Bight, stretching from the mouth of the Elbe to the Dogger Bank, a clammy, dense, dull grey flannel of sodden heaviness which hung over the water; the fog horns sounded on Neuwerk, on Wangerooge, Föhr and Sylt, on Römöe and Fanöe.

The Reverend Timothy Heywood, waiting disconsolately in a dreary boarding house in Gravesend, was told that, although the fog had lifted on this side of the North Sea, it was still thick on the German side and that sailings would be delayed; the Minerva would not sail until visibility improved. He walked the wet streets and gazed at the lights, dull upon the river, at the three-legged lighthouse on the mud flat, at the gloomy docks, and felt great longing, guilt at this longing, and an inexpressible sadness of spirit.

He had sought solace in Milton parish church, a decorated structure, but his thoughts had strayed to the afternoon in Salisbury when he had walked with her, and he noticed little of the church's perpendicular tracery; the grave of Princess Pocahontas, near the old church, was also seen and forgotten. He returned and lay upon his bed in a chill room, the thin curtains admitting light from the street below. Thus I greet the new year, the new decade. Ten weeks ago I did not know that she existed, I did not know of women. I feared that God would punish me as He slew Onan. I guiltily looked at a female shape carved in wood, I touched her. But then Frances came to the Rock…

He groaned upon the bed, wracked with guilt, self-mortification, disgust. Was I ill, sick, perverted? Did I not once walk on the Düne like a love-sick mooncalf and call the figurehead by her name, pretending that it was she? Frances, Frances, no wonder you fled from me…There he lay, overwrought and exhausted, hearing the sirens of ships in the darkness and holding a small, crumpled lawn handkerchief that he had found on her seat in the Salisbury Arms and kept.

He recalled, miserably, that evening at Her Majesty's Theatre, his brief encounter with Mr Havelock who, impetuously, had told him to wait and had fled. He had waited outside the box, hearing the music of the bacchanal, the surging, beating, delirious frenzy. He heard the shepherd's pipe, the minstrels, the startled recognition, the hunting horns echoing across the Thuringian forests. The act ended in jubilation; he sat motionless in the corridor as people floated past him, intent on refreshment.

He enquired at the desk below: there had been no message. Bewildered and disorientated he left the theatre and made his way by public omnibus to Finsbury Park, fearing his querulous mother's surprise at his early return. She had, however, retired early and Timothy Heywood crept through the musty hall, extinguished the flaring fishtail gas burner and went to his bedroom. Where are you, Miss Prince? he whispered, what has happened to you?

He found Mr Havelock's card in his pocket, a card bearing the Wiltshire address, and placed it on the rickety bedside table next to his bible and the crumpled twist of cambric. In bed, culpably, he masturbated, placing the handkerchief around his erect member. Frances, he moaned, Frances. He slept fitfully and was woken by the smell of frying bacon which hung greasily in the stairwell.

After breakfast he had taken his mother to morning service in St James's; she had reminded him that his sister Lavinia and brother-in-law were coming to Sunday lunch. His heart had sunk; he had wished to go to Capewell House to see if any news had come. But filial duty forbade it; he awaited his sister and her husband Sidney with distaste. She was a vulgar young woman, he felt, shrill and cheerful; she had married a salesman who worked for a furniture company.

They had arrived punctually and regaled him with tales of a freak-show they had recently visited.

'There was a bearded lady,' giggled Lavinia, 'and it wasn't false, you pulled it, didn't you Sidney?'

'I did,' he replied, 'and there was also a sort of elephant-man with an enormous `ead. I tell you, Tim, `e couldn't `ave got it through that front door. Imagine `im in a dog-collar, eh!'

Timothy turned pale.

‘`E was a real ripper, wasn’t `e, Lav, playing on `is banjo and doing a tap dance.’

‘There was a mermaid too,’ said Lavinia, ‘with lovely long hair and a scaly body.’

‘Nice bit of ongbongpwang,’ laughed Sidney, ‘but what good’s a mermaid, eh Tim?’ he winked and nudged his brother-in-law; Lavinia slapped his wrist. Mrs Heywood announced that dinner was ready. He scarcely ate a morsel and fled into the grey, quiet afternoon without helping with the washing up.

Should he have informed the police? He had approached a station with a constable standing outside but veered away, irresolute, apprehensive. What was there to say? To explain? That a delightful young woman who was due to come with him to *Tannhäuser* had not turned up?

He had walked through dull streets and returned exhausted in time for high tea, some boiled ham, stewed pears and jelly. Mrs Heywood had produced paper and pencils to play Double Acrostics.

‘Come on, Timmy, you’re the bright one!’ his sister had cried. The initials, read down, gave the name of one country in Northern Europe and the finals, read down, gave the name of a second.

‘A flower. A robber. A coarse kind of bread corn. A strong motion of air. An animal. Woollen thread.’

Sidney solved the puzzle within three minutes.

‘Easy, Ma. Narcissus, Outlaw, Rye, Wind, Antelope and Yarn.’

‘But what countries are they, then?’ cried Lavinia.

‘Norway and Sweden, of course.’

Sidney also knew a word square:

‘I oft times am seen in the night. My next a story should be. An expression of grief, not delight. My last’s the remainder, you see.’

It was Mrs Heywood who solved it:

‘Star, Tale, Alas, Rest. Cheer up, Timmy,’ she continued, ‘you’ve got a face as long as a fiddle.’

‘Let’s have a sing-song,’ said Lavinia, moving towards the piano. Timothy rose.

‘I’m sorry,’ he stammered, ‘I’m very tired.’

He had climbed the stairs to a medley from Gilbert and Sullivan.

* * *

He had frequently asked himself how he would be able to get through Christmas; sick at heart he had written to Mrs Lovell for news, and a reply came. Mr George Havelock was very worried and making enquiries. The police had been informed and photographs of Miss Prince were to be displayed locally and at Her Majesty’s Theatre. Mrs Lovell could not understand what had happened and feared abduction. But by whom? Fenians? She assured the Reverend that all would be done to find Miss Prince, who was known to be a high-spirited and valiant young woman and not easily cowed.

Timothy kept the letter carefully and caught an omnibus to Her Majesty’s Theatre; there he saw her, and stood transfixed despite the jostling crowds around him. The curl, the curl above the right cheek, the dark blouse and high puffed sleeves…He remembered another gown, scooped low, revealing beauty. Could he, dare he touch the photograph? He reached out a trembling hand but restrained himself when he noticed a gentleman behind the box-office looking at him quizzically. I have fondled wood; I long to touch this photographic plate, but flesh, flesh…

He joined the swirling crowds, aimlessly wandering, gazing at meaningless baubles, gewgaws, fripperies. The desultory vivacity of Christmas would soon be upon him, and he feared and loathed the prospect of spending the festive season with his family. Then he chided himself for this lack of Christian charity, and despised himself. He, a servant of the Lord…Frances, oh Frances.

In the growing dusk of the afternoon monstrous thoughts struck him as he sat on the Embankment, staring at the dark river: that he would rather she were dead than that she should love another. In death she would be present forever as an insect in amber, his, his, his. Sick, he thought, I am sick.

He would find her, he would marry her, become a suffragan, a bishop even, and live in a palace and have servants. Vanity, all vanity. He returned home and helped his mother decorate the small house with holly; ivy he pulled from their sour, sooty back garden.

He spent Christmas Day at the services celebrated at St James's, but also played whist in the parlour with the others after a heavy lunch, drinking port and lemon. He accepted a muffler from his mother and a pair of cufflinks from Lavinia and Sidney. He gave no gifts and craved their indulgence.

'You always were a dreamer, Timmy,' said his sister, 'and if you didn't have that dog collar you'd probably not know it was Christmas. Time you found a good woman to look after you!'

Sidney was cheerful and poured him another drink.

'There's a girl in the office, a real corker, just the thing for you, Tim. I bet you won't find too many like that on `Illygolundy or whatever it's called. Big German women I expect, eh? Eating all that sausage.'

'Let Timmy choose when the time is right,' said his mother, 'as long as it's not a French woman, I can't abide them.'

'Timmy will marry a nice little English girl,' said Lavinia, smiling at her brother, 'and live in a nice vicarage somewhere near Walthamstow. Then we can all go on the train and visit them. And,' she continued, turning deep crimson and looking at her mother, 'when there's a little stranger in our midst, Timmy can christen him!'

Mrs Heywood could hardly believe her ears and embraced her daughter laughing and crying at the same time.

'Lavvie, you kept that a secret! Tim, you're going to be an uncle! When is the baby due?'

It was due at the end of June; Sidney, also blushing, asked for permission to light a cigar.

Timothy Heywood shook his hand and embraced his sister.

'Bless you, Lavinia, I'm so glad.'

'Your turn next!' cried Sidney, 'another grandson next year, eh, Ma? Another soldier for the Queen, eh?'

'Let me get over the shock of this one first!' cried Mrs Heywood, wiping her eyes on her sleeve.

'Tim, lend us your hanky, there's a dear.'

He pulled it out, but a little twist of lawn fabric fluttered to the floor. Lavinia bent to pick it up.

'Didn't know you had such pretty things, Timmy!'

He blushed and took it from her abruptly.

'I – I found it in the vestry of St James's.'

Whist was forgotten and the conversation took the inevitable course, babies and baby clothes, midwives and accouchements. He listened politely, and retired at ten o' clock.

He had waited, waited for news, but none had come; his mother glowed at the prospect of becoming a grandmother, her viduity now transfigured; he walked the empty streets. On December the twenty-seventh he waited outside Her Majesty's Theatre, gazing at her photograph; he had waited till few were near, then kissed the cold glass. Frances, Frances.

Mrs Lovell, in her letter, had given him the Eaton Square address, and he approached the handsome house hesitantly; there was no reply. On the following day he took his mother for a walk in the park; it had been cold, and they had sat in a wrought-iron gazebo, gazing at a crowd of urchins playing with the drinking fountain, letting the brass cup on its chain clatter against the stand.

'Go and tell them off, Timmy, I can't stand the noise.'

But remonstration was alien to him and he walked his mother home, filling her coal scuttle and lighting the gas mantle. A leaden inertia overcame him. His mother had broached the subject of his compassionate leave and when he had to return to Heligoland; he had been evasive. The Governor had kindly given him two months' leave; this would soon be up.

He knew, he knew that she would refer to the possibility of his giving up his tenure on the island, of seeking an ecclesiastic authority in London which could bestow an advowson. He had sat with her after the evening meal and played patience with her. I am dying. My life is dribbling away. I shall never see Frances again. But then the second letter came from Capewell House.

He had heard the postman call on the morning of December the thirtieth; he descended the creaking stairs and picked up the letter that lay on the threadbare mat. It was from Mrs Lovell, and there had been exciting news. She had heard from Mr Havelock that his cousin was alive and well and that she had returned to Heligoland.

He had scarcely taken in the description of how this information had come to light: an aristocratic friend had been duplicitous; a flower girl had seen the photograph and remembered Miss Prince; Mr Havelock had ascertained from servants in Regent Street that Miss Prince had spent the night of the eighteenth and subsequent nights in the house; there had been talk of Tilbury Dock; the consul in Hamburg had confirmed that Miss Prince had arrived there. Mr Havelock had set off immediately.

Heligoland! Alive! He fell against the banisters and gripped the finial for support; his mother, alarmed, had led him into the kitchen. He must depart, he had moaned, immediately. But where? To Heligoland. He could not explain, the matter was complex. A dear friend, presumed dead, was now restored to health and back on the island. His compassionate leave was almost over and it was only proper that he return to his post on the first of January. The Governor wished him to officiate at a ceremony to celebrate the re-dedication of a church. There was to be a christening soon, also a funeral. The young curate, Mr Eliot, was inexperienced. It was imperative that he go. But they had already agreed to visit Lavinia and see in the New Year with a bowl of punch, his mother reminded him. He would have to go now, he retorted, and he would have to beg her to lend him the money for a ticket. His mother, bewildered, had replied that she only had a few shillings in her purse. He, likewise, only had a guinea or two, but he would repay her within the month. She had said nothing more and had helped him pack a small suitcase. She gave him the shabby purse with two pounds fifteen shillings. Take it, she had said. He had kissed her, and hurried from the house.

Now here, in a chill bedroom in Gravesend he waited, excitement having given way to fear, to apprehension, to terror. For she must needs reject him, a sick, morbid clergyman, inadequate, prey to prurient fantasies, without money, without virility, without prospects. But to see her, oh, to see her once again! And then? A piece of cambric, a scrap of lawn, that is all. He pressed the crumpled fragment of cloth against his flaccid member, and grey, unwholesome sleep invaded him.

* * *

When a strong south-westerly had blown the sodden rags of mist from the island, Rasmussen, Henk and two others retrieved the damaged figurehead from the base of the red sandstone cliff and rowed her across to the Düne and fixed her once more onto the lifeboat shed. Henk humorously suggested that he should paint the damaged breast and wooden hair; Rasmussen gruffly put him in his place. That would be for the gentry, not for the likes of us.

They rowed back beneath the wheeling gulls; Frances, from the top of the steps, saw them depart, return. She buttoned her coat around her throat and thrust her hair into her tammy; the index finger of her left glove was split, she noticed, gazing at the white flash of skin. As the Reverend Heywood passed the Clapham lighthouse, ignorant of what had happened, for he read no newspapers and spoke to no one; as her cousin gazed in impatience at the mist thinning over Geestemünde, she left the settlement to one side and walked along the sodden Falm to Government House, its flag flapping wetly. The sea churned and glittered in the weak, low January sun; a few fishing boats rose and dipped on the swell.

She dared not visit the house, dared not enter it; it stood grey, four-square and alien, on her right. And yet I had much happiness there, she thought, and much tribulation. Did a curtain move upstairs? A pale face appear? She walked on, past the lighthouse where two men were polishing the reflectors, grateful for her stout boots in the wet grass and the cold day, past that crack, that grassy mouth of moss and bracken in the earth, into which she had fallen – when? A week ago? A year?

She walked on, careful to avoid the friable crumbling sandstone of the cliff's edge and made for the Nathuurnstak, the tusk, the mighty fang, circled and streaked by thousands of cackling gulls, the sea surging below at its base, tossing and tangling the heaving weed. The wind buffeted her as she stood and gazed at its elemental rust, its fissures, excrescences, striations.

Charlotte was unwell here; I was exultant; Miss Lavender helped us. She clapped her hands over her ears to restrain the tugging tammy; her skirts flapped wildly. He will live, I know it! Again, a strange exhilaration seized her: was it the wind? The screaming clamour? The surging tide beneath? She seemed to be surrounded by streaming presences, engulfed by a vertiginous sense of terror, yet terror somehow transcended, transfigured. She stepped forward, yet rapidly drew back from the crumbling edge, her cheeks tingling, her heart pounding wildly.

One woman drowned in the sea below; one threw herself down here; a figurehead is hurled into the darkness. A woman is killed when a madman shoots at my Master and his son, his daughters. But my Master still lives! This stack affirms it!

She saw herself and Teddy walking arm in arm through dusk, owl-light, gloaming, walking in radiance, in transfiguration. A dazzling light struck from the waters as the sun glittered upon them; she shielded her eyes with her hand. One bade me dance and sing, the other calls me now. And, smiling to herself, she turned and walked to Government House.

A butler opened the door after she knocked. No visitors were permitted. The Governor was still gravely ill.

'I am known to the house,' Frances insisted, 'I am a good friend of Sir Edward. I wish to speak to Lady Augusta or any of the children.'

It is impossible, he responded. If she would leave her card he would see to it that Lady Augusta were informed of her visit.

'I have come a long way, from London,' Frances continued, 'my father and Sir Edward are old friends.'

It is impossible, he repeated, quietly attempting to shut the door. But behind him a tall figure appeared, dressed in black. Lady Augusta, pale and imperious, stared at Frances.

' Come to tea this afternoon. If my husband is any easier you may see him.' The door closed.

* * *

Dressed severely in an aubergine silk blouse and dark grey skirt, her hair in a chignon with a golden comb, she entered the drawing room; Lady Augusta rose to greet her.

'Please sit, Miss Prince.'

'Where is Frau Stoeven, Lady Augusta?'

'She is unwell, unable to work after what happened. The manager of the Princess Alexandra sent Wylie to me. He was in service in the vice-regal residence in British India.'

They fell silent; the only sound was the crackling of the fire and the ticking of an ornate clock. At last Frances spoke.

'It is kind of you to invite me. What has happened was appalling, and I have no right to intrude on your grief. But your family has grown very dear to me and I had to come. Forgive me if my visit is importunate, burdensome.'

'You showed great fortitude,' said Lady Augusta, 'I admire that. To have gazed into the eyes of a murderer, to have heard the shots, seen the death of Miss van Egmond and my husband's terrible wound – this requires courage. You are your father's true daughter. Your time on this island has not been happy, I fear.'

Your husband has given me so much,' said Frances, gazing into the fire, 'your children also. How is poor Charlotte? And Beatrice? And William?'

'Charlotte is in pain. The bullet splintered her shoulder blade and the use of her right arm may be impaired. But she is strong-willed. She will not let this prevent her from studying in Zurich, which I find incomprehensible. She used to be rebellious, even insolent, but has matured. The suffering she has experienced will not crush her. In her the Prussian virtues of discipline, service and dedication will come to the fore. I am concerned about Beatrice. The trauma which you all experienced has been exacerbated in her case by an unsavoury relationship with the disreputable Kapitän von Kroseck, a disgrace to the German Imperial Fleet. This has been terminated. She was always emotional and wore her heart on her sleeve: I believe this is the English idiom? Von Kroseck behaved abominably, and the sooner she can forget him and the death of dear Miss van Egmond the better it will be. But she does not have her sister's strength of character. I am sending her to my relations in Kurland where a pastor will take her in hand. Martin Niep recommended him to me. Plain food, long walks and earnest discussions on the Kantian concept of duty will restore her equilibrium. And my son? The death of that unfortunate young woman whom I wished to welcome as a daughter-in-law affected him very deeply. It may sound hard to you, but his obvious grief brought me comfort. He has learned what true sacrifice is. She gave her life for his, she interposed her body. This he will never be able to forget, and I am sure that his life will be transformed by it. His path was one of feckless irresponsibility; I almost despaired. But now I see a chance for him. He will accompany the coffin to Amsterdam and wait for the arrival of the parents. Meditation and contrition will oust self-indulgence. His way will not be easy, but he has found the path.'

A maid brought tea, which Lady Augusta poured; dainty sandwiches and petits fours were also served.

'I am afraid there are no muffins,' Lady Augusta said, with the ghost of a smile on her lips, 'Sir Edward would not be pleased.'

'Is he - ?' muttered Frances, 'Will he - ?'

Lady Augusta sat bolt upright, her hands in her lap.

'He will live. There is no need for surgical intervention. Dr Graevenitz, Dr Saphir and I saved him. His speech may be affected, I do not know. But the expertise of the two and my own knowledge of infusions and poultices, the gifts of God's apothecary, restored life and healing. It was Dr Saphir whom I must thank above all, despite my aversion to his race, also equisetum arvense and agrimonia eupatoria. The man whom I honour and love will recover.'

Frances, numbed, placed her cup upon the table.

'I think I should go,' she whispered.

'No. He was fond of you, he told me this. Stay for three minutes, then leave.'

Lady Augusta arose and pulled her visitor to her feet; she led her up the familiar stairs and towards the bedroom where Teddy was lying. She opened the door, looked in, then turned to Frances.

'Please enter. I shall leave you to say what you wish.'

And Frances entered.

* * *

The room was cold, dim and smelled of unguents and tinctures; she looked at the bed and saw Teddy propped against the pillows or, rather, a figure which turned and stared at her with large, baffled eyes.

'Teddy,' she whispered, 'it's me, Frances.'

He wore a white nightshirt, but his face was equally white; his throat was concealed by a column of thick bandages which tilted his wasted face upwards. She approached hesitantly.

'Teddy, dear Teddy,' she murmured, gazing at his huge, bewildered eyes, his thin hair scraped across his scalp, his straggling greyish whiskers. Dare she sit upon the bed? His hands were outside the quilt, they were limp, papery. Dare she embrace him? But then she was sitting on the bed, holding his right hand, which felt very cold.

'Teddy, Teddy,' she crooned, 'come back to me, grow strong, love me. Your blood was on me, the flowers of your blood, I saw the wound, the dreadful wound, but you will live, grow strong and laugh again.'

Did a flicker of recognition pass across that face of parchment, that suffering lily upon its ravaged stalk? The figure breathed raspingly; she leaned forward and smoothed its lank hair.

'I love you, Teddy, we shall be happy together. I shall be your fair toxophilite, I shall defend you, you will never be wounded again, there will be no more horror. I shall hear your dear voice again and your laughter. You loved my mother, I know, but now you will love me. For no man has known me carnally, I am chaste. *One* adored me, but he died. You will live, Teddy, and we shall have years of happiness. Teddy, why is your hand so cold?'

And she took the pale, transparent hand and cupped it about her left breast. The figure opened its mouth to speak, and breathed stertorously; it pulled its hand away and pointed to a table where paper and pencil lay. She placed the pencil in his hand and laid the paper on the bed; the figure drew the pencil across the paper but then dropped it; it rolled to the edge of the bed, where Frances caught it. She put it back in his hand; the figure slowly wrote four lines in jagged, skewed handwriting, then fell back exhausted. The writing was barely legible, but she made out the following utterance in that dim room, four lines that would remain with her until her death:

'By merciful will, dear Augusta,
We've come through a bit of a buster,
Teddy was nearly sent below –
Praise God from whom all blessings flow…'

* * *

On the pitching deck of the Viktoria George, debilitated after his illness, cursed the wind that beat the sea yet blessed it for driving away the sodden shrouds; the boat had set forth on the day advertised, but had had to put in at Geestemünde because of the fog; he had spent the night in the Hotel Hannover opposite the quay of the Norderney steamers, and brooded long on the fearful events that had taken place on Heligoland. A maniac, so the rumour went, had opened fire indiscriminately in a crowded ballroom, killing a young woman and wounding the Governor; terrified, he feared the young woman was his cousin, but the Hamburger Abendblatt, a normally reliable paper, had described the victim as Swedish. One of the Governor's daughters had also been shot, as had his son.

Now, as the red sandstone cliffs drew ever closer, and his

stomach heaved and fell, he longed for nothing more than to see her smiling and to laugh at her astonishment; his trusty hipflask, full of Scotch whisky purchased in Hamburg, was raised to his lips.

Fanny, Fanny, I shall take you home and we'll call the banns and be done with it. Heywood can marry us for all I care. You needn't tell me why you stood me up at the Theatre and what made you come back to this ships' graveyard. Must be quite a few wrecks here. Was it here that Deutschland went down with all those nuns? This tub I'm on now should have been scrapped years ago, good shipyard though, Blohm und Voss.

He put his binoculars to his eyes to search for signs of life, but the horizon, now above his head, now beneath his feet, caused him to desist. The hot flush, the greenish bitterness brought rushing, rising vomit which he projected over the railing; again he gagged, and his mouth was foul with acrid puke. Damn you, Fan, for dragging me here, he thought, but then, guilt-ridden, he blessed her.

He watched the island draw near; the ship stopped, bells clanged, small boats appeared. He paid his one German mark, was helped down the steel ladder and into the bobbing craft, then rowed across to the duckboards. So this, he thought, is Heligoland, British territory. A group of people was standing on the shore; there was a thin drizzle in the air and he gazed up at the looming sandstone cliffs hanging above him. Mr Samuel Dawson had recommended the Stadt London at the top of the steps; he walked slowly upwards, out of breath and carrying a small Gladstone bag.

At the halfway point he stopped and gazed down at the grey scene beneath, the Viktoria on a sea of liquid steel, a small gloomy island, the riding gulls; he struggled on and asked a figure in homespun and sou'wester where the hotel was. The figure pointed to a large house standing amongst a cluster of smaller dwellings. He reached the hotel, entered and felt reassured by the prints of Balmoral, of Victoria and Albert in Scottish dress. The manager approached, and George explained that this hotel had been recommended by a

Mr Dawson; he had arrived unexpectedly, he knew, but hoped that nevertheless a room would become available.

How pleasant, said Mr Russell. He remembered Mr Dawson well, and a room was certainly available for a friend of his. Had the newcomer heard of the appalling incident? Terrible, terrible. The Governor was, however, making progress. To think that such a thing could have happened here! Dinner would be served at six o' clock: he recommended the excellent seafood, especially lobsters and oysters. Lobsters, perhaps, George thought queasily as he followed the boy with his bag along a dark corridor, but never again oysters! He felt extremely tired and the crossing, as well as his uneasy stomach, had sapped his spirits. He lay on the bed without taking off his boots and gazed at the dusty chandelier above. He would have a light meal, no wine, a nip of whisky, perhaps. He would retire early. Tomorrow he would present himself at Government House and ask for information about his cousin's whereabouts. He heard distant laughter below, the sound of crates and rattling bottles. It's all guano, George, guano.

* * *

The Reverend Heywood, in wintry dusk, climbed down the steps of the Prinz Eitel-Friedrich, stepped into the bobbing Börteboot and was rowed to the duckboards; he walked the slimy planks to the esplanade. Here he approached a figure in homespun and sou'wester and pressed one Thaler preussisch Kurant into his palm; the figure rowed him across to the Düne.

He walked across the dark wet sand to a small cottage and pushed open the door: an elderly woman, Rasmussen's mother, sat staring at him. He looked at the tiny room, a room decorated with white porcelain tiles and enamel blue figures, at the curtain which concealed the box bed in the wall, at the brass clock on the shelf, and sat opposite the woman by the turf fire; the familiar smell of train oil, fish and rancid butter made him feel faint, but here he could rest before beginning the search for Frances on the following day.

This was his hideaway on the Düne, a place to which he fled when life became too much for him and from where he used to walk to the chapel, to Russalka. He knew also that the small house on the Falm which served as his vicarage would be locked and the key stored in the Rathaus; he could not face encounters, importunate prying, solicitous enquiries which, he sensed, concealed a rebarbative hook.

Frau Rasmussen, a deaf mute, brought weak coffee and fish soup into which he knew, shuddering, that train oil had been added; he scarcely drank any. The elderly woman sat opposite him and sucked on her pipe; he threw more sticks onto the fire; the sea ground in the darkness. She leaned across and spat: her features, repellent in their ugliness, twisted and shifted as the fire flickered. His gorge rose and he nodded goodnight, rising and drawing back the greasy curtain.

The box bed was little more than a wardrobe, he knew this. He lay there fully clothed, apart from his shoes, and pulled the rough blankets over him. The wind, he thought, the endless wind and the sea. The ugly, incomprehensible Frisians, the omnipresent stink of fish, of oil, the endless monotony, the dwindling, ignorant congregations, the cold, the damp. Martin Niep is robust, whereas I…

He shivered and drew the blankets closer, he heard the old crone shuffling across the room. Frances, Frances, where are you? Up in Government House? In an expensive hotel? I lie here cramped and cold, warming myself with happy memories of Salisbury, and your handkerchief is here in my hand. I am poor, but you are well attached, I know. Your family might know a beneficiary with an advowson: we can be happy. I was priggish, limited, inhibited, but I can learn, can change. We spoke once of *Parsifal*. You who knew its creator can help me to understand. I shall visit Russalka tomorrow for the last time to say farewell, for I shall feel your warmth against me as we walk together. The pleasant meads of Hertfordshire or Essex, or a lovely church in Norfolk, St Andrew's in Colton, say. Away from this dreadful place, away from the sea and the wind…

He listened as it moaned past the roof, rattling the makeshift shutters. I shall seek her tomorrow. I shall find her. A poker clattered in the room and rolled across the uneven wooden floor, its sooty tip projecting beneath the bottom of his curtain. A gnarled, dirty hand retrieved it.

* * *

EPILOGUE

They walked arm in arm to the Hotel Belvedere whose pleasant pavilion faced the beach and which, in good weather, afforded splendid views of sunsets; they walked through the late afternoon dusk of winter, listening to the distant raking of gravel from the municipal gardens. Her father gazed down at her and smiled; her cheek brushed against his damp tweed ulster; in her free hand she grasped her elegant swan-necked umbrella studded with small jet beads.

'I might have known,' he laughed, 'that no daughter of mine would open a dainty parasol for fear of spoiling it! I should have brought you a solid, stout umbrella when we had that day in Scarborough, but you'd set your heart on this one!'

She said nothing. They entered the hotel, agreed to dine at seven and departed to their separate rooms.

He was sitting patiently at twenty past seven in the foyer, a handsome man, she thought, still youthful, tall, dignified, by no means a masher but courteous, kind and honest. He stood and accompanied her into the dining room which was almost empty.

'Cuxhaven in January! And I promised you the Riviera, didn't I, Fan?'

She smiled quietly.

'As long as I'm with you, Papa, it doesn't matter where I am.'

He bowed in gratitude and insisted on adjusting her chair behind her as she sat down. She faced the large windows: a moon of grey glass hung in the west, fronds of dark cloud drifting across it.

'Lobster?' he suggested, 'or did Teddy stuff you to the gunwales every night with them?'

'He will live, won't he?' she asked, not daring to look at him, but gazing instead at the moon.

'I'm sure he will. I'm sending the best medical man over to keep an eye on him, despite Augusta's objections. She's convinced Morell Mackenzie killed the last Kaiser and prefers to boil up strange infusions, but I'm told they're efficacious.'

He took her hand over the table.

'You poor thing, what you must have suffered to have him shot right next to you. And to see that poor girl killed in front of you as well. What was going through that maniac's mind God only knows, it's certainly beyond my comprehension. You're a brave girl, Fan. And to think that it was I who sent you over there in the first place! Get all that Wagner nonsense out of your head, I said, get rid of that silly idea about making his wife jealous and giving him a heart attack and go for a holiday on a sliver of British territory that's been asleep since the blockade. But it won't be British for much longer.'

She turned to look at him, puzzled.

'It'll be in the papers soon, I expect, so there's no harm in telling you. You probably wondered what I was up to in Berlin. Well, I was engaged in high-level discussions with Bismarck and Caprivi and others on the desirability of exchanging Heligoland for Zanzibar. I won't bore you, my daughter, with tedious details, but it's bound up with German colonial expansion in East Africa.

'Carl Peters has been seeking, despite the provisional agreements of eighteen eighty-six and eighteen eighty-nine, to extend German hegemony beyond the line drawn from the estuary of the Umba river and the island of Pemba and extending eastwards to Mount Mfumbiro. But it's finally been agreed that, although the German Empire should keep German East Africa as a legitimate sphere of interest, Britain should be given the island of Zanzibar. We have also, therefore, graciously agreed that Heligoland should be German territory. It'll take most of the year to sort out the various treaties and legalities and so on but by the end of eighteen ninety Heligoland will become Helgoland.

'Obviously I haven't told Teddy – how could I? – but Lady

Augusta is in the know and will explain it to him when the time is right, as will the British and German advisers, who will be going to the island soon. Knowing him he'll be mortified at first but then stage an elaborate masque on the official handing-over ceremony. Beware, Fan, he'll have you as Britannia with shield and spear handing over the Rock to Augusta as Germania! You can sing your Thomas Arne and we'll invite the old Queen over and her grandson the Kaiser and have a grand ceremony. I'm only sorry it's fallen to me to negotiate all this when Teddy's involved, especially with the state he's in now! He'll probably think I'm getting my own back for the way he used to beat me at tennis!'

She toyed with her halibut and scarcely touched her wine; her father ate with relish and enjoyed his Chablis. He smiled at her tenderly, but her gaze wandered to the moon, now almost hidden by cloud. Augusta, she thought, Augusta. I am nothing.

Suddenly her father was tapping her on the arm.

'Now, my girl, what's all this about George going across to the island? There is a dark mystery here!'

'George?' she gasped, 'on Heligoland?'

'Indeed he is. He sent a telegraph this morning to Charlie Dundas which I picked up when I passed through the consulate. He said you'd fled from London and he's now looking for you on the Rock.'

'It's a misunderstanding,' she whispered, her face ashen, 'I told him at Capewell House that I was invited back to Sir Edward's for Christmas. Perhaps the Reverend Heywood invited him over, I don't know. They seem to get on well together.'

He laughed out loud.

'No more mysteries, Fan, please! If I hadn't requisitioned the North Sea Fleet to pick you up at the crack of dawn this morning you might have met your cousin and your clergyman strolling along the promenade arm in arm! I'm sure you've wreaked enough havoc on that island, it was high time I got you off it!

'Now, my girl, how about this? I mentioned Zanzibar to you. Well, your dear father has been invited to go out there and oversee the transfer of power, to liaise between the Sultan, the

German authorities and the British interested parties on the coast. The French can have Madagascar, we're not interested in that. Zanzibar will become a British Protectorate. I don't know how long it will take, but it should be fascinating seeing how things shape up there.

'Now, would you like to come along? The climate's good, the Sultan is a reasonable sort of chap and you can dazzle the Germans with your knowledge of their language, their culture and Heligoland – you can tell them how marvellous it is and how good a deal they're getting. You can preside over tiffin and bathe modestly in the Indian Ocean.

'Think about it, Fan! I'll buy you a white parasol this time and you can turn all heads, become Sultana one day, that would suit you very well! Didn't you tell me once that the Bey of Tunis lavished gifts on you? But I mustn't make you swollen-headed! And let's think about poor old Teddy. I've taken his island from him and reclaimed my daughter, and there won't be any more rantipoling on the Rock.'

He raised his glass.

'To Teddy, and Augusta, may he be restored to health, and enjoy great happiness with a wonderful wife.'

But her tears were uncontrollable and, shuddering with sobs, she fled from the room.

* * * * *